PREVIOUS BOOKS BY WILLIAM BARTON

Hunting on Kunderer
A Plague of All Cowards
Dark Sky Legion
Yellow Matter
When Heaven Fell

COLLABORATIONS WITH MICHAEL CAPOBIANCO

Iris
Fellow Traveler
Alpha Centauri

WILLIAM BARTON

ASPECT®

WARNER BOOKS

A Time Warner Company

WARNER BOOKS EDITION

Aspect® is a registered rademark of Warner Books, Inc.

Cover design by Don Puckey
Cover illustration by Sean Beavers

Warner Books, Inc.
1271 Avenue of the Americas
New York, NY 10020

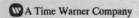 A Time Warner Company

Printed in the United States of America

First Printing: January, 1996

10 9 8 7 6 5 4 3 2 1

to

Edgar Rice Burroughs,
Olaf Stapledon,
E. E. Smith, Ph.D.,

and all the others
whose shadows,
despite a certain amount
of bad press,
still reach out
to infinity

As I walked through the wilderness of this world,
I lighted on a certain place where there was a den, and
I laid me down in that place to sleep, and as I slept I
dreamed a dream.

Pilgrim's Progress
John Bunyan

Here about the beach I wandered, nourishing a
        youth sublime
With the fairy tales of science, and the long result of
        time;

When the centuries behind me like a fruitful land
        reposed;
When I clung to all the present for the promise that
        it closed:

What is that to him that reaps not harvest of his
        youthful joys,
Though the deep heart of existence beat for ever
        like a boy's?

Knowledge comes, but wisdom lingers, and I linger
        on the shore,
And the individual withers, and the world is more
        and more.

Not in vain the distance beacons. Forward,
        forward, let us range,
Let the great world spin for ever down the ringing
        grooves of change.

Let it fall on Locksley Hall, with rain or hail, or fire
        or snow;
For the mighty wind arises, roaring seaward, and I
        go.

—stanzas from "Locksley Hall,"
by Alfred, Lord Tennyson

One.

From the Earth to the Moon.

God is great.

God is great.

Omry Inbar awoke and, as always, opened his eyes slowly, morning lethargy filling his arms and legs like a weight of heated sand, looking up at the ceiling, at an interplay of random shadows in the steely half-light of *subh*.

God is great. The Caller's voice echoing, hollow and eerie, from the cosmodrome's public address system, *Allahu . . .* a long, mournful wail, crossing the stony desert land of the Maghrebi back-country, *akbar* chopped short, decisive.

I bear witness there is no god but God.

Omry Inbar stretching, feeling the rubbery muscles of his back arch, spinal cartilage crackling softly, rubbing the side of his face against a soft silk pillowslip, enjoying those last minutes of half-awareness, those last cloudy moments of sleep.

I bear witness that Muhammad is the messenger of God.

Surrenderers of the Path rising, tardy if they hadn't already risen, completing their ablutions while the People of the Book slept on, getting out their rugs, preparing to submit . . .

Come to prayer.

Come to contentment.

Prayer is better than sleep.

Those interesting words of the *adhan*. Prayer is better than sleep. Sitting up now, feet on a soft, dark, intricately-patterned rug, listening to words that were infinitely more familiar than the prayers of his own long-lost faith.

There is no god but God.

Thinking, but here I am, merely a Jew, able to sit comfortably on the edge of my bed, while the Faithful scramble to prayer. The public relations people needed one of the six to be something other than *Sunni*. A Christian, perhaps, as a sop to the United Arab Republic's powerful fifteen percent minority. There were forty million of them, living in city ghettos and rural villages, stretching across the land from the Tigris frontier of Iran to the Maghreb's Atlantic shore.

No. Too obvious. A *Shi'ah*, perhaps? Someone from the small Levantine population, clustered around Beirut, a goodwill gesture to our supposed ally Iran, all that buffers us from the might of Green China . . .

But it needed to be someone who would fit in with the crew of *al-Qamar*, someone who could do real scientific labor, this not being a public-relations expedition. What they found was a Jewish planetologist, a Jew who could stand in front of the TV cameras and reassure the world that this was a fair, democratic, *secular* UAR. A Jew who could be counted on not to embarrass them with inappropriate Jewish prayers. Are we bitter then, Omry Inbar? Do we feel like some twentieth century American nigger, condemned to stand at the back of the bus?

That's the way *il-Masihhiyyin* feel, it seems. TV news only yesterday, sandwiched between *al-Qamar*'s launch preparations and film of the ongoing bloody war between Argentina and Brazil, proxies in the battle for preeminence of the UAR and China. Christians insisting they could *so* use the library of the Great *Masjid* in Qahira, where the Dead Sea Scrolls were kept.

Bitter smile.

No Jew would dare ask, much less demand.

And *Yisraël* has been gone for a hundred years already.

He stood and walked to the open window, pushed the heavy draperies aside, looked out on morning light. The sky was bright blue-gray overhead, cloudless, tarnished by a high haze of tawny desert dust, the concrete and rocky sand below pale tan and gold, the air still cold with night, though, in another hour, it would be hot. Low, stuccoed buildings in the foreground, concrete basins with imported desert plants from around the world, an extravagant little fountain, spraying its pretty, rainbow-tangled mist.

Faithful taking up their positions, more or less lined up, facing the *qibla* of Islam. Open hands raised to shoulder height, uttering the Magnification together, dissociating themselves from all earthly affairs for the duration of the prayer. Over here a few Partisans of Ali, praying together.

Beyond them, a little knot of Faithless. Atheists and Secular Humanists standing idly by, because nothing compelled them to prayer, but the rules said you must stand politely, quietly while others prostrated themselves before God.

Three Christians kneeling beside the fountain, heads bowed over clasped hands. Here in the Maghreb, they'd be Roman-rite Catholics. Maybe there'd be a Jew standing safely among the atheists. Maybe not. *Muslimin* below, saying, "God is One, the eternal God, begetting not and unbegotten; none is equal to Him."

Omry Inbar raised his eyes from the little square with its fountain and praying workmen, looked out across the desert to Hammaghir Cosmodrome's main launch complex, and felt his heart pulse once, very hard, in his chest, felt the hair on the back of his neck prickle with anticipation.

There, amid the gantries and cranes, the golden cone of *al-Qamar* rose out of the desert dust. Waiting. Waiting for me. My God. We're going to the Moon again at last. Three generations since the Americans had so suddenly closed their moonbase and brought their people home. Three generations since they'd closed their country like a fortress. Letting no one in, so very few out. Tourists, scholars mostly, exiting through the big rural embassy southwest of London. Serious men and women with bombs in their heads, scattering around the world.

There would be Americans here to watch the launch tomorrow. A small gathering the government had reluctantly let in. Historians, they said. People would avoid them, like carriers of some loathsome disease.

Paris, of course, had had to be evacuated, had never really been completely restored, after the *Sureté* arrested that man, put him to the question with implements of torture. Four-tenths of a kiloton, they said. Only four-tenths. Like four hundred tons of dynamite. Not much radioactivity. Fragments of police headquarters strewn far and wide, the Seine's waters filling up the little crater, carrying bomb debris down through Normandy to the sea.

And the Tower went down. French will never forgive them for that. Not that it matters, anyway. Who are the French, these days, now that Brittany and Provence and Aquitaine have their independence? Nothing. Just the snobbish overlords of some tiny, poor Ferenghi principality. Italians with funny accents, that's all.

We pretend. We pretend the Americans are no more. We pretend they're . . . irrelevant. We pretend, but . . .

Down below, the prayers of *subh* were finished, a sliver of sun brilliant on the eastern horizon, men and women hurrying off to do their jobs, for, in only seven hours, *al-Qamar* would rise above the Sahara.

Seven hours, and I go to the Moon.

Shema Yisraël, adonai elohanu, adonai ehod.

I remember, after all.

Ling Erhshan was proud of his moonship, hardly able to believe the deed was nearly done, but knew *Ming Tian* was a pathetic little beast, nonetheless.

Look at her, standing on this century-old launch pad, surrounded by the girders and struts of the service tower assembly. A bell-shaped reentry capsule, all that would come home, just four meters across its base, a little less than that high, sitting atop a landing rocket the same diameter that was little more than a restartable hypergolic upper stage, newly equipped with extendible legs, a stage basically identical to the one China had been using to deliver large comsats to geosynchronous earth orbit since the late forties of the previous century. Had been using since America abandoned the Moon.

And all of it mounted atop a *Shadow-2b* launch vehicle, a hydrogen-powered sustainer with modified plumbing so its fuel could be topped-off on orbit, white-painted core obscured by the slimmer black shapes of six solid-fuel strap-on boosters. Synthetic rubber. Purified fertilizer. Powdered aluminum. Twentieth century technology, dating back a hundred-sixty years and more, to the days of Apollo and those first flights to the Moon.

You had to hand it to those Americans. Not every people would have had the will to go to the Moon twice, then turn around and abandon it twice. Amazing folk. Inscrutable.

And, of course, no Americans—those few who traveled abroad—were ever allowed inside China, not with their country closed up like a giant fortress, not with those few, "scholarly tourists," wandering the world with nuclear weapons secreted in their heads.

When that woman blew up in Tokyo, back in 2104 . . .

It'd been repaired of course, the Ginza rebuilt, but still . . .

Keep them out of China. Please.

Ling stood on the upper access arm for a while, looking out over afternoon desert, past the buildings nearest the launch complex, toward glimmering Lop Nor, freshly refilled as part of the latest reclamation/resettlement project. It had been a beautiful day, with the bluest of skies, the freshest of desert breezes, really a rare day for the old Taklamakan, where once the Tarim Darya had flowed down to the Sarmatian Sea, on the old, dead west coast, from whence ancient Chinese mariners had set sail for Atlantis of the Mist.

You've come a long way for an orphan boy, old Mr. Nothing-from-the-Mountain. A long way from orphanage to scholarship to professorship to bureaucratic power. Built your moonship, arranged to fly it yourself.

Too bad it's come to this.

Too bad about the Arabs.

Imagine the historical tension, the world-wide wonder, if people *knew* we were here, knew that we too were about to fly. But they didn't know. No one knew. And no one *would* know until tomorrow. The UAR program had been conducted quite openly, with regular reports in the global news media, just the way those similar Americans of long ago had conducted Apollo, taking their triumphs, making their mistakes, before the eyes of the world.

Strange to think of the Arabs and Americans, supposedly so different, behaving in such similar ways. Different? No. The old Americans, the Americans of the last millennium, were accounted the second most religious folk of the world, second only to the prayer-mumbling millions of Hindu India. Why should we be surprised that they failed to see the crystalline logic of *Tao*?

Americans and Arabs alike, driven not by cool, considered, rational self-interest, but by the torrid heat of their impossible dreams and wanton fantasies. How much difference is there, really, between Sindbad the Sailor and Dirty Harry? Go ahead, then, make my day.

And, meanwhile, we, we supposedly free, supposedly dispassionate, mighty, capitalist Chinese, people of what the world chooses to call Green China . . . all in secret. Hidden. Why? Because we might fail? Or because we feared the Arabs might hurry then, might beat us to the goal?

Yet it's come to this, here and now, as we rush against the clock's blinking cursor, hurry to launch on the same day after all.

Down at the distal end of the access arm, technicians were working on the capsule, beginning the task of buttoning *Ming Tian* up for her voyage, now only hours away. They stopped to shake his hand, Chen Li and his crew slapping him on the back. Laughing. Wish I could go with you, Professor.

I wish you could too, old friend.

Chen Li had been his chief technician since the project's inception, in secret, fifteen long years ago. If it hadn't been for the Arabs, he'd be boarding her now, to fly by my side. He and four others, the originally planned crew of six.

Ling sighed and stooped, climbing through the open hatch into the capsule's interior. Light green paint, polished metal struts, matte black control panel with red-LED readouts and color-LCD monitors. Colonel Chang Wushi reclining in the pilot's chair. Da Chai, an agent of the government's nameless security agency, next to him as flight engineer. My place. Chen Li's place.

Still, the two, with their backups, had trained alongside the real crew for three years now. Ever since the government decided it couldn't let a crew of peaceful academics race UAR to the Moon.

Because who knew what the Americans had left behind at

their old base? They'd come out of there in an awful hurry, they had. Gone home in a rush, flight after flight ferrying passengers and cargo home. Then nothing. Then America closing its doors, letting no one in, only "tourists" out. Tourists with bombs in their heads. Ling Erhshan had been to the American embassy outside London just once. It was, in some ways, the twenty-second century's biggest tourist attraction. Come see America's face on the world.

Every now and again you'd see a strange plane take off or land. And you'd have to wonder just how, *how*, these ancestorless Americans could build a silent, wingless aircraft that could take off and land vertically, could transition to horizontal flight like *that*, could accelerate at ten gees, rising steeply into the stratosphere, turning away west, leaving behind some thin rumble of an impossibly quiet sonic boom.

There were stories, all right, about what was inside Fortress America. Tourists' tales, told to people more curious than wise, stories leaked from the security agencies of the UAR and China, who still flew spy satellites overhead.

America the Consumer Paradise. America of the magic toys.

But the toys seldom escaped. Aircraft that approached her shores found themselves unaccountably turning away. Ships that came within a hundred kilometers simply stopped. You could go to Mexico and stand by the Rio Grande, could go stand in the Canadian woods, and marvel at those walls of solid air. Could marvel at fairy castles visible in the distance, like something, yes, very much like something out of some American fantasy movie of the 1930s.

Could go stand on Vancouver Island and watch the magic planes go back and forth between the mainland and Hawaii, or on up to Alaska. Seventy years. Now this.

Ming Tian no longer had room for a crew of six because the government had decided that, in place of three men, in place of her principal scientific instruments, she would carry a collimated particle beam weapon and storage battery of some advanced design, the same sort of weapon Chinese warships carried to knock down incoming missiles.

What do they think? The Arabs are going to shoot anti-shipping missiles at us from the Moon? Maybe so. Who knows what governments think? If anything.

So he sighed and sat down on the edge of his acceleration couch, began going over his own checklists, making his own preparations. Soon it would be time to suit up. Suit up and fly away to the Moon.

Sergeant-Major Astrid Kincaid, late of the Third Division, USMC Lunar Expeditionary Force, slid the middle and ring fingers of her right hand into the gyndroid's vagina, began palpating the pretty machine's clitoris with the ball of her thumb, slowly, gently, a small circling motion, clockwise little ohs. Tissues were swelling inside, moistening, ridges of pubococcygeus muscle tightening on cue, gripping her fingers with delicate strength, rippling back upward to a cervical os that she knew would slowly descend.

Ought to, anyway, if I've done this right . . .

She rubbed her left hand slowly back and forth across the gyndroid's abdomen, just above the thing's patch of sparse black pubic hair, feeling muscles there tighten, looked over at the holodisplay floating above the progtool's input pad.

Hmh. Not quite right.

She reached out and tapped the spinal ganglion feedback loop icon, numeric spinner adjusting appropriately, and listened to the gyndroid's soft sigh.

Looked up at its face.

Pretty, black eyes, classic almond-shaped eyes, slitted with deepening passion, mouth open just a little bit, delicate sheen of sweat on its brow, neutral North-Asian complexion just beginning to flush as its faux hormones surged.

Hmh. She tapped on the plateau icon, and the gyndroid's back arched a little, pressing harder against her hand, pelvis cupping forward, straightening its vaginal path so the fingers could go a little deeper.

And Astrid Kincaid found herself looking into those loving black eyes, eyes she'd painted with such care, watching them sparkle with pleasure, flood with faux happiness, with faux life, with . . .

The gyndroid's head went back, thrashing against the pillow, mouth opening, "*Oh . . .*" hips pushing forward, vaginal muscles clenching, massaging as no real woman's unmodified vagina ever would, cervical os coming down, right to where . . . She looked over at the display, where Amaterasu's response graph was compared to a feedback normative derived from Roddie's MedDep records. Well. If he doesn't like *this* for his birthday, the ungrateful little bastard . . .

She could feel the gyndroid's muscles relaxing, gripping her fingers ever so gently. Just the way Roddie would like it. Amaterasu opened her eyes, looking down at Astrid, eyes filled with sleepy, loving softness, and whispered, "Thank you, Mother. It was wonderful."

She nodded slowly. Tell it, You're welcome, Daughter? A small twinge there. Old mammalian conscience speaking. From the days when the Goddess had us care for one another. She slid her fingers out, wiping her hand on the front of her lab smock, still looking into the gyndroid's haunting eyes.

I remember. I remember when I was so bored with men. What? Twenty, thirty years ago now. When I had MedDep adjust my hormones so I'd love women more than men. When this thing . . . But then I grew bored with that. As I grow bored with everything. As Roddie will grow bored with this new toy. A year. Two years. A decade. And another, another . . .

And so little brother Roddie, who was an infant when I was a teenager, is 114 years old today. And, in another six weeks, I will be 130 . . . The avalanche of time, opening up a gulf of years between then and now. Between that old, young life, when we all expected to die, and this . . . immortality.

She reached out for the progtool's input pad, and the gyndroid's hand reached out to touch her arm. "Mother . . ."

Astrid looked at it again, at the almost-suffering, faux suffering, in those beautiful black eyes. She waited.

The gyndroid said, "Will I remember this moment?" Pleading in those eyes.

A long pause, then Astrid shook her head. "No, Amaterasu. You'll forget." Beautiful black eyes filling with a mist of tears. Of sorrow. Faux sorrow.

Astrid finished her movement, fingers reaching out to tap,

just once, on the master-switch icon. The light of life in the gyndroid's eyes faded, the eyes closed, the lovely, responsive body went still, arm relaxing, resting gently on the edge of the workbench.

Well, it was a wonderful new toy. And I had a wonderful time building it. Something to interest me, if only for a little while, experience defining the latest fad, the rash of hobbyist kits appearing everywhere, people looking for something new in a world whose offering of experiences grew increasingly sparse.

She reset the gyndroid's memory table, punched in the codes that would bond it to Roddie as soon as it awoke and beheld itself in his arms. Amaterasu's vagina would moisten with anticipation as soon as it saw his face.

It? She? I wonder how the gyndroid perceives itself?

She searched through the datasets until the ID matrix came up. He. She shook her head and smiled. They'd probably programmed this off some two-generation-old piece of industrial machinery, from the first flush of development, when the Scavenger records were first made public. She tapped in new code, and Amaterasu became a woman.

Roddie would like that.

Astrid powered down the progtool, holodisplay sliding out of existence, disappearing through a slot in thin air, closed the input pad, then stood and went around to the gyndroid's head. Popped the sensors out of its, no *her* spun-fiber brain tissue. Closed the skull, slid the pate, with its long, silky black Asian-girl hair into place, let it reattach itself, let the sensors reel back into their progtool sockets.

Stood looking down at Amaterasu the Gyndroid. Almost in sorrow. Real sorrow? Hard to know. My feelings may be faux feelings by now. What's left of the woman I was so long ago? Or the girl who came before her? The child who played soldier, who grew up following the American Renaissance. Who excelled in athletics, who toughened her spirit and joined the Marines and went off to the Moon when the . . . Event happened.

Long gone, I suspect. Erased by decades of change. Change and sameness. Brief memory of Dale Millikan, lost and gone forever. Brief pulse of regret. Was I ever that innocent? No. Never. She came around to the gyndroid's side, reached down and dug one finger into its, her navel, push and twist just so, and pulled open the carapace, delicate breasts rising on a hinged chest wall.

Hardly anything real in there, all the parts necessary for pure robotic function so terribly miniaturized, beyond anything we could ever have imagined when I was young. Monofilament muscles. Stepper motors the size of a housefly that could lift a house from its foundation. A fusion powerplant fueled by atmospheric condensation.

Without her human parts, her woman parts, Amaterasu would be an empty shell. These bellows just faux lungs, so she could pretend to breathe. *So she can blow out the candles on her birthday cake* . . . A nice, compact faux digestive system so she could eat and drink, confront her lover with the excitement of faux elimination, on demand. Big canisters of concentrated chemicals down where the intestines ought to be. So she can manufacture lubricants and sweats, filled with pheromones to excite Roddie's senses, enhance his every pleasure . . .

She snapped the hull shut and, once again, Amaterasu was a sleeping girl.

The shower room, brightly lit, was all shiny chrome, white porcelain, black tiles, Astrid Kincaid getting undressed, not quite oblivious to its stark, utilitarian symmetry. Its beauty. Yes. I'd call it that. Standing in the middle of the floor, dropping her clothes in an untidy pile while the shower hissed behind its frosted glass door, stray bits of steam starting to roll up by the ceiling.

The image in the mirror.

A tan, Caucasian woman, mature woman of indeterminate age. Not young, you understand. But not old. Tall. Robust. Limbs lined with smooth muscle. Belly flat above neatly outlined pelvic bones, padded enough to hide the hardness there. Breasts large enough to be . . . womanly? Hair of spun gold, shining like metal in the sun. Eyes of molten silver.

Is that my face? I can't remember.

A pretty face, yes. But strong. A soldier's face, perhaps.

Suddenly conscious, just then, of the faint tang of her own sweat. Hardly there at all, but reminding you of other sweaty days, sweaty days and nights that seemed to go on and on, 'til you thought you'd have to die to escape. She got into the shower, turning her back to the spray, feeling the water sluice down over her skin, rushing over her shoulders, little waterfalls forming, water streaming off the ends of her nipples.

Bar of soap, soft in her hand, pale violet soap with a smell of lilacs, wet soap going round and round between her hands, soap foaming up white. Slick foam rubbed on her skin. Rubbed in her armpits, around the base of her neck, where sweat would accumulate. Soft, slick soap foam rubbed on her belly and down between her legs, wet hair matting suddenly, golden hair like metal wire growing spiky and strange.

Dull thought—Playing with the robot should have excited me. Didn't. Hands motionless down between her legs, fingers . . . not even tempted?

No.

I haven't felt like it in a long damned time.

Tired. I'm tired.

Tired for years. Maybe even decades.

A soft sigh, hands resuming their washing, then turning round and round under the showerhead, clean water carrying away the foam, not carrying away the sense of . . . exhaustion? No. Impossible for me to be tired. Little symbiotes in your blood, inside your cells, symbiotes substituted for organelles.

Tipping her head back under the shower now, letting the water run through her hair, down over her face, closing her eyes, feeling it run over her lips. Not lost. Nobody's ever lost anymore.

Image of a face. Of many faces. Lost.

Faces falling down through all the unending universes, down to the bedrock of Platonic Reality and beyond. Bitter smile. We understand so much now. And so little.

Hard pang of despair. Oh, God damn you, Dale Millikan. Why did you have to go and die on me? Image of his face, aging face, face from the days before immortality engulfed us all. Crisp gray hair. A hint of jowl line. Neutral grayish-brown eyes. Eyes full of . . . full of telling. Of . . .

Image of Dale . . . *snap* . . . reduced to a little pile of clean white bones. Is that what happened? Is it? That old, old panic, that old sorrow, welling right up, then . . . You don't *know*. You weren't *there*. What if he *didn't* die? What if he's out there, somewhere, wandering, lost, waiting for you?

That pathetic upwelling of hope.

Ridiculous hope.

Dead and gone. You know that. Dead and gone, like all the others. What's this hard lump in your throat then, Astrid Kincaid?

Then, sitting in the living room, hot mug of black coffee cradled in her hands, settled into her old red favorite chair beside the big, open bay window, window facing the sea. Pale gray ocean out there, sky slowly brightening, soon to be fired by sunrise, sun just below the horizon. In the night, it'd looked like a slow-rolling landscape of molten licorice.

Dark candy sweeping up onto my beach.

Out there, somewhere, just a few thousand miles away, lay the shores of Africa. Morocco, we used to call it. Now the coast of the UAR state of Maghreb. Where *al-Qamar* rests poised on its forbidden launch pad.

By God, they are really going.

Too bad.

Alone in her room then, her room of many years, undisturbed years. Shelf on endless shelf of old things. Ancient things. My father's books. My mother's books. Because they died not long before the gods granted us immortality. Momentary pulse of agèd, fading horror. *The last generation of Americans who had to die* . . . My own books, from when I was young, from the last dying days of real books, when I was a child.

Cardreaders from the years after that. From when I was in school, from when I was a young soldier. The little black cube of her library tap, which held all the books in America. Her . . . artifacts.

A Scavenger transliterator. Next to it, a modern analysis

device, with a neat input pad and polymetric display system. A government-supplied cerebroanalikon engine tying them together. One of the benefits of having been in on it from the beginning. You already *knew.* Knew everything the government wanted to conceal. They had to let you in on it, or kill you, imprison you, something . . .

Waste not, want not, Sergeant, the smiling politician said, after she finished her closed-door Senate testimony in the last days of the Closure Hearings. Set her free, put her on half pay, with access to hardware and a license to do direct research on Colonial artifacts brought back from . . . well. From the Moon. That was all they ever said.

And the e-mail message on the library tap holodisplay, message already three days old. Recalled to active duty, Sergeant-Major Astrid Kincaid. And you know why. Yes I do, damn it. Because none of the God-damned *officers* are willing to go back . . . out there. But something has to be done, and done now. They should never have let it get this far.

Americans never change. We always wait until there's nothing left to do but . . . act.

Outside, the sun was rising, making a bright, shimmering path over the no-longer wine-dark sea. Four thousand miles away, in the deserts of Maghreb, it would be mid-morning now.

Not long after the built-in hold for prayers at *zuhr,* summer sun standing high overhead, waves of heat making the desert shiver like an illusion of itself, Qamal ibn-Aziz Alireza stood in the white room atop *al-Qamar*'s gantry, letting the technicians help him into his flight suit, a familiar, already time-worn ritual.

Tall and thin, handsome, regular of feature and dark of skin, with dark brown eyes and coarse, short black hair, a close-cropped chin-strap of a regulation Air Force beard. Picked as commander, perhaps, for the image he'd make on TV.

Image. That's me.

A not-quite-bitter thought.

Bitter? Why bother? I am going. That's all that matters.

This is the historical cusp of all that we've worked for, worked already for half a generation. Because we perceived the end of human civilization—the end of history—coming over time's horizon, we chose now to go to the Moon, then beyond. To save ourselves, and ultimately everyone else. Everyone living outside the invisible walls of Fortress America.

Historical cusp.

Strange notion.

What if we hadn't decided to go?

What if the UAR's politicians had squabbled and argued and fought until it was too late? Imagine, for just a moment, some other history, where the world's population grew while its resources dwindled. Images of war and famine. Green China reaching out with all its might and all its people to take over what's left of the Earth.

Image of some remote day, only not so remote now, image of a time no more than a century or two down the historical road. Image of squalid survivors, battling desperately for the scraps their ancestors left behind, facing an empty future, looking now at their own images of a dead, empty world. Unless . . .

Unless the Americans emerge. Emerge with their magical, inexplicable technologies to save us all. Or emerge with brooms of fire to sweep us all away.

The other members of the crew had already gone ahead. Mahal and Tariq, Rahman, Inbar and Zeq, already aboard, already strapped in their seats, running the engineering checks, getting ready for launch.

We keep telling ourselves about the future we imagine. Images of the Space-Faring Civilization to come. Images of escape. Escape from the forces of History. But you know, you just know, that somewhere in the councils of government, there are men who harbor darker dreams. What was it the Americans found on the Moon, three generations ago? What was it that sent them flying home, sent them into hiding?

When we go to the Moon, first, foremost, we look for the sources of the Americans' magic. Why else target our first landing for the site of their old polar base? Because we know they found ice there? Hardly.

Grimace of distaste. Like scavengers. After scraps.

Hard for me to concentrate today, despite decades of military discipline, despite years of piloting discipline. Despite the fact that I've been to orbit six times before, though I know the rituals.

This is different. Today, I'm going to the Moon.

Hard to imagine . . .

Head filled instead with memories of the night before. Of taking his two daughters to bed, tucking them in, kissing them good night. Thinking, I'll already be gone when they awaken in the morning. They'll see me on TV. See me fly away into the sky . . .

Memories of taking his fretful wife, of taking lovely Amîna to bed. Of making love to her, then comforting her while she cried. Nothing will happen. You'll see. It's just one more flight into space. Almost routine. Every part has been tested. But, if something goes wrong, you'll be so far away . . .

He'd smiled and held her and lied to her.

The technicians finished zipping him in, then, smiling for the cameras, he shook hands all around and they opened the door to the catwalk, escorted him across open space to the ship. Searing desert sun, and yet it was cold out here. Would be cold to men not cocooned in spacesuits. Frosty smoke drifting off the sloping sides of the ship, just the way they had on his other launches. He stopped and looked down. Men still on the concrete below, though the ship was full of liquid oxygen and hydrogen now, checking out the first stage's great annular engine structure.

Al-Qamar was a brilliant engineering design, snatched from old American books, designs the Americans could have built in the twentieth century. Should have built no later than the twenty-first. The upper stage was a blunted golden cone, not so very different from the experimental SSTO designs the Americans *had* built in the 1990s.

So we went ahead and built a real aerospike engine, complete with a gas-layer heat-shield, so we could descend tail-first all the way from orbit, but it's still the same design. Little six-man SSTO ship, able to haul a mere 20,000 kilograms to low earth-orbit.

Until we made a much larger one and made this ship its cargo.

The lower stage was chopped off, ending in a frustum on which the upper stage would sit for the ride above the atmosphere. They'd covered that with a temporary fairing for the radio-controlled booster's one ride to orbit, its one test flight.

Almost lost her, too, when we had trouble with the comsat link.

Today, the booster wasn't going all the way into space. After placing *al-Qamar* on a 12,000-kilometer suborbital trajectory, she'd brake and come down at at-Ta'if airfield, not far from Mecca. The Faithful, on their *hajra*, would see her fly overhead, would see her land.

A moment of remembering that other desert, the desert of his childhood, far to the east, the land beyond the sunrise. An adolescent moment, sitting astride his horse, hooves clattering on a rocky stone desert of degraded lava flows, dry gunpowder smell in his nose, smell of the desert wind.

A rich man's son on a rich man's horse, on weekend holiday from a rich man's private school. Pretending. Pretending. And yet . . . Wind in my face, sharp, abrading skin surface. Brilliant sun glaring in my eyes, beating down on a Bedawi's *ghutra*, cloth headdress topped with a golden *igal* it was true, but a *ghutra* nonetheless . . . Surge of the horse between my legs, chuffing bellows of its breathing as we rode along.

Pretending. Pretending. Yet sons of the desert still.

Southern Hejaz, the ancient land, the heartland. Not so very far from where I was born. In the old days, before the Republic, they would've called me a prince. He turned and walked toward *al-Qamar*'s hatch, where more technicians were waiting, and thought. Prince? *Wállah!* Colonel suits me just fine.

Just a memory within a memory, momentary, almost elusive, almost illusory. Ahmad Zeq could recall sitting in a hard wooden chair in the hallway at school. Hallway in the engineering building. Sitting with the other graduates. Mostly silent. Hot, sweaty silence in the hallway. An occasional soft murmur, one sufferer to another. Mostly silence. A stir of cloth, a rustling whisper of linen as someone shifted uncomfortably. An involuntary intestinal rumble, someone trying desperately not to fart. The soft cluck of a dry swallow.

My own thoughts. Desperate. Silly. Childish. Pleading.

If it please you, O God, this poor, unworthy homosexual man would like to pass his Engineering Board Orals.

And then. Back then. Those ridiculous inner words triggering a memory of the previous night. I should have been studying. Or sleeping. So I'd be fresh and rested for the ordeal. Just one thin beer, to put me at my ease. A thin beer, like I was a European or a Christian or a Jew or an atheist, I said, because a good Muslim's coffee will only keep me awake. And that fucking Englishman grinning up at me from between my legs, down some dark and stinking alleyway, kneeling there, grinning up at me, smacking his blubbery lips and croaking, "Jism-Allah!"

I should have kneed him right in his weak English chin.

Then, back in the hot, stifling hallway. Wishing he'd slept instead of partying the night away. Tired. Tired. Tired. And then the proctor's voice. "Zeq? Your turn." Exhausted, unworthy homosexual man, shuffling off to bare his neck for the headsman's sharp sword. Passing the Oral Boards anyway, examiners seeming to accept his occasional helpless giggle in the midst of some serious problem as if it happened all the time.

Nerves, they'd be thinking. Just nerves. I passed. Passed, and put my feet on the road that led to *al-Qamar* . . . Flash to present. Attention to task at hand. *Al-Qamar* . . .

Ahmad Zeq put his hand on the master switch, let his neck fall back onto the headrest, eyes on his readouts, and listened while Alireza counted down. Counted down like a hero in some old adventure movie, Arabic numbers like sharp little snarls.

It-neyn.

Wehid.

Sif.

He snapped the switch in with his thumb, and muttered, *"Yibtidi."* Soft, hardly audible, yet seeming to echo through the ship. *Begin.* The mission clock, set to 00:00:00:00, began to advance, red numbers flickering, seconds on the far left, which would lead to minutes, then hours, then days on the far right. Two weeks. Fourteen days. Then we'll be home again, our little ship setting down on a broad concrete pad off the end of the military runway . . .

No noise. Nothing so dramatic. Just a faint shivering at first, movement transmitted through structural members, through his chair and into his body. Everything all right so far, sensors from the booster's annular combustion chamber reporting temperature and pressure, reporting the results of stratified ignition. Thrust stabilizing, pressure building up . . .

Zeq looked up from his console, looked out through the pilot's window, and the bright yellow landscape of the Sahara desert just went down, dropped out of sight, as *al-Qamar* rose on its pillar of translucent fire, like an elevator into the sky.

What shall I say? thought Ahmad Zeq. To the world, he whispered, *"Alhamdulilah."*

From a little more than 200 kilometers up, the Earth turning below was, for Ling Erhshan, an unbelievable sight. No amount of preparation, the viewing of any number of old films and tapes and VR sensies . . . Not Mercury-Gemini-Apollo, nor all those old IMAX films, nothing the Russians had done, nothing from the American Renaissance and their return to the Moon in the middle of the last century . . .

Nothing. That was it. Absolutely nothing.

While Chang Wushi twiddled his pilot's controls, muttering singsong under his breath, a man caught up in the heavy work of talking to himself, while Da Chai monitored the ship's systems and struggled with a recalcitrant rendezvous radar, Ling stared out the window, spellbound.

Below, the Pacific was a featureless expanse of shiny blue water. Glittering. Shimmering. Catching sunlight off the wavetops. Not a cloud in sight. How can that be? Not a cloud in sight, and I can see for ten thousand miles. Down by the horizon, where a little band of light blue air separated the dark blue of sea from the black of space, moonrise. Full Moon bulging up from the wall of the world. Somewhere, out there, my Arab comrades are halfway to the Moon. Regret? No. The more who go, the more likely we are to stay. This time.

The image of their ship, seen on the video net just hours before the first Chinese tanker was due to lift off had been . . . well. "Futuristic" was the word he wanted to use. Though they were all living in the future now, that was certain. A legacy from twentieth century America. A legacy from all those pathetic old writers who dreamed of space and more space, of impossible things like time travel and silly things like pills taking the place of food . . .

Da Chai said, "Professor. I need your help."

Terse. Sharply spoken. A rebuke.

But the view out the window . . .

He turned away with a sigh. "The problem?"

Da Chai tapped the radar CRT. "The periodic update is leaving ghosts. Well. I think they're ghosts. But they also get updated, and now I can't tell . . ." Frustration in his voice.

Ling looked at the screen and shrugged. "Yes. We never did solve the sprite problem. If Chen Li were here . . ."

"But he's not. Can you fix it? Do we need to get him on the radio?" Tapping on the screen again, angrily. "One of these things is the Tanker. I need to know which one."

A slow nod, another sigh. Pull yourself together. Transcend. This is an adventure, yes, with so many aesthetic qualities, but . . . he folded down the radar computer's hidden keypad and tapped, blanking the image, scrolling numbers, reading stored values, data from error traps they'd left in place when the schedule slipped and the software wasn't quite ready. Yes. Not quite ready. Just ready enough.

The radar control subsystem had been whipped up from a twenty-year-old Japanese design. You'd think, they could come up with a *new* design, somehow, sometime . . . But, under Chinese tutelage, the Japanese seemed to lose their spark of usefulness.

Tap. Tap-tap. The screen blanked and came up again, this

time with only one image of the tanker, bracketed by glowing white numbers. Range. Relative velocity. Offset vector . . .

Chang Wushi said, "Never mind. I've made visual contact."

A look of repressed hostility from Da Chai. Ling Erhshan smiled and shrugged. I told you, if only Chen Li were along . . . No point in that. By the living spirits that inhabit everything, we're going to the Moon! Going last, it's true, but going. He felt the skin of his face flush, warm with delight as he turned back to the window . . .

Sudden pang. The unmanned tanker was hanging in space, motionless, a few hundred meters away, sunlight almost blinding on its featureless, white-painted hull.

I can't believe I am actually here.

Chang Wushi muttered, "We crash into that thing, you'll believe it."

If only for just a moment.

"It looks," said Kincaid, "like an old MiG-21 standing on its tail."

The little techie, who'd said his name was Bruce, stood quietly at her side, looking at the Scavenger scoutship, hands in the pockets of his artfully roughed-up blue jeans, hair blowing in the warm, humid Pacific breeze. "Guess so."

Tall, thin, aerodynamically clean hull. Flat nose inlet with a shock-deflector cone poking out. Smallish triangular wings midway up. Four skewed-vane landing legs around the base. No bubble canopy, though. Little round windows, like the windows on an old-fashioned airliner, arrayed in neat little rows. And sixty meters tall, four meters in diameter. Painted silver. Other techies clustered around that base, doing something to the engine. Men in uniform going up and down a ramp that extruded from between two landing legs, leading to a small, brightly-lit hole near the bottom of the hull.

If this was a *real* rocket, they'd be walking into a fuel tank.

Real rocket. Like the ones we had back then.

Not this magic thing.

I wonder how much this is like the one Ethwŷn Nasóól found, when he came through the stargate on Æghóng and found his first abandoned Colony? Maybe like this, maybe not. Visuals in Scavenger literature were hardly evocative. More like exploded diagrams, interladen with numbers and subillustrations.

Language hard to read too, even when you knew it well. Not like a human language. Even the driest technical literature more like some complex form of poetry, vertical rows of complexly structured pseudo-ideograms, with parenthetical remarks strung out on either side, paragraphs, if it was fair to call them that, more or less like a Scrabble board after the game is done.

The techie, a scrawny man with thin, sparse sandy hair who looked like he ought to have thick glasses covering his washed-out blue eyes, elbowed her hard in the ribs, standing way closer than he needed to, and said, "Sure are glad you folks decided you need this. We've had her ready to fly for fifty years."

Looking up at her, eyes sparkling.

Not looking into my eyes, no. Looking at my tits, the way they push out the front of this old uniform tunic. Well, you little shit . . .

The man had a habit of ostentatiously pissing in public, too, bellying up to the side of whatever building was handy, unreeling a pecker twice the size it ought to be, looking around to see who was watching.

All right. You can have anything you want, these days, so little Brucie here bought himself a big dick. All right. So why is he still only five-three? My toy soldiers all look like fucking Neanderthals and gorillas and comic book monsters. Is that any better?

Brucie elbowed her in the ribs again, standing closer still, and said, "Ah, say, Sergeant-Major?" She looked down at him. Sudden thickening of a fake Southern accent. "I wonder if y'all'd like to go off with me fer a quick fuck?" And now, eager like a puppy.

Disbelief. Here I am, standing next to a man who may be a hundred-fifty years old, and he says . . .

"Come on, Sarge. Be a sport."

All right. Hundred-fifty-year-old teenager. Sudden memory of Roddie opening up his birthday present. Amaterasu awakening, filling up with ersatz love. And Roddie bending her over the table, mushing her lovely little tits down in the birthday cake, cornholing her right in front of everyone, while his guests clapped and cheered him on.

A whole country full of centenarian teenagers.

Because never dying means you don't *really* have to grow up.

Brucie reached out, as if reaching for one of her breasts.

"In your fucking dreams, asshole."

A sudden crafty look. "Yeah? Well, I'm sure your specs are in the net somewhere, Sarge. In my dreams, as you say."

If this was some old movie, I'd reach down now and rip that pretty little pecker out by its bioengineered roots. Still, no rule says you *can't* grow up. If you want to. She glanced at her chronometer, and said, "You just get my ship ready, Brucie. You've got about four hours left."

Craft displaced by ingenuousness once again. He said, "That so, Sarge?" A shrug. "Well, we get to fly our toy. That's all that really matters." And a serious look, gazing fondly at the little Scavenger spaceship, superimposed against the broad, flat blue Pacific.

Something, Kincaid thought, we have in common. She looked up into the sky, and said, "Yeah. We shouldn't have stayed home. There's more to life than living forever."

Softly whispered: "No shit, Sarge. No shit."

Floating. Floating in the softest sea. No weight. No where. No when. Just floating with my eyes closed. Floating on my way to Heaven. God, I could stay like this forever. Just drifting, alone and unafraid . . .

Soft whisper of machinery somewhere. Faint hum of electronic something. Whisper of a turning motor. Soft tickle of air blowing in my face, just under my arms, coming from somewhere behind me. Faint itch of clinging sweat, drying sweat, hardly there, hardly there at all, just like me . . .

"All right. I'm ready." Inbar's voice, suddenly loud in her ears.

Subaïda Rahman opened her eyes and felt her insides

clench hard. Bright moonscape sweeping by below, no more than twenty kilometers straight down to the lowest plains, corroded, rolling mountains reaching up more than half that. Going by *fast!* No wind here . . .

Laughter. Alireza's voice, same volume. "Your heart rate was down below fifty-five. I thought you went to sleep."

"Um." Cough. A throat-clearing noise. Smooth, gray-brown plains flying under her now, running north along thirty, Mare Frigoris coming up. Just now over what? Lacus Mortis. She said, "Almost. Not quite."

"I understand *al-Qahira Journal* ran a big article on you in this morning's edition. They said you were very . . . calm, I think was the word they used."

Inbar's voice, fatigued, maybe a little out of breath, said, "*I'm* not calm. I'd like to get this *done.*" Though he'd been trained for zero-gee EVA, against just such an eventuality, Omry Inbar did *not* like this business of floating along in naked space. Rahman couldn't imagine . . . Maybe he was just afraid. Maybe a little motion sick.

Down below, the plains were ramping up into the north polar highlands as they passed by 70N. That wide caldera coming up to the west would be Meton, meaning in another few minutes they'd be over the rim of mountains separating Peary from Rozhdestvenskiy, where the old American base lay in ruins. We ought to be down there already. Timeline shot to Hell.

She toggled the two little hand controllers on her AMU's armrests, listened to the little peroxide thrusters stutter, noise transmitted through various structural members until it was inside her suit. Inertial tugging on her harness destroying the illusion of weightlessness for a moment, Moon moving beneath her, getting out from under her feet, going behind her back, featureless black space, starless space, sun-glare-dominated space coming round.

Al-Qamar's golden cone was about 200 meters away, floating free, skewed at an angle, nose away from her, fore-shortened, broad annular aerospike engine bulging toward her, three landing legs down and locked . . . and the fourth one stuck half open, main joint bent up like a dancer's knee,

Omry Inbar a fat white manikin clinging to the hull beside it, tools in place and strapped down. He said, "I need you to position the jack now."

"All right. I hadn't realized I'd drifted so far." More thruster thudding from behind her back and the ship started to grow. Down near the southern horizon, far beyond the ship, Earth was a tiny blue-white sliver, mostly black and lightless now.

I'll be almost sorry to be down on the Moon, back in gravity again. This dreamlike dance. Image of a woman, perhaps no more than fifty years old, perhaps no more than twenty years from now, dancing this dance out among the asteroids, out among the flying hills of Saturn's ring system . . .

Just the second step, that's all. Remembering President Morwar's speech, twelve short years ago. Twelve years since President Morwar and his scientific advisors decided there was only one way out of the world's inevitable downward spiral. One way for *us*, at any rate, for the desert UAR and its relatively small population. *We* can survive, you see. But the rest of them. They will drag us down. Forty billion people in the world today. Forty billion, of whom the Arabs constitute less than one percent. One percent of the world's people holding five percent of all the land, holding ten percent of all the material wealth.

Compare that to the five billion already starving in the princely states of Hind, to three billion Europeans in their own patchwork quilt of tiny republics. To the seven billion of southern Africa, to the six billion in South America. To the eight billion of Greater China, Green China, which had expanded to fill Siberia and Central Asia, had come all the way to the Ural Mountains.

To the billions of southeast Asia and Mexico and Central America. Even to the hundred million of isolated Canada, to the four hundred million refugees now crowding poverty-stricken Australia's dry red deserts.

You could look at all the old graphs and all the old plans, and you could see that no one ever extended them far enough. Far enough to see that, no matter what you did, no matter how draconian your solution, the world would come to an end, some time in the late twenty-second century, or early twenty-third.

President Morwar looking at his advisors. Gentlemen, that time is now. We have perhaps a half-century to do what we must, for, sooner or later, those starving billions will come for what we have. Come and take it, and then we'll all go down together.

And the Americans? A shrug. Who knows what they'll do? Waiting for them to save us would be like waiting for . . . I don't know. Waiting for the Archangels to come down and wash away our sins.

I was just a graduate-school girl then, trying to pass my courses, make honors, trying to keep grope-handed professors out of my skirt without offending them.

Sharp memory of that skinny, dark Sudanese mathematics professor, the one who held the honors seminar in advanced multivariable topology. Sitting beside her that afternoon in a back corner kiosk at the library, making her suddenly *very* sorry she'd worn that short dress, putting his hand on her thigh, grinning, tucking his fingers between her knees, making that little *prying* motion . . .

What *now*, little girl? An "honor" mark from this greasy little man is your ticket to the next level. And you do *so* want to be accepted into the astronaut corps. Applications have to be in by the first of Hazirahn, and . . .

But the image that called up. Lying on her back, dress pulled up, legs spread, his garlicky hummus-breath in her face.

Mmmh. Mmmh. This feels *soooo gooood*, little girl . . .

Small crunch of revulsion. Not against the act, which had been . . . rewarding, perhaps, the few times she'd tried it with . . . suitable boys. No. Against the implication. The implication.

Fingers prying at her thighs now. That other hand stealing up her arm, headed, perhaps, for a breast or two.

All right. Then think of something, little girl.

She'd smiled and taken him by the hand, patted him on the wrist. "I know just how you feel, Professor Wahid. It's so frustrating when a girl won't just . . . go along with it."

Puzzled look. "What do you mean?" Those fingers between her thighs relaxing just a bit.

"Well. You know I'm a lesbian, don't you?"

She'd almost laughed at his comic gape. "A lesbian? But . . ." A gesture at her body. Sudden quirk of anger. "But you don't *dress* like a lesbian. You don't—"

"My parents. My parents are *very* traditional."

Professor Wahid then, chewing his lower lip in dismay. "Why are we here then?"

Feigned astonishment. "Why, to talk about the seminar. It's . . . so seldom I get to talk to such an . . . intelligent, such a *learned* man." Push a button, pull the chain.

A soft popping of backpack thrusters and the ship was a golden wall before her, Inbar's plump face looking out at her through his helmet faceplate. Pale. Fretful. A face that pleaded, let's be *done* with this . . .

Pale, fat face. Deep, brilliant, penetrating eyes. He was one of the few who'd tried to bother her, during the years of training, as she moved up and up, got on crew rosters, got up in space on orbital missions, got herself named as American Technologies Specialist on the first flight to the Moon. Bothered me. Though I wore the uniform, walked the walk, talked the talk. Told me, fatuously, insipidly, how much he *liked* women in short hair and trousers . . .

All right. One of the few . . . *cosmopolitan* enough to see through the ruse. Well, Zeq of course. But he merely thought it was funny. Offering to get her dates with his female "pals."

She said, "Let's go."

Only gratitude in his eyes now. Let's go.

Looking out one of *Ming Tian*'s small portholes from ten thousand kilometers up, the Moon was a vast yellow circle of light, a circle of harshly-lit landscape, mountains becoming *real* mountains, endless circular craters becoming visible on the face of the shadowy maria.

Over the hump now, over the hump into the Moon's gravitational field and falling straight down. *Ming Tian* was moving slowly, no more than eight hundred kilometers an hour, bare residual velocity. But we're falling. Falling down to the

Moon. Behind them, Earth was a tiny, blue and white crescent. A lost world. I remember staring at the Moon when I was a boy . . .

Little boy Ling Erhshan, lying out on the orphanage fire escape—industrial stinks from the ruinous slums of Shanghai making the old brick walls of a two-hundred-year-old building seem damp and slimy—smelling the stench of Shanghai's close-packed sixty million souls, staring up at the old white Moon. White like death. No. Always yellow to me. Warm and yellow like the sun. Yellow like life.

The orphanage had had a little library, mostly children's primers. A few adult Chinese novels none of us could read. Some books printed in Russian we could do no more than essay, sounding out the Cyrillic characters, getting that Siberian girl, what was her name? Anyushka, to tell us what the words meant.

I remember finding that other book, *Moon Man*, printed in *pinyin Putonghua*, Chinese language in Romanic letters, a translation of an early twenty-first century story by some writer with an unpronounceable foreign name, Dutch, maybe English, name transliterated into simplified Chinese characters that meant "thimble valley."

Cover picture showing a muscular Caucasian hero in torn military camouflage, with sword and pistol to hand, beautiful, half-naked blond woman by his side, the two of them standing in an eldritch landscape, facing a red and blue tiger under a dark lavender sky, sky in which hung a blue-white crescent Earth. Realistic-looking Earth, because people had already seen it thus. Like the Earth hanging outside *Ming Tian* just now. The Moon I dreamed of seeing.

Wonderful, impossible story about a middle-aged soldier, called up against his will to fight in one of his country's wretched foreign adventures, author's anger reminding me how foul the world had seemed to its denizens at the turn of the millennium. They should have known how very much worse it would get. Yet they did nothing.

Story about a soldier standing on a mountaintop, defeated, watching as a cruise missile came in over the sea, smashed into the base of the cliff on which he stood. Nuclear explosion. Unadorned flash of white light. Soldier awakening in his tattered uniform on a dusty plain covered with pale yellow moss under a dark lavender sky in which hung the lost blue Earth. *Moon Man*.

Ling Erhshan lying on the fire escape, looking up at the yellow circle of the Moon over Shanghai, imagining himself to be soldier Dorian Haldane, beloved of the beautiful Goth slave-woman Valetta, blown away to another dimension, rather than merely to the timeless eternity of death. Imagining himself lost on the Moon of the Greek-speaking Kalksis oppressors, descended from Ptolemaic colonists stranded after a nuclear war between Rome and Carthage. A Moon inhabited by Chinese-speaking red Indians, by Gothic slaves and Roman guerrillas determined to win free of Greek dominion.

I would lie there in the stinking darkness. Lie there and imagine myself captaining some creaky pentekonter, imagine myself the pirate scourge of the Five Seas I could see, so shadowy, in the yellow world overhead . . .

The radio speaker set in the main instrument panel suddenly blatted static, then, "*Ming Tian*, do you read?" Chen Li's voice.

Da Chai leaned close to the audio pickup, and said, "We read you poorly, Control."

Chen Li said, "We're having some trouble with your telemetry channel."

Equipment failure. A cold hand on Ling Erhshan's heart. Because nothing had really been ready on time, or fully tested.

"What sort of trouble?"

"Interruptions. A second of no signal, then a second of signal. Very regular. Inexplicable."

Inexplicable. Ling said, "What's in the interrupted signal? Static?"

"Hello, Professor. No. More like a carrier-wave hum. Nothing our equipment could produce, I don't think . . ."

Ling stared at the worried look on Chang's face for a moment. "Maybe. If one of those old transistors is . . ."

The radio speaker, completely free of static, said, "This is

Major-General Morris K. Athelstan, speaking for the Department of Defense, United States of America. All spacecraft now flying in Cislunar Space are warned that the Earth's natural satellite Luna has been claimed as national territory by the United States. Unauthorized landings on United States territory anywhere in the solar system will be treated as a military invasion and dealt with accordingly. This warning will be repeated in one hour, broadcast to all communication systems throughout the world and Cislunar Space. Major-General Morris K. Athelstan, speaking for the Department of Defense, United States of America, signing off."

The speaker said, "<static>opy you, *Ming T*<static>. Do y<static>ead?"

Da Chai turned away from the speaker, mouth hanging open. No words.

The speaker said, "Come in, *Ming Tian*. Do you read? Over." Static fading, fading, becoming no more than a background hiss, the familiar music of the spheres.

Ling leaned forward toward the pickup, and said, "We hear you, Chen. Um. Did you . . . um. Did you pick up the transmission from, um, General . . ." hard to pronounce, even when you spoke English well, "Athelstan?"

Open microphone from the ground, people shouting in the background, jangly Chinese excitement, then Chen Li: "Yes."

Chang Wushi said, "What do you suppose it meant?"

Quite possibly, just what it said, but . . .

No American presence in space for the better part of a century, and . . .

A piece of that message suddenly jumping back out of memory ". . . unauthorized landings on United States territory anywhere in the solar system . . ."

Anywhere in the solar system?

Da Chai said, "A decision will have to be made on how we proceed."

Chang Wushi: "Or if we proceed."

Ling Erhshan gestured out the window with a wan smile at the bright yellow Moon looming huge before them. "We proceed in that direction. Captain Newton won't be letting us turn back just yet."

Da Chai looked over at the beamer's control console and said, "Well. We are, at any rate, well armed."

Another cold hand clutching at Ling Erhshan's heart.

Now, by the splendid shores of the endless blue Pacific, that near-mythical California ocean, Astrid Kincaid and her soldiers got ready to go. Pale blue sky, dark blue sea. Extraordinary. And yet . . . yet I remember so many more extraordinary scenes. Skies and seas without number. Worlds beyond imagining.

Why the Hell did I come home?

Because they ordered me?

Yes. That *was* the reason. Do this, soldier. Do it now. That's an order.

All right.

Now this.

This is an order too.

Line of men and women, filing toward the ship. Following orders. Getting ready. Ready to go.

Corky Bokaitis, Kincaid decided, looks just like a gorilla. A little girl gorilla. Well. Maybe not quite. But the jutting jaw, the dense, reddish-black hair on her arms, the beetling brows . . .

PFC Bokaitis was one of three Neanderthalers in the squad, the other two males, none of them taller than five feet three, each of them stronger than any three "normal" humans. I wonder if there are any normal humans left, these days? Sure there are. Billions of them. *Outside.*

Sometimes, I can't even remember a time when human beings in America were as alike as so many little frogs. Sure, a white one here, a black one there. A yellow one. Every now and again a red one. And picture books showing off the rare breeds. Tall, slim, naked-bodied Nilotics. Khoi-San people with yellow-brown skin and peppercorn hair. Melanesians, Australoids. Hairy Ainu.

What was it, three, four, five years after Closure, when people began toying with the new possibilities? Hey, me, I *can* look like a muscle-bound superhero. Look like the most beautiful woman who ever lived. And all without the torture of dieting, without spending a single moment sweating in the gym.

Then . . . why, I *can* be tall. I *can* be white. Or black, or yellow, or red, or . . . Damnation. It isn't easy being Green. But it's *possible*, you see. Purple. Blue. Rainbow hued and covered with glitter and . . . She remembered going to that nature-park play, what? Twenty years back? Maybe more, maybe less. *Breakfast in the Holocene Dawn*, it'd been called. Five muscular runts chasing that damned aurochs retroclone through the woods, jumping on the bastard's back, knocking him down, animal lowing pitifully, burly blond trolls jabbering as they struggled to break his neck.

After every performance one or the other of the players would be limping from some fracture or another, arm or leg twisted, rib or two buckled. Once, the aurochs, furious about being killed over and over again, had gotten one of the actors down, running one long, red-dripping horn through and through his guts, actor wriggling and squalling in a thick, old-fashioned, very artificial-sounding Yankee accent: "Ow! Ow! Get 'im aaaff me! Ow!"

That day, the audience had roared.

And, just so everything would be "right," they'd let the actor lay there blubbering until he died, before hooking him up to a MedDep terminal. Post-resurrection, we gave them both a standing ovation, man and aurochs alike. Blond. Neanderthalers were mostly blond, PFC Bokaitis rather inauthentic in that respect. It's just that black hair looks so . . . *mean*.

Zappa's Law: "Give a guy a big nose and funny-looking hair . . ."

Jesus. What a fucking waste of time.

Rest of the squad wasn't much better, little gargoyles, big gargoyles, men and women constructed to look like heroes and, um . . . heroines, one supposed, from old, old movies. And post-Immortal, every one. Every one of them born since the Event, and not one of these babies has ever thought he or she might have to die . . .

Remember what that felt like? Remember when you were seventeen, and everyone said, Teenagers think they're immortal? Who the Hell dreamed up that lie? Remember being seventeen, lying in bed at night, thinking about the sick, sorry inevitability of death? Thinking about it. In twenty years, you'd say, I'll be middle-aged. Twenty more years and I'll be old. Twenty years after that, ancient. Twenty years after that, no matter how careful, no matter how lucky, I'll be dead.

Dead. Dead. Dead.

What kind of sorry damn God would rig a game with rules like that?

Fuck you, God.

I'm off to see the Wizard.

Who, it turned out, had immortality for us, after all.

Now, watching her sixteen little playtoy soldiers march back and forth, loading supplies and gear into the hull of the Scavenger rocketship, Kincaid wondered just how they'd face it, when and if, if ever. Hell. Nothing's going to go wrong. Nobody's going to get killed. Fly to the Moon in a fucking invincible alien spacecraft, arrest some fucking Arabs and Chinamen. Make sure the Base is still locked up tight. Come home.

Right.

And make sure the fucking Gate is still shut, its address tables thoroughly scrambled.

Make sure they can't find us . . .

Whoever they are.

Brief, sharply repressed memory of fire, fear, and blood.

We just didn't understand the Scavenger records at first. Space-Time Juggernaut? What the Hell is that? Didn't understand that the Scavengers had combed through all those incomprehensible Colonial records. Combed through them for years and decades and centuries, until they thought, just maybe, they understood . . . that it might be coming for them.

It didn't occur to us to wonder why they were gone.

Until it came for us.

Remember how we waited? Days and weeks and months and . . . no Space-Time Juggernaut. No end of the world. Whew. Got away with it. Generals and politicians relieved. Made it. Safe. Home free. Home.

But I didn't destroy the gate. It's still up there. Waiting.

I used to imagine just a few more weeks would go by. A few weeks, a month, two or three, no more than a year, *surely* . . . and the radios would crackle, crackle on down from the Moon. Dale Millikan here. Sorry I'm late. Could you folks send up a ship?

A year, Two. Three. Five. Ten. Twenty. Forty. Sixty . . .

PeeWee Roth, a noseless, toothy gargoyle just a little more than eight feet tall, came and towered over her, saluting. "All loaded up, m'am." It was amazing he could talk around those fangs at all, much less sound like some old borscht-circuit comedian, making tired jokes about gefilte fish.

"I don't suppose it'd do any good to remind you I'm just a noncom . . ." She looked for some readable expression in those glassy weimaraner eyes. "No, guess not."

The communicator on her belt chirped and she pulled it off, holding it in the palm of her hand, remembering a favorite TV show from her childhood. Why the Hell are we using eighty-year-old junk like this? *Answer*: Because no one bothered to make new ones. Didn't think of it. Didn't think we'd need them. She flipped it open and said, "Kincaid."

"Sergeant, this is General Athelstan."

"Sir." No urge to salute. This bastard had been a little shitass second louie back in the old days, had been with her on the Moon, sure, but never once stuck his nose through the Gate. Now look at him.

"The Arabs have initiated their descent sequence, Sergeant. You are go for launch. Plan Bravo."

Plan Bravo, for Christ's sake. Like they had a full array of tactical paths ready to whip out at a moment's notice. Like they'd actually planned for this.

"Acknowledged." She flipped the communicator shut and stuck it back on her belt, turned to the toy soldiers of her new squad. Bright-eyed, every one, looking at her like, what? Mommy? No, more like Playground Leader. "OK, boys and girls," she said, "Boots and saddles . . ." And, for just one moment, felt a tiny atavistic thrill. *Boots and saddles*. We're going up and out.

* * *

Strapped in his seat in *al-Qamar*'s control room, surrounded by his comrades, hands on joystick and throttle,
Alireza waited for final burn initiation. Waited for Zeq to say
sif and hit the switch. *Not* watching the mission clock. No,
just waiting, staring up at the black sky, nothing, not the sun,
not the Earth, not the Moon visible. Nothing but dead black
velvet sky.

That crazy warning coming in over the com channel.
Consternation in mission control. American observers ques-
tioned. No. Sorry. Don't know a thing about it, fellows. No
one's said a word to us . . .

So what do we do *now*?

Say your prayers. Make the phasing burn. Go down the
pike. Land.

What else *is* there to do? Go home? Cancel the program?
We can't do it without the Moon. Land somewhere else, *other*
than the old American base? But we made that an integral part
of our plans, part of bootstrapping to the Mars colony. Mars
colony, you see, so when the Collapse comes, in thirty years,
or fifty, or seventy, all of humanity's precious eggs won't be
in the same damned basket. Besides, Mars just seems so
damned . . . Arab. Red deserts and all that.

Then Zeq counted backwards to *sif* and hit his switch,
watching his panels, muttering engineering data. Somewhere
down in the bowels of the rocket, pressure-fed ullage engines
growled softly, fuel and oxidizer surging down into pumps,
pumps which whined, pressure building, fuel and oxidizer
mixing, hypergolic igniters jetting briefly, liquid fluorine
spraying into an expanding mist of hydrogen . . .

The control panel vibrated gently under his hands as the
big aerospike engine caught. Somewhere down below, really
below now as deceleration built, dropping him butt-down into
the seat, fiery gases were expanding into the void.

Tariq said, "Landing radar locked on. Three thousand
meters. Fifteen hundred kps lateral velocity."

All right. All right, Colonel Sir Qamal ibn-Aziz Alireza.
This *is* your time. Engine rumbling merrily, sucking up velocity, blowing it away as fire and exhaust gas and radiant energy, ship slowing, dropping, dropping . . .

Mahal, reading the inertial navigation unit, said, "On track, on timeline, on target."

"Zeq?"

"We're doing fine. Just fine." Soft, soothing voice.

Nothing from the other two, Rahman and Inbar just passengers. Until we get down. Then we'll be needing a planetary geologist and an American technologies specialist . . .

Moment of troubled memory: ". . . anywhere in the solar system . . ." Where the Hell else had they gone? Somewhere we didn't know about? If they put up a secret Mars base, maybe . . .

Mahal said, "Tracking four arc seconds west of true course . . ."

And Tariq said, "One thousand meters. Two hundred kps transverse . . ."

Alireza, adjusting the controls, felt his heart start chugging away, faster and faster, beads of sweat popping out on his brow.

Then Zeq chirped, "High gate!"

And the Moon surged up in their windows, flat, bright, yellow-white, reaching out to infinity, suddenly become a whole world.

Inbar said. "*Elohim!* I *see* it!" Voice silly with excitement.

Falling at a steep angle now, down across Peary toward the mountainous rimwall of Rozhdestvenskiy. Right *there*. Patches of burn on Lunar soil. Small, shiny things, strewn here and there. What looked like the wreck of an old spacecraft, some history-familiar American design, all angles and wrinkles of glittery gold. A clear, glassy dome, dome of misty triangles shining in the sun, shadowy shapes within. Rahman whispered, "Still holding pressure, maybe. They built well, those old devils."

Down and down, Lunar horizon bulging up until the toy ruins of the Americans' mooncity were lost again. Down and down. Tariq's numbers coming quickly now, Mahal calling out range and distance to the dome, on whose coordinates the inertial unit had been set . . .

Cloud of thin, flaring dust, lit by fire from within.

Mahal: "Contact!"

Zeq: " Engine stop."

Slam. Rattle. Bang.

Silence.

Then, over the radio link, you could hear the mission control team yahooing like cowboys in some old Italian movie. Alireza took cramped hands off the controls and flexed his fingers. No famous words prepared, just one more murmur of, "Thanks be to God Almighty."

Subaïda Rahman unbuckled her restraining harness and said, "Let's *go!*"

It was reasonable, Kincaid knew, for them to be using a Scavenger ship. And a good thing. Scavengers were roughly the same size and shape as human beings, though they didn't look much like them, not really. Still, they'd had things like hands on the ends of things like arms; were upright bipeds; had their sensory organs clustered on something like a head; head mounted, more or less, on the top end of the torso. Much narrower than us, of course. Narrower and lighter—all hollow bones and muscles like tendons—so a Scavenger really looked like a cross between a bright green parakeet and a walking skeleton.

Brucie's crew had done a good job of taking out the Scavenger upholstery and welding in old airline seats. You'd hardly know they didn't belong here. On the other hand, we'd never even get *in* a Colonial ship, Colonials the size of toy poodles, looking like a cross between a red squirrel and a Chinese dragon, fur and scales and silver fangs and six eyes of molten gold.

But the Colonials had antigravity and hyperdrive and God knows what else, technologies, whole sciences we hadn't even begun to understand, despite decades of trying. Scavengers just a *little* better than us, a little brighter, a little more advanced.

While the Colonials flew starships and then built the Gates . . .

Scavengers.

Hell.

We were no more than the bugs who clean up what the

hyenas and vultures leave behind. Too bad I didn't have a chance to follow up on Jensen's latest article. Evidence, firm evidence, thoroughly referenced in Scavenger literature, indicating that hyperdrive experiments gave Colonial scientists the key to the gates. Which, just maybe, brought down the Jug on their heads. No more than a hint. Because, just when they had it figured out, the Jug fell on them.

And almost fell on us.

Did we close the Gate in time?

Memory of fire and death.

Maybe so. Maybe not.

The ship's jury-rigged human intercom rasped and Brucie's voice said, "General called. Says the Arabs have touched down."

"So. Chinese?"

"Falling straight in. No orbit, apparently. They could be down in maybe ninety minutes."

Ninety minutes. "When the Hell are we leaving?"

"Right now, Sarge."

The Scavenger reaction drive screamed—white light flooding in through the windows, making the faces of her monster-soldier-children glow like demons—and the ship lifted, bulleting into the night sky at better than fifteen gee, leaving behind a splashed, bubbling pool of molten glass where the sandstone launch field had been.

Fifteen gee. Soldiers sitting up, peering out the windows, looking down on the falling Earth, gaping, astonished at the sight. And we feel nothing. I guess the compensators still work. Hell, another few years and maybe the Scavengers would have had antigravity too, then hyperdrive, then . . .

Brucie called out, "Up and at 'em, guys! Three hours to the Moon."

They were falling in now at what seemed like a very steep angle indeed. Left to its own devices, *Ming Tian* would miss the Moon's northern limb by about eight thousand meters, whip around the farside and head out into planetary space, accelerated by a gravitational slingshot, lost and gone forever.

No. Not forever. We'd be back again in a year or so . . .

Imagine that. What if the engines *don't* fire?

We pushed it too hard. Tried too hard to be ready by too artificial a deadline. Sure, they're old, reliable engines we've been using on GEO transfer stages for the better part of a century. Ninety-eight point seven percent reliable. Just imagine the look on Chang Wushi's face as he counts down, hits the toggle and . . . nothing.

Looking out the viewport, Ling Erhshan could watch the Moon grow closer visibly, minute by minute. A quick glance at the mission clock. Seventeen minutes to closest approach. Meaning fourteen minutes to retrofire. No, thirteen now.

Originally, they hadn't planned on this kind of approach. Originally, they'd planned on a leisurely reconnaissance, two or three days in Lunar polar orbit, taking photographs, making telescopic inspections of the seven known American bases, of the dozens of landing sites and hundreds of traverse tracks left behind all those years ago, then go down, probably at Peary, and see what was what. But we thought, with our conservative approach, with our commitment to a "heroic dash," that we'd beat the Arabs here by months, maybe even years. Twelve minutes.

The speaker rasped, full of static, Chen Li's voice: "Recon reports an American launch from California, several minutes ago. Very small. Possibly a missile of some kind." Eleven minutes.

A missile. Bag us with nuclear warheads, take out their old base as well, for whatever reason? *Ming Tian*'s particle beam weapon might be able to deal with such a threat. He exchanged glances with Chang and Da Chai. Not *quite* worried glances. "Well, we should have a day or two." Ten minutes.

Chen Li: "Recon reports they took off at fifteen gee. Accelerated to approximately forty kilometers per second before burnout." Chen Li's voice very flat. Word tones somewhat subdued, attenuated by static as well, making his phrases sound uncertain, ambiguous.

Da Chai said, "*Forty* . . ." Nine minutes.

Chang Wushi said, "Then they'll be here in about—"

Ling said, "Three hours or so." No sense breaking out a calculator. Eight minutes.

And Ling said, "They. But if it's only a missile . . ."

Da Chai said, "Not something we can . . . wager on. Wager our lives."

"No." Seven minutes. Outside, the Moon was looking more and more like a slanting plain, less and less like a round yellow world. Climbing up to meet them now, Peary a bright circle, the squashed ringwall between it and Rozhdestvenskiy forming up into tall, rounded, bulging peaks and dark valleys. Old news stories say the Americans found plenty of fossil ice on the back side of these mountains. Six minutes. Those were the same mountains where the Lakota chieftain Red Hawk and his Mohican ally Chingachgook hid their revolutionary band, not so far from the Lost City of Koriolanis, where Dorian Haldane met his lady love. Five minutes.

Chang and Da Chai turned away, began strapping themselves in, focusing attention on their instruments. Too late now to worry about American missiles. Or whatever. Time now to worry about hardware. And lives. Four minutes.

Ling strapped in, still looking out the window, listening to their technical chatter. Strange to be a passenger in my own spacecraft. A passenger, after all these years. A wonder they let me come at all. Three minutes.

Well. I am the Chief Designer. I suppose they figured if anything went seriously wrong, I could fix it. Should have chosen Chen Li. Two minutes. Moon outside a whole world now, as expected. Rolling hills ripping by below, mountains reaching up to pluck them from the sky. So glad I'm here. So very glad. One minute.

Long, long eternity of fear. Time enough to wonder how I'll feel if . . . The engines fired after all, and down they went to a white-lit Moon.

Through some oversight, *al-Qamar*'s Lunar rover never had a name. Maybe no one thought such a vehicle, like some huge go-kart, like the ORVs so popular with modern Tuaregs, deserved to have a name. Bounding now over the rolling charcoal hills of Peary's floor, the four of them were clipped to their seats, watching the mountains grow larger, watching *al-Qamar*—where Mahal and Tariq stood watch as they knew they must—grow smaller, until it was no more than a golden freckle out on a darkling plain.

Six kilometers, thought Alireza. I could have done better. Now, though, they rolled up in front of the Americans' old geodesic dome, rolled through the wreckage of their abandoned hardware, rolled across the blackened star patterns of their old landing sites, rolled to a stop. The foggy dome was larger than it appeared from a distance, looming over them now.

Silence. Finally, Rahman said, "I don't know whether it's mist or just UV discoloration on the inner panels. Probably the latter."

Inbar, voice very soft: "If it's mist, then there's air."

"Probably air in any case. It hasn't been all that long."

Zeq said, "I feel like I'm trespassing in a graveyard."

Yes. Very much like that. A little bit like the feeling you got, visiting those old gutted tombs hewn from the living rock of the Valley of the Kings. Alireza bit down on that cold feeling, putting it away. No use fretting about superstitious nonsense. No one died here. It's like an abandoned home. Of course, abandoned homes often had that haunted feeling as well. As if the people who'd gone away, unexpectedly perhaps, might . . . Silly. He said, "All right, let's go in and see what they've left us." He unclipped his harness and stood, rolling to one side, wobbling unsteadily for a moment in strange, too-light gravity, struggling with the unfamiliar CG of the suit, which was so much more comfortable in zero gee.

Inbar said, "Check and see if they left the key under the mat. Americans were always leaving keys under mats."

Scratchy voice, staticky in their earphones. Mahal: "Mission control says the, um, Americans have just launched something."

"Launched what?"

"A missile maybe. Control says it accelerated too hard to be a manned ship. It'll get here in about three hours, they said."

Someone, Zeq maybe, muttered *Bismallah*. Nothing else to say, when you heard something like that.

"What about the Chinese?"

"They'll be down in fifteen minutes or so. You should see them as soon as they start retro burn, maybe ten degrees above your southern horizon."

A bright star, falling, falling, growing brighter as it fell . . .

"All right. Keep us posted. We're going in now, if we can."

"Careful."

"Right."

The airlock door, it turned out, was swung open on its hinges, a gaping black hole in the foundation wall of the dome. Lightless inside.

"Something here, stuck to the wall just inside the hatch . . ." A piece of paper, which cracked into two pieces when Rahman plucked it from its place. She held it up to the ambient sunlight, staring at thin old writing, English script. Felt a useless impulse to blow the dust off it.

"What does it say?" asked Zeq.

Long silence. Feeling of unreality. "It says, 'Key under mat. It's your ass, buddy.' "

Another long silence, the Alireza said, "Isn't *Buddy* a popular American name?"

"Sometimes. It also means *friend*."

Alireza said, "Was it taped to a particular switch?"

"Doesn't matter. There's unlikely to be power." Rahman flipped the switch and the airlock lights came on. Another long moment, the four of them looking at each other, pale, strained faces looking out through thick faceplates, then she said, "Their nuclear power system should've shut down long ago, untended like this."

Zeq said, "And yet."

"Right. Pull the outer door shut." A slow look around, at dials and gauges, panels of switches, and typical mid-21st century readouts. "This is familiar equipment."

Inside the dome, there was air: nitrogen, oxygen, carbon dioxide, trace gases in the correct ratios, at just a few dozen millibars below standard sea level pressure. Inbar said, "So. Do we unsuit? It'd make things easier."

Alireza stood looking out through the dome, in the direction of the sun. It was a lot easier to see out than in, what they'd thought mist or discoloration apparently some optical coating. The Earth and Lunar landscape were bright enough outside, but you could look straight at the sun, too. Maybe that smudge was a sunspot? "Not yet. Let's look around." Up in the sky, maybe ten degrees above the southern horizon, a bright spark suddenly appeared. Company. Somewhere else up there, between Earth and Moon, there would be more company. Or maybe just a warhead. Should we do something? What? Nothing to be done. We don't even have a pistol among us. Not expecting to meet anyone on the Moon.

All around them, boxes and crates and piles of hardware, little American moonbuggies in various stages of disassembly. Two large, boxy structures that looked, more or less, like late-twentieth century mobile homes. Rahman was standing by some kind of long bench, looking down at jumbled equipment, silent.

Alireza came up beside her, peering down through faceplate glass. "What is it?"

Rahman turned it over, a complex structure made from what appeared to be thin, thin strands of gold foil. Strands of foil that looped through and through each other, twisted and turned, never seeming to touch one another, never seeming to get closer to one another, even when you put your glove on the object and pushed . . .

"I don't know."

Odd looking, deep inside. Like there were misty places somehow. A little bit like that famous painting of the stairways, stairs leading into one another in impossible ways. "Like," Rahman whispered, "there are singularities here."

Alireza turned and looked up at the sky. Felt a slight shock. Minutes had passed and the Chinese ship was coming down, a little metal spider riding a flower of bright flame. Down, down, cloud of dust . . .

The flame went out and the other ship was sitting out on the plain, much closer than *al-Qamar*. Alireza thought, Whoever it is, he's a better pilot than me. He looked around at the base. All right. So we've found a dome, two house-trailers, and a lot of leftover junk. The equipment in here's not even as good as our own. Old junk. Antiques. Then why would . . .?

Zeq's voice in his earphones. "There's a door here."

"Where?"

Zeq's spacesuited figure, waving from beside a humped up place in the floor, near the far foundation wall. Another airlock? Not likely, given they'd already found three, spaced evenly around the walls. They went over and looked.

Zeq shined his helmet light inside. "Just rock, covered with some kind of spray-on sealant."

Rahman said, "Makes sense they would've built underground. In its heyday, this base had over a hundred people living at it. Couldn't fit that many people under this dome. This is just the construction shack."

"Why didn't they take it down?"

"Why bother? It makes a pretty good work area and airlock system."

Alireza said, "Mahal?"

"Here."

"Keep an eye on the Chinese. Let me know when they come out."

"All right."

He looked at Inbar. "You stay here. We can try to use you as a radio link if the signal gets cut off."

A nod through the faceplate, a look of almost-relief.

The dark tunnel was short, featureless, without anything that looked like a light fixture, ending in another door, an old airlock door set in a hull frame, frame buried in the rock wall. Alireza stood for just a second, looking at it, then reached out and popped the latch. Light, bright white light, like natural sunlight, came flooding through.

"What in *Shayol*?" Rahman pushed past him, pulling the door open, stepping into the next chamber.

Silence. The three of them almost huddling together, spacesuits all but touching, looking down off a rough hewn, stone balcony, down a long flight of fresh-cut stone stairs, at a vast underground chamber—a giant cavern full of sourceless, hazy morning light, with green trees and rosebushes in bright red flower, broad lawns of grassy sward, buildings, like some remote mountain village, clustered in the near distance.

Inbar's voice crackled in their earphones. "Mahal says you'd better come up. Chinese have broken out their rover. At least one individual is driving your way."

Zeq said, "I wonder if this is some kind of optical illusion."

Rahman: "You mean, like the VR art that was popular in America back then?"

Alireza said, "We'll find out in a few minutes. Let's deal with this other problem first." He turned back toward the hatch.

Rahman said, "Are you *kidding*?" Tableau moment, then she turned and went bounding down the stairway.

Zeq looked at him, face framed in his helmet faceplate, then said, "I'll stay with her." Turning away as well.

What? Order them back? Military discipline and all that? No. Deal with the problem yourself. Let them do what they came here to do. He watched them go down, watched them disappear into the shrubbery with a twinge of unease, turned back toward the hatch, regretting its necessity.

Turning my back on . . . What shall I call this? Magic? Or only typical American nonsense? Sell the sizzle not the steak. Magic fountains in a cold gray moonbase. Maybe Ali Baba will come scurrying from the bushes any moment now . . .

Rolling across the rugged plain of Peary's floor, Ling Erhshan felt the makeshift Lunar rover waddling under him, unstable. Unstable, because I'm alone here, an empty seat where my companion should be, but . . .

Chang and Da Chai working over their consoles, tuning up the particle beam device, charging its capacitors, or whatever. Getting "ready," whatever that meant.

"You go on over to the base and talk to the Arab commander. The American . . . missile will be here in no time at all. When . . . Well. When it's over, we'll come over on foot. It's not far."

Riding now through a field of debris, crawling up to park

beside a newer vehicle. Those squiggly lines must be Arabic . . .

Sitting there motionless, staring up at a flat black sky, at brightly lit mountains, low, eroded ringwall mountains, dimensionless, as if painted on black glass. Like a movie set. Rubble of artifacts all around him now. Like an abandoned movie set. And then, sudden exhilaration.

Because I'm really *here*. Because I've been permitted to *see* this. With my own eyes. Whatever happens next, or doesn't happen, there will have been that: A magical thrill I can carry with me from now until the moment of my death. Uneasy stirring, glancing over his shoulder in the direction of a bright crescent Earth. Thinking, A moment that may not be so very far away after all . . . Vision of a missile streaking down out of that starless sky, striking, exploding, bright flare of nuclear fire, then nothing at all. Black eternity.

So. If it comes, it comes. No reason to think about it before that last fearful moment arrives.

He unhooked himself from the seat harness and stood, teetering unpleasantly, getting his footing in the dusty soil, then turning to walk toward the wall, where the outline of a hatchway of some sort was visible. Walking, almost tangling his feet, suddenly remembering patchy old black and white video footage. Kangaroo hop. Use your ankles.

The hatch swung open, bright yellow-orange incandescent light flooding out, spacesuited figures waiting.

Inside the dome, beyond the inner airlock door, Ling stood facing his two Arabs, looking in through their faceplates at swarthy Levantine faces, at beetle-browed, primitive-looking men with round black eyes and enormous noses. Wondering, for an inane moment, how they kept those huge brown beaks from smashing into their helmet glass. But they look more like the heroes from my old American science fiction novels than I do. Why did I never picture Dorian Haldane looking like this? Or lovely blond Valetta with a nose like a ripe banana planted in the middle of her face?

No. My child's imagination made her a pale northern Chinese woman with long, straight yellow hair and unusually big eyes. And, of course, because I was an adolescent boy, a dense forest of curly yellow pubic hair. Yellow like a grocery-store lemon. And big breasts of course. Breasts the size of cantaloupes. American women always had big breasts. You saw that in all the movies.

Ling sighed, pushing away silly old memories. I am here. It is now. Focus. Because the UAR program had been conducted so openly, their suit radio frequencies had been published, and his own hardware was equipped to transmit on it. "Chang?"

"Here."

"I'm switching over now. Will you monitor?"

"Yes."

"The Americans?"

"The missile is no more than an hour out."

The missile. So certain, they are. That cold, cold hand, thoughtfully fingering the spaces of my spine . . .

He touched the button on his chest-mounted control panel and, in English, said, "I am Ling Erhshan," careful to subdue the tones, say it low and flat, so they'd hear something other than *ping-ping pong*, "commander of *Ming Tian*." A gesture, out through the dome.

The narrow-faced man, his English thick and guttural, almost incomprehensible, said, "Alireza, commander *al-Qamar*." He motioned to the other man, whose face was fatter, paler, sweatier looking. "Omry Inbar, scientist."

Omry Inbar . . . recognition. "The author of 'The Oil Shale-like Properties of Certain Fore-Trojan Asteroids'?"

A surprised look. "The paper I presented at the 2133 IAF congress in Teheran, yes."

"I was there. But not permitted to ask questions, sadly."

Inbar, eyes suddenly alight, opened his mouth to speak.

Alireza interrupted, "What of your crew? Why not here?"

Ling looked into his eyes, finally decided they were just too alien to be read easily. All those old American movies. If this was an American, I'd know what he was thinking. "Manning *Ming Tian*. Waiting for the Americans to arrive."

Inbar said, "So. You think it is manned after all?"

Then they did know about it. Silly to imagine the Arabs

would not be tracking objects in near-Earth space. "Perhaps. My companions think not."

Alireza said, "And if it is a missile?"

Long stare. What *are* you thinking, my slim desert chieftain? "Unhappily, my government has insisted that *Ming Tian* be equipped with a collimated particle beam device."

Inbar muttered, "My *God* . . ." Spoken as if he were quite used to speaking English. Still the language of science, after all these years, because no one wants Chinese or Arabic or Spanish or Swahili or Hindustani to predominate.

Alireza said, "What good will that do?"

You could see the fear in his eyes after all. But only in his eyes, otherwise, this was some army officer, like army officers the world over. Like Chang Wushi, for instance. Back in *Ming Tian*, calmly preparing to open fire on an unknown vessel, with unknown powers . . .

Just then, their suit radios crackled and spoke.

First you watched the Earth grow small, shrinking visibly out the viewports, watched, silent, surrounded by gaping young gargoyles who, perhaps, never once, in all their short, immortal, playtoy lives, imagined they would be here. Then you watched the bright Moon grow larger and larger, faster and faster . . .

And then, just then, you felt that savage anger grow large as well.

Hours to the Moon. Days to Mars and Venus and any asteroid you cared to name. A week or two to Pluto . . .

Why the Hell aren't we *using* this stuff? Why are we sitting home? Fortress Fucking America . . .

Because we're *afraid*.

Afraid that ole Boogeyman goin' come git us.

But the gates are shut. Scavengers couldn't figure out how to build a Colonial hyperdrive and neither can we. And the Space-Time Juggernaut won't come for us, so long as we keep our noses out of its . . . business.

We could still have the stars, so long as we're content to take the long, slow route . . .

Memory. Hard, sharp memory of standing underneath a

dark, blue-lavender sky, looking up at a big bright sun and a small dim sun, dim but still too bright to look at. Of standing in an Arctic parka, breathing through an oxygen-boosted respirator because the air was way too thin, thinner than the air atop Mt. Everest. But a lot damned better than the air on Mars! Standing there, staring up at a starry sky full of oh-so-familiar constellations, knowing that yellowish first-magnitude star was Home . . .

But, Sergeant-Major, a starship built with Scavenger technology would take *forty years* to reach Alpha Centauri.

So the fuck what?

We're fucking *immortal*, God damn it!

But we're also fucking *afraid* . . .

Jug might not like it. Might come. Might kill us all.

Brucie's voice over the intercom: "Forty-five minutes, Sarge."

"Right. Thanks." She picked the old communicator off her belt. "Patch me into the comlink."

"Will do," bluff, hearty words, little Brucie now in his technohero role. "Through the translator and out, on one freq in Arabic, the other in Chinese." Unspoken: no sense wasting good English on them gooks. Though, of course, Brucie was probably a gook, most twenty-first century Americans had been gooks, made up now to fill his fantasy role . . .

"Thanks." A moment for thought, then, "This is Sergeant-Major Astrid Kincaid, USMC Lunar Expeditionary Force," What a laugh, like Pershing's Heroes landing in France, come to end the War to End War, "addressing all groups and individuals currently landed on the United States External Territory of Luna. Board your ships now. Begin making preparations for liftoff. If you do so, you will be permitted to depart in peace. If your vessel cannot make trans-Earth injection at this time, lift off to Lunar orbit. You will be taken in tow and returned to low Earth orbit for repatriation." Long pause, then, "If you attempt to resist, you will be attacked by armed infantry. Sergeant-Major Astrid Kincaid, USMC, signing off."

Corky the Neanderthal Girl said, "Way tough, Sarge! Just like in the old TV shows."

Shit. *Just like in the old TV shows* . . . She put the communicator on her belt and kept looking out the window, watching the Moon grow, wishing it was that bright blue moon she'd seen once, long ago, in a galaxy so damned far away they never *did* figure out just which one it was.

Consternation.

Arabs gabbling to each other, big eyes even wider, like white European eyes now, probably saying, "Did you hear *that*?" Fat-faced scientist waving his arms, teetering off balance in the low gee, commander reaching out to steady him, muttering low.

And confusion in me, as well, thought Ling Erhshan. Two voices in my ears. One a woman, snarling nearly-incomprehensible Arabic, a language I only studied for two years as an undergraduate, thirty years ago now. And another woman, hard, barbaric voice speaking Chinese, echoing back through the circuit from *Ming Tian*.

Recognizably the same woman's voice. Metallic, angular and deadly. Well. Not such a difficult trick. The UN computer in Singapore does just as well.

Da Chai, speaking in his left ear now: "Ling . . ."

"I heard."

"Maybe you'd better come back to the ship."

"I . . . think not."

"If there's fighting . . ."

Image of technogenic lightning bolts. "It would appear that it's a manned ship we face, not a missile. I assume you will . . . hold your fire?"

Soft static in the earphone, Arabs still snarling to each other, then Chang Wushi said, "The particle beam weapon will not be much use against infantry, once they've debarked. Other than that, all we have are our sidearms."

Ling was trying to keep consciousness of his own little gun, with its pathetic little bullets, tucked away in the suit's right knee pouch, suppressed. "Still. I think there's no other choice."

"We'll do whatever seems appropriate, when the time comes."

That cold hand again.

* * *

Alireza kept listening to Inbar, hearing his insistent, frightened plea, "Let's just go back and get in the ship. Let's *wait*. What harm can it do?" But the decision was already made, his arguments fading away. "Mahal?"

"Here. What do you make of it?"

Nothing. I make nothing of it. He felt a momentary urge to tell them to get out of the ship and come over to the dome, *stay together*, but, "Sit tight. Um. Maybe you'd better do a preflight."

Tariq: "We'd already started that. Even before . . ."

Right. Memory of a ridiculous woman's voice, grating in his ears. Old fashioned Arabic, full of heavy consonants and sharp sounds. Guttural stops where glottals should be. Like the Arabic of my country cousins in Hejaz, rather than the crisp, modern sounds of *bälädi*, Dialect of the Cities, the Arabic you heard on the nets, were taught to use in school . . .

And Zeq, suddenly popping out of the rabbit hole: "Qamal, Omry, you *have* to come *see* this!" Stopping suddenly, at the sight of Ling.

Inbar put his hand out, touching the arm of the Chinaman's suit. "There's . . . something here. We don't know what."

Alireza felt a quickening surge of . . . what? Ownership? A desire, at any rate, to prevent this . . . foreigner, he supposed, from seeing the underground gallery. Silly. Not mine. Not *ours*. In just a little while the Americans will come and take it away from us. Try to, at any rate.

Sigh. "We've got about half an hour. Let's go look."

Subaïda Rahman was standing by the rear wall of the underground chamber, perhaps a kilometer from the entrance, with its balcony and stone stairs. Anomaly after anomaly. Now this . . . thing. Most of it had been merely strange. Inexplicable. Funny looking bushes and trees. Bits of machinery that were like *nothing* she'd ever studied. Not stuff from the Renaissance, certainly. Not much like the few bits and pieces that had escaped from Fortress America over the years.

Memory of being in the top secret government laboratory

south of Äwbahri, at the terminus of the Fäzzan rail line, buried in the hardpan desert of Idehan Marzuq. Hot desert wind without, cool air-conditioning within, while her colleagues lowered the little silver helmet over her head . . .

Just found it out there, floating in the sea, though something that felt this heavy and dense to the hand should have sunk like a stone . . .

Feather-light on my head though.

How does it feel?

All right.

Can you see anything?

No.

How about when I do this?

Well . . .

Pins and needles at the base of her spine, building, building . . .

The sudden orgasm had made her surge from the chair, ripping the thing off her head, standing almost bowlegged, then almost knock-kneed, crying out . . .

Male scientists staring at her in puzzled astonishment.

Maryam, the one other woman on the team coming forward suddenly, brushing back her short, stiff hair, looking into her eyes, seeming nonplused.

Did what I think just happen to you?

Shaky whisper, Yes. Yes, I think so . . .

Maryam picking up the little silver helmet, smirking, We could make a lot of money, if we could learn to manufacture these . . .

Shaky laughter, ignorant male colleagues gathering round, demanding to know what was going on.

Dr. Saddiq taking the thing from Maryam, saying, Well, maybe we'd better try harder to find an English dictionary with this word in it. Tapping the front of the helmet, where it said, *Orgonogenesis Inc.*

Who wants to be next? Mahmuhd?

Maryam and Subaïda hid their smiles until after the young man went through his version of the experience. Tried not to laugh when a stunned Mahmuhd excused himself to go change his linen. It was a few days before someone figured out the connection to the word *orgone*, which had been in their dictionaries, all along . . .

This thing on the chamber's rear wall though . . . not like that at all. More like an altar to some technological god, some typically American god. Big smooth sheet of what looked like polished black formica, set flush with the rear wall, coated with a thick layer of plastic sealant.

Not quite featureless. If you leaned close, you could see rainbow refraction, an interplay of colors just like the ones you saw on the surface of a twentieth century videodisc. Microscopic pits in the formica? Invisibly tiny bubbles, like dust motes in the plastic coating? Or some property of the plastic itself?

There was a heavy frame around the thing, marking out an area perhaps twenty meters square, things like insulated wires, red and blue and black, marked by various colored stripes, coming out here and there.

Ham fisted. Hardly the sophistication you'd expect from the Great Renaissance. We do better work than this, even now. Almost as if it had been built by those old Germans, building for Apollo. Heavy. Redundant. Brooklyn-Bridge engineering they'd called it.

There was a little chair, covered with fine white dust, a small control panel mounted on a console. Dials, meters, gauges, what looked like dead LCD readouts. Brute force toggle switches and big square push-buttons. All of them carefully labeled, in English, with bits of embossed color tape. Very enticing, that caged switch that said, "Power Main." Flip it on and . . .

"Relaxen und watch das blinkenlights."

Funny memory. Despite years of technical journal reading, that poster, seen in an old British laboratory, had been hard to understand, English words transposed into faux German grammar . . .

This row of twelve rheostat dials now . . .

Big-T.

Little-t.

X, Y, Z.

X, Y, Z all primed.

Little-i.

Plus and minus.

Chord.

Chord? Maybe it was a lunar pipe organ . . .

Then again, why would there be *separate* properties of plusness and minusness?

She reached out, as if to twirl one of the dials, thought better of it, took out her CCDCD camera and took a picture of the whole control panel, then started taking closeups of all the instrument settings.

All right.

Now then.

She hit the power switch and watched the lights light up.

Some of them did indeed start to blink.

Four of them, the Arab astronauts and a stray Chinese scientist, walking down the garden path together. Almost huddling against one another, surrounded by strangeness. Omry Inbar, stopping suddenly by a pile of old rocks. Kneeling, picking one up, muttering something in childhood-abandoned Hebrew. Turning the rock over and over again. Picking up the next one. Then another.

"What is it?" asked Zeq.

"These rocks are . . . weathered."

Alireza said, "Not much weather in here." Looking up at the distant gray ceiling, wondering for the thousandth time just where the light was coming from.

Ling knelt beside Inbar, and said, "I'm not a geologist, but . . . I've spent some time in rocky country." Thinking of the Taklamakan. "These seem . . . exotic. Not like any mineral specimens I can remember seeing."

Inbar looked at him, face still and strained. "I don't recognize them either." Moving on, going back toward the rear of the chamber, where strange light had begun to play. Rahman was back there somewhere. But she had a lot of sense. A careful woman, a thoroughgoing scientist who could be trusted to . . . stay out of trouble.

From Zeq, sharply: "Commander!"

Then, the four of them staring down at a skeleton of clean, dry white bones.

Alireza said, "Not *quite* to the 'clean bones gone' stage." But dusty looking, as if they were about to crumble away.

Inbar said, "The ligaments are gone. If there was wind and weather they'd be . . . scattered." Very quiet voice. Very uneasy.

Ling, some distance away, said, "There are more of them over here."

Them? Bones massed in a pile. Still discrete individuals, not mixed together or anything, but . . .

"As if," said Alireza, "they died huddled together."

"Holding one another," said Zeq.

They went on.

Ling Erhshan standing, staring, at a pretty little shrub, thousands of little yellow flowers, no leaves. Stalks and stems of some odd silvery stuff. Leaning closer . . . Not flowers, no. No pistils, no stamens. Just fleshy yellow material . . .

In his very good academic English, Inbar whispered, "What do you suppose it is?"

No supposition. The rest of the plants here were your standard sorts, straight from someone's idea of an English garden. "Maybe . . . There were plenty of commercial horticultural geneticists working in America, back in the 2050s . . ."

"Maybe."

Then they were standing behind Subaïda Rahman, watching her photograph all the lit-up dials and gauges, watching her record angular Romanic numbers from LCDs and bits of film-CRT.

"Amazing any of this still works," said Zeq.

Alireza: "What is it?"

"How would we even guess?" whispered Inbar, still speaking English, standing beside Ling.

Rahman turned and looked at them. Plucked a piece of tattered paper from the console. Handed it to Alireza.

"It looks a little like the handwriting on that other note. The one in the airlock. Hard to tell . . . I'm not used to looking at English script."

Ling took it from him, read, "Millikan's team at gate

001010. Setting . . ." Numbers and non-alphanumeric symbols.

Rahman gestured. "That last stuff matches the settings on these dials. The binary . . ." Pointing at a row of six mechanical switches, under a piece of tape that said, "Portal Address." Switches 3 and 5, reading from the left, as you would in English, were in the down position, the rest flipped up.

Ling felt a mild pulse of astonishment. "As if they were programming a 1950-vintage digital computer."

A look of measured respect. "That's a good analogy."

Mahal's voice suddenly buzzed in Alireza's earphones, reedy and attenuated, almost inaudible, though they'd left the doors open and made certain radio waves would propagate down into the chamber. "Commander?"

"Here."

"The Americans have begun their braking burn. The engine is . . . very bright . . ." Through the static you could tell Mahal was quite nervous.

"I'll be right up. Try to raise them on the international distress frequency." He turned and looked at the others. Reluctance was plain on their faces. *This is magic*, their faces were saying. *Who cares about mere soldiers?*

He said, "Zeq. And you'd better come too, Professor Ling."

Disappointment, but, "Of course. I'll try to see that my crewmembers . . . stay calm."

Stepping out of the hatch in the ground, Alireza could see what had Mahal so upset. The dome was flooded with bright white light—light coming from a blinding blue-violet spark in the sky—light so bright its contrast had washed away the crescent Earth, washed away much of the Lunar landscape as well. A fusion drive, perhaps? Or something better? Allah alone knew what magic these people were sitting on. Keeping to themselves. Waiting for the rest of us to fill the Earth and die in our own poison . . . Waiting us out. And now come to kick us off their Moon, so we can't even *try* to save ourselves.

Ling said, "I can't seem to get through. I thought I had them, but now there's only static."

Outside, the light suddenly faded, pouring away into the heavens, retracting into a bright knob of flame, flame hovering, licking against itself, high up in the deep black sky.

"My God." said Inbar.

Ling said, "Like a rocketship in one of those old Japanese *manga*." Like a rocketship. Like . . .

Ming Tian suddenly flashed, once, very hard, very bright, and something like a bolt of lightning flew up from the little ship, straight at the hovering rocket.

Nothing. Motionless.

Ling, in Chinese, to himself: "Oh, Chang Wushi, oh, Da Chai, too many army-made, war-mad days and nights . . ."

A long tongue of dull red fire reached down from the heavens . . .

Sky going all white, blinding them.

Crying out, covering their faces.

Alireza peered out through the dome with aching, teary eyes, blinking hard, saw brilliant golden sparks flying away on long trajectories, bouncing in slow motion across the dusty plain, saw a glowing ruby hole in the ground where *Ming Tian* had been, *al-Qamar* still standing there beyond it . . .

Filling his lungs, shouting, full of panic, shouting at the radio, *"Mahal! Tariq!* Get out of the ship! *Now* . . ."

Another tongue of liquid fire. Another blinding sky. Another livid hole bracketed by bounding sparkles of incandescent ruin, fading, fading . . .

The Americans' winged spacecraft dropping slowly now on its column of fire, descending on an empty Lunar plain. Into the long silence, Ling Erhshan suddenly whispered, "We're not going home, then . . ."

Two.

Sartor Resartus.

The view from an infinite height.

The view from the Command Module, like the view from the center of some endless, multi-dimensional flower, petals of bright white light going out and out, stretching like brilliant shadows, shadows cast by the Throne of God, out in directions no human mind can conceive.

I know these directions. Know them now.

Know of colors beyond any prismatic fathoming.

Know of times without number.

Worlds beyond kenning.

Effortlessly, I know everything, everywhere, everywhen.

I know when a sparrow falls.

I feel it in my heart.

View from an infinite height changing, shifting, malleable. The putty of creation molded to my touch. I imagine. There is being. I sigh. The reiterated powers to numbers no mathematician could construct unfurl. I think of darkness. Darkness falls.

Pointless.

Why am I here?

Why do I . . . persist?

Is it because I still fear to go out into the eternal night?

Surely not.

They say God is Love.

I am not love.

That much is certain.

For a long time after I got the job, I feared I might really be God Almighty. Trembled with terror and longed eternally for the surcease of human sleep. No more. Not for me. Maybe the Other had these longings as well. I knew him not, though he almost certainly knew me.

I know when a sparrow falls.

Feel it in my heart.

The Other must have felt my fall, felt it as a pinprick, somewhere inside. If the Other had a heart. One of those things beyond my knowing, though I know all, see all, with a simulacrum of Odin's All-Seeing Eye.

Out the window now, brilliant blue galaxies flow by, blue spiral arms winding round fat red cores. I could reach out and touch the cores. Make them flame with renewed youth. I do not. I could reach out and change the decay rate of protons. I do not. I could reach out, let the ghost wind of the neutrinos sift like dust through my fingers. Could tell them all that their mass was changed, that the history of this universe or that one, or all of them put together, was changed. I do not.

Stars, like dust. Galaxies like grains of sand.

Let them be.

Let them live out their lives.

They don't know.

Let them live on in the darkness, with their small fear, their fear of inevitable oblivion. I can remember when I feared that oblivion. Oh, God, I remember! Remember when I wished for the reality of God and feared it at the same time. Must I die? Now? Forever? *Unfair*. Damn you.

Sometimes, when I take these moments alone, when I look out through the Command Module's infinite windows, I remember those fears and laugh. If you'd told me then, what was to become of me, I don't think I would have had the sense to feel horror. No. I think I would have felt joy. First, no death. Then, the infinite power to create. The power to change.

I will . . . and it is so.

Sometimes, even when the work of Creation presses on me, I remember and, remembering, I laugh, striking fear in a million, billion, trillion . . . transfinite number of souls. I point to the idea of an idea, the spirit of a notion, I murmur, "Make it so . . ." and I laugh. No one gets the joke, though I could will them to understand.

Then the black despair descends.

I could will this all away.

I could make an End to All Things.

I didn't ask for this job. It fell upon me, unbidden. (Oh, that lie! That lie!) Sometimes I tire of the task, as the Other must have tired. I thought of that, before I had more than an inkling of the Truth. I could let it all go, let it fall away into the darkness and be done. I *could*.

And yet.

I know when a sparrow falls.

I feel it in my heart.

Even God can't imagine the pain of Creation's End. If He had, He might never have spoken the Word. Might never have let there be light. Certainly, knowing what I know now . . .

Well.

In any case, I am still afraid of the Dark.

Three.

Children of the Lens.

Underground, continuing to work their way through all the dials and switches of the control panel, Inbar and Rahman were uneasy, ignoring their feelings . . .

Should we be up there now?

What good would *that* do?

Our duty . . .

But . . . *this*.

Thoughts universal, however unspoken.

Next to the "Power Main" switch was another one, almost identical, similarly caged, with a red label tape that said *Link*. Subaïda Rahman eyed it, knowing there was nothing left to do. Either we act, or we do not. Fretful fears: Only a fool does things like this. Meanwhile, up on the surface, the Americans would be landing about now.

Inbar said, "We'd better wait for Alireza. Maybe we should go up and see . . . ." The ground twitched under their feet, a barely perceptible movement, fine dust sifting down from the ceiling.

Nothing. Motionless. Looking at one another, faces drained of color, filling up with fear. The ground twitched again. More dust. Rahman thought, That's it then. I'll never know if . . . She reached out and uncaged the switch, reversed its position.

Pale golden light, a luminous hint of rainbows splashing at their feet. Abandoned scrap of paper with its cryptic numbers and scrawled English words suddenly lifting off from where it'd been set on the edge of the console, blowing away out over the bushes. Dust flying off the ground, gusting around their space-suited ankles.

Inbar turned toward the wall, gaping, and said, "In the Name of God."

It felt *very* strange to be standing on the familiar, dusty surface of the Moon after all these years. Standing there in old-fashioned combat tans, mottled desert-warfare fatigues of the sort she'd worn, way back in the late 2020s, when America had what turned out to be its penultimate foreign adventure, the destruction of Morocco's nuclear weapons capability.

Soldiers, if you could call them that, gathering in a ragged row at the foot of the ramp, by the Scavenger ship's landing jacks, each muscular dwarf, each tall, grinning gargoyle, shouldering pack and rifle, each surrounded by a pale, intangible nimbus of silvery light.

Take a deep breath. Nice, clean air, at standard temperature and pressure. Faint smell of gunpowder. Lunar dust sifting in through the curtainfield, where it's compressed by our boots. Brucie and his boys were standing in a little knot nearby, grinning, goggling around at the scenery, staring over at those two bubbled craters, cooled already to the point where they were just black glass, little rims of dull red light showing through here and there.

Brucie said, "Man, that sumbitch really *worked*."

Kincaid turned over a bit of twisted metal with one foot. Sure did. No way of even knowing what this used to be part of.

One of the other techies said, "Radio traffic seems to indicate there were two crew on each vessel at the time of attack."

Four dead then, which meant there were five more somewhere else. Looking up at the dome, which should have been dark. Someone has turned on the lights, then. Four more Arabs. One last Chinaman. Poor fucking bastards. The communicator on her belt chirped. She put it to her ear and said, "Here."

"This is Athelstan. Thought you should know the Arabs assaulted our observers at their launch complex. We've blown their autodestruct mechanisms. Hammaghir is gone."

Observers. Teleoperated androids, with bigger-than-usual bombs in their heads. Cooling radioactive holes in the sand.

So why did we wait? Why did we let it get this far? Who knows? Politicians and generals make their decisions. Maybe they argued about Pearl Harbor or something. Argued 'til it was too late for anything but . . . this.

"We saw your explosions. Are you finished up there?"

"No. We've got to go inside the base and catch five survivors."

"Inside the base?" You could hear the upset in Athelstan's voice. "Too bad about that."

"Yes sir. Too bad." As you say sir. She put the communicator back on her belt, not bothering to sign off. All right. Time to go.

Looking out through the dome, Alireza whispered, "Trust to the Americans to send Djinni for us."

Zeq, voice fainter still: "Djinni are saved as well, some of them. Allah sent a separate revelation to all their kind, to be accepted or rejected, just as with men. Djinni, the Book says, have their own *Quran* . . ."

Ling, edging backward, feeling fear curl through his abdomen, said, "Something more has been going on in America than we ever suspected." All those years of satellite photos, of skulking along the borders with Canada and Mexico, spies trying to get in, always failing, never a chink found anywhere in the walls of Fortress America. Watching the embassy, with its magic planes. Shadowing the tourists here and there. Picking mysterious flotsam from the ocean. Now, here were the Americans, like things from some old movie, bounding toward them across the Lunar plain. Coming for us.

Why am I afraid? Why am I so afraid? I've played out scenes like this in my imagination a thousand times. American scenes, from old American books, old American movies. But this is real. And Chang Wushi is dead. Da Chai is dead. Blown away to . . . not even dust. Blown away into the sky as vapor and fire. Soon, most likely, I'll be dead as well. This is real. That's why I'm afraid.

Even Dorian Haldane would be afraid.

Alireza said, "We'd better get back down to Inbar and Rahman. We should face this together . . ."

Then . . .

Trying to run, pretending to run, in a spacesuit of hundred-year-old design, Ling Erhshan imagined he could feel every one of his fifty-five years. Could count them, see them flashing before his eyes like still frames from his personal movie.

Such a simple movie. Confused scenes of infancy. Those people who might or might not have been his parents. Ice and snow. Mountain scenes. I never knew my name, or who I might be.

Then the fast drumbeat: Orphanage. School. Books. Scholarship. College. Politics and grantsmanship. Graduate school. Science awards. Doing real science. Working toward a goal. Bureaucracy. Politics. Moonshot. Politics . . .

And monsters running at you across a dusty black plain, Earth hanging bright in the sky.

That inane voice, refusing to shut up as they scurried into the tunnel, closing the door behind them: You're having an Adventure, Ling Erhshan. Having an adventure at last. I wonder if Chang Wushi and Da Chai were afraid, in that last moment of theirs. If they had an instant of regret, just before being burned away to nothing, being torn to pieces and . . .

Then they were out on the balcony, closing another door behind them, as if, somehow, its flimsy metal would keep the monsters out on the plain at bay.

That one *thing*, out in the lead, *taking* point they'd call it, looking like the cover illustration from my old paperback of *Number Thirteen*—the one I stole from the orphanage library the day I went away to school, so I'd have something to read on the train—all eyes and long, sharp teeth and dark, ragged hole of a nose . . .

Running through all these crazy bushes now, crazy American bushes in a cave under the Moon, while dust swirled around them on winds of . . . winds of . . .

Scientist mind waking up.

Winds of what?

I'm in a cave, buried under the surface of an airless world.

Winds of what?

And that soft golden light, coming from the back of the cave, where they'd left Inbar and Rahman . . .

Rahman, who'd already had the temerity to touch those mysterious controls, put power to whatever it was that had lain here, silent and alone, for three long generations. Whatever it was that had . . . given the Americans their magic. And made them into the things you saw up there. Things coming for us now.

They came out of the bushes and stopped. Stared. *There.* Almost as if you *knew* this would happen. As if the old stories had *prepared* you for it.

Inbar and Rahman, bulky in their spacesuits, standing together, facing what had been a featureless wall. Staring out through it. Long, long vista of rolling yellow hills under a pastel pink sky that could not, could *not* be making this mellow golden light. Pale silvery clouds up in that sky. Small, pale, metallic sun, fiery disk of molten gold.

Fine yellow dust, blowing in through the opening in the wall, drifting across the floor, seeming to hover above it, swirling like liquid. Alireza's voice, dry, very dry in their earphones. "Well," he said. "I wonder where they parked the flying saucer?"

Ling Erhshan suppressing an urge to giggle, suppressing a momentary fear that he would have one of those "nervous breakdowns" Americans in old books and movies loved to fret about. Not I, not I, because this is . . . He said, "This explains a lot, doesn't it?" His own voice so very laconic, English so very precise and crisp. Calm now. Because this is . . . looking out at that golden-pink world, because . . . because this is *glorious.*

There was a crack of thunder behind them, making them turn away from their window. An explosion, gouting flower of crimson fire, the door above the balcony flying outward, tumbling as it fell down into the garden, leaving behind a pale contrail of faint gray smoke.

Ah, yes, thought Ling Erhshan. The monsters. I did forget about the monsters . . .

Kincaid up on the balcony with her troops, looking out across the lush, level expanse of the Pierre Boule Memorial

Lunar Gardens: Always wondered if that was a penname, French "boule" the source of English "bull," nothing to do with manure after all, merely an old-fashioned word for "lie." Garden looks well too, looks just like it did when we shut the door here, seventy-six years ago.

Except, when you looked over your shoulder, one last time, on that long-gone day, there was no golden light spilling across these beautiful lawns . . . God *damn* you, Stanley Krimsky. You were supposed to *spin* the fucking dials before you shut off the gate. *Spin* them, then kill the power and *run* . . .

But Millikan's team is still out there, Sarge . . .

I'm giving you an order, Corporal. Spin 'em.

Yes, ma'm.

Hell. I should've done it myself. Right. And you should've obeyed fucking Major Grimaldi and emptied your clip into the gate's control console too, while you were at it.

Dale Millikan would've understood.

Brilliant golden light on the far wall though, making you remember what it'd been like the first time you saw those yellow hills, that pale pink sky, that sun of molten metal . . . Or the last time. Angel of Death hovering over those yellow hills, thrum of a thousand wings, Angel of Death like a flock of half-invisible birds, taking on some strange, indefinite shape, hovering over the ruins of Koraad.

Snap. Snap. *Snap*.

Human artifacts disappearing from the landscape, like *that*.

Men and women bringing their weapons to bear, opening fire . . .

Snap.

Men and women gone.

Sergeant-Major Astrid Kincaid, USMC Lunar Expeditionary Forces, ordering her soldiers to turn and run away. Live to fight another day. Sometimes a better soldiers' motto than good old *Semper Fi* . . .

Turning to run herself, but not before casting one long, regretful glance at old Koraad, tasting a memory of making love with Dale Millikan far into the alien night . . . Made me giggle by calling me "Astrid Astride," the silly bastard. Cried my last tear ever on the flight home from the Moon.

Brilliant golden light on the far wall now, shadows of humanoid shapes moving within it. Kincaid motioned to her soldiers and went on down the stairs. Too late maybe. Or maybe not.

Down in the garden below, Alireza watched the Americans descend, and formulated his command decision. Not much of a decision, really. Hope their officer was a reasonable fellow. Hope he'd let them surrender. Chinese had *fired* on them after all. Destruction of *al-Qamar* merely a reasonable precaution. Which didn't make poor Mahal and Tariq any less dead of course.

Mahal and Tariq, who'd never see this . . . this . . .

Maybe the American officer would offer some kindly explanation, before he shot them down like offending dogs. He glanced at nonplused Zeq, who glanced at frightened Inbar, standing beside bright-eyed Ling—bright-eyed, curious, seemingly unafraid, standing there, staring through this magic portal, at what appeared to be some other world. Appeared to be . . .

In English, Ling whispered, "So much trouble to go to, for a mere diorama." Wind still whispered around their booted feet, stirring the vegetation of the garden.

Subaïda Rahman said, "Too much trouble, yes. Far too much trouble."

She glanced at Alireza, a daring look, daring him to do something—as if the American soldiers were forgotten—and stepped up to the image. Hesitated. Looked at Ling. Eyes wide, full of unnamed fear, but . . .

Took one step forward, stepped through into the diorama chamber. Stood stock-still, stood looking around. Turned, looked back through the portal at them, then looked up, above the portal, at something apparently far away.

Alireza said, "I don't want to believe. I do not."

Ling said, *"E pur si muove."* Shuffled forward, clumsy in his antique spacesuit, stepped through the portal to Rahman's side. Turned to look around. Broke into a grin of obvious disbelief.

In English, an amplified voice bellowed, "HALT! DO NOT PROCEED!" It was the voice of the barbaric woman. There was a crisp, muffled report, a sparkling explosion from the ceiling above them, small rocks falling, spattering on the ground.

Alireza to Zeq to Inbar. One last look back at the soldiers, visible now through the bushes, silvery light sparkling around each one. They went through the gate together.

Kincaid burst through the bushes, still thinking, Maybe not too late, rushing forward to the Gate console. Golden light still flooding through, soft wind still blowing, crossing the curtainfield boundary to stroke her skin, just as it had so long ago. Five people in old fashioned space suits standing there on the other side, outlined against yellow hills and familiar pastel pink sky. She leveled her rifle, opened her mouth to bark one final warning.

One of the interlopers, smallest of the five, stepped to one side quickly, stepping out of the Gate's image area, probably ducking her impending fire, just getting out of the way . . .

Good that they're afraid.

The image inside the Gate shimmered and dissipated, replaced by rainbow-spattered black formica. "*Shit!*" Not afraid enough, apparently.

Her soldiers gathered behind her, looking around curiously, then fanning out like they'd been taught but still entirely too much like a bunch of huge, friendly puppies. Corky Bokaitis said, "What's going on, Sarge?"

This is a *bad* thing. Why the Hell are you grinning, Sergeant-Major Kincaid? Why the Hell? Just because. Because. She walked over to the console and sat down, started running the scanner, watching numbers scroll across its little LCD screen. Grin flattening. "Well. Sons of bitches were crazy enough to give the tuner a little spin before they cut power." But I know where they went.

PeeWee Roth said, "Yuh mean, we lost 'em?" A little relief in his voice. Maybe he'd read up on the mission beforehand.

Smarter than he looks? Hard to tell, with a face like that. She said, "Gillis, go up to the surface and put through a comline link to the ship. I'll need to tell somebody what's happened." Pointing, then. "You six will set up a base here and stand watch on both sides of the gate. The rest of you . . ."

Bokaitis handed her a scrap of old paper. "Found this in the bushes, Sarge."

Millikan's team . . . Krimsky's handwriting. I wonder if Krimsky's still alive? Maybe I'll kill him a few times after we get back. When. If. She reset the boards to what was, after all, an unforgettable address, and powered up the Gate. Soft wind rising. Pink sky. Yellow hills, Golden sun. Silver clouds. Empty and bare. "All right. Let's get going." A bad business, then. But what is this thrill I feel? Hell. *You* know what it is . . .

No more than an hour and the five of them were standing together on a shallow-sloped hillside looking down on the city, sweating in their spacesuits, puffing at each other through the common radio link. Alireza said, "Nothing moving down there . . ." English clumsy, spoken out of politeness.

Nothing moving anywhere, except that golden fleck of sun, which continued to drift at an angle toward the far horizon, except the silvery clouds, pale and diaphanous, drifting slowly, north to south apparently, across a pastel-shaded backdrop. Faint mother-of-pearl layering, like those first images from Mars . . .

Dust? Fruitless speculation. Ling listened to his suit vents hiss, the air's sound, along with his breathing, almost overwhelming the noise of whining motors behind his back. Almost. He wondered if the others could hear it as well, or if their own suits . . . Probably not. This suit was based on an old Russian design, life-support hardware actually inside the suit's pressure vessel, and he could fancy feeling a bit of excess warmth through the beta-cloth shield at his back. A quick glance down at chin-level dials. He said, "My pump-motors are redlining. There are circuit breakers that will trip if the bearings start to overheat."

Rahman said, "Can you reset them?"

He shrugged, felt a little torrent of sweat go down through his neck ring. "Yes." Tapping the panel door on his chest pack. "But . . . if the bearings burn out . . ."

Zeq said, "Maybe it's time to make that decision now."

Snarly, guttural Arabic from Alireza, reply like a hissing whisper from Rahman. He'd gotten little sense of their argument back at the gate, though Inbar, with his fluid, skilled English had thoughtfully provided snatches of translation, between his own participatory remarks.

Shock when Rahman shut the magic portal in the face of those impossibly monstrous American soldiers. The four of them watching her snap a quick series of photos of this second, identical control panel. Consternation when she reached out and spun those dials.

Inbar's panicky scream crossing the language barrier easily.

Rahman waving the camera, insisting they *could* get back.

Zeq: But how do you know . . . *that*, gesticulating at the randomized dials, will prevent them from following us?

Rahman's face very serious, very dark-eyed behind her glass faceplate: I do not.

Now, Ling said, "I am very hot in here."

Alireza: "We do *not* know what we're dealing with here. Poison gases. Microorganisms."

Ling said, "If your analytical instruments are accurate, there are no poisonous elements in this air." He watched Inbar look down at the instrument pack strapped to his chest. Doubtless, the same numbers still glowed in their little windows: 740 millibars in a gravity field that seemed to be a little more than one-half gee. Oxygen partial pressure about like Earth's at four thousand meters. A little bit of nitrogen, not much. Rather more helium, which seemed unlikely, making their voices sound strange. A little too much CO_2. Not enough to do them permanent harm. Maybe just enough for headaches. Argon. A lot of argon. Inexplicable.

Ling listened to his backpack whine for another minute, then reached up and popped the helmet seal, listened to his air hiss out. Slid the faceplate up into its receptacle. Felt his nostrils crackle as he breathed in. Dry. Extremely dry. Cold. No jetting breath, though. Not all that cold. Maybe five degrees Celsius. Maybe a little higher. Faint, flowery smell. He shut off his suit coolant flow, opened the vents, turned off the oxygen valve, left the fan motor on. Felt his suit temperature go down, sweat evaporating rapidly into the sudden dryness. Stood looking back at four pale-faced Arabs. He said, "Seems all right."

Still fear in Alireza's eyes. And, surprisingly, Inbar was the first one to reach up and twist his bubble helmet loose from its moorings. He sneezed. Shook his head briefly, irritably. "Smells like wild carrots . . ." he said. Image of European hill country in the fall. White flowers with their little red dots growing everywhere. Hay fever. Inbar sneezed again. Grimace of dismay.

Silence of a sort. The distant wind, very distant wind moaning. Distant wind, perhaps, that lifted the dust that colored this *most* peculiar sky . . . perhaps. We know . . . nothing?

Finally, Omry Inbar said, "God damn it."

More silence, underscored by that soft, distant sighing. Alireza said, "Maybe you'd better keep your Jewish profanity to yourself, Dr. Inbar."

Said in English, thought Ling. For my benefit? Or just common courtesy? Or . . .

Inbar, face seeming to darken, said, "Colonel, we've been here for something like an hour already and no one's said a God-damned *word* about what's happened."

Ah, yes. The lot of us walking across this dusty . . . *alien* landscape, staring, silent, baffled, eyes full of fear and wonder and . . . if this were an old American movie or an old book, what would we be doing. Reacting mightily. Screaming and crying. Running in circles like some Italian buffoon . . . huffing and puffing like an Irish washerwoman . . . Americans were good at reacting mightily . . .

Quietly, Rahman said, "I think it's been obvious to all of us since the beginning. The Americans came to the Moon not to find fossil ice so they could be a self-sustaining base, but to locate their test center someplace safe. The energies necessary to operate a teleportation system . . ."

Awesome. They would have to be awesome. And. Yes. That other thing. Several other things. He said, "I don't think I can make myself believe in faster-than-light transference."

Rahman, eyes on his face: "Why make that assumption? Assume that sun," a gesture at the bright bead overhead, "is, oh, Tau Ceti. Why assume it took less than eleven point two years to get here?"

Slight prickle of fear on the back of his neck. Do we tune the transceiver for home then and discover our friends and relatives are a generation older? Assuming we could get down from the Moon, of course. Zeq said, "How much energy would it take to transmit a human being from the solar system to a planet circling Tau Ceti?"

Right. That's the other thing. Ling said, "Approximately the same as it would take to accelerate him to the speed of light, push him through the interstellar medium to Tau Ceti, and decelerate him to relative rest."

Silence.

Then Alireza said, "That can't be right. Assume they found some way to convert us to radio waves, then convert the signal back to matter again. It'd be the same energy required to punch a high-powered laser to the receiver."

"With," said Rahman, "sufficient redundancy to get not less than something like ten-nines reliability?"

Ling thought, Been reading our science fiction, have we Colonel Alireza? The genre had been increasingly popular in the UAR since the inception of the Lunar program. Popular in Green China as well. He said, "How much data processing power would you need, how fast a switching system, to scan and transmit something as complex as a human being?"

More silence.

Zeq: "Too much. Too damned much."

Right. The problem of information density.

Rahman said, "There are other ways. A wormhole, for example . . ."

Inbar snarled, "Have you all become unhinged? Where the Hell *are* we?"

Silence resumed, the wind seeming a bit louder than before. Maybe I'm just imagining that. Goosebumps on the back of my neck. Fear suppressed because . . . there's no other choice. I . . .

Alireza said, "We just don't know."

People doing no more than looking at one another. Not, Ling told himself, reacting mightily at all.

Zeq said, "Do we really think the Americans really built the Stargate? I mean, the English labels looked like they were affixed later."

"And," said Rahman, "those bones . . ."

Stargate. How easily we slip into that old, old jargon.

After a while, they started walking again, walking along the narrow, rutted track, the same one they'd been following since deciding to move away from the . . . what? Transmitter station? The little cluster of hardware and corrugated vinyl buildings out in the middle of a veritable nowhere.

Someone's been going this way. Or did, in the past. Yellow dust drifted over the tracks now. Walking toward the distant city whose spires they could only glimpse 'til the first row of hills was surmounted. Not a normal city. Not an . . . Earthly city.

Ling smiled to himself, feeling sweat trickle across his forehead and gather in a wet left eyebrow, wishing he could take off his suit. But the suit was his water supply. His oxygen supply, if necessary. His armor. His warmth if it got colder than this at night, as it likely would. Nightfall. Golden sun sloping toward the edge of the world.

At least, I wish I could take off my helmet like everyone else. Even Alireza, who'd scowled and shrugged and given in last. Reminds me of Chang Wushi. Regulations. Always regulations. Chang Wushi, who was dry scraps of leather and bone now, lying under an airless sky, baked dry, cooked by a naked sun.

Below, as they walked down onto more level ground, the city was resolving itself. Big tan buildings, looking like they were made from brick, coated with sandstone stucco maybe. Smaller ones, shiny yellow-gray, more in tune with this world of not so many colors. An occasional colored hut, red, green, orange. American buildings, he suddenly realized. Things they put up for themselves, when they were here.

Lost cities. Lost cities in the desert. Xian? No. Old stories. Stories from Arabia and Persia and Europe. The only other book I ever read by Mr. Thimble Valley, book found in the graduate school library, translated into old-style literary Chinese ideographs, difficult to read even by an educated adult, with its thousands of interrelated signs.

Desert Rider. About the dying world of Il Xad, of how its savants struggled to build spaceships, so they could colonize the neighboring world of Yttedra, seize it from its barbaric inhabitants. How interesting, I'd thought, that he chooses to show us these worlds through the jaundiced eyes of a high-ranking nonhuman scientist-bureaucrat. I can almost remember the made up name, spelled out in grass writing, footnoted in *pinyin*. Yes. *Rondar i'Huiôn.* Impossible to pronounce. Ideophonic characters in the text going "*lóng-bah lǐ-wi-yàng.*"

Strange that I remember these things, when so many other details of my youth have faded into the mist. Renewed moment of thrill. I was so happy, merely to be going to the Moon. What would I have thought had you told me, back then, that one day I'd be going to a *real alien world* . . .

Nothing. I would have laughed. These things are impossible. Can't happen. There are no *real* alien worlds. Oh, maybe out among the stars, worlds so alien that nothing would be familiar, comprehensible. But out of reach. Forever out of reach . . .

Scientist-mind speaking up: What does this mean for the Standard Interpretation? Answer: Big trouble. Impossibly big trouble. No matter how things resolve themselves, we're going to have to take a look at that.

Near the edge of the city now. They stopped, mopping their brows, shadows growing longer as the sun scraped the top of the hills. Stopped and looked at the wreckage. Wheels. Crumpled white wings. Cockpit with jumbled bones. Tilted tailplane, rudder broken away and lying on the ground nearby. Traces of fire here and there.

Numbers on the crushed fuselage, black paint on white metal. NCD4044. Meaningless. They went on into the city,

Ling Erhshan looking up at the darkening pink sky once again: Just where the Hell *are* we?

Sunset on Mars-Plus. That *was* what they'd called the place, back in the beginning, when they'd popped open the Gate for the first time and there it was. Sunset. Sky deep pink, swiftly darkening to lavender. Bright stars just beginning to wink on, sun no more than a golden-purple shine on the haze above the horizon where it'd gone down.

So many sunsets like this. I was just a girl then. Happy young girl, though I didn't know it. Thought of myself as the old-bag noncom lady, pushing forty . . . Image of the soccer field they'd set up in one of the deserted plazas of Koraad, kicking the black and white ball around. *Futból* in those days, because so many of us were . . . Hispanic. We said Hispanic. Later image, standing, watching the lavender turn to lilac, to purple, to indigo, to black. Fields of unfamiliar stars spangling the night, magic jewels. The pale white lozenge of a nearby spiral galaxy spread out, eight degrees across, behind that starfield. Dale's arm around my waist, just holding me, watching, not saying a word . . .

Corky Bokaitis coming up to stand beside her now, looking at the sky above the hills, trailed by her two blond brethren, handsome blond Neanderthal Men whose tunics said Fred and Barney in neat white letters against black cloth tape. All right. I get the joke. Everybody gets the joke, even people who weren't alive when there was still TV, complete with fifty-year-old reruns, get the joke. So why do *they* think it's a joke? Playacting at being soldiers. Playacting at being cavemen. Playacting at everything.

Bokaitis said, "Where is this place, Sarge?"

Good question. In the old days we brought in astronomers, big telescopes, bigger telescopes . . . Memory of bringing through a mobile launcher, of using a portable lightsat launcher to pop arrays of instruments into orbit. Scientists looking farther and farther out into space, not seeing a damn thing they recognized. "Don't think they ever figured that one out, Corky. We wound up calling it Mars-Plus. Because of the pink sky."

"Hmh." Swarthy cavegirl looking up at the stars, one arm around each caveman's waist. "That so?" Polite amazement.

But then, I was first out the gate on Alpha Centauri, looking up at familiar stars, watching two suns come up, thinking about it, realizing, God damn, I *knew* where the fuck I was . . .

Then scientists coming in, jubilant, setting up their instruments . . .

And one of the first things they'd done was point those instruments back at a bright star on the constellar boundary between Perseus and Cassiopeia, peek-a-boo, I *see* you! Because, you see, we have to, just *have* to have moved some four-plus years into the temporal past right now . . .

Jubilant. Expecting to find a brilliant radio beacon in the sky, astrometric binary oscillating back and forth, with a period of just one year. Close enough, in fact, that we'd be able to pull meaning out of the static with our computers. Scientists already planning what messages they'd soon be handing to their past selves. And then back, through the gates, to their now-selves, and then . . .

Jubilant. Fucking *time* travel, God damn it!

Time travel? What the fuck are we talking about here?

She'd gone to Dale Millikan, science-popularizing journalist, for a simplified layperson's explanation.

Dale hemming and hawing and scratching around the roots of the dense gray beard on his throat. Well. Duh. Hmmmm . . . Well, look at it this way: When we come through the gate to Alpha Centauri, we must be moving 4.3 years into the past.

We do? Why? I mean, when we go back through the gate . . .

Well, that's it. The rules of relativity, I think they call it "composition of velocities," or something like that, say if you move faster than light, you have to be moving into the past . . .

I don't understand.

Shit. Um. Take my word for it, then.

All right. So where does time travel come in?

OK, we're four years plus in the past, right now, on this

side of the gate. So the light from the Sun, up there in the sky, left the vicinity of the Earth four point three years before we stepped through the gate to come here. Right?

I guess so.

So. What happens if we build a *new* gate, here at Alpha Centauri, and punch through to the Earth?

Well, assuming we figure out how to build gates of our own . . . Oh. We arrive on Earth eight point six years before we left.

Dale Millikan's eyes brightening with pleasure. Pleasure because I turned out to be smart enough to get it, sort of, or just pleased because he could explain it successfully to a dumbfuck noncom girl?

Still puzzling over the whole business, she'd gone to one of the scientists for another try, sitting with a bird-like old man who seemed to take great pleasure in eying her breasts while scribbling equations on the screen of his electronic notepad, things with lots of x's and y's and u's and v's and Greek *gammas*.

Look, Sergeant, this business is really very simple. I don't know *why* it gives people such fits. Einstein's principle of relativity states that the analytical form of physical laws is the same in all inertial reference systems. And the principle of the constancy of the velocity of light states that the speed of light in a vacuum is a universal constant. Does that make sense?

Duh. Sure.

Well now, Sergeant, Einstein understood that two spatially separate localized occurrences are simultaneous when the readings of two identical clocks adjacent to the events are the same, and it is known that the clocks are synchronized. However, when the clocks are not near each other, their synchronism must be defined. Right?

Bright, bright, beady lizardman eyes staring at her tits, as if they held her sentience somehow.

So, Einstein's *particular* genius was understanding that two identical clocks, cee and cee-prime, situated at two distant points, pee and pee-prime, fixed in a given inertial frame ess, synchronize *in* ess, when the respective cee and cee-prime times tee-one and tee-one-prime of the sending of a light signal at pee and its arrival at pee-prime are connected by the formula tee-one-prime minus tee-one equals tee-two minus tee-one-prime with the cee time tee-two of its return to pee after reflection at pee-prime *back* to pee . . .

Holy. Fucking. Christ.

Lizardman writing on his little flatscreen, holding it up for her tits to see, going, Now, *gamma* is equivalent to one divided by the square root of one minus vee-squared, *divided by* cee-squared, *times* delta-ecks-prime, so . . .

Maybe if I just pop my shirt open, I'll be able to see better and . . .

Lizardman: On the *other* hand, if you-sub-ecks-prime equals cee, and hence, you-sub-why-prime equals you-sub-zee-prime equals *zero*, then you-sub-ecks equals cee and you-sub-why equals you-sub-zee equals zero, in accordance to the principle of the constancy of the velocity of light. Clear?

Duh. Sure.

OK. That cee *does* represent the maximum speed of energy propagation is indicated by Einstein's 1907 argument using these same equations, Lizardman tapped his screen, pointing at all the various yous and vees and ekses and gammas, which, he said, shows conclusively that in the *contrary* case it would then be possible to transmit information into the past. Q.E.D. Smug little lizardman, shaking a finger at those selfsame tits.

Time travel. Right. I get it now. Thanks, Doc. Be seein' ya.

Only one little problem. That bright, first-magnitude star on the edge of Cassiopeia was silent. Solar radio waves, sure. Oh, you could even pick up Jupiter, farting and whistling away, but . . .

First order fear: Did something . . . *happen* to us? A reassuring glance back through the still-open stargate. Second order fear: Is the Copenhagen interpretation of quantum cosmology wrong? What if?

Impossible.

But what if?

Dale brought up Bohm's alternative first, but he wasn't a scientist and they were too afraid to listen anyway. He'd be pleased to see the literature now, learned articles in journals, by men and women with degrees dating from the twentieth century . . .

Still afraid after all these years.

General Athelstan, his cronies on Earth in a panic, ordering her to destroy the Gate, plant explosives that would collapse the cavern. God damn it, woman, we gave you fucking nuclear weapons for a reason. *Use* them!

Calling me "woman" like that, for Christ's sake. What old fantasy can he have been living in for the past three-quarters of a century? Well. I hope he shit his pants when I told him I was making a router call to the trace packager routine, reopening the Gate to Mars-Plus.

She patted a breast pocket, where her own annotated copy of the ten-thousand gigabyte Scavenger manual on the Colonial Stargate operating system nestled, a flat square the size of a turn-of-the-century floptical disk. More than a million toolbox calls into an information system that, apparently, lay snuggled against the keelblocks of Creation, of which we humans have learned to understand and manipulate precisely six.

Just enough to let us get around. Sort of. Get back to places we've found by accident, that's all.

Because we were afraid, and still are.

Because the Scavengers hinted, in their literature, that the million calls they knew were no more than a billion-trillionth of the total. How many possible quantum states are there, for the Universe as a whole?

Toolbox. Jesus. We gave it a name so we could imagine we understood it, as if the universal gate system were some old-fashioned computer and its operating system no more than software calls to some kernel ROM written by a conscious mind . . .

Cold chill there.

What if?

Then . . . *who*?

Well. You *know* who, don't you?

She turned around, looking back toward the gate, through into the bright, yellow-lit space of the cavern under the Lunar base, her soldiers setting up equipment, some of them, others just standing around gaping at the now black sky. One of Mars-Plus's moons was up now, a little bronze jewel glowing softly as it sailed low over the hills. I remember the exhilaration I felt when I first saw this place. Like magic, an alien world, right out of a book. Like a child's dream, somehow. Exhilaration now. I'm glad to be back.

Will I be so glad if . . .

Brief memory. Suzy Panetta dying in front of her. Maybe dying, maybe something else. Angel of Death sizzling overhead. *Snap*. Suzy's startled look, wincing, not quite pain. *Snap*. Suzy rolling up like a windowshade. *Snap*. Rolling up into nowhere at all. *Snap*. White bones raining down, rattling down from that same nowhere, making a dry, brittle pile on the dusty ground.

Suzy? Kneeling, picking up a pale skull. Looking, full of disbelief. But Suzy had had quite distinctive front teeth, projecting a little forward, with that little gap, just so, the crooked, slightly malformed, slightly yellowed canine . . .

Just like the teeth in the skull. She'd dropped it. Dropped poor Suzy on the ground and run.

Shadows falling on them out of a dull, red-purple sky, shadows of the tall tan buildings masking the shadows of the smaller, metallic yellow ones, which seemed, somehow, ever so much older, masking the tiny shadows of the colorful, new-looking American structures, so obviously temporary.

Level yellowish pavement under their booted feet, dust sliding, just above the ground, on a wind that chilled their faces. The five of them gathering round a boxy, greenish-brown car, looking at cracked black vinyl upholstery, plastic steering wheel curdled by years and years of dry sunlight. Paint faded and peeled, but no rust. Tires flat, dusty looking.

Ahmad Zeq reached down into the back seat and picked up the little white ball, fingering its dusty, crackling, padded surface, trying to make out faded words in what appeared to be Romanic script. "Is this a baseball?"

Ling poked at it. "Softball, I think. They were a little bigger, couldn't be hit quite so far . . ." The wind gusted—blowing dust up around them, evoking a soft nightmare whoosh from the blunted edge of the nearest stone building, moaning on American vinyl—then died down, silence restored.

Zeq said, "We must have been insane to do this. What did we gain?"

Alireza: "Maybe our lives. They were starting to shoot. That golden-haired woman . . ." One of the few in the squad of monsters who even *looked* human, if you discounted those soulless, chrome-bright eyes . . . He felt a familiar cold shiver recurse up his spine.

Inbar: "What're we going to do?"

Rahman: "More important, where are we?" Conscious again of the camera clipped to her spacesuit harness, with its precious images of readouts and control settings. Which might, or might not, mean anything. And I did take a picture of that scrap of paper, the one with the scribbled numbers . . .

Zeq felt a sharp wave of something like despair. "Even if we get back through the . . . gate. Even if we do, there's nothing waiting for us on the Moon but those . . ." Those *things*. No djinni at all. Nothing so familiar.

Almost to himself, Ling whispered, "Famous monsters from movieland." No one seemed to hear him. Or know what he meant, at any rate. No matter.

Inbar said, "Even if they're gone, even if they just packed up and went back home, there's *nothing* on the Moon for us now. All we could do would be stand there in the dome and stare up at Earth and wait until we starved to death."

Rahman: "A rescue mission, perhaps . . ." Because, back in the UAR, there were other orbiters, the lower stage even now being cleaned up for its flight back from Hejaz to Hammaghir. But, wistfully, We are *here*. This is . . . more important than . . .

Long silence. Finally, Alireza, looking up into a swiftly blackening sky, said, "In any case, it is about *maghrib*. And we have, some of us, missed too many prayers, Travelers' Rule or no."

More silence, eying each other, then Ahmad Zeq whispered, "Praise be to God, Lord of the Universe, The Compassionate, the Merciful, Sovereign of the Day of

Judgment . . ." Fear. Fear makes us small. And yet there is no power and strength, save in God.

Ling stood quietly to one side, watching the three of them posture and pray, the two men with their expansive gestures, standing, kneeling, foreheads in the dust, the woman, more . . . closed. Hands at her sides. Memory of all those years spent in Turkestan, a land of Muslim tribes, Muslim nations, for a millennium before the Chinese conquest, before Soviet rule, before Russian conquest. Muezzin calling the faithful to prayer, people falling to the ground, groaning out their rituals.

When I was young, I held them in contempt. Primitive savages, believing in gods and demons, devils and angels, no better than Hindus, with their cows and red dots and epicycles of despair . . .

Sudden memory of the American "tourist" he'd met one day while wandering the sightseeing places of Agra, the year they held the LPSC in India. What year? The 175th, I think. Tried to talk to him, get some hints about . . .

Jolly fellow, tall, slim, suntanned, dressed up in white linen, told me his name was Laredo. Shook my hand. Very cold fingers. Cool, despite the summer's oppressive heat. Referred to our hosts as *Hindudes*. Talked my ear off about nothing at all, classic American bullshit. Told me the declension of special American words: *dude* a male, *doodah* a female, *dudlet* an immature male, *dudette* an immature female. Stories about breeding them as livestock on something called a *dude ranch*, watched over by cowboys known as *doodads*. Treating me like an ignorant child. As if I hadn't been studying American movies, reading old American books all my life . . .

Aw, shoot, yew little Chink. Ah'm jest pullin' yore laig. Making me think of that cowboy bomber pilot in *Dr. Strangelove*.

He glanced at Inbar, standing quietly by his side. An atheist, perhaps. Even in Arabia.

Almost apologetically, the man whispered, "I'm a Jew."

Ah, of course. Suddenly remembering Alireza's remark

about "Jewish profanity." Silly and insular of me. Jews. Christians. Plenty of those in Chungkuo too. All of them busy praying to their apocalyptic God.

What if Tao had a face and name? Peasant masses out there even now, in the hills and misty valleys of China. To them it does have a face and name. *Tao-Chiao* not merely the philosophical *Way*. Who am I to judge people's prayers?

By the time they finished praying it was full dark, stars brilliant overhead, night wind cold on their faces. Ling closed his suit vents, felt his body heat start to bring up the temperature inside. Pretty soon, he realized, I'll be too hot again.

Just as well. Tired. Hungry. And, soon enough, I'll be thirsty. When the last of the suit's water bladder is emptied. What will we do? Starvation could take weeks. Dying of thirst only takes days. Arabs slightly better off, of course, with their compact recyclers. Trust a desert people to think of water.

Alireza stood looking up at the sky, dark face shadowy and mysterious in the starlight. He said, "Though, of course, we used inertial guidance units, we were taught celestial navigation at the academy. Bringing home our aircraft at night, with failed instruments. Walking home through enemy country, trackless desert perhaps, after being shot down, bailing out, surviving a crash." No more then than a gesture up at these stars, here and now.

Ling knew the stars as well, stars watched night after night, year after year, through a decade and more out in the Taklamakan. Bright stars over a stone desert. Stars by which I hoped, one day, to navigate my ship to the Moon, maybe on to Mars if I were lucky enough.

Zeq pointed up at a bright spark, down near the horizon. Small, almost showing a disk, not quite. "This thing . . ."

Rahman said, "Satellite . . ."

Inbar: "Not a spacecraft, I don't think. A small moon."

Small moon. Sharp pang in the chest. *This is an alien world!* Another planet, not the Earth, not the Moon. And . . . somewhere else.

Alireza said, "There's not a constellation in the sky. Just white dots and more white dots . . ."

Not, then, some world circling Tau Ceti? How very comforting that would have been. *Close to home*. Ling, very softly, said, "No *Via Galactica*, but . . ." Looking now at a bright smudge, many times the breadth of a Full Moon, so obviously a spiral galaxy. If it was a normal-sized one, with average surface brightness, it might be no more than twenty or thirty thousand parsecs distant. And no Milky Way, no river of stars . . . "Perhaps we are in a globular cluster, and that is . . ." *Home?* Impossible, of course. Quite impossible.

Inbar said, "Those might be the Magellanics over there. And that smaller, much dimmer spiral Andromeda."

Alireza: "Slim evidence, indeed."

The nearest building, the one behind the parked car, one of the Americans' vinyl quonset huts, proved to be unlocked. First discovery: when you flipped the switch just inside the door, the lights came on, little incandescent bulbs filling angular American-style rooms with a warm, homey glow. Second discovery: when you turned the taps in the little galley, water gurgled down the drain. Cold water. Hot water. Even a little sprayer attachment, and this box by the sink would be a dishwasher. Full of clean dishes.

Zeq went into the lavatory and pushed the handle, watched the gleaming white porcelain toilet flush. Turned and looked out through the doorway. Smiled. Started unclamping the waist-ring of his spacesuit. "Rest of you," he said, still smiling, "can wait in line." Closed the door in their faces.

Ling opened a kitchen cabinet. Boxes. Cans. Packets of this and that. Jars of spice. He took down a big blue box. "Kraft Deluxe Macaroni and Cheese. Best if used by: Jan 61."

Inbar said, "Probably nothing but dust inside now."

Rahman said, "The dried pasta would keep. Might taste a little flat, of course." She switched on the stove, watched one spiral resistance element start to glow, dull orange, then bright red.

Alireza opened the refrigerator. White walls stained with green and black. A very stale smell. But the little light still came on. The plastic milk bottle looked like it was full of cottage cheese. Would bacteria and mold organisms have survived and prospered in here for more than seventy years? Unlikely. All we see is their mass grave.

He picked up one capped, dark blue can and read the label: *King Kuts*. Picture of a contented-looking tan and white terrier. Sudden, alarming shock, bringing the whole business alive for him: Crazy Americans bringing their pet *dogs* to the Moon, then taking them out to the *stars* . . . Further shock. Stars. You know the scenario we've been imagining. American physicists figured out the secret of teleportation. Came up to the Moon to conduct their experiments as far from home as they could get, just in case it wasn't so *safe* . . .

But you know the Americans flew to the Moon, a hundred years ago, in primitive rocket ships. You know they didn't build those machines. Know they didn't build this city.

What else do we know?

Not enough.

He said, "Well. At least we won't die of thirst. Buys us a little time. Let's . . . have a look around."

They got out of their suits then, shivering a little in the dry cold, following Zeq's impromptu lead, walking around, at first in a little knot, turning on lights, poking around quasi-empty rooms. A mixed bag of offices, living quarters . . .

The uneasy feeling of looking at people's unmade beds. Room with a pair of men's white-cotton underpants abandoned in the middle of the floor. A single athletic shoe, soft-soled, bright red, turned-up toe style popular across the world of almost a century ago, label on its sole "SuperSlipper Deluxe." Inside, on the white insole, you could see faint dark imprints where someone's toes had made the shoes home.

They found the thermostat in the hallway, clicked it to "on," set the temperature. There was a distant hiss, a faint smell of burning dust. After a while, they wandered apart.

When Rahman walked into the little library, she was mainly interested in the antique American desktop supercomputer perched in the corner, next to a little Japanese 3V display unit. Old stuff, old technology, the twentieth century's last dying gasp. Surely, if the refrigerator still worked, the computer would too, would hold, perhaps, in its crystal memory, some hint as to what had gone on here, all those years ago.

She flipped the switch. Nothing. Checked the connections. Checked the power supply. Made sure the damned thing was plugged into the wall outlet. Switched to another outlet, just in case . . . Looked at the blue and white "QA Inc." sigil in the upper left hand corner of the box's facade with a slight sinking feeling.

The Quantum Access chipset, all the rage worldwide in the 2050s, had turned out to be notoriously unstable. It hadn't mattered back then. The computers would be long obsolete, long discarded before it would matter. But this computer had simply forgotten how it worked. And the tools I'd use to bypass its amnesia are back aboard *al-Qamar* . . .

No. Scattered in bits and pieces across the surface of Crater Peary.

She sat back in the chair, looking around the room. Not really a library, just looking like the old image of one. Maybe someone's office? Shelves above the desk, with rows of bulky twenty-first century crystal memory cards, really old fashioned optical book disks. Even a row of paper books.

Perfect bound, it was called, signatures glued to spine. If I picked one up now, its pages might fall out on the floor. Maybe even turn to dust and ashes, they used such poor paper in those days. But . . .

A black Christian Bible, bound in something like leather. That would be intact, printed on clean, durable stock. An English translation labeled *The Koran*, published by someone called "Penguin Classics." She glanced at the optical books again, saw that most of them were references, mostly physics, and mathematics. Quantum mechanics and cosmology. A big, slick black book called *The Perennial Dictionary of World Religions*. Seventeenth edition.

A row of what appeared to be three-ring binders, neatly placed, alternating spine and opening out. Someone with a neatness fetish, who wanted them to sit properly, not fall together . . .

She took one down. Blew dust off its gray, unmarked cover. Set it flat on the desk. Opened it.

A printout of a manuscript. "EkaReferenced Toolbox Calls to the Colonial GateNet OS: Were the Scavengers Kidding?" Several dates written in, in a variety of pen colors, a variety of hands. Dates from the 2060s, near the very end of the American tenure here. She flipped through the pages. Text. Pictures of control panels, variations on the ones she'd already seen. Diagrammatic descriptions of settings. Equations full of integral signs.

Lots of annotation, colored pen marks, some of it neatly printed, others a cursive scrawl, illegible, looking more or less like Arabic script written the wrong way round. The daily working notes of a multi-person research group.

Printout page dated 02/14/59: " . . . we suspect that if you make a direct call to the Window Manager, using the above setting, you do not *need* to have both gate consoles set the same way. How else could it have worked? Did they telephone ahead and ask someone to tune them in? There's *no* evidence to support a conclusion there were FTL communications independent of the Colonial transport net. (Unless, of course, it was something the Scavengers simply missed. JB.)"

Above that, in a neat, emerald green hand: "So Beasley thinks the Window Manager is the key? Not if my reversibility algorithm for MenuBandwidth is even *close*!! DM."

To one side of that, in small, crabbed black: "You still don't understand the math. JB." Someone else had drawn a red smiley-face beside that, quick strokes of a delicate pen, emblematic of all that had been twenty-first century America. Rahman shifted in her chair, staring at the page, at the old notes. All right. The secret is here. Somewhere.

She took down the next notebook. "Imagery of the Space-Time Juggernaut in Late Scavenger Eschatological Literature, by Dale Millikan." No annotations this time. No dates. Mostly text, a few pictures that looked like exploded diagrams of machinery, decorated with something like Chinese ideograms. Ling . . . No. She'd seen enough Chinese to know this was something else.

She flipped to the last page, where a final paragraph had been slashed through in a bright green pen. There was a note, strokes heavy, as if the writer had been bearing down angrily, also in green. "What the fuck if this *isn't* the Scavengers' version of SF? What the fuck if it's *real*? Where the fuck are the Scavengers now? On fucking *vacation*?"

There was an old-style paperback book on the shelf too, once-garish cover faded, showing a muscular man with a sword. When she opened it, the pages came loose, cracked and smoking under her fingers. Hundreds, thousands of people, writing these things for each other, rather than posterity . . .

A third notebook, this one bound with a tan plastic spiral, lined paper, full of handwriting. Scribbles. Doodles. Drawings of this and that. Spacecraft. Green ink landscapes. A muscular naked woman. Some of the sketches were rather good, closeups of the woman's face where you could see it was an attempted likeness. One sketch that seemed to be of the woman's crotch, a few anatomical omissions implying it might have been drawn from memory, rather than the live model . . . His lover? Or just a fantasy?

On one page, alone, surrounded by a circle of green that had been drawn over and over: "If it's real, we're fucked." On the next page, startling, a careful drawing of a gate control panel, each control arrowed and labeled in neatly printed English. On the pages beyond, a terse explanation of what each control did. God almighty . . .

She went back to the first notebook and began looking at the control-setting diagrams, comparing them to the pictures and explanations in Millikan's notebook, time starting to slide by, unnoticed.

Kincaid stood in a cavern on the Moon, just inside the yawning Gate, looking out at the nighttime stars of Mars-Plus, bouncing lightly on the balls of her feet, almost taking off in low-gee. Muscular tension. A wish she could reach through the antique communicator pressed to her ear and . . .

Athelstan was saying, "Now you listen to *me*, Sergeant-*Major*." Arrogant, overbearing, self-inflating tones: the Man In Charge. Listen to me, Sergeant-Major, or I'll huff and I'll puff and I'll . . .

Outside, Corporal PeeWee Roth, fangy monster-man, was

directing people, getting them to line up their gear. People. Sheesh. That big guy next to Roth right now, arguing with him, waving his arms—curtainfield sparkling like pixiedust—tall, maybe over seven feet. Big, square head, dead white face, angular bones in his neck.

Sepulchral voice: Me? Francis Muldoon, ma'm. No, ma'm. I enlisted just for this mission.

Jesus Christ. Why would someone want to look like a giant polio cripple from some old movie or something? And that laugh of his . . .

Athelstan: "Now, you pull your people back through the gate. You set a demolition charge at the control console on Mars-Plus, set the time, and you shut the gate. Then you set the timer on the 200 megaton weapon we gave you and leave it in base. You lift off, loiter until the weapon detonates, then you come home."

Or you'll what?

What difference does it make, what they do or think?

Outside, outside in the real world of Mars-Plus, the alien galaxy was sliding slantwise down through the horizon now, magic glitter on the other side of the sky. She looked down at the little man by her side, Brucie Big-Dick she'd begun to call him, and . . . what the Hell was the name of this other little shit, his systems engineer? Chuckie. Buck teeth. Blond fuzz flattop. Jesus Christ. *Chuckie?*

Pressed the mute on the communicator.

"How long'll it take your buddies back on Earth to launch the other ship?" Still standing in the hangar, surrounded by scaffolding, hull access panels gaping open.

Chuckie looked up at her and smirked, bumped Brucie with his hip. "Jeez, Sarge. We took the drive apart twenty years ago, to see what made it tick. Never did figure out how to get it back together. Sorry."

Brucie, looking up at her. Knowing. He said, "You know, it'll take 'em three weeks or so to program up our macrovacuole to make a conventional scavtech commuter transport like the ones you fellas found on Winkie. If there's anyone willing to program it for 'em . . ."

Winkie was one of four residential planets where the

Scavengers actually seemed to live, among the thousands upon thousands where they merely . . . mined. Tract housing for about eight billion skeletonbirds. Never did find Emerald City, what we'd called the Scavenger homeworld in the early days, still called it later, even after we learned to read their language, learned they'd called it Æghóng.

"What's a macrovacuole?"

Brucie eying her. "Haven't paid much attention to consumer tech, have you?"

"No." Busy with my memories. And my books. Twenty years spent translating the *Héláq* encyclopedia, among other things. What a fucking waste of time.

Chuckie said, "You got a foodserver in your house?"

"Sure."

"Vacuole's what makes all those nice, tasty goodies out of your shit and piss and bathwater. We've got a big one can make anything. One of the original models, copied from the wrecked factory you guys found on Munch."

I remember Munch. Like the empty ruins of a planet-wide slum. Technicolor forests growing over everything. And fucking giant hurricanes, savage earthquakes, because something blew the planet's big moon into a steep elliptical orbit. A bizarre sight, hanging in the sky, like Earth's Moon, but swollen, blackened, a fucking enormous bite taken out of its side . . .

Outside, Roth was through with Muldoon, was now talking with PFC Tarantellula. Skinny black gargoyle, three and a third meters tall, just shy of eleven feet. Hairless. Huge, clawed hands. No nose. Beak for a mouth. Big white eyes. A fucking professional spiderdancer. Surprised to see her in the squad, someone I'd actually run across in real life, on one of my few "vacations." Watched her dance in Central Park. Graceful. A dancing demon. Saw her at a party after the show. Saw her palm a basketball and pop it with a squeeze . . .

She punched the mute button again, listened to Athelstan's furious squawking. "God damn it, Sergeant . . . God damn it, Sergeant . . ." Sputtering hiss, like he was spitting into his microphone. Christ. Foaming at the mouth.

She said, "I'm sorry. General. Reg 4314A. An officer outside the direct chain of command, in combat, is required under law to use his or her own best judgment to . . ."

A scream, classic, banshee scream, rising in pitch: "God damn it you're not an officer God damn it you're not in combat God damn it to Hell, Sergeant, you're *not* outside the fucking chain of *command* . . ."

She snapped the communicator shut. And Brucie Big-Dick said, "Such refined language. They give special courses at West Point?"

She smiled at him. "Don't know. Never went to West Point. Just a scumbag sergeant."

Later, Kincaid stood out under the stars of Mars-Plus with her curtainfield shut down, breathing the strange air, smelling those familiar smells, feeling its cold wind on her face, like fingers stirring in her hair. Stars in the sky, the little moons sailing in their low orbits. Dwarf galaxies so much like the Magellanics that, at first, the scientists were fooled.

Like most fools, easy to fool . . .

Oh, God, I remember. Memories put aside. Pain surrendered, then forgotten. No. Not forgotten. Never forgotten. Walking up onto a low hill, looking back toward the bright area around the Gate, looking back through into a yellow-lit cavern under the Moon. Just like old times. Shadow shapes of soldiers back on the Moon, moving things around, setting up their basecamp, other shapes, distinct, on this side, Bokaitis posting a guard, for Christ's sake, following regs.

A look around in the darkness. Arabs and Chinaman not lurking out in the dark. They'll have followed the track over to Koraad. Dark buildings in the distance. Is that a gleam of light I see? Or imagination? More likely, complex, reflected moonlight.

Brucie and Chuckie, glittering inside their silvery armor of harnessed quantum inference. Curtainfield not a *field*, as such, just . . . an artificial spacetime configuration where the air atoms are likely to stay . . . because they want to?

Brucie and Chuckie still looking up at the sky, pointing things out to each other. Brucie Big-Dick had an arm around Chuckie's narrow shoulders now. Well, well.

Another couple holding hands. Gillis, who was, perhaps,

the most human looking of the lot, once you discounted those ... *sinews*. Not muscles. Like steel bands and cables crisscrossing under his skin. Gillis went for function, not appearance like the rest of these idiots. Gillis, able to bend steel in his bare hands ... Holding hands with a tiny, wiry black and yellow tigerstripe girl with glittering, faceted eyes whose uniform tunic said "Honeybee." Christ, look at that. She's got her hand in his back pocket.

Kincaid switched on her curtainfield, felt its warmth spill around her like a magic shawl, lay down on the hard rock of the dusty hillside, looking up at the night sky. Sometimes, it's summertime here. Sometimes. Winds warm and lovely.

Can't have been far from here ... Lying naked on a scratchy green wool blanket. He was fat and flabby, gray and scruffy, fifteen years older than me, a *civilian*, for Christ's sake. Belly like a skinful of soft margarine. Hand on my hard stomach, rubbing back and forth, eyes sparkling right through the warm darkness, looking at my pussy instead of me, like a man contemplating a steak dinner ... Not even very good at it. Not at first. But Jesus could he talk.

I never knew I was starved for that kind of attention. Not 'til old Dale Millikan got hold of me. Hell, I decided he was all talk and no action, but ... Well. Got better at it, once he decided I wasn't going to run off before he could throw a few quick fucks into me. Wry smile. You'd think a man in his fifties, a man who could whisper sweet nothings so *well* would have things figured out a little better than that.

I just have a way with words, he'd said. Not much else.

A way with words.

I wonder what happened to him, after ...

I wonder what his last moments were like ...

I wonder ...

Long pause.

Jesus, don't be so stupid, you old bag. Over and done with. Long gone. Bullshit. She sat up, stretched. Yawned. Four hours to local dawn. Might as well tell them to take a little break, get some rest before we head out. Catch them Arabs over in Koraad and ...

Then what?

Yeah. Good question.

Just bomb the gate and go on fucking home?

Bullshit.

Never thought you'd see this place again.

Now, here you are.

What do you want to *do*, girly-girl?

Finally, late at night, the five of them sat sleepy-eyed in the prefab building's little lounge, perched uncomfortably on American couches and chairs meant for sprawling. Toileted. Bathed. Brushed and combed with the combs and brushes of men and women long departed. Full of freeze-dried food long gone stale. Rahman's notebooks were propped open on the room's big, transparent plastic coffee table, astronauts and scientists flipping through them, finding bits of knowledge here and there. Mostly though, mere bafflement. Questions and more questions.

Rahman said, "I don't know. The simplest explanations, for the impossibly fantastic . . . What the historical record seems to indicate is that the Americans came to the Moon a little more than a century ago for the same purpose as we did: to bootstrap a space-faring civilization so humanity, their part of it at least, could escape the coming disaster. Their instruments told them Peary was sitting on what seemed to be a big pocket of fossil ice, maybe some trapped gas."

"They don't seem to have understood what they'd found at first, either." Ling was flipping through one of the printed hardcover books, marveling at the feel of its slick, sturdy, old-fashioned paper. "This business about thinking they'd found an old Nazi base . . ."

Alireza shrugged. "The Peenemunde team *could* have gotten to the Moon."

Inbar said, "Didn't, though."

Rahman: "In any case, they found the Stargate, with its controls preconfigured to take them *here*. Mars-Plus."

"Interesting name," murmured Zeq, turning, staring out the window into featureless darkness.

"So they found a system of teleportation devices, devices of extraterrestrial origin, apparently. Somehow worked out a methodology for *using* them. Found hundreds, maybe even thousands of abandoned worlds . . ."

"And," said Ling, "they, for some reason we don't know, decided to come home and leave it all behind."

"Not quite all," said Alireza. "At least now we know the secret of their magical consumer technology."

Inbar: "What a waste. What a damned waste."

Ling: "There was a time when that was considered the American Way." He kept flipping the pages of his book. "This business about Scavengers and Colonials . . ."

Rahman said, "As near as I can figure out, *Colonials* is what the Americans called the people who built the system of gates. *Scavengers* are a later folk who, like the Americans, spent some time exploring the abandoned transport net."

Zeq said, "So. And where are they now?"

Inbar: "Maybe that's what sent the Americans scurrying for home, ill-gotten booty clutched in their hot little hands."

Ling said, "What do you suppose is meant by the phrase, 'Space-Time Juggernaut'?"

Long silence, then Rahman sighed and pushed one of the big notebooks to the center of the table. "Well, we've got one thing. This appears to be a working text on Stargate net operations. In it, I found this." She flipped through the pages to a columnar table and shoved the book across to Ling.

" 'Hypothetical Terrestrial Gate Loci.' "

She said, "As near as I can tell, the only way to move is between two physical gates, a transmitter and a receiver. There are instructions for how to call a downed gate and do a remote power-up from here."

Staring at the columns of figures and words, picked out in some fine Romanic sans-serif font, Ling said, "I wonder how the . . . Colonials set up the system in the first place. Surely they didn't fly the gates all over the universe in starships . . ."

"No answer."

Alireza slid forward off the couch and kneeled beside the table, running his finger over the figures. "Does this note say 'Old Red Sandstone'? I wonder what that means?" More figures, latitude and longitude figures. "This one is somewhere in southern Libya." Looking up, looking around at a circle of faces.

Finally, Zeq said, "In the morning, we could go back to the gate. Set its console according to these directions . . ."

And go home? Rahman said, "If there are gates all over the Earth . . ." she pointed to a set of figures that seemed to be somewhere in North America, "why did they come after us in a rocket ship? Why not just pop through the gate and be waiting for us under the Moon?"

Why indeed? "Cowboys," muttered Alireza.

Maybe, thought Ling. Or maybe not. Sometimes, when it was important, Americans could . . . act decisively enough. He said, "We shall uncover something of the truth when morning comes." And, if there *is* a gate buried in the Libyan desert . . .

Looking out the window again, Zeq said, "Morning. I wonder how long that will be?"

Omry Inbar awoke and, as always, opened his eyes slowly. No muezzin now. No wan morning sunlight. Dark night. He sat up, half awake, suddenly came alert with a pang of . . . not terror, no. Just . . . surprise. Folding upright in unexpectedly low gravity, dusty, unfamiliar bed creaking softly under his weight.

He pushed open the draperies and looked out on cold, dark night. The windowpane was slightly fogged, moisture from his breathing condensed out of the warm room air on cold ersatz glass. Outside, the stone street was all shadows and blotches of . . . imaginary somethingness. No movement. No haze. Moons gone down, sun not risen. Sky full of stars.

He glanced at his watch. Pale blue numbers, barely visible. 0440. No wonder I'm awake. Summer sunrise in northern Maghreb not so far away. No telling how far away it is here. Still tired, though. Dreams awakening me. Idle thoughts, percolating merrily away.

Old Red Sandstone. Should've answered his question. Let it go though. Old Red Sandstone is the name of a hypothetical Paleozoic continent, out of whose skeletal remains, embedded for a while in Pangaea, then Laurasia, formed the embryo of North America and Europe and parts of Africa. Appalachians and Atlas all that remain of the mountain range pushed up when Old Red Sandstone collided with the edge of a forming World Island . . .

Be interesting, if . . .

Well. Morning will come. And, outside, the stars were still turning. But slowly. He lay back on the bed for a while, listening to the silent darkness. No, not completely silent. Someone else is up and walking around. He got up, stood on the cold floor, dressed in his underpants. Somewhere here, my socks, my suit liner coverall crumpled in a pile. The door opened silently, on its still-perfect American hinges, and he padded out into the dark hall.

Back to the common room. Slim silhouette, outlined in pale starlight against the big bay window, curtains drawn aside. Rahman standing still, looking out at the shadows of the city. *Koraad*, the old book said it was called, in the language of the Scavengers. No indication of what the Colonials had called it, if anything. He moved up behind her, marveling that she still hadn't heard his approach. Deep in thought.

Subaïda Rahman, always so lovely and slim in her trim Lesbian business suits, her short, neatly combed Lesbian hair. I always knew she was faking it. Could tell she knew I knew. Too bad . . .

Slim now in . . . yes, still dressed in her coverall. Too bad, again. It would have been . . . nice to come out here and find her wearing no more than briefs and brassiere, looking, just maybe, like some European catalog model. Maybe, if there was enough light, I'd be able to see the shadow of her pubic hair through sheer white cloth, see the outline of her mons where the cloth pressed up against her . . .

Conscious now of an erection pushing out the front of his underpants. A thousand choruses of, If only . . .

Those images of women, not like real women; women who would turn and behold your desire and . . .

He reached out and touched her softly on the shoulder.

Subaïda Rahman jerked hard, lurched toward the window, reaching out, smudging the pseudoglass with one damp hand, spun, staring up at him, mouth open, dark, liquid eyes so very wide . . .

"By God! *Inbar* . . ." Hand on her breast, gasping for breath.

He grinned. "Sorry. I didn't think you'd take me for a . . . um." Spindly, feathery alien from those lavish illustrations we've seen, stalking you in the night . . . He could see she was looking him up and down now, the whole front of his body, to her dark-adapted eyes, probably well lit by starlight. Can she see . . . probably. And, in your dream, she reaches out for the waistband of your underpants, reaches inside . . .

She said, "You should put something on." Dark eyes glittering, mere wet reflections in the dark, unreadable.

He reached out to touch her again, unexpected, unplanned, felt her push his hand away. Ah, well. Erection subsiding now, all by itself. He turned toward the window, and said, "Seems to be getting a little lighter over that way. Must be east."

She stood beside him, looking out at stars soon to fade. She said, "Maybe so. We'd better wake the others. They won't want to miss *subh*." And she thought, My heart is still pounding. Silly bastard, sneaking up on me like that, like some kind of skulking rapist, with cock at ready . . .

Sunrise. Golden drop of sun coming up behind them, throwing streamers of garish pink across the purple-black sky, wiping away the stars, lighting up the silver clouds. Long, angular shadows flowing down the hillside ahead of them, their own shadows, walking toward the Lost City of Koraad.

Shadows of my monsters. She'd taken eight of them with her. Left the other eight back at the gate. Four sitting in a cavern under the Moon, griping at being left behind, four sitting it out this side of the gate on Mars-Plus, also griping, Why can't *we* come, Sarge?

Because you never know.

Just a simple raid, Round up the bad guys and bring them home.

Then blow the gate?

Above, over the square towers of the old city, the sky was a full, glistening pink now. Magic sky. Magic world. Magic universe. We never did figure out how any of it worked. Not the gates, not the worlds . . .

Memory of Dale Millikan, slowly mutating from journalist to scientist, sitting, looking at the atmosphere comp figures. Saying, This isn't possible. Why is the helium still here?

What the Hell was that baggy old lady geophysicist's name? Thalia something. Memory of Dr. Meninger cackling, saying, Because God *wants* you to talk like a cartoon character, sonny.

He'd grumbled. Then put it in his next article. Jesus. An article a week for all those years, every one of them held up by the military censors. Glad we published them as a book after closing the door on the rest of the world. The rest of the universe. Too bad Dale never knew.

No. God damn it. I do not want to blow the gate.

Crazy shadow of the soldier on point, soldier walking down onto flat ground now. Why the Hell would someone want to look like a mountain gorilla, like an silverback male? And that silly name. *Realmodo?* Why the Hell Realmodo?

Shoot, Sarge. 'Cause *Quasimodo* wuz just a character in a book.

No, I don't want to blow the gate.

Then they were standing by the wrecked plane, staring into its dark and dusty interior at dark and dusty bones. NCD 4044. Kincaid said, "Well. Hi, Georgie."

Beside her, Corky Bokaitis said, "You know 'im, Sarge?"

A slow nod. Georgie Polychronis, little shit Greek boy from southern Maine. Stupidest-sounding twang, almost as bad as some of those mushmouf Southerners.

"How'd this happen?"

"He fucked up. We all did." Then the car and its old softball, evoking more old memories. Then the building with its open door. Hell, I was the last one out of there. I remember turning out the lights, closing the damned door. You think . . .

No. You don't think that.

A quick look around. Her eight soldiers. Brucie Big-Dick and his little friend Chuckie, who'd squirmed with him far into the night, staying in the background like they'd promised. Aw, come on, Sergeant-Major. We'll stay out of trouble. Donnie'll watch the ship for us. What could go wrong? Well . . .

She said, "No sense any of you biggies coming inside. Um. Honeybee." Fast. "Fred and Barney." Stronger than any two oxen. "Rest of you take a look around. Don't go too far."

Inside then, rifles at ready, slipping in like characters on an old police show. Flip on the lights. Spacesuits on the dining room floor like five dead men, lined up in a careful row, folded just so, backpacks powered down . . .

Then, she was standing in a back bedroom, looking at a rumpled bed.

I made my bed on that last day. Made my bed, got up to face the Judgment Day, though I didn't know it yet. Got up, whistling, changed my sheets and thought about how they'd gotten so messy. Hmh. No sign anyone fucked in this bed last night.

Quick memory of lying under Dale for what turned out to be the last time, while he bucked and humped between her legs, thrusting into her with short, quick movements, almost below the threshold of perception downdeep downdeep . . .

Could've been better for a last time. Maybe if we'd *known* . . .

Better memories, of other times, of time taken, of desires oh-so-carefully fulfilled. You could get him to be oh-so-gentle, soft, grinding, round and round and . . .

She turned and walked away, walked down the hall to Dale's office, stood looking at his computer, at his disks and books. Tracks in the dust where someone had been looking things over. Which one. The Chinese scientist? The Arab woman, their "American Technologies Specialist"? What a job title.

Places where some books were missing. Which ones? Would I remember? Fingering them now, looking at titles. Dale's notebook is missing. Maybe he took it with him when he left. He usually did. Or maybe those nice Arab boys are looking at his drawings of my cunt, snickering and nudging each other . . .

Another memory, of flipping through his notebook for the first time, half research notes for his articles, half private diary, half . . . What the fuck is *this* supposed to be? And laughing. Green ink sketches of my crotch, for Christ's sake. What the Hell did he think he was going to do, forget?

He'd shrugged, half-embarrassed. It's just . . . how I do things. It's not real until it's on a piece of paper I guess. They'd wound up fucking on the floor of his office that day, which was just damned silly. For Christ's sake, we're middle-aged. What if somebody walked in on us?

Dale had smiled then. Well, they'd've just had to be fucking jealous, is all.

Sure. Jealous. Back out into the front room, gathering up Honeybee and the caveboys, back out into the square by the jeep, where the soldiers had gathered. Sigh. "All right, let's go. They can't have gotten far . . ."

Then, a sudden, terrifying thought, image of certain pages from Dale's notebook surfacing. *Shit!*

With daylight flooding in through big windows made of something that was, curiously, almost like fine, layered mica, "glass" changing the alien sky from that horrid, gassy pink to a warm almost-tan, Ling, Rahman and Inbar worked through the contents of a room in one of the middle-sized yellow-gray buildings. Scavenger buildings, if the American books were to be believed.

Why would they lie, thought Ling? Why would they make all this up? Just because they were known to make things up, because they were famous for their insidious fantasies? Rahman, book open before the console, said, "I can make neither head nor tail of this. It's sort of like one of those big gates, but . . ."

Inbar muttered, "Doesn't look like it's eight million years old, either." No it doesn't, but . . . hints in the American notebooks, just hints, mind you, that the Scavengers had come prowling through the ruins the Colonials had left behind, maybe eight million years ago. Colonial ruins themselves abandoned maybe a billion years before that. Not that the tan stone buildings looked like they could possibly have sat around weathering for a billion years . . .

So is this a Scavenger gate, or one of the very old ones, the ones the Colonials left behind? Does it matter?

Maybe. Hints in the green-ink notebook, though, that those figures had no meaning. Millikan. Dale Millikan. Something about that name . . . Well. No matter. Whoever he was, he cast doubts on the time figures. His question, repeated over and over, making no more sense with each successive iteration: Where do these gates really *go*?

And when? Does *that* make any sense? Maybe. I keep reminding myself about what relativity and simultaneity really *mean*.

Rahman was flipping through the notebook, pausing once again to look at one of the pages with drawings of the naked woman. Inbar smirking. Something I don't understand going on here. "It doesn't seem quite appropriate for a scientist's notebook somehow."

Rahman said, "No." Put her finger on a scrawled passage, lips moving as she made colloquial twenty-first century English into colloquial twenty-second century Arabic. "Parts of it seem more like a diary."

Inbar said, "Maybe it was his girlfriend. I envy him if it was."

Rahman gave him a sour look.

Ling thought, Envy? Because some long dead man was having sex with a woman who looked like a South American pornnet star? Maybe I've missed an important part of life. Who knows? Pleasant memories of the occasional odd girlfriend, usually a pudgy young lab assistant, who'd give up after a few weeks or months, when it became clear she could never be more than . . . secondary, at best. He looked over her shoulder and tried to read crushed-together lines of Romanic script.

" '*Times* says they won't pay any more if I don't write something the censors will let through. At least the check for 'Haldane in Love' finally came. Pays a semester of Ginger's college tuition. Wish she'd gone to NC State instead of Duke.' "

Rahman flipped through more pages. "Part diary, part something else. I'm not sure this guy was really a scientist. More like a . . . Mmm. What? A *newfaq* reporter maybe?" Flipped to one of the diagramed pages. "This."

Ling looked from the drawing to the machine. "Close, but not quite. Maybe close enough."

Inbar said, "If we're not sure . . ." Very uneasy looking.

Rahman looking at Ling, seeking confirmation. He said, "We might as well try. Where are the settings for the one in Libya?"

Inbar said, "God. I don't know if . . ."

Rahman handed him the notebook, then took out the binder with the printed pages of charts and pictures. "Here."

All right.

Power main.

Blinking lights, scrolling screens, these LCD screens, if that's what they really were, much different from the ones on the larger machines, the ones that had brought them from the Moon. Labels in what looked like ideographs, but weren't. No English-language tapes, this time.

He said, "We'll have to assume the switch order is the same."

Inbar said, "If it's not?"

Rahman: "I've been through the Libyan outback. I'll recognize it if . . ." Soft, crackling hiss, smell of burning dust, and the flat wall behind the console spilled rainbows, flickered, shimmered, opened out on a distant vista.

Inbar: "My God. My *God* . . ."

Ling thought, Any god you wish to name. Any god at all . . .

He said, "Even I know this is not the high desert of Libya."

Rahman. "No."

Long, low hill sloping away into the distance, brown dirt covered with shaggy, scruffy green vegetation. Distant trees, widely spaced, a little odd looking. Winding silver stream down in the valley. Yellow-tan boulders. Brilliant, clear blue sky. Shadow-patched full Moon hanging low over the horizon, looming, as if huge.

Our Moon. Recognizably *our* Moon.

Ling said, "Not Libya. But it is Earth."

Inbar said, "Eight million years. Continents haven't drifted far in eight million years."

Ling looked at him, momentarily surprised, then . . . Well, of course. A geologist, after all . . . He said, "But if it opens through a Colonial gate? A billion years is time enough." And *why* are we assuming Scavenger and Colonials gates . . . *no!* We've tuned them in. The gates go where we *tell* them to go. The rest of it's just fantasy. If the address we've dialed up . . .

The door opened and Alireza burst in, followed by Zeq, the two of them stopping short at the sight of the open Stargate. Alireza said, "Earth?"

Zeq laughed. "Where, the public gardens of Tobrûq?"

Alireza stepped close to the gate, staring through at the blue sky, sniffing at a soft breeze. "An odd, flat smell . . . but obviously the Earth . . ." He turned away, taking them all in with his glance. "We came to tell you, there are . . . things in the city . . ."

Pulse of excitement. *Things*. Ling whispered, "The aliens?"

Zeq said, "Might as well be. Only Americans, though."

Alireza: "Coming this way. I think they know where we are." He looked at Ling, "Your pistol?"

He tapped a coverall pocket. "Here. But, Colonel, these people have military rifles of unknown . . ."

"*People* . . ." Alireza spat. He looked at the gate again, then over at Rahman. Gestured at the console, then the window, open on a familiar world. "Take your pictures. Then we'll go." He turned and stepped through the gate, staggered under an obvious increase in gravity. Staggered and looked around, muttered some exclamation to himself.

Inbar murmured, "God . . ." once more, eyes alight with fear, then stepped right through the gate after him.

Fear, thought Ling. Full of fear. But also filled with a desire to *see*.

Bursting into the room then, door slamming open, rebounding from the old metallic wall with a resounding *crack-clank* . . . Remember when you thought it was so odd that Scavengers and Colonials *both* used doors on swinging hinges, just like us? Bursting into the room in time to see a brilliant play of rainbow colors on the floor, the walls, to see the gate screen behind the control panel coruscating with a complex pattern of silvery sparkles, see the silvery sparkles coalesce and go dark.

Kincaid stood still for just a second, rifle held at port arms across her chest. Killed the curtainfield and took a deep breath. Flat, musty smell, smell of dry vegetation. Smell of old mold. Nothing sweet. Nothing flowery.

These are bold, crazy bastards, doing something like this! Through the big, rebuilt gate under the Moon, then right on through an unreconstructed Scavenger gate to God knows where . . .

Well. Maybe *you* know where. You remember that damned smell. And you know now they've probably got Dale's notebooks with them. Probably the Gestalt Manager instruction manual with them too. So they've figured out the address-code notation. And seen Dale's notes about the Terrestrial Gates. Thin, humorless smile. Sons of bitches in for one big damn surprise, whichever one they jumped. She bent forward over the console, looking at the settings. Address switches were, of course, still set, but the dials would have tumbled when the connect was broken from the other side. If they spun the controls again . . .

Bold, *crazy* damn bastards.

All right. So why are you so insufferably pleased, asshole?

PeeWee, standing next to her, stooped under the Scavenger-height ceiling, said, "Something funny, Sarge?"

She glanced up at him. "Yeah. Take Fred and Barney, go back to the main gate. Pull through two men. Leave two guys back on the Moon, and two on this side. Set up a microwave relay and come back with the other four guys."

"What's going on, Sarge?"

Hmh. She said, "Get busy. We're going for a little walk." Slipped the disk out of her pocket and triggered it, watched images of controls form on its flatpane display. Poked around a little until she got to the address dictionary, started looking things up. OK. Four Arabs and one poor little Chinaman. Most likely headed for Libya, then. Right? Shrug.

Another look over the control console. All right, you've got the spatial settings. You know God damned well they won't have wound up out-of-skein. So what about the fine tune? Same thread or some other one? Temporal?

Boy are they in for a fucking surprise . . .

Long, long look at the set of small dials under the mechanical-switch address row. Hmh. Murmur: "Maybe if I had a fingerprint kit I'd know if someone'd touched this thing recently . . ."

Honeybee said, "I can see near-ultraviolet, Sarge."

"So?"

"The big switches and these things over here are wet. Like with oil from someone's fingers."

Oh. "How about these little ones down here?"

"Dry. But . . . Well, the dust is disturbed. Like something jiggled them a little bit."

A little bit . . . Jesus. What was it my Grandpa used to say? "Fuck a duck . . ." Get busy then. Not that difficult. That's your heart going pitter-pat, isn't it? Just so. Excitement? Or just fear? A little of both?

What will really happen if they're left on their own, loose in the Multiverse? What if they find their way home? What if the rest of the world finds out about the gates and . . .

Hell. Maybe the Jug will come for us after all.

Sunset again, a few small, high clouds striated with red-orange, sun setting beyond distant mountains, throwing the land into deep shadow. Distant mountains, blue mountains, with high, snowcapped peaks, towering—though far away—over rugged, dry, rolling highland plains.

Like no mountains, Omry Inbar thought, anywhere in the world. Standing on top of a tall hill, looking out over an impossible world, looking down on the others, watching them try to build a campfire, he felt a tightness in his chest, a . . . shortness of breath? Something like that. Just fear? Or real?

If we were on a plateau high enough to reduce the air pressure, it'd be getting cold now. Doesn't feel like the air pressure's abnormal. Coming through the gate from Mars-Plus . . . Step forward. Stagger under what felt like a full gee. Feel your ears pop. Not even painful. Just a little internal *crinkle* of sensation. Still, short of breath . . . Like I have pneumonia, or like the partial pressure of the oxygen's . . .

Sky growing darker. Something's wrong with the Moon. Same shadowy pattern of bright highlands and dimmer maria. *Familiar* Moon. But . . . Right. Something wrong. Can't quite put my finger on it.

Something skittered by in the dusky light, making him jump. Another one of those running, bipedal reptiles, a little bit like those Australian lizards. This could be Australia, couldn't it? Another look at those tall, snowy mountains. Well, no. Not unless they moved the Himalayas south for the winter.

They'd seen four or five of the lizard-things during the course of a four hour walk. A few bugs. Once what looked like a big dragonfly. Hard to tell how big it had been in the distance. Still. A *big* dragonfly. Maybe the size of a small bird. Where did they have dragonflies the size of sparrows? Not much life here, this place a landscape slowly turning to desert. Southern California? That'd be . . . interesting. Could those be the Sierra Nevada? Maybe. No part I've ever seen depicted, though.

Sparse fauna. Sparse flora. Green weeds, growing in clumps out of dusty tan soil. Soil raising in puffs at the wind's command. No grasses. Which seemed a little strange. Lots of woody brush. Some things like tumbleweeds blowing along, evoking some odd commentary from Ling about American cowboy movies.

Tumbling tumbleweeds? A shrug, dismissing the whole business. No birds. And this kind of desert should be full of rodents. Things like mice. Hyraxes, maybe. Snakes. Where are the snakes? Another long look up at the Moon. Inferences resisting hard, resisting the call to clarity. Something about this I don't want to . . . think about.

Once, they'd seen something that looked like a tarantula. Where there are spiders, there ought to be wasps. Bees? Not a damned flower in sight. Some trees around that little stream they'd followed for a while before going up onto high ground, heading for the vistas. Mostly scruffy little pine trees. Conifers, at any rate. Unfamiliar things with broad, waxy leaves. Once, something Ling swore was some unknown species of ginkgo.

And that other thing. That other fleck of light, twinkling like a star, but too . . . big to be a star. What could that be? I could *swear* it's moving . . .

"*Inbar!*" Hoarse whisper. Alireza.

The four of them clustered round a small depression. They had a fire going now, but . . . all looking away from it. Ling on his knees, binoculars pressed to his face. A gesture from Alireza, pointing, down into the shadows, a depression where a small pool, possibly a slow-bubbling spring lay.

Something moving. Something big. Can't quite make it out . . . He walked down to where Ling crouched. Ling, whispering, "Look at those *teeth* . . ."

Inbar kneeled down, reached out and gently took the binoculars, unfamiliar, old-fashioned, Chinese characters glittering dim red on the internal displays. Adjusted the traditional knurl . . .

No more than a gasp as the image jumped up at him.

Something *big*. Smaller than a camel, maybe the size of a pony. Dark, gray-green, it was hard to tell in the failing light. Big eyes, glittering with sunset red. Demon's face turning toward him . . . Slanted eyes, like a Chinese dragon, long, narrow muzzle full of . . . *teeth!* Long buck teeth, crushing, crunching . . .

Eating a tumbleweed? You could hear the dry stuff crackle. See the big head dip down, see the fat front limbs paw at the ground, uprooting something. Crackle. Crunch.

"What is it?" whispered Rahman.

Inbar thought, It's *not* a *moschops*. It *can't* be. I'm dreaming all this. In just a minute I'm going to wake up in my bed at Hammaghir Cosmodrome, safe in Maghreb, wake up and hear the muezzin calling the Faithful to prayer. I'll get up, snug in my robe, look down on them and smile, glad I'm Jew.

Then I'll look up into the sunrise and see *al-Qamar* waiting to take me to Geologist Heaven . . .

Alireza said, "Tomorrow, I guess, we should go back to the Stargate and try again. This isn't Earth, no matter how familiar looking . . ."

Omry Inbar took the binoculars away from his eyes and sat down suddenly on the hard, dusty ground. Sat down and started to cry, sniffling softly, big tears rolling across his cheeks, dropping down onto his coverall, the others turning to stare at him, astonished.

There. Kincaid watched the old Scavenger gate ripple, rainbows playing in her face, seeming to chase each other across the old black wall, watched the wall shimmer and fade away, opening up on a black, starry night, on a big white Moon. Familiar Full Moon. She looked down at the settings, at the Scav readout plates. The Scavenger recursive numbering system annotated itself, hard to translate into anything with human meaning, but . . .

Two-hundred-fifty million years. On the nose. A sharp look through the Gate, at the big, old Moon. Hmh. Even without binoculars or altered vision, you could see Tycho was missing. Not to mention Copernicus . . .

PeeWee Roth whispered, "Where's this, Sarge?"

Where indeed? She stood, going around the console, and stepped through the Gate, knees locking for a moment as the increased gravity clutched at her, curtainfield hardening gently as it reacted to the changing atmosphere. Stood, staring at the sky, sky of a hundred thousand stars, or so it seemed, sky with a bright Full Moon. Spun, looking at the world around her. Two-hundred-fifty million years!

Remember the first time? Not here and now, no, but . . .

We should have *known* it was possible, given the nature of the quantum-holotaxial universe the Scavengers described, given the hints we got from what little we could decipher of Colonial records. We? The scientists should have known, the physicists, the cosmologists. Hell, even I should have known.

Dale knew. Suggested it in a meeting. Suggested it, looking up from his notepad. Scientists staring at him. Then smiling at each other. Time travel? Impossible. But. But what? Tipler? Derisive grins. *Tipler*. Sheesh. Go write your article, journalist. Go write another fantasy epic for your legions of fans. Ain't no such thing as time travel, Mr. Millikan.

Until, one fine day, we stepped through a freshly tuned Stargate, a recently refurbished Scavenger Stargate, one the Scavs had apparently rebuilt from some old Colonial junk. Stepped through, me and my troopers, Dale, with camerakit, Dr. Beasley, Professor Wingmann . . .

This is the forest *primeval* . . .

What the Hell are these funny-looking plants? Look like *ferns*, for goshsakes . . .

Well. Convergent evolution?

Then.

A soft growl.

Soft. But . . . big. Yes. Big. Deep. *Nearby*.

Slowly I turned . . .

Jesus. Professor Wingmann's scream was almost ultrasonic, looking at a head the size of a small car, teeth like . . . Steak knives? Hell, no. Teeth like God damned fucking *railroad spikes*!

Bet you didn't know a dried-up old biddy like that Wingmann bitch could run like an Olympic sprinter, did you, Dale? Nope. Can't say as I did. Credit to Dale, kneeling, shooting video, panting with excitement. Credit to my soldiers, who waited 'til they had a *reason* to shoot. Even credit to that old fart Beasley, who'd stood still for a moment, then whispered, "Well no, not *Tyrannosaurus rex*. But a close relative. *Surely* a close relative . . ."

Surely, Doc. Surely.

Wonder why it let us walk away like that?

Hell. Dale grinning, once they'd got safely back through the gate. Hell, maybe it was just a nice guy.

Or, said Beasley—sitting down now, getting over the shakes—maybe it just had a fat belly full of nice, juicy *Maiasaura* . . .

Then, the arguments.

Go *back* through the gate? You've gotta be nuts!

But . . . Dale gesturing at marines, with rifles, standing in a neat line.

Professor Wingmann, looking somberly at Beasley, who was sort of on Millikan's side. Sort of. Professor Wingmann going, Well? What about causality?

Beasley nodding. Clearly, something wrong with all the theories. Every damned one of them.

Millikan staring at them, odd look in his eye. Not all of them, Doc. You know about Bohm's Alternative. And you know what I think.

Beasley nodded. Sure, but . . .

Wingmann: But we don't know if it's right.

Lying in bed that night, cuddled with my fat, angry old lover. Listening to him mutter and stew. God damn it! The *Cretaceous,* Astrid. We went to the Cretaceous!

And now these pitiful *scientists* are afraid to go back.

Afraid they might get eaten?

Nope. Afraid they might come back through the gate with their specimens and find themselves gone. Remember that little mousething you stepped on as you popped through the gate? *Grandpa.*

That's silly.

It is, isn't it? But they can't be *sure* you see . . .

Kincaid looked back through the dusty old gate, back into the ruddy light of Mars-Plus. "OK. Fred and Barney on that side . . ."

"Shoot, Sarge . . ." Almost a whine, like a little boy told to clean up his room.

"Gillis and Honeybee over here. Rest of you saddle up . . ."

A fresh breeze was starting up, blowing down off the mountains, cool, invigorating, full of wonderful smells. Christ. Two-hundred-fifty million years! Athelstan will shit. He'll just *shit.*

Then, a colder voice, speaking from within: He'll shit if you ever get back to tell him about it. And somewhere, back on Earth, techies would be hurrying to outfit another transport. This time, Athelstan would bring the bombs himself. No doubt about it.

Omry Inbar awoke, this time with a little start, crawling sensation in the pit of his stomach, eyes opening on a black night sky speckled all over with bright white stars, luminous band of the Milky Way twisting above, like some impossible, translucent, monochrome rainbow of dust spread across the face of the void.

Dark.

Moon is down.

Wind sighing softly, rustling dry weeds.

Fire a dim bed of coals now, a smell of woodsmoke in the air.

Sound of people breathing.

People around the fire no more than dark shapes, almost invisible, huddled in on themselves. Who knew, when they stocked *al-Qamar*, we'd be needing sleeping bags? If we'd known, we could have taken blankets from the Americans' bedrooms . . .

Cold.

They all think I'm crazy.

What do you mean, they'd said, the Permian?

Just that, he'd said, the Tartarian Age of the Late Permian Epoch. Somewhere between 253 and 248 million years ago.

Long silence after that.

Years . . . ago?

Quite right, Ling had whispered. The last five million years before the End-Paleozoic Extinction Event.

A gabble of useless talk after that, people getting mixed up, puzzled, talking about the KT Extinction, Inbar finally rousing himself to point out that the End-Paleozoic Event had obliterated ninety-six percent of the then-extant species . . .

Another silence, then, softly, Alireza said, Wait a minute. Are we talking about time travel here?

Rahman: I thought modern physics finally laid that notion to rest a hundred years ago.

Ling, thoughtful: Sort of.

Zeq: Sort of what?

Inbar: Sort of agreed they wouldn't worry about it any more.

And I saw a moschops yesterday. A moschops! Good God.

He lay quietly, hands linked behind his head, and looked up at the sky, at the glittering . . . pebble that had caught his attention earlier. What if tomorrow's the day? What if?

But it looked a little smaller now, as if getting farther away. Still, it really *was* moving. Otherwise it would have set with the Moon. On the horizon, in a direction that most likely was east, the darkness seemed a little less absolute now. A . . . grayness over there. False dawn maybe.

Subaïda Rahman awoke, fuzzy headed, bright morning sunlight filling her eyes, blue, cloudless sky overhead, right in the middle of one of *those* dreams. This time it was a dream about a woman, a big, husky woman, clad in black leather, jacket with ragged sleeves cut off, some kind of tattoo on her left shoulder.

She sat up slowly, looking at the far away mountains. Clouds over them now, obscuring the peaks. Was it snowing up there? Probably.

More and more, the dreams were about women. Women from movies, of course. I even recognize that one. Some Italian, Mia something-or-other. Right. But now I don't remember the name of the movie. Just remember going with some of the girls from Mission Control . . . I enjoyed dreaming about men. I wonder what's become of those dreams? Maybe the pose is struggling to . . . Lash of hard anger. Nonsense. But . . . Softer memories. I wanted to get married. Have babies. And fly to the Moon. Faint, horrible sigh. Despair. Not in the United Arab Republic in the second quarter of the twenty-second century. But a lesbian girl. Why, yes, of course. Almost as good as a man, you see. Almost.

Not quite.

And then, a sudden, slight shock. Memory reminding her. It's been two years since I last snuck off for a date with a man. Someone my cousin Zainab set me up with. He was *so* shocked, when I asked him to . . .

Still, he'd done it, startled though he was. And a little grim afterward. Spoiling my delicious feeling of sheer *sin* as he drove me to Zainab's house afterward. Silent. Pecking me on the cheek good-bye. Getting in his car and driving away.

But it was all right. Delicious while we did it. Fun later, sitting up with Zainab, giggling about the silly ways of *men* . . .

"Wish I could offer you coffee."

Sudden start, back to reality. Alireza sitting on a rock not far away, next to the ashes of the long-dead campfire. Smiling. Smiling at her. I wonder if I made noises in my sleep . . . She could feel her cheeks start to heat up a bit. Probably imagines me dreaming about his chubby little wife . . .

The bright world forming up like hard crystal all around her. Sun in the sky. Pale daytime Moon, piece of glitter, *something*, in the sky beyond it. Inbar's crazy deathstar . . . Shrouded mountains, rolling plains. A dark speck in the sky, moving, far out over remote, tan hills. Ling sitting on another rock, watching through his binoculars.

"What is it?"

He said, "I can't tell."

"What does it look like?"

Silence, still watching the thing, then, "Well. A little bit like a World War I biplane. Sort of." They were using that handy English phrase a lot. And that other phrase, a favorite of Inbar's: We must have been *crazy* to do this.

Inbar seemed to be sleeping, still lying on his side, breathing heavily. "Zeq?"

Alireza said, "Went down to the pond to wash up."

She thought about the creature they'd seen down there the previous evening. *Moschops*, Inbar'd called it. Harmless plant eater. Well. A bull's a harmless plant eater too . . . She stood, shaded her eyes, looking down the hill. "Where? I don't . . ."

Alireza stood beside her. "Odd. Maybe I'd better . . ." He glanced at Inbar. "We need to get started back. It's a good four-hour walk back to the gate."

She nodded, said, "I wish we'd brought some food from Mars-Plus. I'm hungry." Alireza smiled, nodded. "Thought this was going to be Libya, didn't we? Stupid. Lot of nasty places to get lost in Libya, starve to death while you wander around, right outside Benghazi." He kneeled beside Inbar and shook his shoulder.

Inbar rolling over, looking up at him, bleary-eyed. "Wha . . ."

Then, a long, hard scream, a strangled scream, the scream of a man caught, perhaps, in a large piece of industrial machinery. A man being ground away to dust.

Paralyzed tableau, Ling with his binoculars, Rahman standing, Alireza kneeling, Inbar lying on the ground. Tableau lasting for a just a few seconds, seconds stretching on to eternity, filled by the scream. Then they were up and running.

Alireza whispered, *"Wallahil'azim . . ."*
It looked like some kind of great, thick-bodied crocodile, a little shorter than the surviving Nile crocodiles you saw in the zoo, maybe a little heavier. Bigger legs. Thicker chest. A crest of spines on its back, tall masts of bone webbed by scaly, green-black-pink skin, skin through which the sun could shine. Round head. Face like a tiger . . .

No. Face like the ghost of a tiger. A tiger's skull, cheek teeth exposed. Face smeared with bright red blood. Ahmad Zeq lay on the ground under its face, looking up at it, staring, staring, motionless . . .

Alireza's whisper, *thing* suddenly looking their way, bright yellow eyes ablaze.

Not the eyes of a tiger, no.

More like the eyes of an eagle.

Then Zeq turned his head and looked at them too. Eyes wide, astonished eyes, eyes bright with . . . something. Some emotion, unreadable. Mouth open, a black hole in his face. Mouthing words.

Ling muttered, singsong Chinese, went down on one knee, pulled the little pistol from his pocket. Snapped the slide. Aimed, fired.

The thing jumped a little, snarled, odd bubbly sound, maybe just startled by the bang. It stepped forward and Zeq gargled something, a horrid, wordless shout. The animal was standing on him, left hind leg planted on the great rip in his abdomen.

Inbar, voice high, babbled, "Not the sail! Shoot him in the eye!"

Of course, of course. Voice whispering through Ling Erhshan's head, reminding him to be calm. Focus. Focus now or you die. He took his wrist in one hand, aimed. Squeezed. Bang, and a bullet bounced off the animal's head, ripping a long, pale furrow, then red blood starting from white meat.

Another animal sound, half from the thing, tossing its head, cry combining a dog's yelp and a cat's snarl of rage. The rest, of course, from Zeq, clawed foot grinding him in the dirt, spreading him open.

Alireza stepping forward, reaching for the pistol, but . . . Aim. Squeeze. The left eye vanished in a gout of ichor. Animal screaming now, sound more human than Zeq's faded cry. Aim. Squeeze. Bang. Two eyes gone now, animal tossing its head, gnashing its teeth, twirling, long, fat tail passing over Zeq once, twice.

Inbar said, "Now. Behind the left shoulder!"

Bang.

Animal bucking, arching its back, spiny sail rippling.

"Again."

Bang.

It slumped. Slumped, rolled over on its side.

Just like that.

Motionless.

Ling, staring at the little curl of smoke rising from the stubby barrel of the handgun. Pattern of disbelief forming. This must be a very *good* little pistol. Inane now: I wonder where they bought it?

Then, the four of them standing over what was left of Zeq. Shreds of clothing. Tatters of skin. Smears of blood. Assorted things that must be guts. White of bone here and there. Still in one piece, sort of, but . . .

He turned and looked at them, eyes open, but blind, looking through them, speaking choppy, truncated Arabic phrases.

"Oh, God, Yussûf. Like white light. Like rivers of white light, Yussûf . . . ?"

No transition. But the blind eyes were, suddenly, looking at nothing.

Alireza said, "Yussûf . . .?"

Rahman, turning away, looking toward the mountains. "Boyfriend."

"Ah. I remember now."

Ling went and stood beside Inbar, who was standing beside the animal. "So. What do they call this? Is this a *dimetrodon*?"

A loose-shouldered shrug, almost apathetic. "Some kind of sphenacodont, yes, but . . . It's very late for those. They should be extinct by now."

Alireza said, "How much ammunition do you have?"

Ling looked at him, not comprehending for a moment, then popped the clip. Counted. "There are four left."

Then Rahman said, "We better get back to the gate." Very softly now, turning away, just walking.

Inbar, looking after her, whispered, "Useless. So useless . . ." Poor damned animal probably just looking for a nice, fat moschops to gobble up.

Kincaid then, under a clear blue sky, walking through the desert scrub country with a handful of soldiers, watching Realmodo *en pointe*. Holding his M-80 in one hand, like a long, skinny pistol. Ambling away, shoulders rolling, a characteristic three-legged gate. Why would anyone want to look like a damn gorilla?

Son of a bitch has a nice-looking butt though. Makes me want to run up and . . . what? Pet him. That's it. Memories of a puppy she'd had as a kid, a scruffy little terrier whose coloration had been more or less the same, black with a haze of gray. What had the dog's name been? Jesus. I can picture her plain as day. But . . . A hundred-twenty years has gone by. Memory of frolicking with the dog, out in the woods. Other memories. Sitting on a rock, out in the woods somewhere, sad for some long-forgotten reason, dog cuddled against her side, soft under her hand.

Overhead, the Moon was a pale, blue-gray shield, almost featureless. I remember wanting to go there as a kid, remember looking at old Apollo films, images of heroic deeds done when my grandparents were young, deeds already two generations dead.

Another memory, of standing, spacesuited in middle age, at the *Apollo 12* landing site, of getting out of the rover, standing, looking at all the footprints, the tattered LM descent stage, the ALSEP package strung together with cables, the old flag on its tilted pole. Surveyor 3 standing in its little crater . . .

Ahead of her, Realmodo recoiled as a small lizard-thing ran in front of him, scuttled away in the underbrush. He looked back over his shoulder at her. "This place gives me the willies, Sarge."

Funny turn of phrase. *Willies* are the ghosts of dead virgins. "Get used to it. There are scarier places than this."

Beside her, Bokaitis said, "Yeah? Where at, Sarge?"

Kincaid turned to look, wondering. Sarcasm? No. Wide, ingenuous eyes. These are children, whose world was circumscribed by the net. She said, "Hell, maybe if you're unlucky you'll get to see some of them."

But we've almost caught up to them now. What then? Put the silly bastards in chains and go home? I'll probably spend the next ten thousand years in the stockade for disobeying orders.

So. Where else then? So many worlds. So little time. That's what we used to say. Memory of Dale, sorry he was "getting a little long in the tooth, just when things have gotten . . . interesting." So. Did he mean the Many Worlds? Or just my cunt?

Dale pissed off because he couldn't go back to the Cretaceous and play with the dinosaurs. Then we found another world with things a *lot* like dinosaurs, a world clearly *not* some past incarnation of the Earth. Pissed off, though, when they wouldn't let him go hunting. Talking about all his favorite dinosaur movies, about dinosaur toys he'd had as a kid. Christ. Memories of my own toys, of my own cherished moviediscs. Remember *Jurassic Park 3D*? Dale shrugging it off. By then, he'd said, I was getting jaded. Too sophisticated. The original version of *King Kong*, now . . .

Good old Fay Wray, screaming, screaming . . .

People always scream in movies, screams never like the real screams you hear in combat. Sudden memory of a day out in the Moroccan desert. Rattle of automatic weapons fire in the distance. Somebody screaming, high, shrill, a man, terror plus horror plus pain. Somebody screaming like that, with all that energy, just has a minor wound. Ow, ow, it *hurts* . . .

All over but the shouting, standing there in the hot sunlight, talking, Lieutenant Ramirez taking off her helmet as they talked, discussing the next order of business, wiping sweat from her brow . . .

Whack.

Ramirez staggering, eyes astonished, blood coming out of her nose, running over her lip. Turning away, little black hole in the side of her head, below the temple, in front of her ear. Reaching up to touch it, then falling to her knees . . .

Christ. I thought she was dead.

Bullet lodged on the underside of her skull, though. Still intact.

Visiting her in hospital a few weeks later, when I was rotated out. Ramirez grinning through her bandages. Telling me, *fuck*, how bad it hurt, having your damn sinuses all burned up . . .

Bang.

Far away. Soft echoes.

Realmodo up ahead, stock-still.

Ain't no damn guns in no damn Paleozoic.

Bang-bang.

Long pause.

Bang-bang.

Realmodo looking over his shoulder, shapely rump tipped to one side.

Bokaitis: "Sarge?"

"Yeah. Let's go."

Ling, crouching among the rocks with his comrades, heart pounding softly in his chest, struggling to keep his rapid breathing quiet, looking down a long hill at the Stargate. An odd-looking, muscular man lying on the ground, two rifles lying beside him, pants ripped open, blood pooling under one leg. Crouched over him, working on the wound, a shirtless, tiger-stripe girl.

Of course it's a girl. Look at those nice little breasts. Standing over both of them, rifle held at port arms, a squatty blond fellow with a strange-looking, beetle-browed face. There was another beetle-brow visible just inside the open gate, standing, watching them, alarm visible on his face.

Alireza whispered, "What in the name of God is *that* thing?"

Scaly, greenish brown animal the size of a big dog, lying curled on its side, rib cage burst open, obviously dead, looking rather like a cross between a wolf and a monitor lizard. Inbar, voice like a breathy sigh: "Theriodont of some kind. They survived into the Triassic; things like *Cynognathus*. Descendants of *dimetrodon*. Ancestors of mammals . . ."

The tiger-stripe girl and beetle-brow number one picked up their fallen comrade and carried him through the gate. A moment, then beetle-brow number two came through and picked up the two rifles, went back to the other side.

All alone, here in the Permian, just now . . .

Alireza: "Rahman! *No!*"

Subaïda Rahman on her feet, leaping over the rocks, sprinting down the hillside. Alireza, foolish, on his feet, shouting at her to come back. Then another shout, this one from beyond the gate, from inside it. Rahman, standing at the console, reaching. Blond beetle-browed soldier stepping through, just as Rahman started twirling dials, punching buttons.

Thud.

Ground slamming at their feet.

Rainbows and fire jetting from the Stargate.

Wisp of oily smoke. Gate going black.

Ling reached the bottom of the hill, panting, more with fear, more with excitement, than exertion, striding over to the gate. Stopping, standing still, looking at things on the ground. Bits and pieces. Not bloody, no. Cauterized.

This thing a hand and forearm. This thing a knee, with attached pieces of thigh and calf. The front half of a boot, toes still inside. Some cloth. Desert camouflage. Standing with him, Inbar whispered, "You'd think they'd've failsafed against something like this . . ."

You'd think that, wouldn't you? No parachutes on airliners, though.

Alireza walked up slowly, stooped, picked up the last piece. "Hmh. Hundred year old M-80 assault rifle." He popped the clip, took a close look. "Sixty HE rounds." Slid the clip back in, hefted the weapon his hand. "UAR Marines still use a version copied from this. American military technology at its best."

Ling walked over to where Rahman was sitting on the ground, leaning against the gate console. Looked down at her. Face almost green, faded pale under the tan. Reached out. Waited for her to take his hand. Helped her to her feet. Stood looking into her face. Finally: "You had to do it, you know."

Wan smile. "Did I? I suppose so."

"There're most likely more soldiers out there somewhere," gesturing at the wilderness. "Do you think we should wait for them? Surrender?"

She glanced at Inbar and Alireza. "I don't know."

Alireza said, "Let's try again."

Inbar, angry, afraid: "So? Where to? Some other past era of the Earth? Maybe we'll be lucky this time and wind up in the days of Harun al-Rashid. Maybe we'll meet Sindbad!" Angry. Bitter. Sarcastic.

Silence. Then Alireza said, "Set it for Mars-Plus, vary one parameter by the smallest amount possible. Maybe we can sneak back past them . . ."

Sneak back to *where?* Our ship is . . .

"It'll give us breathing space, at least. Time to think."

Ling said, "I don't know. They seem to have some method of finding us."

Then Rahman found the address in her camera's registry. Called up the image. Set this gate's controls the same way. Put her hand on the last rheostat in the bottom row, nudged it slightly. Looked up, straight at Alireza.

He said, "Hit the button." Voice flat, emotionless.

Colors swirled on the gate surface, swirled and cleared.

Rahman: "Guess we didn't break it."

Rocky red desert, reaching out to a mountainous horizon under a pale orange sky. No clouds. No visible sun. Was that bit of glitter up there one of the tiny moons?

Inbar said, "I don't know. That doesn't really look like . . ."

Alireza: "Let's go. What have we got to lose?"

Four.

Tale of a Tub.

In those last few weeks, those few weeks before the Jug, I think I knew what was coming. Maybe we all did. But the NASA/NSF bureaucrats, the military authorities, politicians greedy for wealth and power, university scientists so wistful about the possibilities of their new knowledge . . .

And me?

Gone mad, absolutely mad, with the splendor of it all.

If I'd known what was to come, would I have done the right thing? Would I have known the right thing when I saw it? I still don't know. Maybe I did the right thing after all.

Maybe, if I'd known what was to come, I would've gone right through the gate, following poor Astrid Astride and her fleeing troopers. Would have helped her shut and wreck the gate under the Moon. Would have gotten aboard the ship and ridden home to America in her arms.

Maybe. Just maybe. We could have lived happily ever after.

Is it too late now?

Could I step back into the byways of the Multiverse and lead her home?

Or even lead her here?

I feel the great pang of her in my heart now.

The pang of a sparrow falling.

My own personal sparrow.

She deserved better than the likes of me.

Too late now, even in the Multiverse. Even in the land where all things are possible. When I came here, the datatracks merged. All the universes where Dale Millikan lived converged. Converged on this spot. Others have their separate infinities. All I have is infinite Oneness.

I remember how Jesus laughed when I said it: *I am that I am.*

Oh, you fool. You arrogant fool.

So we fooled with the infinite knowledge base. That filthy knowledge of good and evil. Found the gate under the Moon, went out in the footsteps of the Scavengers, in the footsteps of the Colonials, walked the byways of the multiverse . . . and so the Space-Time Juggernaut came to set things right again.

The Bird of Fire coalesced in the sky, and we wondered if we were looking on the face of God, if this was indeed the bright Angel of Death.

Death, it seemed then, was the right answer.

Troopers become bones, clean bones gone . . . a smile, even then, in the face of eternity. I never can stop thinking these things.

Somehow, the scientists and I were trapped, wise men and women wide eyed, looking to me for guidance. Imagine that. You. You, Mr. Millikan. A man of action, someone who can *do*, while the rest of us merely *be*.

Now, we can't go back through the gate on Mars-Plus. Can't get back to the cavern under the Moon. The Jug is there now. Fire in the sky. Snapping up the trooper-girls one-two-three . . . are you alive, my beloved Astrid Astride? Or will I find you no more than a pile of clean bones one day?

I fancied I heard her voice, *I still live.*

On a little desert world in a galaxy far, far away, where we'd been following the trail of the last Scavengers, reading their words written on scraps of this and that, I stood before the gate controls and considered. Stay here? Wait it out? What if the Jug takes Earth? What do we do then? Go back to Mars-Plus? No. Jug is there. Waiting for us, perhaps.

Will he find us here?

No way to know.

Have to *do* something.

Please, Mr. Millikan. We trust you.

Well, shit. Fancy that.

So I spun the dials and snapped the switches and watched bright rainbows spill out on hot, white-lit gypsum sand, and looked through at a red sandstone world, pink sky above a rubble-field of frosty red stones, sky dark toward zenith. Men there, inside the dome we'd set up over the gate, turning to look at us, wide-eyed with fear.

Outside the dome, I could see one of the new Scavenger-model spaceships we'd been fooling with. The one that had brought this gate hardware to Mars. The real, red Mars, our own Earth a blue-white spark in its sky.

"Let's go!"

Watched the scientists scuttle through, until only I was left.

Now me.

Go home, you fool.

Go to Mars. Destroy the gate. Fly home to Earth in the spaceship. Wait things out. Maybe the Jug will just pinch off our gates, once we've all gotten home. Maybe it won't finish us off.

Like the Scavengers, apparently.

Like the Colonials.

Go home, Dale Millikan. Go home to Astrid Kincaid.

Maybe she'll love you, even without the romantic back-drop of the multiverse to fool her. Go home. So what if the multiverse is closed to us now? We still have the Scavenger technology. Still have . . . my God. Spaceships! We have their spaceships. Go home.

One day. One day perhaps. You'll stand with Astrid Astride on the surface of Iapetus, looking up at brilliant, yellow ringed Saturn and . . . oh, God. Those old dreams shrunken away to nothing at all in the face of all we'd found.

If I go home, I abandon the land of all my dreams and . . . I stood staring through the gate at them for a long moment, scientists and technicians looking back at me curiously, wondering what was keeping me. I spun the dials, punched the buttons, watched rainbows spill back into the gate, and then Mars was gone.

Stood alone for a long time on the white sand surface of a world with no name, fallen Scavenger ruins half buried in the background, low mountains rising above the distant horizon under a pale, blue-white sky in which hung three small, bright white suns.

What do I do now?

Go.

Go back to the world of your dreams.

Cringe of fear.

What about the Jug?

What if the Space-Time Juggernaut finds you?

So what? You're almost sixty years old now, Dale Millikan. Not going to live forever . . . I thought that then, used it to soothe my fear. What if I'd known that, going home, I'd've walked into an immortal time-frame where I could, truly, live with Astrid Astride, happily ever after? What would I have done?

But I didn't know.

Just knew that I couldn't bear to lose all the worlds of all my dreams.

Somewhere, out there, perhaps, Valetta the Slave-Girl waited for Dorian Haldane to come. Or maybe, somewhere out there, Valetta the Slave-Girl waited for Dale Millikan to come. Somewhere out there was a dream that overshadowed reality. Somewhere out there was a dream that washed Astrid Kincaid away.

So I dialed up a world of bright lavender skies and stepped on through.

Maybe, later, I would change my mind. Go on home. Live out my life and die. Maybe she'd forgive me. Maybe she'd understand. Oh, Astrid Astride, you deserved better than me. And now I feel the pang of your fall . . .

Sometimes, I try to imagine what it must have been like for God Himself. (Herself? Itself? Bits and pieces of my old selves coalescing from different cultural surrounds. How many Academic Phalangists does it take to screw in a light-bulb?)

Not the fact of being an all-seeing, all-knowing, all-pervasive omnipotent deity. I know what that's like, now, being able to send an infinite number of probabilistic doppelgangers to an infinite number of times and places. Send them out, take them back, absorb and emit them like so many photon packets.

I can't imagine how I adapted to this reality.

Nor can I imagine what it must have been like for God.

Imagine exploding out of nothingness, into being, into infinite being, just . . . just because there existed, *a priori*, a finite probability that God and Creation *could* exist? Hell. Simpler to say *just because*.

The records are here that that's what happened. The paper trail led from the Scavengers to the Colonials, easy for us to follow from Day One. And the Colonials seem to have figured out that Somebody, Somewhere, built the whole shebang. They even seemed to understand, in the end, that the fact of that understanding was what called the Jug down on their sorry little asses.

And, of course, having come to the Throneroom, having become All-Knowing myself . . . for a long time, if duration can have any meaning in a multiplex plenum, I refused to call the primordial force God. Not my *style*, you see. For a long time I orbited various attractors in Denial Space.

But . . . the force that through the green fuse drives the flower? What's not to be God about that? Especially since no crooked worm ever found *my* winding sheet. Then, seeing what faces were gathered round me . . .

So God's records are here for all to see, the whole eternal tale of how He/She/It/Whatever grew from a tiny seed, His substance and Platonic Reality and, ultimately, the whole of the Multiverse emerging from the less-than-Planck-length event horizon of a more-than-infinite singularity in something less than Planck Time.

Let there be Light? Hell, more important that He let there be Darkness.

A simple story, compelling, evocative, mythopoeic and more, reminding me a bit of a story, *Universe and Beyond*, that one of me made his life's work, one of me who somehow escaped the channel that led most of us down into the abyss of hack work and pseudo-science journalism.

God emerges from Nothing At All. Pops into deterministic being from some nondeterministic probability. Sits around For Ever and Ever. Knowing Everything. Doing Nothing. And after an Eternity of that Timeless Time, it occurs to this logbump of a God that, perhaps, just perhaps, the problem is He's a tad lonely.

So God builds a universe that brings forth sentience, that evolves to omnipotence, so God can have a Pal. The universe, it seems, and everything in it, is no more than God's womb, gestating Supreme Being, Mark II, over billions of years. Sheesh. That version of me was a bit of a sap. No wonder he died penniless. (Well, sort of died. Somewhere in here/out there, he cruises the byways of the Multiverse, doing Our Thing, having stepped from death to infinite life everlasting in no time at all.)

I used to wonder if this sort of thing would piss people off. Oh, well. At least now I don't have to wonder anymore. Certainly pissed me off.

But the Real God in the Real Multiverse, *did* emerge from Nothing At All, and really *did* build Something (all right, *Everything*) from that selfsame nothingness. Cool. Far out. Fetching. Far fetched. Hell, if you like, I've got an infinite number of infinitely sophisticated metalanguages from which you may spend all eternity picking adjectives.

But, God damn it, the Answer is still not here. Where the Hell did God come from? Probability? Okay. Fine by me, folks. So where the Hell did Probability come from? In the Beginning was the Word, and the Word was *with* God, and the Word *was* God? What the fuck is *that* supposed to mean? And, of course, no record of where, pray tell, God went when he left. Or why.

Bob likes to remind me it's *just a job*. I'm not supposed to have Time to wonder Why, I'm just supposed to keep the God-damned gears oiled and running smoothly.

Bob thinks he should've been given the Job, instead of me. Claims he thought up the whole idea first, exploited it more thoroughly, in every iteration that either one of us possessed, back when we were finite. Likes to tell me if I've seen farther than other men, it's merely because I've stood on the shoulders of giants like him.

I always tell him I thought the correct phrase was, "pygmy typing on a giant typewriter."

He turns sour for a moment, says, Whatever.

Bob's shadow popping up in the hereafter/nowandthen, shadow cast down through Platonic Reality, down to the abandoned and dusty Netherworld Throneroom of God All Mighty, from all the iterations and reiterations cruising the Multiverse.

Hey, Pops. Can I have the keys to the Jug?

Someone building a crooked house are they?

Crooked smile. Well, you know, Pops. I *told* you we shouldn't have been sentimental about Origins. Now your damn girlfriend's loose in the Multiverse again, spalling iterations as she goes. You should have let me pinch Earth off back at the Beginning.

Sigh. Just a sentimental fool. Maybe *that's* why I've got the Job.

Five.

Last and First Men.

Fucking blood all over the place.

Kincaid stood in the open Stargate, soft Permian breeze blowing across her back, tunic damp with sweat, looking into the room on Mars-Plus. Christ. Gillis lying on the floor, grimacing, bands of muscle standing out all over, lithe little Honeybee bending over the bloody task of applying a pressure bandage to the ragged wound in his thigh.

Scared the shit out of me, finding the damn gate shut, dead whatsit on the ground, pieces of human meat scattered around . . .

Soft, soft whimpering. Gillis? No. Troglodyte Fred kneeling beside the chopped up remains of brother Barney. Crying, Oh, Barney, Barney . . . Fucking mess all over the floor. Out the window, Mars-Plus's sun was setting, just as high noon came to Permian Earth.

Heart pounding as she'd run up to the dead gate, sharp tang of burnt *something* in the air, an electrical smell. Momentary image of herself and her pathetic little band rushing down the hill. Staring. Brucie Big-Dick by her side, eyes wide, voice . . . uneasy. "Jesus, Sarge. It's not broken, is it?" That faint tremor saying, *Please* tell me it's not broken . . .

One thing to be loose and free in the Many Worlds. Quite another to be stuck forever in the Permian. What a strange notion. Stuck forever? No, not quite. Every damned one of us, fucking immortal. Wait patiently, boys and girls. A mere two-hundred-fifty million years and . . . we'll be back. Heh. But what world lies in the future of that particular Permian? Our presence alone enough to break a major cusp and start a new thread.

Horrid awareness. Every possible history has its own singular thread, every quantum-event complex its own subset of strands and plies. You know that. Everyone whose ever thought about it knows that. On the other side of the cusp, I'm back in the Permian, wondering if I can live through the End-Paleozoic Event, just a couple of million years down the road . . .

A couple of million years? Shit. Something eat you long before then, asshole.

Memory of being a child, of reading an old book about brain lateralization. They cut the corpus callosum, you see, to interfere with the propagation of impulses leading to epileptic seizures. And, over time, each side of the brain develops a unique personality. One on the dominant side in control, non-dominant side sort of stuck in . . .

What a fucking *nightmare!*

Cut your brain in two, maybe OK if you wind up on the dominant side, but what if I wound up on the . . .

I?

What the Hell does *that* mean? I *would* be stuck in that particular Hell, because both sides would be *me*.

Cusp.

Poor little Fred, Barney's bits gathered to his breast, smeared with brotherly blood: "I don't like this, Sergeant-Major. I need to go home now . . ." Faint itch of pity and contempt, of remembered compassion, threads of feeling commingled. Tired of playing grown-up now? Tired of this game? Nobody warned you it might be a little . . .

Fred said, "I just didn't think we'd get . . . hurt. You know?"

Jesus.

Honeybee, finished with Gillis, muscleman now dazed from old military anesthetics, said, "These men need medical attention, Sarge."

Especially the dead guy, huh?

Honeybee stood, facing her. "There's a modern DocLocker on the ship. And a freezerpac for Barney."

Cold meat. Get him home, even in pieces, they'd soon set him to rights. Tired. Quite tired now. Kincaid said, "Sure. Get a bodybag for Barney and tote him on back to the other gate. Gillis, I guess you . . ."

Honeybee, angry: "Why don't you just tune in the Moon from here and let us put them through?"

Kincaid leaned her rifle against the side of the gate console, closed the portal to the Permian—locking my other self into its timeline—started punching up the scanner subroutine. "The other gate's locked open. Just haul Barney over in a bag. He'll keep."

"Not without some memory loss, damn it. Lemme call back over the link and have them shut the damn gate. All they have to do is power-down, right?" Communicator already plucked from her belt.

Kincaid turned and stared at the small . . . woman? No more alien than *I* used to be. Honeybee still had her tunic off, lovely and fit despite the odd coloration and patterning. Damn-all smart, too. And walking into mutiny. All right, you know what to do about that. Image of herself shooting the woman, quickly dismissed. Hardly reasonable. "I'm going to use this gate's hardware to track the other party now."

Fury rising: "Who gives a *fuck* about some Arabs and a Chinaman? For Christ's sake, something will eat them, sure as shit. Let's just get *out* of here!" Angry glitter in faceted eyes.

Murmurs from some, agreement, silence from others. Go home? Kincaid thought about it for a second. No. Not home. I'm home now. Home out there. She said, "Hell. I can reroute the gates from here. Let me open up on the Moon, then we'll . . . decide."

The audible sighs of relief, people seeming to relax, we get to go home and . . . Hell. Irritation? More than that. This is what's *wrong*, damn it. When they granted us eternal life, they took away everything else . . .

A passage of time; not much time wasted. A mere resetting of dials, warning called out over the comlink, Honeybee helping Gillis limp through to the Moon, a weeping Fred carrying away his sack full of Barney. Unlink. Scanner routines uploaded from the Toolbox, wherever *it* was, nobody'd ever figured that one out, and Kincaid sat back in her console chair, staring out at an orange sky—sherbet sky over blood-crimson desert—stark red mountains beyond.

Could have been worse. That was clever, tuning in Mars-Plus, then nudging one damn control. But stupid, too. They've got some of the books, enough to guess. Not enough to know. "Well," a soft murmur. "Out-of-thread, of course. But still in the same skein, it seems."

Bokaitis: "What the Hell does that mean, Sarge?"

Kincaid turned and looked, room now full of thoroughly bewildered soldiers. So. Give them a quickie primer in the theory of the Many Worlds? Tell these ignorant babies about my days on the Moon, about finding the gate, finding out where it fucking went? Christ. It was years before we figured out it *wasn't* just an interstellar-range matter transmitter.

Softly, Brucie Big-Dick said, "You ever read much alternate-history fiction?"

Read? What's that?

Bokaitis said, "Oh, sure. You mean like that 3V series *TimeSwap*?"

Brucie: "Yeah. Like that. A strand is a tiny, highly-localized bit of alternate history made from a quantum-state cusp. A ply is a personal alternate history made from a conscious mind's cusp-complex. A thread is an alternate world, spun off by a whole array of conscious-mind decision processes, the consequence of a historical cusp. A skein is a bundle of similar threads spun off from a geophysical cusp. I don't know if they come bigger than that."

Kincaid: "I didn't know anyone cared anymore."

"Do they come bigger? I don't have a license to . . ."

She nodded. "A little bit. Terminology never settled down. We closed the door and came home before we had much chance to look outside a few nearby thread-bundles." A soft snort of laughter, remembered mirth. "Dale Millikan wanted to call the eka-skein structure a scarf, bundle of scarves a sweater. Pissed the scientists off something fierce."

Brucie said, "Millikan. I used to read his stuff when I was a kid."

Bokaitis, looking through the gate: "So where's this place? When? I don't know what to ask."

Kincaid stood up from the console, picked up her rifle and slung it over her shoulder by its old webbing strap. "I don't think there *is* an answer, Corky." She looked round the room. "I don't think I can order any of you to come with me. I'm going to be court-marshaled for this anyway."

Tarantellula, spider lady, was standing beside Bokaitis, featureless white eyes on the orange sky. "I'll go, Sarge."

Muldoon, after a moment's hesitation: "Nobody ever accused me of having much sense either, Sarge."

A long silence, then gorilla Realmodo slumped back on his hindquarters, looking away from them. "I think maybe I over-estimated my courage when I signed up for this, Sarge."

Another silence. Kincaid said, "Sure. No problem. You and Corporal Roth stay here and stand watch over the gate. Keep it open 'til Athelstan shows up, I guess. Or until we come back . . ." Relief in the Monster Man's eyes as well, saved from having to say anything. "Yes, Sergeant-Major."

"Corky?"

Brief pause from Bokaitis, eyes big. "Well. I guess so."

Brucie Big-Dick: "Hey, we'd sort of like to . . ."

Chuckie Crew-Cut: "Ah. No. Sorry, big boy. I guess I'll be getting back to old Donnie now, if you don't mind."

Brucie looked at him for a second, surprised, maybe biting his lip. "Well. OK. Just me then, Sarge."

"Fair enough. Let's go."

The air is too thick, thought Alireza. Thick, a little hard to breath, as if it were denser than the Earth's air. The gravity seemed a little low. Maybe a lot low. Somehow hard to tell. We seem . . . light on our feet, and yet . . . Memory of those stale old rations back on Mars-Plus. I am getting *very* hungry, just now. How long will it take us to starve? Days? Weeks?

They'd been walking for a few hours already under a warm orange sky, sweat trickling inside their clothes, like the delicate tracks of gentle insects. Walking now, all done with bickering, just moving slowly, steadily down a rutted, dusty trail between two tall, angular bluffs of dark red . . . sand-stone?

Sandstone. Maybe. Inbar not willing to say with any certainty.

Tired of the damned arguing. Useless back and forth. Obviously, this place is *not* Mars-Plus, let's go back, let's press ahead, *someone's* been here, gesturing at the flattened surface of the path. There were things that looked like hoofprints. A little . . . large maybe. And something with three fat toes. Not quite like a lion's track, though none of them were really familiar with wildlife signs . . . and, of course, staring down at the footprint, memories of the thing that had killed Zeq sharpening.

Is this a human footprint? Maybe. Distorted. Wind's been blowing the sand around, of course. Remember *yeti*? Let's not jump to conclusions . . .

Inbar just staring at him. Finally: *Jump to conclusions*, you say? Waving his arms, flapping them at rocks and mountains and fantastical sky with its fat, pink sun. Look *around* you, Colonel. Where *are* we?

All right. So I have to give him that. Just trying to hold onto my . . . sanity. Then, with the sun slipping across the tops of the mountains, the moon had come up . . . *Moon? Wihyaht rabbína*, don't call it that! Pale, pale blue sphere rising in what they supposed must be the east, disk against the sky, shocking contrast of pastels, making it look as if the thing were *inside* the sky, orange color far beyond, making it look huge . . . and about to fall upon them. Delicate swirls in its substance. Banded like a gas giant. Darker swirl there, in its southern hemisphere, just like . . .

Ling, speaking his soft, delicate English, had whispered, It looks just like Neptune. Another spark of light visible nearby. Someone, Rahman, asking, Would we be able to see Nereïd, or the rings? Probably not. Ling's sudden laughter shocking in the stillness: This cannot possibly be Triton beneath our feet.

No. This cannot possibly be Triton. Can not. Impossible. They'd all agreed on that.

Where *do* you think you are, then, Colonel Sir Qamal ibn-Aziz Alireza? Keep asking yourself that. Desert country here, dry in your nostrils, wind dry on your skin, whisking sweat away. No desert like this in North Africa or the Middle East. Not the yellow-sky Gobi. Australia? Perhaps. More likely the old American southwest. Someplace with a name like Roan Mountains?

So. Is America in orbit around Neptune, then?

Image of American cowboys, riding the interplanetary range. American Indians, ki-yiing under intergalactic stars, slicing off extraterrestrial scalps.

So what do you think this is? Did we stumble into some latter-day American entertainment production company's back lot? They do fantastic things with VR and special effects, even in backward old UAR, where you fly into space in old-fashioned rocketships.

Maybe, if we keep walking, we'll eventually come to a little door at the base of the sky, open it and find ourselves departing some vast soundstage, coming out into a cool, damp blue evening, palm trees waving in a Pacific Ocean breeze, and it will be California, California of the old movies, Los Angeles . . . No, Hollywood. Maybe we'll go out the door and it will be 1927, gangsters and bootleggers and Elliot Ness and Al Capone and . . .

Even here, even now, a momentary particle of awareness, of just how thoroughly their plastic claptrap culture had infected the whole world. He felt himself smiling. Why not? No less unbelievable, no less plausible than what's already happened. They walked up a steep hill, a narrow cut between two tall red cliffs, Inbar panting audibly, less fit than the others, Ling starting to fall behind, showing his age. Came to the top of the ravine, just where it opened up on darkening orange sky, on a narrow, sterile valley, lit pink by the setting sun.

Alireza stopped dead in his tracks. Ling, coming up behind him, head down, bumped into his back.

Finally, Inbar, querulous whine marking his voice, said, "I kept thinking if just one more thing, just one more ridiculous, inexplicable, unanticipatable thing, happened, I would take Ling's pistol and shoot myself."

Alireza, carrying the American rifle, found his own voice loud in the stillness: "Perhaps I'll join you."

Below them, a long, rocky defile, a tumbled mess of boulders and shards, streaming away from shattered cliff faces, down onto level ground, beyond, a level red plain stretching out to a distant, flat horizon. And, sprawled across the rocks, broken, crumpled, what looked like the hull of a crashed airliner.

Not an airliner. You know perfectly well . . .

Cigar-shaped body, a bit like an ancient V-2. Painted silver-blue, with some kind of angular design in a darker blue. Windows in the nose. No wings. Fins around the tail. Four visible, bent and torn, crushed metal under the hull that might be two more.

Instead of a rocket engine, instead of an expansion bell or two or three, there was a long, bronze-colored pole, bent sharply in the middle, leading out to a banged-up cylinder of gray metal mesh, indistinct, complex shapes not quite hidden inside.

They picked their way slowly down the hillside, slipping on loose rocks, stuff like shale scattered in the sandy dirt, walked toward the thing. Big. Maybe sixty meters long. Lettering now visible on the side. Romanic lettering, sort of, painted in dark black. More or less unreadable because it was . . . ornate. Decorated, little lines everywhere, extraneous lines, disguising the letters. Only numerals at the end of the row of words easily recovered: 0-220.

Inbar stood looking up at the buckled metal wall, now bulging over their heads. "Gothic blackprint, like they used to use for German."

Alireza: "And . . . are the words German?"

Rahman: "No. English. Sort of. It says, 'GalactoLight HyperNews Channel 0-220.' "

When they climbed up the red rocks and through a big rip in the ship's hull, Subaïda Rahman felt as if she were tingling all over. Anticipation. Excitement of discovery. A prickle of fear crawling on the back of her neck.

There's an inescapable conclusion here. Conclusion that matched the cryptic notes Dale Millikan and his colleagues had scribbled all over their notebooks, had written in the margins of their printed texts.

They walked down the dark companionway, forward,

more or less bunched together, silent. Passed through hatch-
es, past the open doors of compartments, everything a sham-
bles, lockers burst open, their varied contents spilled across
tilted decks.

Came into the control room.

Obviously the control room.

Two bucket seats, upholstered in dark brown leather, broad
arms festooned with buttons and switches. A padded black-
leather joystick on the right arm of each chair. Console
between them, with more switches. Two horseshoe banks of
instruments/controls under big, cracked crystalline windows,
windows looking like they were made of the finest quartz, not
glass, cracks long and straight, the shear-plane cracks of
stone, not the crazed, intersecting lines of a supercooled fluid.

Alireza sat in the left-hand seat. The commander's seat.
Sat staring at row on row of dials and buttons and gauges.

Ling said, "This looks very strange. No CRTs. No LEDs or
LCDs. Nothing even so modern as the turn of the millennium."

Rahman's attention suddenly refocused on her specialty,
her education. She said, "A spaceship built by Europeans
from the 1940s."

Ling nodded. "Something in between *Frau im Mond* and
Destination Moon."

Alireza pointed at a set of controls mounted in the center,
just above the console, below the middle of the windscreen.
More buttons, like old three-position circuit breakers. Lots of
circular dials with electromechanical indicator needles.
Alireza tapping a label. "Am I correct in reading this word as
hyperdrive?"

Rahman dropped into the right-hand seat, staring, baffled,
starting to work back through . . . theories. Can't do it. Too
much . . . She said, "I wonder how a *mass proximity indicator*
works?"

Ling, staring through broken transparent stone, out into the
red desert, at a darkening sky now the color of cooked pumpkin puree, where a few stars were beginning to glimmer:
"Gravity waves, perhaps . . ."

Alireza tapped a console to his left. "I'd like to fly a spaceship that had one of these . . ." Alireza the pilot speaking. Alireza with a faraway look. Alireza in the land of fantastic dreams.

Rahman bent forward and looked. *Graviton polarity generator.*

Ling said, "The technologies indicated by the labels on these controls presuppose processes that are simply not possible. Unless everything *we* know about the nature of the universe and all its laws is . . . incorrect."

Moment of silence, then Omry Inbar said, "So, you're assuming the same rules are valid *here*."

"Well . . ."

Rahman turned in her seat and looked at them, first Inbar, whose face was very pale indeed, then into Ling's thoughtful eyes. That inescapable conclusion. "Maybe just . . . a *little* different. Different enough."

A nod, first from one, then the other.

The rest of the ship proved to be a mixture of the known and the unknown, the easily comprehensible, cabinets full of crushed cans and old food dried away to brittle scraps, then the impossibly antique. Rahman felt elated when they found the ship's computer, mounted in a little cabin all its own aft of the control room. When they opened it up, the others seemed offended. No electronics, you see. Just a maze, a fuzzy mass really, of tiny, tiny, *tiny* little gears and wheels and whatnot. The machine Babbage would have built, had he been able to manufacture microscopic hardware.

So, what runs this? How does it work? Alireza was almost angry.

In other parts of the ship, they found what purported to be the hyperdrive machinery, and something claiming to be the gravity polarizer that so amazed Alireza. Labels telling what it was, strange instructions printed on little white plaques. Twist this, turn that. Move this lever to . . .

It looked like no more than a mass of plumbing, like something you might see in a World War II German *Unterseeboot.* This can't possibly be right, but . . .

Then the bedroom. There'd been a waterbed, of course, now no more than scraps of torn vinyl, a pile of paper and cloth in the corner that had once been wet, had gotten a little moldy before it dried. Books and clothes and bits of this and that strewn everywhere.

Inbar bending, plucking a little rubbery disk off the floor, turning it over and over in his hands. "What do you suppose this is?"

Ling looking at it, then smiling. "It's a pessary. An old-fashioned birth-control device. North Asian women still use them sometimes, because they can be washed and used again."

Inbar, still staring at the thing: "So we're talking about a people here who have faster-than-light starships, but don't know about reproductive biochemistry?"

"Not to mention electronics," said Alireza.

Rahman, picking up dress after slinky dress, all made from watered silk, in an array of subtle colors and hues, some with metallic glitter mixed into the cloth: Slim-hipped slacks. Lovely clothing, but . . . I couldn't have fit into any of these things since about age thirteen. Moment of regret. I wouldn't mind having a change of clothes right now. We're all starting to smell.

She lifted a floor-length dress that flowed from a tight bodice, something with an improbably high waist, and held it against herself. A dress for a woman of 180 centimeters perhaps, weighing no more than forty-five kilograms, at best . . . "What we have here is the wardrobe of some twentieth-century American fashion model, I think . . ."

Inbar picked up a pair of tiny silk panties, no more than a triangle of cloth for the woman's vulva, the rest of it just thin ribbons. Held it up against himself. Frowned. "Unless this thing used to stretch a bit . . ."

Alireza snickered and said, "The woman who wore that must have had to shave a bit, here and there . . ."

Or it would have looked a little strange. Right. Men so easily distracted by . . . The thought of clean underwear a distinct wish now. And my period's not so far off . . . Maybe this woman left a few tampons behind . . . Seeing as how these people didn't seem to know much about . . . Why didn't I just get those shots when it was suggested? No reason. Just . . . same old reason. Every woman's reason.

Ling said, "Well. Perhaps she was Chinese."

Rahman picked up a thick hardcover book, book bound in expensive-looking red leather, gold printing embossed on the spine. *Crimson Desert*, by Passiphaë Laing. Flipped it open. A novel of some kind, written in . . . English? She read aloud: "Whann, in the fulnes of time, I chose seaking of Rhino Jensen, newnes without number it would be, but supposed not I."

Ling took the book, flipped through the pages, a phrase here, another one there. "English. But not English."

Inbar said, "So we're in a parallel world. So what else is new?"

Rahman began laughing. No hysterical edge to her voice. Not quite.

And Ling whispered, "Like *Glory Road*, then? Have I fallen into a book about falling into a book?"

The five of them were glowing softly in the alien dark, curtainfields shimmering like delicate Kirlian auras on the edge of vision. Getting cold out, now. Desert night cold. Switch off the field and your breath is a brief white flag against the night.

Déjà vu experience because strange is as strange does, not because I've been here before. So many strange worlds, under so many strange skies. Scavenger bases, some established, some ramshackle. Colonial worlds like so many planet-wide urban projects here, in other places like little steel fortresses defying eternity. I wish we'd never gone home. Where would we be now if . . .

Listen to me. Like my grandfather, whining about Apollo. Americans on the Moon in 1969, maybe on Mars by 1984. Mars colonies. Asteroid mines. That story he used to talk about, astronaut-prospectors finding something like oil-shale out in the Fore-Trojan cluster. Little did he suspect what would *really* have happened if . . .

If and only if.

This sky now, beyond fantastic, looking like some kind of

CCD astronomical photo. *Colors* up in the sky. Stars picked out in pale red and blue, yellow and white. Look there. A green one. Wolf-Rayet Star? Impending supernova? Globular clusters, balls of white, tinged with the faintest pink, hanging far beyond the sky. Look closely. Those little things you see are distant spiral galaxies, with their reddish cores, arms stained with the blue of youth. Gas giant hanging in the sky, some other little moon sparkling nearby. Dale would've loved this place.

That old, romantic image. Just the two of us here. That would've been nice. His arm around me, talking softly, far into the night; holding each other for warmth . . .

Wry smile. Like it was only yesterday.

I remember my great grandmother from when I was a little girl. How old was I then, twelve? Something like that. She must've been something like eighty-five. Maybe a little older. Staring at the wreckage of her face, wreckage hard to relate to the pretty face in all those old photographs. Old lady whispering, "I can't believe it sometimes, Astrid. Inside, I still feel like a girl of eighteen. It seems like I'm . . . sick, that's all. Like I'm sick and, soon, I'll get better. Go out again. Boys. Dates." Old lady looking at her with a shy grin. Probably remembering her first fuck.

And here I am, older than she ever dreamed of becoming, mooning away about a lost love, a distracted fat man who screwed me a bit when I was already middle-aged.

The great-grandmother had died not long after that. Regretting its necessity. My father telling me, wistfully, that her last words, whispered just as she slipped away, were, *I wanted to live forever* . . .

Must have been a pretty deathbed scene. Like in a movie.

They were all afraid to die. We all were. Mass hysteria in America, in the weeks and months after the interdictions were set up. When the . . . "Lunar Discoveries" were announced. Headline on the *Times* that just made me laugh and laugh. Banner covering half the front page: *Eternal Life* . . .

Eternal life, then wave after wave of suicides. Religious folk. Madmen. People afraid that *now* they'd be depressed and sad for damn-all forever . . . I wonder how many people turned it down? I wonder how many people just lived until they died?

I remember how sorry I was then that we'd left Dale behind. It was a long time before I figured out that, somewhere, on the other side of one cusp or another, there was a world in which Dale came home, in which we lived happily ever after. Or maybe a world in which I was left behind too, in which we went out and out, on in the many worlds until . . .

Until what?

Shrug.

Until something.

Until the Jug caught on and wiped us away.

Space-Time Juggernaut. Nice turn of phrase . . .

Looking up at the sky, Corky Bokaitis said, "That's not Neptune, I guess, is it, Sarge?"

Another shrug. "Well. Probably not. Not *our* Neptune, anyway."

Muldoon said, "What other Neptune is there?"

Silence, then Tarantellula, white eyes on the sky: "I know what you mean, Sarge. I guess we can't be making too many assumptions here."

"Guess not." That was the mistake so many of the scientists made, back in the beginning. Too many assumptions. Just assumed that they *knew* . . .

Muldoon lifted his rifle and aimed at a little point of glitter in the sky—twinkling thing just below the curving limb of "Neptune"—peered through the gunsight-rangefinder of the guidance system. Just one more little moon that . . .

He said, "Huh. I figured it was going to be just a rock. Damn thing looks like a *building,* tumbling end over end. Lookit all them lights . . ." Impossible to believe that he'd had himself *programmed* to talk like that . . .

A quick look through her own scope. Long, dark-skinned cylinder, full of what looked like windows, thousands of tiny, yellow-lit windows. Turning slowly, complex motion about two axes of rotation.

Tarantellula said, "You know, Sergeant-Major, this place is kind of . . . interesting."

Brucie Big-Dick, long silent, said, "No shit."

* * *

In the morning, when the sky was a bright orange verging on pink, the sun a brilliant ruby spark throwing long red shadows all along the cliff face, they abandoned the starship, stumbling down the long ravine, teetering, slipping on shattered rocks, until they were out on the face of the desert, standing in the lee of some tall, russet cliff.

Here, there was nothing more than red sand and blowing pink dust, dust you could see best down by the horizon, like a layer of distant fog, blowing in the wind. A crashed starship, thought Ling. Confirmation, and yet we learned nothing we hadn't already known.

Alireza said, "We might as well go this way." Gesturing to their right, along the cliff-face, in a direction that seemed like south.

Seems like south, because the sun rises in the east. Because we define east as the direction of sunrise. Brief memory. Sunrise over the East China Sea. Dirty gray water. Ramshackle boats, as if I lived hundreds of years ago, rather than in an ever-so-modern twenty-second century sort of China. How old was I then? Fifteen, maybe? Getting too old for the orphanage. Wondering what would become of me.

Inbar, standing still, frowning, looking uncomfortable, as he had all morning, said, "Why that way? Why not some other way?"

Alireza just stared at him. Stared, then turned and began walking.

Silence. Then Inbar muttered a soft word in Arabic, a single clipped syllable, and started after him. Sigh from Rahman. She said, "There's nothing to decide anymore . . ." Started after the others.

Nothing to decide anymore. Ling began walking as well, thinking about that. We could go back to the gate. Go back and try again. Try again. And again. Maybe, sooner or later . . .

What? All sorts of possibilities. Maybe, sooner or later, the gate would open onto the surface of some airless world, would open on a Colonial mining station, or some Scavenger techno-resource. Imagine: a ripple of rainbows, a black sky, roaring wind, our shouts of surprise as we're sucked through, blown out into the void, or onto the surface of a place like the Moon. Sunlight pins and needles on my skin, vacuum a stabbing of knives in my head, my sinuses, my ears . . .

Old stories. Old stories of trapped astronauts daring their thirty allotted seconds of vacuum, crossing from ship to ship. Remember the scene from *2001*? Should Frank Poole have been bleeding from his nose and ears and mouth? Where were the petechiae on his skin? Where were the bruises?

Soyuz 11. Three men dead in their couches. Three men who died while they listened to the air whistle out through a malfunctioning valve. Three dead men who'd had more than thirty seconds, a lot more, in which to unstrap, to reach up, to struggle for life, to at least *try* to close that valve. Why were they still strapped in? Maybe you don't get thirty seconds.

Lots of reasons why the Soviet's Lunar program came to a bad end. Clumsy technology. Insane political system that encouraged bureau managers to wreck each others work. But *Soyuz 11* . . . if nothing else, that made them think, *Maybe we can't do it*.

Imagine. Imagine the Russians making it to the Moon in nineteen seventy-four. Imagine the Americans deciding, just maybe, they'd keep that Saturn production line open after all, refund Apollo Applications, build a wee little moonbase maybe, while waiting for that damned crazy Shuttle to come on line. Imagine. Maybe imagine somebody landing up at the pole around 1980, maybe prospecting for a pocket of fossil ice. Would they have found the gate then? Or does it lie only on our side of that particular cusp?

Rahman, speaking English, said, "What the Hell is that?" Pointing at the sky.

Alireza said, "I've been wondering."

Ling stopped, squinting upward, looking where she indicated. A distant, metallic sparkle against an apricot sky. Inbar said, "How long has it been there?"

"A couple of minutes."

Fighter pilot. Eyes caught by the barest fleck of light, shiver of motion. Ling shaded his eyes, trying to see. Middle-aged eyes still pretty good, never nearsighted, though he'd be needing corrective surgery for hyperopia sooner or later, a twenty-four hour nuisance he'd been putting off for years. This thing now . . .

Rahman said, "You know, it looks like a nineteenth century passenger liner."

Inbar said, "Yes. Yes it does."

Still subtending less than a minute of arc, the thing was shiny metal, its lower half featureless, long, relatively slim, perhaps six times as long as it was wide. No telling how big. No telling how far away. Above, some kind of superstructure, made of darker stuff, details indistinct. Were those tiny, fluttering bits of color flags?

Alireza said, "Maybe. I think . . . gun emplacements?" Squinting hard now, hands folded like binoculars around his eyes.

Inbar sighed, unclipped the real binoculars from his belt, put them to his face. Made a slight choking sound.

Alireza snorted, leveled his stolen rifle at the sky, peered through its gunsight. Silence. Then a muttered exclamation, a short Arabic phrase in which Ling thought he could hear the word *Allah*, emerging from a language that sometimes seemed to be little more than strings of ells separated by muddy, half-swallowed vowels. Alireza passed the rifle to Rahman, who merely gasped. Ling stared at distant, glinting metal until Inbar nudged him, handed over the binoculars.

Focusing, and . . . *Impossible*. Ship sailing through the sky, two broad, six-bladed propellers turning lazily at the stern. Gun turrets. Tiny figures moving about the canted deck, colored flags fluttering from invisibly thin rigging. And a radar dish. That's a radar dish turning atop the mast.

Sputt.

Loud, shuddery sound, like some huge gas burner igniting from its pilot light. Ling lowered the binoculars, turned and looked at another part of the sky, the part above the mountain cliffs. Long, thin trail of reddish smoke, smoke hard to make out against bright orange sky, pointing to a dull red flame, small black object racing out over the desert.

Alireza's voice terse: "*Missile.*"

Sputt.

Another one rising, chasing the first.

The people on the ship . . . People? The crew seemed to see them right away, ship slowing, wallowing, seeming to turn. Dots running around up there, tiny mites clinging to their host, turrets turning, turning in their direction.

Flicker-flicker-flash. Twinkles of bright green light, light almost too bright to look at. Light from the muzzles of those aerial guns.

Bang.

Missile exploding, falling in a shower of golden sparks. Flicker-flicker-flash. Flicker-flicker-flash. Alireza crying out in Arabic, voice urgent. Telling them, perhaps, to tighten their aim. Red flame merging with the ship and . . . Gorgeous blossom of silvery fire, an explosion, a gout of incongruous brown smoke. Ship staggering against the sky, turning, turning, moving in toward the cliffs, listing to one side.

Those tiny dots. Tiny dots against the sky. Falling men. You could hear a dull, grinding roar now. The engines struggling perhaps. But one propeller was stopped, the other one whirling faster and faster. Ship still distant, coming closer and closer, lying on its side in the sky, falling . . . It passed over the cliffs, out of view. A moment later, a plume of gray smoke began to rise.

Silence. Soft wind blowing over the desert sand, lifting tiny particles that stung on the skin of their faces. Alireza was looking around, at all of them. "I'd like to go . . . see."

Madness. We should go back to the gate and . . .

It was Inbar who said, "Yes. Let's do that."

They began walking again, following the line of cliffs, watching as the gray plume grew to a tall tower, rising thousands of meters until it was sheared away by high-altitude wind.

The starship was, somehow, no surprise. Looking at it from the top of the ravine, Kincaid thought, Why is this place so familiar to me? Certainly no place I've ever been before. No place I've even dreamt about. Something Dale said? Memory of standing with him on a windswept crag. Where? Gilligan. No, that's just what he called it. A joke. The Stargate

Commission's official name was Gilliken. A joke. Private joke piled on top of a public joke. Gilligan's Planet. But then, Gillikens, Millikens, Munchkins and Winkies, origins of the names we selected for the four principal Scavenger colony planets. Look, Dale. A planet of your own.

Something, though, about the design of the ship, the topography of the planet. The topography of the sky. We were standing atop that cliff on "Gilligan", surrounded by yellow-green forest, looking out across a plain of grass like ripe wheat—ripe wheat waving in the wind like the surface of some strange yellow sea—looking toward the city. Tall towers surrounded by a light pink mist, city shining against the backdrop of a pastel blue-green sky, tall towers connected by fragile-looking aerial runways, flying roads, pedestrian corridors, whatever.

Dale looking at it through his binoculars, we two, part of the first party to come through, first humans to look down on this vista. Dale whispering, Every dream I ever had. Every God-forsaken dream . . .

We followed a path down the cliffside, Dale wanting to hold my hand for some reason he couldn't explain. Wouldn't explain. You knew that. Wouldn't. He had a way with words. Said what he wanted to say: I keep hoping, he'd said, that we'll open a gate one day and find *my* world. One of them at least.

"Sergeant!"

Bokaitis, pointing southward, at a point not far above the horizon. Something flaring in the sky, garish green fire, a puff of dark smoke . . .

She lifted her M-80 and looked through the gunsight. Jesus. What the fuck is that? Like a dirigible, but . . .

Sharp-eyed Tarantellula said, "I spotted it just a fraction of a second before the explosion. Thought I saw missiles tracking."

Away on the edge of the world, the thing went down, crash smoke rising into a tall, dense plume. Rising, blowing away on the wind. "Let's go." Shouldering her rifle.

Brucie, fascinated technician, scowled and said, "What about this?" Gesturing at the starship.

"Forget it." Forget about spoiled wonders. Fresh wonders waiting for us. Waiting somewhere. What else is waiting? Are you out here, Dale? Is that really what I'm doing, looking for my lost love, my lost gray fat man, like some silly schoolgirl mooning over a romance novel? Fucking Christ. "Let's go."

They made it about halfway to the crash site, running along the base of the cliffs, following an obviously fresh trail, before Muldoon, bringing up the rear, eyes behind them, raised the alarm. Kincaid, on point, was looking down at well-scuffled sand, surface turned over, lighter than the well-settled sand everywhere else. Obviously just the four of them. The three surviving Arabs. The Chinaman. What the Hell do I do with them when I catch them? Put them in irons and drag them back through the gate to the Moon? Drag them back, bomb the gate, go home and face Athelstan's wrath? Maybe. Or turn them over to Bokaitis. Little cavegirl's smart enough to get this silly patrol back home. Probably smart enough to know she should just blow the gate and get the fuck out of there. Go home. Athelstan'll pin a fucking medal on your pretty left tit, cavegirl.

Where the Hell would I go? He's not really out here, you know. And even if he *is*, it's been a long damned time. We aren't the same people we were then. Not even in our memories. Just remembering the last time I thought I was in love. Maybe the only time I ever *was*?

How the fuck do I know?

I thought I was then.

So long ago . . .

Muldoon's moron voice was urgent, with just the right touch of impending panic. "Sarge?"

She turned and looked. "Holy shit . . ." Big green things. Dark green. Big bugs, with long, stalky legs. Things like praying mantises the size of dinosaurs. Big bug eyes looking right at them, triangular heads, mandibles opening and closing on squirmy darkness, insectile grins.

Things on their backs, too. Skinny things, also green. Like skinny green ants, standing on their hind legs, holding the reins of their mantis mounts. Skinny green ants holding what looked like guns. Flicker-flicker-flash.

Something thudded into the sand nearby. *Bang.* Brilliant flare of green fire, like a pulse of ball lightning at their feet, grains of sand whispering through the air, sharp grains crackling on their faces and bare hands. There was a brief feeling of static electricity in the air, a familiar ozone smell.

"Curtainfields up!" Silvery shadows forming around them.

Kincaid lifted her M-80, sighted in, quick image of a green ant man in the scope, looking back at her, green ant man with something like a face, impassive. She fired, knocking him backwards off his mantis. Him? It.

Rapid pop-pop-pop as Bokaitis and Tarantellula fired in counterpoint, Muldoon just standing by, rifle dangling from one hand, looking bewildered. Ripple of return fire, flicker-flash, from the ant men, green fire boiling the sand around them. Missed us. Missed. Bad aim? No. Projectiles curving away at the last instant. Curtainfield fucking up their guidance systems. Good.

Pins and needles inside my belly, though. Bad news, I think . . .

She said, "Let's get the Hell out of here."

Muldoon turned and ran, surprisingly light on his feet, in his polio-cripple boots.

They didn't quite make it to the nearest ravine, the nearest route up into the cliffs, before the ant-men woke up to what was wrong with their aim and started firing on them with unguided solid shot, dumdum slamming into Muldoon's back, knocking him off his feet, rifle spinning away into the dust. He'd gotten up, bawling wordless terror, and run for a pile of rocks, angular red rubble of big sandstone shards nearby.

Stopped to pick up his weapon, though. Not as bad as he seems.

Crouching down now, shooting through the chinks of their little fortress, watching the ant men ride round and round, ducking the little green explosions, explosive light reflected off the faceted, clear, metallic eyes of their mounts.

Images of what might happen. Of being held in those hard bug hands, of giant mantis heads bending down, so very delicate, you see, bending down, grasping mandibles gaping open, gaping, chewing, chewing.

3V educational video image, of a mantis man continuing to fuck a mantis woman, though his head was eaten away, his arms and shoulders gone. What the Hell was it my friend Jenny said? Look at that. Amused disgust in her voice: Men are all the same.

Another bright green explosion on the edge of their sanctuary, rock fragments whining around, making them flinch, though the curtainfields continued to do their job. More tingling inside. Each time, Kincaid would look at her combat monitor, dusty old thing with a crude old battery, clipped neatly to her old web belt. With every explosion, there was a burst of hard gamma radiation.

Curtainfields taking the brunt of it, but . . . Right. Symbiotes'll be busy tonight, dealing with the damage. If they get the chance. Enough hard radiation and the symbiotes'll die. Wonder what the symbiotes'll do when they wake up inside a giant mantis? Eat it? Remanufacture it into me? That'd be . . . odd. All sorts of philosophical bullshit welling up.

Bang. Green fire. Bits of rock rattling around their cage. Strange buzzing behind the eyes, energetic photons going one-two one-two and through and through . . .

"Jesus, Sarge . . ." Bokaitis suddenly up on her knees, M-80 poking out through the rocks, going pop, pop, pop, skinny green ant men flying off their mounts, bowling through the air like so many wriggling green pinwheels.

Brucie Big-Dick, mighty hero of the starways, cowering on the ground now, weaponless Brucie, covering his head, uselessly, with his arms. Tarantellula starting to squirm over to the next hole, figuring, maybe, she'd do the same. Maybe, in due course, the ant men would give up and run away. Or maybe we can just kill them all. Clicking her own weapon to full automatic, rising to one knee . . .

WHAP.

Bokaitis sitting down suddenly, hard on her backside, mouth hanging open, face full of surprise, ripples spilling around the sides of her curtainfield, ripples crossing over each other like ripples in water, making little crisscross interference patterns of light and dark.

"Corporal?"

Just sitting there.

"*Corky?*"

She fell over, leaning backward slowly, then falling in a little puff of red dust—dust billowing up around the curtainfield—little black dart sticking out of her right eye, keeping the lid propped open, surrounded by slivers of what looked like broken glass.

Silence, then Tarantellula said, "Oh, *shit.*"

Then, *bangbangbang*, green light flaring outside, pouring through the cracks in their rockpile, washing out the silvery screen of curtainfield light, creating a bilious world.

Muldoon made a great, wordless shout, jumped up, banged his head on the rocks above, fell down, groveled, dropping his rifle, jumped up again and squirmed out through the nearest hole.

"God damn it, no! *Muldoon . . .*"

You could hear him out there for just a moment, hear the thudding of his heavy feet, hear that huge, silly voice crying, "Lilly! *Save* me, Lilly . . ." Scuffle of running feet, praying mantis feet, then silence.

The two of them sitting in their hole, Kincaid feeling ill, suddenly wishing the whole world away, Tarantellula's alien black face, featureless white eyes, unreadable. The dancer said, "Well."

Right. Kincaid patted her rifle and said, "You watch a lot of old war movies, do you?"

Impassive stare, then a slow nod. Right. She said, "I . . . guess that's why I'm here."

Kincaid said, "You remember *Back to Bataan?*"

"I remember that guy with the bayonet through his throat . . ." Right.

"You remember *They Died With Their Boots On?*"

Another slow nod. "*Garryowen.*" Right.

Kincaid put a fresh clip in her M-80, put it on full automatic and . . . White light flooded through the holes in the rockpile, strobe light, light closing their eyes. White light again. Blink. White light again. Long, slow rumble of fading thunder, far, far away, shuddering across the sky.

"Fuck." Kincaid got up on her knees and poked her head out the nearest hole, almost wishing her deadly dart would come, would come sailing in through her eye.

Silence. Stillness. Dead praying mantises lying in motionless heaps. Dead green ant men lying scattered all around. Wisps of smoke, pale white smoke, almost invisible smoke, rising here and there, something dead at the base of each wisp. You could see Muldoon out there too, scattered around on the red sand in what looked like six or seven big bleeding pieces.

Tarantellula, crouching at her side, said, "Well fuck, Sergeant."

Sudden movement, down at the base of the red cliff. Tarantellula lifting her rifle, taking aim. Kincaid putting out a hand to make her hold off. Two small figures walking out onto the desert sand, heading right for them. A smallish man with black hair. Built like a small man, anyway, short legs, long waist, big head with straight black hair, long hair confined by a white headband on which was painted some blood red design. Man in some kind of dark military uniform.

Tall, slender woman beside him, dressed in a neat white pantsuit, the sort of thing a casual-minded woman might wear for a night out on the town, might wear to a nice restaurant, might . . .

Kincaid lifted her M-80 and looked through the sight. The man appeared to be Oriental, maybe Chinese. That was definitely a Chinese character on his headband. The woman? Oddly familiar-looking, also something of the Oriental about her. High cheekbones. Lovely dark eyes . . .

The woman waved. Waved and called out, *"Mother?"*

Tarantellula whispered, "What the *fuck* . . ."

Lovely voice calling, "Mother, are you in there?"

Brucie suddenly came out of his fetal cower, kneeling up, bright-eyed. "Someone you know?"

Kincaid looked again, feeling slightly dizzy. It was the gyndroid Amaterasu, the little fuckrobot she'd delivered to brother Roddie less than a week ago.

* * *

Back up in the hills, on a cliffside overlooking the crash site, Subaïda Rahman watched what was going on down below and thought, We've avoided thinking about it, avoided talking about it too much . . . thinking about where we are. About what's *happening* to us. If it wasn't obvious before, it's obvious now. Obvious from the things we saw in Dale Millikan's notebooks, the books filled in by his colleagues. Obvious from this . . . this . . .

No handy phrase you could use to characterize it.

Not in English. Not in Arabic.

Down below, the ship was wrecked, smoldering, the fires going out, tower of dense smoke thinning, dissipating, blowing away into that impossible sky. Impossible. What kind of atmosphere scatters white light to bright orange? No atmosphere we can breathe. Dust, like on the *real* Mars? Doesn't look like it.

The airship was lying more or less on its side, hull crushed in, gaping holes opened on black interior compartments, superstructure twisted and toppled. Swarms of giant praying mantises circling round, things on their backs like huge green ants firing green fire guns into the ship. Little beings spilling out, much smaller red ant sort of beings, trying to run, trying to fight back with red fire guns of their own. Every now and again, a mantis creature would burst open, would fall down dead. Mostly, though, it was the red ant men who fell and died. Are those swords they're wielding?

Big green ant riding down on little red ant, scimitar swinging, little red head rolling in the red, red dust, green ant riding on.

There is a version of the Many Worlds cosmology that allows time travel, the version that says, You Can't Go Home Again. Travel into the past, you've broken a cusp. The past you go to does not lie in the past of the time you left. Travel back to your own time, you've broken another cusp. The home you return to is not the home you left, nor does it lie in the future of the past you visited.

So do you come back and find another you living in your house, mothering your children, giving your husband a nice little blowjob on a sweaty weekend night?

Well, no. She left on her own time-trip some time ago, you see. Do you notice any differences, small or large?

Maybe, maybe not. Depends on the nature of the cusp-set you broke.

But her husband is probably expecting his regular weekend blowjob, nonetheless. Men are like that, the pigs.

Go back in time and kill your infant self. Go home. It's not the same home, of course. And it is not a universe where you were killed as an infant. You can't get there from here. Or can you?

From every cusp, an infinity of histories spring. Every history is real, even the ones that are impossible. Every time you say, "When pigs have wings," a cusp opens on a world in which, just then, pigs miraculously begin to fly.

And Many Histories, Many Worlds implies . . .

No. I don't believe it.

I don't.

Nobody believes it.

Not really.

Down below, the green ant men were just finishing off the red ant men. Men? Alireza, watching through binoculars, said, "They're not killing all of them. The green ones are . . . doing something to some of the red ones." Something odd in his voice.

Rahman took the binoculars and looked. Big green ants, two or three, sometimes four together, holding little red ants on the ground. Green ants squirming, squirming. Red ants held still for whatever it was. She took the binoculars away from her eyes.

So, you've come to an alternate universe. An alternate universe in which everything is different. Except one thing. Well . . . Except one class of things. The red ants already dead must be the males.

Scrape of noise. Alireza, with a muttered exclamation, bucking up off the ground, spinning round, aiming his American rifle. Ling bug-eyed, drawing his little pistol with its four little dimetrodon-slaying bullets.

Subaïda Rahman sitting on her heels. Merely staring.

They were a handsome couple, the woman tall and very

thin, clad in sleek black leather, leather with that skin-wrinkle buff finish that only real leather can possess. Handsome, smooth white face, dark blonde hair with just the right waviness-property. Blue on blue eyes. Wide eyes. Big girl eyes. The sort of big girl eyes you knew men fell for, even in deepest, darkest Arabia.

She thought, Well. Here's our fashion model, perhaps . . .

The man. Rahman could feel her cheeks flush. A squat, muscular white man, a well-tanned Caucasian with curly black hair, curly, black, with sharp red highlights. Mulberry bright eyes. Square jaw, clean-shaven of course, but with just the right touch of stubble, stubble that said, My blood boils with manly manly juices . . .

Muscular man dressed in a leather harness, all rings and clips and carabiners, sandal straps running up his calves almost to his knees, baldric over shoulder, supporting a long, curved sword. A long-barreled pistol here, a short sword there. A jewel-handled dagger.

A lot of hair on his chest. Really, a lot of dense, fluffy, black pubic hair below his ridged, muscular belly. Scrotum a large, weighty, wrinkled brown bag; thick, circumcised red penis dangling down a good fifteen centimeters . . . I wonder if I'm blushing? It feels like it. His bright blue, big blue eyes on me now. Probably seeing . . .

Slight shock. Behind them, three red ant men, slightly shorter than the humans, slimmer than ants of course, their body-plan details really *very* different. But the hard integument, the six jointed limbs. And stiff red faces, humanoid faces, frozen into place, expressionless masks of faces.

The man looked over his shoulder and said something to the ants, a hard, metallic, tone language sort of speech, rising and falling, almost yodeled, *clangclangclangclangclang* . . .

One of the ants reached out and put an arthropod hand on his shoulder, squeezing gently, *clangclangclang* right back.

Ling stepped forward, fear making his eyes dart back and forth, looking from face to face, looking at the woman, the ant people, down at the man's genitals, back up at his face. He held out his hand and said, "Hello. Ah . . . We've come from far away and, ah, don't know this world."

The man stared at his hand. Stared. Glanced at the woman. "English Three, na? Awdd."

The woman looked them up and down, curious, obviously mystified. "Nawt herein, but . . ." A shrug, very pretty. "Are you with the Imperial Terran Navy? There's not supposed to be anything . . ."

Interesting. Not the slight Brit accent popular in the scientific world of the twenty-second century. Flat mid-American. Twenty-first century TV American. Rahman said, "Who are you?"

The woman looked her in the face then, hard-eyed, aggressive, speculative. Woman to woman. "I'm Passiphaë Laing. This is Rhino Jensen." Expectant then, waiting for some standard reaction. Nothing. Puzzled look. "Don't you follow *Crimson Desert*?" Crackle of gunfire from below, flare of green, green light. Red ant people stirring nervously, *clangclangclang* . . .

The man, Rhino Jensen? What a peculiar name . . . said, "We'd better get out of here. Not far to Kanthol. There'll be another flight to Halian soon . . ." and *clangclang* to the ants.

The woman, Laing, said, "I don't know who the Hell you are or what the Hell you're doing here, but you're welcome to come along. In fact, you'd better. If the Beanies get hold of you . . ." Gesturing at the carnage below.

The path led upward, farther back into the hills. Following the man and woman and their ants, Rahman thought, When the answers come, will they make any sense? Somewhere. Somewhere deep inside, a stark fear: What if this isn't really happening? What if I merely went mad? What if I'm locked in a cell somewhere, in some hospital, maybe in Cairo? Locked in a cell, drugged to make me calm. Calm and ever so tractable.

Image of a disheveled young woman, strapped in a straitjacket, foam on her lips, lesbian hairdo growing out ragged, eyes wide, wide enough for the whites to show all the way around, staring and staring.

What if?

Just follow the ants.

* * *

Sing around the campfire. Then what? Join the Campfire Girls? Or, in my case, maybe the *Kampfeuer Mädchens*? *Mädchenen*? Hell. Kincaid smiled to herself in the darkness, watching the flames of their little cooking fire, small red and green flames playing with one another as robot Amaterasu took things out of the packs she and . . . Genda? The packs she and Genda'd stashed back at the entrance to the nearest ravine.

A wok. Slotted spoons. A fork. A knife. Magic cans that opened on fresh ingredients. Crispy vegetables. Bits of dark meat. Robot Amaterasu. Domestic Amaterasu. Brucie Big-Dick sitting in the darkness, watching her, big-eyed as well.

Image of us standing out in the desert under a darkening orange sky, long rays of sunlight sloping down, making the shadows grow. Kincaid facing her creation, stunned, and then, unable to suppress a crazy, crooked grin: "Last time I saw you, you were tits-down in a birthday cake."

Pretty, young Oriental-girl face crossed by a shadow, a distant look, a remembering look. "That was . . . long ago, Mother."

Long ago? Cold chills, classic icy fingers playing touch-and-go on her spine. "Why, it was only a . . . a . . . couple of days ago?"

Long look from those dark, soulful, man-swallowing eyes. "It was nearly two thousand years ago, Mother. I've missed you." Pale, pale smile. Do you love me, Mother?

"You aren't supposed to remember me." Maybe from the party? A memory of me watching brother Roddie stick it up her ass while his buddies laughed and cheered?

"But I do remember."

Um. "Not supposed to know who I am . . ."

The sultry little-girl voice said, "Yet I do."

Tarantellula: "What's going on here, Sergeant? You know these people?"

Brucie the Technician's voice, dry, remarkably unafraid: "Yeah, Sarge. Inquiring Minds Want to Know."

Robot Amaterasu looking at the little dark man, the two of them exchanging glances full of . . . what? Full of data? No. Little pang, deep inside Kincaid. Exchanging glances full of grace. Amaterasu looked back at Kincaid and gestured at the man: "Mother? This is my friend, Lord Genda."

The little man stepped forward, offering his hand, grasping hers, surprisingly, close to the fingertips, holding them gently, Kincaid's hand like a massive paw in his small, delicate fingers. He said, *"Genda Hiroshige-desu. Hajimemashite."* Sharp. Alternating hard and soft. Genda Shroshgeh-dess. Hajj-meh-mah-shteh.

"Pleased to meet you, sir." A little smile. "I once spoke a bit of Japanese. Not any more." But I remember enough to know that was rather . . . brusque. An imperious look in those cold, dark eyes.

Imperious look, but . . . a shrug, a smile, a glance, suddenly very warm glance at Amaterasu. "Merely an affectation, Madam. Your daughter makes me speak the English of your day."

Darkness now, the campfire flickering, casting long shadows of robot Amaterasu as she cooked, watched by the others. They'd helped bury the chunks of Muldoon, Bokaitis's whole body, helped them pile a cairn of stones over the grave, Tarantellula all the while wondering if they shouldn't just carry the remains back to the gate and send them on through to the Moon for bagging and retrieval.

But, by now, Athelstan may be there. On his way out here to get us, drag us back for trial? Or just setting up to bomb the gate shut? No matter. Kincaid silent, then motioning them onward, following Genda and Amaterasu off across the red sand, past the carcasses of giant mantises, green ant men, on to the bottom of the nearest ravine, then on up into the stark red hills.

So where have you been . . . daughter mine?

How'd you come to be here?

Impossible. *Impossible* screaming inside her head. You know, of course. *You* know, but . . .

Lovely young robot walking beside her, sleek woman-shape in fashionable white clothing moving gently to those special rhythms. Amaterasu walking beside her shyly. Shyly taking her hand. Mother. My mother . . . Tarantellula, tall, angular black spider dancer, white-eyed, hardly woman at all, more monster-man than anything else, taking point. Lord Genda and Brucie Big-Dick falling behind, falling in side-by-side, walking together but not touching, walking silently. You know why. So they can watch us. Men's sly eyes on women's gently rocking backsides, watching those hips tilt and sway, hips draped in clothing, perhaps, designed to accentuate that sway, make it . . .

Men's hormones stirring. Bubble, bubble, toil and . . .

Robot Amaterasu holding her lost mother's hand, walking up into the red mountains as sunset turned the pumpkin sky dark brown, as the stars popped out in magnitude sequence. Amaterasu speaking. A small story. A simple story. Programmed love for brother Roddie. Uncle Roddie, that same old story. Uncle Roddie trifling under the little girl's dress. Uncle Roddie making the little girl cry. What happened to the programming I left? What happened to the programming that would make you love him?

Uncle Roddie fucking me, making me cry, programmed orgasms making him smile and smile.

And be a villain still?

Amaterasu smiling sad-eyed at her mother. Shakespeare had it right.

Uncle Roddie tiring of his robot girl. Putting her back in the box. Putting her in the closet. Putting her away.

What about *me*? What about . . .

Mother, you and your comrades never came back from the Moon.

So. Robot Amaterasu lying still in the darkness, huddled in her box, remembering, over and over, every second of her life, playing it out from beginning to end. Every joyless orgasm. Every surge of hateful programmed love.

Glad to be in my box. Glad to be here forever.

How long? Program counter delivering a no-event event-code once every Planck time for fifteen centuries. Even in powered-down mode, I began to sleep, sleep without dreams, for longer and longer stretches. I'd awaken, and remember, and sleep again, awaken . . .

From behind them, Genda said, "I found her in a rubbish

dump, on a world called Tano's Planet, some two thousand parsecs from Earth, about four hundred years ago."

Kincaid standing to one side, watching the two of them set up camp and make their colorful cooking fire, thinking, You found her in a rubbish dump . . . some time in the eighteenth century?

Well, no, madam. On Tano's Planet, in that particular universe, it's the Gregorian Year 3954 A.D. I found her, opened the box and found her. Fell in love, you see . . .

Robot Amaterasu's eyes somehow shining through the darkness.

And you, Lord Genda Hiroshige. How did you come to be on Tano's Planet in the year 3954 A.D., seven thousand light-years or so from the Sun? Long walk?

A smile. A polite shrug, Genda lifting bits of seaweed-like this and that in daintily held *hashi*, chewing reflectively, looking up at the sky. I came there in my spaceship, *Baka-no-Koto*, but . . . Well. A long tale. Not a merry one.

Brucie Big-Dick, voice very soft: "We are interested."

Dark eyes on him, frowning. "Perhaps . . ." Long silence. Then:

"There is a time and a place where the West died stillborn. I know you understand, or you wouldn't be here. So. In China, in the days of the Tang Empire, having driven the Hiung-nu away, while the West went barbarous and was lost, they sailed ships around the edges of the Fat Flat Ocean. Sailed according to the principles of Tao, and went to the Desert Land, where they saw lizards the size of yaks and hopping rats the size of men. Went to faraway islands of lissome women, to mountainous islands where there were no men at all, only walking birds ten feet tall and eagles who killed them for sport. Sailed on ocean currents to a land beyond the sea, where dark men built stone temples and sacrificed to bloody gods.

It didn't last forever. Nothing ever does. The Mongol overlords came and threw down the Tang, ruled over us, and your kindred as well. Your Marco Polo and mine are doubtless the same man, living before cusp on endless cusp drove our worlds apart. Then the Ming came and made their empire, and sailed the thousand seas and traveled all over the world. The cusp of cusps was the persistence of Tao, the withering away of the Confucian State.

A thousand years before I was born, a fleet of one hundred great ships pulled up before the Lisboa roadstead, her grand admiral firing his guns over the water, his emissaries demanding tribute from Prince Henry.

Lord Genda smiling over the last remains of his dinner, smiling at robot Amaterasu. Prince Henry thought of resistance. Thought about it for minutes on end, perhaps. But Prince Henry was a canny ruler. He and Chen Ho made their deals. Prince Henry, in due course, became King of Europe by the pleasure of the Great Universal Emperor. And Chen Ho, trade monopolies in hand, became the richest man in all history.

In due course we made our machines and saw the use of steam. We made our aircraft and, in what you'd call 1864, a party of Chinese explorers set down on the Moon . . .

Did you find the Stargate at the pole?

No. That came much, much later. Our World State formed and we filled the Solar System with life. About a century before my birth, we discovered the true nature of the space-time continuum, which led to hyperdrive and the colonization of the stars.

Kincaid sat back, leaning a against a warm rock face, watching him, eyes reflecting bits of dying firelight, knowing what was coming.

Genda said, I was a young man then, twenty-seven, not long out of the Space Academy, commander of a small three-man scoutship, *Baka-no-Koto*, about to leave on an extended exploratory mission, out in the direction of Sagittarius Arm . . .

Interesting name for a ship, Kincaid thought. Polite Japanese way of saying *bullshit*.

Soft laughter from Genda, who seemed far away, far in the past. We were looking forward to that mission, Bannerjee, Raimundo and I, three non-Han military officers out to prove our mettle. It would have been . . . a fine life.

Soft whisper from Amaterasu: And now you'd be centuries dead. And I'd still be alone in my cold, dark box . . .

A slow nod, a gaze in her direction. True. But we had the hyperdrive, and all such cusps break in the same direction . . .

Kincaid said, "How did the Space-Time Juggernaut manifest itself?"

Long, long silence. Then Genda said, "The stars fell out of the sky. Every one of them."

Compelling image. "Fell?"

"Like bits of paper falling from a bulletin board. Then . . . in the darkness, as people screamed and ran, though there was nowhere to hide . . . *something* came to the pretty little colony world of Xiaohuà bù Liáng, came and rolled the world away to nowhere at all. Something like a . . . cloud of light? To this day I can't quite recall its exact shape."

Angel of Death sizzling overhead, like a flock of migrating firebirds. My friends rolling up like windowshades. *Snap.* Replaced by dry, rattling old bones . . .

Genda said, "I got the ship away. Left my friends behind. Flew through empty space . . ." Suffering in his voice now. Regret. "Only the gates, which we'd just begun to investigate, remained, out of all creation. I went on through the nearest, starship and all, and . . ." He fell silent, leaving behind an image of those gates, large gates it seemed, floating alone in empty black space.

Amaterasu put her hand on his shoulder, and said, "We've been in this skein of universes for four hundred years, exploring."

Brucie Big-Dick: "Looking for what?"

The robot looked at him for a long moment, then said, "The way out."

Tarantellula: "Out into what?"

"Out into reality."

Though she knew it wasn't the answer, Kincaid asked, "Back home?"

Genda said, "There is no home. My home is gone. And this . . ." Hand waving at a sky full of impossibly colorful stars, "This is just a dream. Somewhere, some . . . thing is dreaming it all for us. That's the reality we seek."

Sitting in her darkness, back warmed by cooling stone, Kincaid thought, Looking for the Jug. Fools.

Hard memories. Old memories. Memories not so old after all. Memories of sitting home, year after year, slowly, painfully deciphering the bits and pieces of Scavenger literature they'd brought home from the Multiverse, a way of . . . thinking about lost Dale without *thinking* about him.

Out there. Somewhere.

Hutùnûq's Story. Because, you see, it didn't happen all at once. No. A little bit, then a little more, then all of it, seemingly at once but really no more than just one more iteration. What is this thing in the old, hard-to-understand Colonial records? What is this Space-Time Juggernaut they've come to fear? Why do they want to hide now?

Like a cloud of fire. Like a cloud of fire that descends into first this Colonial sky, then that one—one at a time—in bunches and clusters, ringing down some improbably final curtain on hundreds, thousands, even millions of Colonial worlds, following them wherever they went in the Multiverse until . . .

The Colonials, for whatever reason, never gave up, never retreated, never went home to hide and die. And the Jug, our word for the Scavengers' own pet name for the Monster, hunted them down. A world at a time, a universe at a time, in this spacetime and that one, until . . . Scavengers puzzling over those last historical records. Records left by lost individual Colonials who wandered the Multiverse until they vanished.

Hutùnûq wondered if the Jug was hunting the last ones down individually. Wonder if any of them escaped to survive, like Flying Dutchmen, like Wandering Jews, over all those billions of years.

I think he hoped, one day, he'd track down the Last Colonial. Certainly, he searched and searched, until . . .

Hutùnûq's Story. Hutùnûq and his party of explorer archaeologists, wandering an empty world of crisp, white gypsum sand. *This*, the story said, this is the place to which we tracked the last Colonial. Nothing here now, you see, but some very old ruins. Very old ruins and . . .

Through the rebus-puzzle writing, through the alien thoughts of a very alien Scavenger language, you could hear Hutùnûq's Scavenger hearts pounding as he told and retold his survivor's tale.

A cloud of fire forming in the sky.

A million, billion, trillion bits of light, twisting on high, corkscrewing down out of nothingness, into being. A million, billion, trillion predator eyes looking down on them from on high and . . .

Snap.

First this one rolling up like a windowshade, then . . . *snap* . . . that one and . . . *snapsnapsnap* . . . a hand-ful, then a score then . . . Hutùnûq's breathless Scavenger voice: I and two others escaped back through the gate to Llerwerrûqqel—the world we think may have been Gilliken—closing the gate behind us, scrambling its address table so the . . . thing could not follow us through.

The thing we think may be the Space-Time Juggernaut, the thing that ate the Colonials, one by one. Waiting. Waiting at just the place where last it feasted. Waiting. Perhaps for us.

Fools, she thought.

Looking for the Jug.

You get used to living in a book, Ling told himself. Get used to living in a dream. Question is, which book? And whose dream? I never had enough time to read or dream. Not after I got to be an adult, a student, a scientist-engineer, man-ager . . . not after I put my nose to the grindstone, nose so quickly ground away.

All those simple, simple dreams. We go to the Moon, you see. Open the old American moonbases, take up where they left off. Maybe something up there that made what happened in America . . . happen. But most likely not. Vinge's *cusp* you see. America turned the corner on tomorrow and simply accelerated out of sight. We can follow them. We can, if only . . .

Cusp. Prophetic word.

Long walk cross country, across dark red landscape under a nutmeg-seasoned pumpkin sky. Silver clouds at night, wanderers delight? But it was a clear sky now, a sky filled with what he supposed must be stars. Stars fallen out of a book as well, a book by Bonestell, maybe, or from some atlas of sky photos, deep sky false-colored from long exposure times. Neptune high in the sky now, like a midnight blue balloon, dark eye of a fresh storm looking down on them all.

I remember when I was a child, thinking how wonderful it was that the planets, the real planets, had turned out to contain such stark, incredible beauty. I wondered how the people of the 1960s and '70s and '80s felt, seeing them all for the first time. Now I know.

The long walk up through the mountains as night fell: walking away from the little valley where the ship had crashed, the cruiser *Vanator*, Jensen called it. In what language? Certainly not *clangclangclang*. Walking away from a valley of death, red ants killed, or pinned to the ground, green ants squirming on top of them. Hollow echoes fading behind them, echoes of explosions, much fainter echoes that must have been green-ant war whoops, red ant screams.

Maybe, somewhere in there, green ant cries of passion? Green ants fulfilled, red ants raped. Same old story, from a hundred thousand books, a hundred billion lives.

And this sleek, trim, leather-clad Passiphaë Laing, walking by his side, talking to him, while Subaïda Rahman followed and listened and frowned. Something going on here that I don't understand? Probably. Rueful smile in the darkness, smile full of memory. I never understood any of them. Not something I could grapple with, grip with an engineer's mind.

Where is this place?

Laing exchanging bemused glances with Rhino Jensen of the ridiculous cognomen. Well. Saying it almost like that old actor. A sigh. Quick staccato back and forth with the man in a language that was almost English but not English, almost comprehensible but not. Trying to decide where this is? Don't they *know*?

And she said: *Technically* speaking, this is the desert planet *Arrasûn*, located in the unclaimed space between the Terran Empire and its chief ally the Bimus Ascendancy, on the outskirts of what's left of the old Parahuan Imperium, about 2400 parsecs from Sol. The nearest human colony is Tano's Planet.

So what does that mean? And why *technically*?

Well. A little grin. That's just what it says in the script, of course. There really is no such place as Arrasûn.

Long silence. Ling walking, Rahman still listening. The others walking some little distance away, Inbar talking with Jensen, Alireza just walking, staring at red ants. For a moment, Ling had imagined he could see the shadow of Ahmad Zeq.

He said, Script? What script?

Laing laughing, shaking her head. Somebody's going to have a hard time explaining *this* one. Asses will be on the carpet. Boy.

What are you talking about?

Look, I don't know what program you folks are from, but this is the software substrate for *Crimson Desert*. There's been a pretty good malph, somewhere on up the line.

I don't understand.

There'd been a troubled look in her eyes, a long deep shadow reaching away into her soul. You don't *know*? It was plain she could see he didn't, her upset deepening swiftly. So they programmed you all the way through? Boy, that's not *fair*.

Life's not fair.

This isn't life.

Look, I don't know what you're talking about. Where is this place and what's *Crimson Desert*? And now, a stark fear of what he was about to find out, rose.

Laing said, If there was somebody to complain to about this, I'd sure as shit complain. But there isn't, as usual. She looked away, took a slow breath, looked back at him, face full of obvious sympathy. *Crimson Desert* is an interactive story background in the Ohanaic Pseudouniverse. We're all AI modules assigned to act out various roles within the flexscript.

Silence. Then Rahman gabbling in Arabic, all walking stopped, the other Arabs turning, staring, astonished, Inbar's eyes large with interest, Alireza's large with unmistakable fear. Fear and disbelief.

Ling said, "I almost guessed that. Almost guessed it."

Omry Inbar awoke to red-orange sunrise, and thought, A videonet drama. I'm inside a videonet drama. In just a minute, the director will shout Cut! and we'll all break for lunch . . . No. Not quite. Just a dream. He sat up on one elbow, feeling cold and stiff, joints almost creaking after lying out on the hard ground all night, looking around. Sunrise. Brilliant sun a squashed, streaky pink disk, quite oblate, on the far horizon, out over the desert, Neptune pale blue, almost washed away by the morning light. No sign of smoke anywhere. People and red ants lying strewn on the ground around the dead fire, some of them stirring, some not.

Jensen huddled against the little red ant he'd squirmed with the night before. What *is* he doing to that thing? Ling's voice then, in a hushed whisper. Passiphae Laing's throaty, sexually-charged chuckle. What do you think?

But . . . but . . . *why*?

Well. She's his wife.

Oh.

I forget you all don't know the story. Jensen's a Sector Explorer for the Ohanaic Fleet. He crashed here about twenty years ago; went native.

Um. I see. And you?

I'm an investigative reporter for GalactoLight News.

Ah. Dr. Livingston, I presume?

Quite. I always liked Henry Stanley. Not to mention Spencer Tracy. She laughed, a merry sound, a likable sound.

Inbar sat up, sat cross-legged on the ground, rubbing his hands together, wriggling stiff fingers and wishing for a good, hearty cup of the very best Ethiopian coffee. Caffeine to jump-start my soul, sugar to power the transformation.

So, here we are inside the programming track for *Crimson Desert*, the most popular, longest running interactive hypernet saga accessible by the citizens of the Terran Empire of 3954 A.D., somewhere in something she calls the Ohanaic

Pseudouniverse. Why *pseudo-*, I wonder? I have a feeling I'm not going to like it when I find out.

Inbar stood, stretching, listening to the gristle of his neck and spine and shoulder joints crackle, wishing now for a hot bathtub, a professional massage. Hell, why not simply wish for a warm bed with satin sheets and my own private, paid-for whore?

Everyone was stiff, stretching, murmuring complaints, Ling, oldest, perhaps the worst. Laing reaching down to help him to his feet, help him brush the red soil from his coverall. Even the ants were stiff, rolling around on their little globe-shaped hips, bending and straightening thin, angular arms and legs, hard plastic faces expressionless. But their eyes. You can see something in their eyes. Just a hint.

Everyone was stiff but Jensen, who'd slept more or less naked on the bare ground. Jensen bounding to his feet, yawning, laughing, bright-eyed and bushy . . . well. Not quite bushy-*tailed*, exactly. Jensen slapping his little red wife on her red plastic bottom with a flat, hard sound, like a man's hand striking a block of wood. A hollow block, at that, little red woman murmuring *tingytingting* like a little bell, as if in protest.

And then another voice, not one of theirs, loud, harsh, with that oh-so-flat and unBritish accent, "Well. Caught you at last." Flat voice echoing round the low crags surrounding their campsite. On the cliff above stood five . . . people? Four of them people at any rate. A short, rather unkempt young man. A slim, handsome Asian couple, man and woman, man in military uniform, woman looking like a video star . . .

Quite at home here, I suppose, mused Inbar, unsurprised, at himself, at them. A thing. Thing of some kind. Not a person. Not really. Person-shaped, but thin, spindly, black, something over three meters tall, with huge, featureless, glowing white eyes. Not glowing. Reflecting the morning light like mirrors.

And the American soldier woman, she of the flowing golden hair, she of the bizarre, *alien* silver eyes. Alien? The word's taken on new meaning, deeper meaning. How familiar, how *comfortable* she looks just now. Something from home.

Up on the cliff, the Asian-looking man said, "Jensen and Laing? I wondered if we'd run into you two in here." *In* here.

Alireza stepped forward, just one step, a half-step perhaps, and called out, "Sergeant-Major Kincaid, is it? Come on down. You and your friend can . . . explain things to us."

"If she knows, herself," Inbar heard Ling mutter.

"If there's anything to know," said Rahman aloud, voice quite cold.

Kincaid laughed and stepped off the cliff, landing like an acrobat in front of them. "There is," she said.

Alireza sat then and ate his breakfast, hot, sharp flower-scented orange tea sipped between little spoonfuls of some crunchy grain cereal that had quickly soaked up a splash of tart, lime-green milk, and wondered for the thousandth time, if he really understood. Wondered, and listened to the talk, mostly between little soldier Genda, strapping newswoman Laing, and this metallic American Amazon, Kincaid.

Do I *finally* understand this world *Multiverse*? Maybe. Most likely not. Easy to understand its comic book implications, of course. You make a decision, yes or no, the universe splits and two of you go their separate ways, one yes, one no.

But it isn't as simple as that, nothing ever is, especially with physics. It was demonstrated almost two hundred years ago, with all those crazy slit experiments, that a particle plainly follows all possible paths, until someone *looks* and nails down true history.

What about *us*? Who's looking? Who collapses *our* wave function?

A good Muslim knows. No need for some godless Anthropic Principle.

Always gave me a headache to think about these things, back at university. Never understood why an aerospace engineer in training should have to study these things, even in brief. Give me good, honest, faithful machines. Always the same, no matter what. Unless they're broken. In which case you fix them.

Now listen to them talk.

How in *Hell* could we be inside a story? Look at Ling. Chinaman *gleeful* at what he's hearing.

Listen to Kincaid's questions now. She understands the Multiverse well. Understands how, if something is possible, then, somewhere, sometime, in some history or another, it is. But, still, *Crimson Desert*? A story is just a story, you see. Sure, there can be a history in which there exists a story called *Crimson Desert*, which includes a meeting between . . . us. But. The characters in a book are just characters. They are not conscious entities. They don't experience the story themselves.

A story, you see, is just a story.

Then, that other being . . . do I understand correctly? Is this woman Amaterasu a robot, built for men's pleasure, no more than some complex masturbation toy?

Amaterasu interjecting, very quietly, No, Mother. A book is, I think, a Chinese Room.

Ah, now there's a notion. A locked room. Inside, a man who speaks only Spanish. With him, an elaborate library containing all the rules for translating between English and Chinese. A slip of paper is passed under the door, bearing a message in Chinese. The Spanish man goes diligently to work. In due course, a slip of paper is passed back under the door, bearing the English translation. To the man inside, there is no message, only the following of rules, directing mechanical tasks. To the people outside? *Something* has understood the message.

Does the room itself then, speak Chinese and English? Certainly, the Spanish worker inside does not. His presence is irrelevant and could be taken by an insensate machine. All those Hard AI arguments of centuries past, arguing that the Chinese Room is indeed imbued with sentience and must, in some sense, be aware.

Even I know it isn't so.

The intelligence of a Chinese Room lies with the mind that laid down the rules for parsing the message. An information processing machine is nothing more than an extension of the intelligence that programmed it. At best, the fossilized intelligence of its creator.

Kincaid staring hard-eyed, dismayed, at the robot.

Then the soft sound of Ling, swallowing gently, eyes troubled.

Oh. I see. The fossilized intelligence of its Creator.

You follow a line of cause and effect, backward through time. The reader reads. The writer writes. The writer came from somewhere. Somewhen. Each step in the chain no more than one more insensate link, back to some First Cause. And there you find the intelligence that imbued all the rest.

Of course we can be inside a story now. What's the difference between once sort of Creation and another? A matter of degree, not kind. Very funny, really. Look at how uncomfortable this notion makes the empiricists among us. They don't want, you see, to be mere . . . creations.

Later, when the sun was past noon, crossing beyond the zenith, afternoon advancing as it settled down the western sky once again, sky darkening very slowly from bright orange to dun, they walked and walked, Inbar's feet in agony now, the cheap patent leather of the thin boots that he'd worn inside his spacesuit starting to tear here and there, creasing and tearing, exposing stuff like gray cardboard.

They were on the western slope of the mountain range now, the side away from the flat red desert, the sun always in their faces, but you could see the city in the distance, Kanthol, the City on the Mountain, Jensen called it with obvious pride. Kanthol, towering above lesser peaks in the foreground, some great Himalayan range visible beyond it, peering over the horizon, washed out pink with distance and haze.

On Earth, the distant mountains would look blue, this . . . *pinkness* enhances the alien feel of Arrasûn, the imaginary world of *Crimson Desert. Imaginary*. My God. And what had Ling meant, when he'd said, Gathol, it ought to be called Gathol? And the other one should be Helium, not Halian.

Soldier Kincaid laughing with delight, heavy American

breasts shaking on her chest: Not *quite* Barsoom, is it, Professor Ling?

Ling staring at the red ants, listening to them *clangclang* away. No, he'd said. I suppose not.

But still wishing it was?

I'm wishing it was *Moon Man*'s Moon. At least it'd be Earth, hanging up there in the sky, not Neptune . . .

Kincaid silent then, for a long moment, odd expression on her face. She'd whispered: I wish it was too. Maybe that's where he went, off to join Iulianos and Red Hawk and Valetta. Off to join them and fight the Kalksis together . . .

Obvious pleasure on Ling's face. Has he met a kindred spirit? Maybe not, something else in the American woman's face, in her face, not in those liquid silver eyes. Torment? Maybe.

Kanthol, the City on the Mountain, glittered atop its crag, as if its buildings were made from the purest of white marble, as if its domes were plated in gold, platinum, silver, electrum. Like some Hellenistic city of old. No. Not quite. Hellenes painted their marble cities in pastels, reds and blues. and in rich browns, greens. This city, Kanthol, was like the Greek cities as eighteenth century European tourists imagined them to be, dreaming among the weathered ruins.

Walking and walking. And listening. Listening to the American woman . . . can she really be 130 years old? Look at those luscious breasts, those broad, fertile hips . . . Listening to her tell the story. Can it really be true, this story of the Colonists and the Scavengers, the old abandoned system of Stargates, beginning with the one under the Moon?

Of course it can. We're *here*.

It was some time, she'd said, before we understood they *weren't* Stargates, leading nowhere anyone could see. Gateways to other universes, to other times in other universes. gateways across creation itself. We'd had the mathematics, the quantum cosmology to understand it for more than fifty years before we went to the Moon. It just didn't seem like the highest probability explanation. Besides which, we *wanted* them to be Stargates.

And why did you come home, after finding such a thing? Why did you create Fortress America? Why did you . . . *hide*?

She'd said, Let me tell you a little bit about something the Scavengers liked to call the Space-Time Juggernaut. We just like to call it the Jug . . .

So. Is there really something, an entity of some kind, loose out here in the . . . the Multiverse, cosmologists call it, something which doesn't want us probing out among the gates?

Something, Kincaid told them, which destroyed the Colonists on all their worlds. Something which destroyed the Scavengers when they went looting among the worlds. Something which almost destroyed us.

Something, said Lord Genda Hiroshige, which erased the very fabric of the universe I called home.

Possible?

Why not, considering what's turned out to be possible so far?

Rahman, long quiet as they walked and walked, said, Why has it left the gates open then? Why not close them all and keep us all home where we belong?

Home where we belong.

Genda only smiled, and said, "Good question. When my own universe was destroyed, utterly destroyed, apparently down to its very atoms, though I got away before then—all that remained were the gates—floating alone in the black void."

"A wonder you survived."

"A wonder indeed. I was on hyperdrive as the stars fell. I got through the gate. Call it luck."

Call it anything you like.

By nightfall they were down on the dusty plains and rolling hills west of the mountain range, but the city of Kanthol, lit now by a hundred thousand twinkling golden lights, hardly seemed closer at all.

A long walk, a long night's walk, and Subaïda Rahman sat in a little outdoor cafe in the heart of Kanthol, City on the Mountain, wishing mightily for fresh clothing, and thought, *Butyl mercaptan*. That's it. My armpits smell like a natural gas pipeline leak. Any minute now there'll be a little spark and I'll explode, taking this whole silly world with me. We few, we band of heroes . . . I'm thinking like a madwoman again.

They sat at a nice round table, the twelve of them together, drinking from little sake glasses of what tasted like DeKuyper's Peppermint Schnapps. White marble buildings towering all around them, towering from crag to crag, slanting rays of brilliant, late-afternoon sunlight throwing long shadows down a red brick paved avenue, avenue thronged with hordes of bustling red ants, ants going *clangety-clang* as they maneuvered around one another, going *clickety-clack*, plastic skin on plastic skin.

City On the Mountain? Mirth. Ought to call it Kanthol, City of the Living Fire Engines. All we need now is to hear the hoo-hah of a French police car tootling in the distance and my life would be complete . . .

Pity the red ants aren't people. At least I could get some fresh underwear then . . .

Image of herself, like Jensen here, dressed in red-ant harness. How would I look? I'm in good shape, nice breasts, not too large, not too small. Firm waist. I wonder if I have a nice-looking rear end . . .

Inbar leaned close, peppermint breath masking the fact that he hadn't brushed his teeth in a week, and whispered, "What're you smiling about?"

Soap bubble popped. By the one person here who'd be ever so glad to advise me about my rear end. "Nothing. Daydreaming."

He said, "Not really necessary. Not here." Looking up at that orange sky, that brilliant pink sun.

Across the table, Ling and Laing, Genda and Kincaid were sitting together, talking. The others. Jensen tinkling away with his . . . wife? How very odd that seemed. Not quite the way it is in children's storybooks. The pretty Oriental girl, a robot incredibly, sitting to one side, talking with that little American who called himself Brucie, little man bright-eyed, focused on her in an obvious way. The big black thing with the white eyes and strange name sitting with them, with some strange interest of . . . her? Stranger and stranger. In any event, with some interest of her own. And Inbar. And Alireza. And me. Rather like outsiders here. I wonder why?

Genda, voice rather forceful, rather certain, was saying, "You're not *going* to get home. *None* of you are. It is almost certain the Juggernaut is sniffing along your trail even now, making what rectifications it can."

Hard pang. Hard pang inside. *Not going home.* And that other possibility, the possibility that home is . . . gone. A deep hollow forming within her. Rahman thought, This is *not* what I wanted. Remembered image then, the excitement of going into space, going to the Moon. Space-Faring Civilization. Mars of the red sky, black at zenith, lit by a cold, faraway Sun. Voyages to the asteroids. Jupiter a fat orange ball, hanging over Callisto's black-ice horizon, hanging over the spires and domes and steamy smokes of the new volatiles plant they would one day build.

Image of an old woman. Subaïda Rahman, life winding down, spending her last productive days among the moons of lovely yellow Saturn.

Cold sense of despair.

That dream is lost.

And . . . this one?

Unknown. Perhaps unknowable.

Ling said, "How can you be sure? It's been almost a century since the Americans first found the gate system. They haven't been 'rectified.' Maybe if we just turn back . . ."

Kincaid, quiet, reflective: "The rectification—a good word for it—is retroactive. The Jug will have pulled our whole timeline."

Ling, with obvious disbelief: "Then why were the Scavenger worlds left behind? Why are the gates themselves still in place?"

Genda: "I don't know."

Kincaid: "The Scavengers didn't know either. They knew about the Jug itself from Colonial literature they'd read. We think they kept on pushing out into the gate system on the assumption that they'd simply misunderstood. After all, the Colonial worlds themselves are still intact, if a little beat up.

The Jug seems like . . . well. Like eschatological literature. You know: like the last chapter of the Bible. I am the Alpha and the Omega. I am coming to punish every one for what he has done. That sort of thing."

Rahman heard Alireza whisper, *"When the sky is rent asunder; when the stars scatter and the oceans roll together; when the graves are hurled about; each soul shall know what it has done, and what it has failed to do."*

The others, fallen silent, were staring at him. Had he spoken in English or in Arabic? She couldn't remember. Probably the latter. His English wasn't really that good.

"And yet," said Kincaid, "I know the Space-Time Juggernaut is real."

"And I." Somber-faced Genda said, *"Al-Infitahr* 82:1. I've had a lot of time to think about this business." He turned back to the main conversation, and said, "We're safe enough, here in the Pseudouniverse, whether inside the script manager, or back in the main thread. I don't think it matters."

"Unless," said Amaterasu, "the parent Creation that led to the Ohanaic subset is rectified."

Strange. I didn't notice she'd moved away from Brucie, had come to sit by Genda's side again. The little American was focused on the tall black thing now. Tarantellula? Quite focused, in fact. Surely he wasn't thinking . . .

Laing said, "No one knows what that is. Beyond the audience track, there may be no more than some prehyperspatial variation of Earth. As long as they keep their noses out of other people's business and stay home where they belong, we're safe enough."

Genda said, "I've had time to sample a number of the script manager's alternate histories. In most timelines, Earthmen stay home."

Laing said, "In most timelines, Earthmen are extinct. Or never existed."

Rahman thought, *Script manager.* Interesting concept. How does he knows those timelines aren't just more . . . stories?

Kincaid said, "Scavengers never figured any of this out. They treated the Colonial gate system more or less like a set of interstellar transporters, even though they knew that wasn't the case, knew they were loose in the Multiverse. That's why it took us so long to figure out what was really going on. I think maybe the Scavengers thought if they stayed away from the probability manager, the Jug'd just let them be."

Genda stretched, leaning back in his chair, reaching out to put his arm around Amaterasu's shoulders. "Come with us. My ship's up in the hills. We can reach one of the deep space gates and get out of this skein entirely."

Alireza: "And go where?"

He smiled. "I've been trying to figure that out for the last four hundred years. I've picked up a clue here and there, even some good ones right here on Arrasûn. I've got a good idea where to go next."

"And do what?"

Rahman thought, Good question. Go off to God knows where and find . . . what? Why? We're just *lost*.

Genda said, "I think maybe it's the Space-Time Juggernaut we're looking for. I'd like to go home again. Or at least to somewhere, somewhen I can pretend is home. Somewhere I can imagine is safe. Jug alone knows where that might be."

Alireza's voice was oddly strained: "You sound like you're talking about God."

Genda merely stared at him, not quite smiling.

Is that what he thinks, then? Does he believe this . . . Jug is God? Cold thought. Could *I* believe that? I never *really* believed in God. Not in my heart of hearts. What if . . . just that. What *if*?

Laing said, "I think you're right. Let's go."

Jensen: "*Us*? We can't do that. We're not real."

Laing said, "Sure we can. And, out of skein, we're as real as any of these *people*."

"Well . . ." Red ant wifey tugging on his arm, going *tingety-ting*, Jensen making *clangclang* right back. He looked at Laing and said, "She doesn't want me to leave. I think."

Laing smirked. "Bring her along, asshole."

A glance at his ant, a worried look. "But . . ."

"Look, we're damned well off-script now. Have been ever since these people showed up. Someone *else* is living our lives. We're dead. If we don't go with them, *you* go back to inactive routine status 'til somebody needs parts for a hero. Think about it."

"Um. Well. You've got a point there." And *clingety-cling* to the antwife.

Rahman leaned forward slowly, feeling the intensity build. Going forward now, forward into . . . ? Not exactly the unknown. Forward into another dream? Subaïda Rahman, loose among all the worlds that could ever be? No so much like that other dream, a dream in which I ranged forward in the name of Humanity, but . . . she said, "How can you leave the story for which you were made? Characters in a book are . . . fixed."

Laing smiled at her. "In a book, yes, it would seem so. But *Crimson Desert* is . . . was an interactive drama. We're not characters in just this one story, you know. There are others."

Jensen, wistful, "I wish I could remember them now."

Ling said, "I find myself imagining that I can somehow access memories from all the many histories in which my . . . total self has participated."

Total self. Rahman thought, In the fantasy concept of Many Worlds, variations on *me* are, even now, living out their lives. What would it be like to know all those lives at once?

Laing said, "From within, the story of *Crimson Desert* is real; from without, merely a story, however mutable. On this skein, the characters may not leave the story, may not become *real*. But, when we pass through the Stargate to another skein . . ."

Kincaid laughed. "Somewhere, even now, there are eyes on a page."

Rahman thought, Somewhere, eyes on a page, a mind imagining that it will, like *that*, fall into the page, join the story, become one with . . . Cusp. Is that what they call it? With that mind's imagining, a cusp is broken. And, on an infinite number of worlds, the reader falls into the story, is caught up in the storm. Which becomes real. As all things possible must, somewhere, be real.

The Kantholian flier, a rusty, shuddering old bucket flown by some crusty-looking red ants, dropped them at the head of a deep ravine back up in the mountains, left them atop the cliff and took off again while the pink sun was still high overhead, flying away into the cloudless, bright orange sky like an iridescent golden soap bubble making good its escape on dry winds scented with emery dust. Down below, nestled among the tumbled red stones, lay Genda's starship, *Baka-no-Koto*.

Shading her eyes, staring down at the silvery glitter of its hull, Rahman muttered, "A flying saucer. Why am I not surprised?" *Because the public fantasies of the Americans are part of their technological history.*

Passiphaë Laing put one hand on her shoulder, the feel of those strong fingers making her jump slightly, making her skin crawl, and said, "So. *I'm* a little surprised, Mr. Genda. You said this was the ship you brought from your own timeline. Looks just like an Ohanaic Fleet scoutship to me."

Genda said, "Yes. Well. Not quite a coincidence, I suppose. Perhaps why the gates led me directly here. Turns out the technology of my twenty-fifth century led to the discovery of our version of your Type One hyperdrive. And, of course, when it comes to faster-than-light transport, function presupposes form."

Laing looked at him, frowning. "Maybe."

Alireza, thinking of the way high-performance supersonic fighters tended to resemble each other, said, "What does all that mean?"

She said, "In the Ohanaic Pseudouniverse, on the skein containing the audience-track thread for *Crimson Desert*, at least, FTL travel was developed in the late twenty-first century, during the age of the Zarinist World State, more or less unexpectedly. The technology, now called a Type One hyperdrive, was kept a military secret. Still is. Later on we got into a scrap with another species, the Krü, who had their own hyperdrive, what we called Type Two. Beat them."

Rahman thought, *Audience-track?* Reminders, from one moment to the next . . .

Genda smiled mirthlessly. "The Type One hyperdrive can hit metavelocities of around four hundred cee. Type Two is limited to something like ninety. Of course you beat them."

Rahman said, "Was that your ship we found crashed up in the mountains?"

Pause for a heartbeat. "Yes. It had a Type Two drive," said Laing.

Genda said, "There's a Type Three, the human commercial drive developed at the dawn of the Terran Empire, not quite as good as Type Two, but something you can just buy, so long as you've got a good line of commercial credit. And we mustn't forget the Bimus drive, better, by a tad, just maybe, than the Fleet's Type One . . ."

Jensen, arm around his wife's shiny shoulders, still looking down at the ship, said, "Not to mention the Niijold drive, faster still, and whatever the Hell magic it is the Mydhra seem to be . . ."

Laing, angry: "God damn it, we aren't that far into the story yet! We're at *least* a half-century from the first Niijold military encounter."

Rahman heard Kincaid mutter, "Jesus Christ . . ."

Later, four of them sat in *Baka-no-Koto*'s parlor-like control room, looking out through a transparent patch of hull-metal. Ling gazed out over a fall of sun-splashed flat rocks where the others languished over a late picnic lunch, lunch prepared, seemingly without labor—without effort at any rate—by Amaterasu, bustling about in the ship's tiny, magical galley.

Genda said, "We're going to be in each other's laps for the whole trip. Unpleasant possibly, twelve people crowding into a ship intended for three, built for five in a pinch."

Kincaid snorted. "I thought you Japanese liked togetherness."

"On your Earth, maybe. On mine, each terrestrial inhabitant is a wealthy person, living alone on his or her landed estate, surrounded only by mechanical servitors."

A sharp whiff of familiarity. Ling said, "Like in *The Naked Sun*?"

The others looked at him, faces blank, then Laing said, "So. Where's this special gate of yours sitting?"

"There's a very big tunable cargo gate about eight parsecs

from here. I think it's the one we want. Certainly indicated by the old Orovar records I came here to look at."

"Just floating in space, all by itself?"

"In solitary galactic orbit, yes."

Kincaid: "And you can make this trip at four hundred times the speed of light? Eight parsecs seems like a long way."

Genda frowned. "This ship's drive is not . . . as good as it could be. Three weeks, maybe. A little more."

Kincaid gestured out the window. "Your life support system up to that?"

"Of course. I'm more concerned about the lavatory than anything else."

Ling, watching the way that strange little American, Brucie, was following the robot around down below, said, "Some of us will probably mind being in each other's laps more than others." A glance at frowning Lord Genda, thinking, *Or maybe not.*

Kincaid said, "You keep telling us about a universe in which people fly around in various sorts of sluggish, hyperdriven starships. What are these gates *for*? Why aren't they part of the story?"

Predictable, thought Ling.

Laing said, "They're not part of the story, just part of the infrastructure."

Kincaid: "And what about the audience track?"

Laing: "I don't know. I'm not part of the audience track."

Genda said, "There are no gates, of course. No way to get out there from in here."

Odd. Ling said, "Then how . . ."

Genda: "*Crimson Darkness* is programmed into a hyperspatial information network that operates through something called a Level Six hyperdrive generator. It can move physical objects like the lower level drives—the audience track universe can't muster the technology for that—but it can be used to transmit information. Their whole knowledge base is in here with us. I can get at that, even though I can't get at *them*."

Then . . . "Then these gates are just packet switching cards in an old-fashioned wide-area network?"

Laing said, "Sort of."

Sort of. Pulse of fear. "Then how do we know . . ." He suddenly felt very short of breath. No way in. No way out. "How do we know there's any reality beyond this network?"

Laing, grinning, "We don't." Something mean-spirited in her eyes.

Kincaid said, "Some of us got in here from an external reality."

Ling said, "If that's all the gates are, then it must be an 'external reality' that's . . . part of this network." No. I do not wish to believe that I'm not real. I . . .

Genda said, "That's an easy inference to draw, professor. It'd simplify things no end. But the fact is, all quantum processes are linked through the Toolbox to Platonic Reality. It's why you have an experience you call consciousness."

Laing said, "And why I do, though I'm just a subroutine in a star-spanning information network."

Genda: "And so, when we go through the gate, we link to the other parts of the *real* gatenet, access the Multiverse, and what was real in here is also real out there."

An hour, then a day, another day then another, while *Bakano-Koto* spun through the dark between the stars, that classic dark of song and story, the stars still no more than jewels against the sky, unmoving. Unlike, *most* unlike all the old images . . .

Robert Bruce Tanner Davidson the Third sat alone down in the hyperdrive bay, sitting stripped to a pair of black-and-gold paisley briefs, sweating into the drive bay's hot, dry air, air like the inside of a kiln, looking out through the hull at the motionless sky.

Sky with the power to entrance. The power to entrance me, magic me away from everything mundane, though I'll soon be two hundred years old . . .

He kept glancing back at the Type One hyperdrive, technically the Harveson Translight Overdrive Generator unit. That had the power to entrance as well. The power to call forth memory of emotion, of remembered fancy. Little gears and spinning disks, disks that cast forth rainbows, disks that sang as they turned to mist. Little masts projecting here and there, turning spindles bound together by silvery bits of whirling Möbius strip.

More mist. A whiff of distant suns. Did Seacaptain Chandler tell us true? If I fall in there will I come back inside-out? Will my comrades have to shoot me out of my misery? Or will the ghostgirl do for me what she did for the German soldier's glove?

Too many close calls with death. A man my age should be long dead. Maybe I am dead. I don't even remember the Korean War, though I was already a school-age boy, though my unremembered father died in that faraway land.

Far away? He never knew. I never imagined. So many different lives. So many possible histories. If I hadn't studied aerospace engineering, I'd never have grown rich building rocket engine components for the American Renaissance. And if I hadn't grown rich, I wouldn't have had the medical care I needed, two heart transplants, an artificial liver, three new sets of kidneys as I grew older and older still.

I was 112 years old the day I sat with my shawl in my lap, on a balcony overlooking the garden of my country home, when that cute little nurse brought me the paper, *Times* was it? Little nursie shaking with excitement, and I read the headline, "Eternal Life."

I almost died laughing that day. Almost. She had to defib me twice before the medevac Moller came to cart me away for treatment . . .

Outside, the stars were ruby and amber, sapphire and bright, bright gold. The magic hatch to the drive bay dilated open and an immense, angular black shape wriggled in, filling the room with the sound of breath, the faint scent of living flesh. Tarantellula said, "Wondered how you managed to disappear."

Brucie Big-Dick looked at her and smiled: "I never really enjoyed crowds." She'd gotten out of her Marine combat fatigues, was wearing what looked like a pair of white silk briefs and some kind of thin halter-top. Black breasts concealed there? Hard to tell. The girlclothes looked incongruous on her. Like Godzilla dressed in a pink lace teddy. King Kong in a bustier.

But it's not hot back in the crew cabin, no matter how many people are breathing up the air. Why is she dressed down? Silence between them for a moment, white eyes so featureless you couldn't tell . . . Christ. Is she looking at my crotch? No. I'm just imagining things.

He said, "Why'd you do that to yourself?"

Tarantellula stared, reached up and ran one spidery hand over her face, feeling its hard, rough texture, the pores and granules of an obviously artificial skin. "It's not the only thing I've been. Why'd you do *that* to yourself?" Gesturing at the front of his shorts.

He smiled, shrugged. It was down there, all right, waiting like a coiled-up snake. Or maybe like an uncooked kielbasa? He said, "When I was a boy, all I ever wanted was a big dick, you know? Something to show off in phys ed class, when we went to the showers."

White eyes looking at him, unreadable.

He said, "Muscles. Money. Power. Enough brains and determination, you can get all that. All I ever wanted was a big dick. One day I got rich enough to buy one."

A nod, as if she understood. "Most women don't like that, you know."

"So what? Most don't, some do. I'm only interested in the ones that do." Besides, doesn't she remember dear little Chuckie?

She said, "That robot's not going to fuck you, you know."

A shrug. Yes. Too bad. If I was home I could get a kit and build one for myself, but . . . outside, the stars. Impossible stars, of course, but . . . He said, "Tarantella. That's the dance you do when you're bitten by an Italian wolf spider, right?"

"I guess." She said, "Sergeant Kincaid's not going to fuck you either. Pining away for some dead guy or another."

Do tell . . . "Tarantellula, that's just a little one?"

A shrug. "Arab girl neither. Supposed to be a lezzie."

I wonder. Did she check to make sure Rhino Jensen

wouldn't loan me his ant? "So. You ask Ms. Laing for me yet, Miles Standish?"

Staring white eyes, hard mouth expressionless. She said, "I'm not sure that one even has a cunt."

Such language.

Tarantellula said, "She won't fuck you, but I might."

Brucie Big-Dick smiled, and thought, Well. All things come to he who waits? He said, "Times sure have changed . . ." Watched that big, angular black head nod. "Most women aren't quite so forward, even now."

Thin black lips opened, showing teeth as white as the eyes. Teeth and a narrow, flickering black tongue. A grin? She said, "How do you know I'm a woman?"

Hmh. "How do *you* know I'm a man?"

"Fair enough."

"OK." He put his thumbs under the waistband of his briefs and slid his shorts off over his rump, let that enormous schlong unfurl and lie full length, flaccid on the floor of the drive bay.

One long look, then she said, "What the Hell is that in your pubic hair? *Lips?*"

Brucie Big-Dick looked down and grinned. Opened that extra mouth and extruded his extra tongue, wiggled it around, licked his crotchlips, moistening them. "The first new girl-friend I had after I bought the big dick thought this'd be a nice touch. Turns out she was right. I just have to be careful not to get it pinched between our pubic bones. You'll like it, I think . . ."

Were those white eyes, somehow, brightening at the thought? Maybe she'd never met anyone with a decent erotic imagination before. She said, "If you had little eyes down there, it'd make a cute little face."

He opened his other eyes, grinned from both his mouths, and made the crotchmouth whisper, "Well, I *do* like to watch . . ."

When she slid off her own shorts, he had the decency to gape before he grinned. Those . . . *teeth* of hers were a nice touch, too. Yes indeed.

* * *

*We are all animals. You may reject that animal self as a
personal choice, but doing so does not make you more of a
person, or less of an animal.* Dale Millikan's words. When
did he say that? Just to me, whispered, in the middle of the
night, maybe whispered while his head was resting on my
thigh, just before or after . . .

Or was it in one of those damned silly books and stories
the scientists were always twitting him about? Sophomoric
bullshit. Dr. Jessup said that, scaling Dale's latest opus
toward a trash bin. Pissed him off no end. I told him if he was
going to say *asshole* so much, he'd need to cultivate a men-
acing accent.

Sitting on the sofa beside her, Ling Erhshan said, "I didn't
think that'd make you smile. The sketches are supposed to be
of you, aren't they?" Ling's voice reticent, almost embarrassed. Not too embarrassed to keep on looking.

Kincaid had one of Millikan's old notebooks, one of the
ones the Arabs had stolen from the barracks on Mars-Plus,
from Dale's room, open in her lap. Flipping from page to
page, reading bits and snatches of his familiar old words in
that familiar green ink. Solid, accurate diagrams of gate control systems, Dale's own speculations about what the gate
system meant, where it'd come from, who the Scavengers
were, the Colonials. Wild, unscientific guesses about the
nature of the Space-Time Juggernaut.

Right now, it was open to a fairly detailed green ink sketch
of a woman's crotch. She glanced over at Ling. Right.
Looking at the crotch, not at me, just the way you'd expect
any man with the correct gender-orientation to . . . Kincaid
grunted, looking away, exasperated.

More pages turned, more diagrams, more green words.
Dale Millikan always scribbling in his notebooks, pen and
paper in hand, hardly ever using the palmtop he'd been
assigned. Not *real*, you see. Not real at all.

"What was he like?"

Kincaid looked at Ling, at the honest curiosity in his eyes.
What was he like? What's anyone like, when you fall in love?
As long as you love them, the sun never sets. When you stop
loving them, it shines elsewhere. But what about when you

lose them? What about when they go away and love someone else? What about when they die and leave you behind? Sensible people learn to put those things aside. You're supposed to shrug and say, Life goes on . . .

She shrugged and said, "Overweight. Middle-aged. Clever. Fun to be with. A surly bastard, sometimes." No. You can see that's not what he meant.

Ling said, "I read some of his books when I was a child. Part of the reason, maybe, why I'm here."

"Which ones?"

"Well." Eyes far away, searching his childhood, flipping the pages of those lost books again and again. "*Moon Man*, principally."

Kincaid snorted. "I never liked that one. The women in it were just whores. Mattresses for the men."

Ling felt a slight breathlessness. A whore? Gothic Princess Valetta? Remembered image of Dorian Haldane, middle-aged white male American soldier, stealing Princess Valetta from the mansion of her Kalksis lord, stealing her, taking her away to the mountains. Princess Valetta so passive, so serene, lying naked upon the lush Lunar grasses, purple grasses, mauve grasses under a dark mulberry sky, sprawled just *so*, while soldier Haldane stared at her nakedness, stared in surrogate for the readers.

Princess Valetta lying just *so* while Haldane and the readers fucked her. I used to read that scene and masturbate. Ling suddenly realized he was smiling. "Well," he said, "I can . . . imagine, I suppose, why you might feel that way."

Kincaid snorted again. "No you can't."

Ling Erhshan said, "Perhaps not. I had a girlfriend once who was an avid reader of English Romance novels. I tried to read a few of them once."

Clean underwear is a many-splendored thing. Not something you give much thought to, ordinarily; but, like regular sex, something you really miss when you haven't got it.

Subaïda Rahman sat alone in *Baka-no-Koto*'s ventral gun turret, watching the stars' silent float, imagining all the worlds out among those silent jewels, imagining herself among them. Worlds of the future in all the stories, worlds of humanity, thousands of worlds scattered all down one long galactic arm; worlds of non-humanity, millions, billions, trillions of worlds, filling up an entire universe of light.

And, yet, here I sit, happiest of all because I've got clean panties to wear. That made her smile, looking out at the stars.

Four days to go. Can't get there soon enough for me. Enough of this. Little cubbies and hiding places not enough anymore, time hanging on all their hands, putting them back in each other's laps once again. Hard to avoid people, even when you hide. Even when they hide.

Hard to avoid sulking Inbar's shadowy eyes, watching you, making you remember him coming to you in the night, once again and . . . Hard to avoid things you never thought you'd do. Slinking about the almost-dark ship in the middle of that "night," starlight flooding in here and there, making shadows, shadows in which to lurk.

The door irised open and there was a shadow out in the corridor. Shadow just standing there, looking in at her. Alireza's voice said, "May I come in?"

She felt the urge to say no, to tell him, *Just go away*. But . . . "Of course. Come in."

He came through the door, which closed itself behind him, slid down the curve of the far wall, positioning himself in the little space beyond the gun control console. Not looking at her. Looking out through the transparent hull. Eyes on the stars. Her stars.

I feel like he's . . . taking something from me. Silly. This has become my space. That view . . . an integral part of this space.

He said, "You seem upset, Rahman. Subaïda. Is there something . . ."

Ah yes. The good military commander looks out for the psychological well-being of his troops. But he called me by my first name. Not a good sign. Not a good sign at all. "Nothing important. I'm having a little difficulty with the long confinement. I'll be glad when it's over."

His eyes were bright, liquid looking, shining in reflected

starlight. "It's hard, isn't it? If this . . . if *this* hadn't happened, we'd've been home a week ago."

A week ago. Does that mean anything now? Where are we now? When? Now? Lost in a place that isn't even *real* . . .

He said, "I've had a talk with Inbar. He really is sorry he bothered you. This kind of . . . close confinement is hard on a man."

But not on a woman, you silly bastard? She said, "I really wish you hadn't . . ." Now, when I see him, see him looking at me, I can't pretend it didn't happen.

He glanced at her, then back out into the sea of suns. He said, "This is your fertile period now, isn't it?"

Rahman felt her insides clench, tension, anger welling up, threatening to spill over into the confined space of the turret. What *right* do you have to invade my . . .

He turned and looked at her, stared, something on his face, almost a supercilious grin. "When I was sitting in the command chair this evening, you came and stood next to me for just a few minutes, with your hips about on level with my face . . ."

Nothing then but a moment of anger welling within, threatening to spill out through eyes and mouth and . . .

He held up a hand, palm toward her. "You think I'm just taking a turn vying for the prize of your . . . *favors*, don't you? You imagine me telling myself, the fat Jew wasn't good enough for her, but I, a nobleman, military officer, man among men . . ."

"Colonel Alireza." Her voice was sharp, very abrupt. Implicit *please stop* unspoken.

Suddenly he was looking out at the stars again, smile faded away to nothing at all. "I wish I could tell you I didn't feel those things. I wish I didn't feel them, for my soul's sake. But the truth is . . ."

A feeling of dread, a feeling of horrid disappointment. Here it comes.

He said, "The truth is, I love my wife, my children, my home, the service, my country, the world. I love God. I have His Word to guide me. That's enough to contain all the evil that lurks in every man's heart."

The anger continued to build, feeding on itself, confronted now by this *superior* bastard. But the angry words were contained.

He said, "Most of my friends, my close military friends, people I've lived with all my life, still don't want to believe in the reality of human reproductive pheromones. It just seems so . . . dehumanizing? So out of tune with our culture, with our history. With life itself."

An understandable truth. If a woman doesn't want to regard herself as a dog in heat, would a thoughtful man want to see himself as part of a pack of slobbering hounds? *Kalb.* An insult among insults, insult with a long, filthy history. Humanity transcends. Without that transcendence, you are no more than a dog.

Alireza smiling at her again: "Their lack of belief doesn't stop the pheromones from being real, from reaching out of a woman's body and putting dirty thoughts in a man's head."

Rahman remembered a phrase from a hundred-fifty-year-old American sociology textbook she'd read as part of one of her early courses in the history of technology.

Blame the victim.

He said, "They're like atheists, in a way. Atheists think if they don't *believe*, then the reality will . . . go away. And yet they understand that our *faith* has nothing at all to do with the existence of God. You'd think intelligent people would be able to make that logical inference, wouldn't you?"

You'd think that.

She remembered reading about early American attitudes toward the possibility of nuclear war. If we *talk* about it, you see, if we talk about it like it *can* happen, maybe it *will* happen . . .

An implicit belief in something like synchronicity. As if the effect could somehow invoke the cause. After a while, he left, leaving her to wonder why she hadn't spoken up.

He's not a bad man. A good man, a sound man, trying to do what he thinks is right. The rest of it's in . . . in me. I have to accept that. People . . . All of us just people.

For a brief moment, a fantasy image welled up, unbidden, out of some intractable depth. What if he *had* come in, looking for . . . What if it'd been Alireza, also aware of her silly political pretense, instead of wretched Inbar, come to . . . proposition her in the night?

Image of herself, for just a moment, grappling with Alireza, the possible thrill of it a creeping buzz somewhere down below. Because it always was no more than just a pretense.

Image of sweaty grappling followed by a sudden, harrowing image of herself cooing over babies, a sudden, intense, horribly undeniable longing. A spark of feral understanding. Hormonally-driven desire.

I remember somebody saying it, once upon a time. Was the speaker a man or a woman? I don't remember. Just remember the notion suggested, that women are horny for babies precisely the same way men are horny for women. All I remember is how angry that idea made me.

No way, in this world, for me to be both a woman *and* a person.

Damn them.

Outside, the cargo gate was floating superimposed against the velvet black of deep space, no more than a collection of silvery loops and rings and squares of magic wire. No auras. No fields. No spectral surfaces. You could see the distant stars right through it.

Genda Hiroshige said, "When I arrived here, four hundred years ago, I arrived through one of these gates. Came sailing on through while darkness snapped at my heels . . ." Remember that image: stars falling from the sky, falling into the abyss, like bits of white rice paper fluttering through the night.

Ling Erhshan thought, We have all the pieces at our fingertips now. But we still don't have any answers. We go through this gate and find . . . what? Yet another universe? A new world? Another skein, some thread or another? Why?

Amaterasu rising, walking away, going somewhere else in the little ship. Conscious of men's eyes following her, focused on hip movement? She's a robot, why should she care?

Genda said, "There're old ruins down on the *Crimson Desert* set. The planet has been inhabited, according to the baseline script bible, for something like two million years. Terrestrial years, of course." He glanced at Ling, looking for understanding, perhaps. "We've been following a common knowledge thread through these old worlds, out near the edge of what used to be the Parahuan Imperium, before humans and Bimus got through with it."

Kincaid said, "So where do you think the gate leads?" Implicit: anywhere worthwhile? How would you define *worthwhile*, under these circumstances?

Amaterasu came back, carrying something that looked like an oversized bronze briefcase, handed it over to Genda, resumed her seat.

"Well, well," said Passiphaë Laing. "What're you doing with a portable Bimus military computer?"

Genda said nothing, orienting the thing across his knees, opening the case to reveal oversized bronze keys, arrayed like a standard keyboard, embossed with miscellaneous, unrecognizable characters, a flat, blank screen . . .

Ling whispered, "So the Bimus have five-fingered hands, do they?"

Genda looked at him. Nodded. "Quite." He snapped the lid back against the hinge-lock and the screen lit with a mellow chime, white light scrolling upward, colorful icons placing themselves one by one.

Brucie Big-Dick, sitting in Tarantellula's lap, snickered. "Two thousand years in the 'future' and they still use those things? I haven't seen a powerbook since I was . . . Hell, since I was middle-aged."

Genda ignored him, tapping at this key and that, rolling the little brass trackball around with his thumb, going *clickety-click* on first this icon, then that one.

Flicker of light from outside. Colored mist swirling out of nowhere, swirling, filling the gate, blotting out the bright glitter of faraway suns. Staring out into space, out into a universe flooded by rainbows, Kincaid said, "Now, we go through this gate and emerge into the Multiverse. Off-skein, out-of-sweater, or whatever term you want to propose. I still do not see . . ."

Genda smiled at her. "If the Orovar records are correct, it will lead us straight to God's Machine."

Ling thought, *God's Machine?* Lots of remembered discussion, about the focus of Genda's Quest. About the possible structure of the Multiverse. But no one's used the term . . .

Genda smiled and laid his hands on the controls, tilting the ship, nudging it forward, until they fell through the gate and . . .

Blink.

A new view out the control room "windows," black space gone, Stargate and rainbows, replaced by a blue-gray-green field, brilliant, violet-white spark just off-center, obviously closer, closer to them than the . . . backdrop. Distant backdrop, but not infinitely distant. More like "purple mountains' majesty."

Ling Erhshan felt the couch vibrate under him, soft, suggestive movement, and heard Rhino Jensen mutter, "What the Hell . . ." Saw Laing put her hand on Kincaid's shoulder and say, "Right through the gravity polarizer field?"

Genda seemed aghast, staring down at his instruments, then back up at the view, chattering something, a brief comment in Japanese. Hard shudder now, crockery breaking somewhere in the background, and Amaterasu's arms became a blur, hands flying over the control console. Her own controls, Genda's controls.

Outside, the world flared incandescent pink, brightening to white, tinged with purple-red. Kincaid said, "Plasma sheath . . ." Another hard shudder, something going *clunk* under the floor.

Genda's voice, a whispered hiss: "This doesn't make any sense at all. Four thousand kilometers from a planetary surface, under one-gee, but a dense atmosphere . . ."

Amaterasu looked, said, "In all directions," kept her hands flying. The brilliant spark ahead of them approached fast, slid to one side, swept on by, going behind them, warping their trajectory, but the view ahead stayed more or less the same, detail on detail, patches of brown and green, silvery patterns like forked lightening, things that looked like broad river systems of white . . .

Those are mountain ranges I'm seeing. Seeing from far, far above. Old astronaut films . . . and my one brief moment of glory, looking down from *Ming Tian* as it swept around the world toward TLI. Mountains growing fast, pimpling up into 3-D reality.

Brucie, leaning forward, staring out at an approaching wall of *world*, said, "Good thing we weren't moving fast relative to the gate."

Ling looked into the control console, found a set of numbers that seemed to represent some kind of relative velocity. Numbers getting smaller as *Baka-no-Koto* rammed through air. We must look like some vast falling star . . .

Kincaid said, "What the Hell is that?" Pointing.

A tiny, silvery speck in the . . . sky? Hard to call it that. Sky is empty space that goes on forever, colored sometimes by scattered light. Here, there was ground everywhere you looked. Silvery thing growing larger: *Aircraft*. Sort of. Cigar-shaped hull with four long outriggers, cylindrical objects at the end of each strut jetting longish orange flames. Silvery thing growing larger, turning, turning, orange flames growing much longer as it turned. Trying to get out of our way.

It suddenly became huge, blotting out the view for a moment, and *Baka-no-Koto* shook, roaring like a gong from the collision. They went on, trailing bits of the whatever it was. In a small viewscreen by Genda's elbow there was a view aft, a view of that ship, tumbling now, red fire coming out of it in odd directions, falling away, falling away trailing a plume of gray smoke. Sorry. Sorry, whoever you are.

A distant keening sound now, mournful wail from a thousand sorrowing tongues. A familiar sound, rising in pitch. Sound familiar from a thousand old movies. Sound few people live to remember having heard. Ling felt a small, soft regret start up as he realized it was the sound of the air planing across *Baka-no-Koto*'s hull as they fell and fell. Surely, this isn't how it ends. It's as if all our lives are a scripted tale. Hero never dies. Hero lives, prospers, gets the girl, lives and loves, while only the spear-carriers fall, only the villains are erased . . .

Outside, the landscape grew, mountains rearing, forests passing swiftly underneath. Ling Erhshan watched, entranced as the black shadow of their ship, racing across this strange new world, became larger, keeping pace beneath them, growing from a tiny dot to a big black circle in the twinkling of an eye. Watched it grow vast, a pall of deepening regret, shadow swallowing the light outside, until the ship crashed.

Six.

I Am the Only Being.

Opsimath. One who begins learning late in life.

I learned a lot of words early in life. A lot more toward the end, when I began to understand it was the knowing itself I treasured, rather than the utility of knowledge.

Lots of words flooding out of my many minds now. Omnipotence, the quality of Almightiness, you see. Omniscience, strictly: infinite knowledge, hyperbolically: universal knowledge. In the there and then, I remember puzzling over that one. Did the man who wrote the Official Definition have some basis for thinking *infinite* was more all-encompassing than *universal?* I mean, the Universe is supposed to be *everything*. Maybe he thought there was a limited supply of things and ideas, somehow less than infinity . . . maybe he'd been listening to Georg Cantor.

Omnipresent? That's me. Present in all places at the same time. That's me. God is not ubiquitous, but omnipresent.

One of the bits of me forwarded its favorite word. *Omnify.* To make everything of; to account as all in all. To make universal. Yes, that was what had happened to me, all right.

Bits and pieces and doppelgängers and iterations, all of them out there, all of them in here. At first, no more than a confused medley, a babble of voices that seemed like it would never settle down. Then, a pattern, imposing order on chaos. Maybe real, maybe no more than illusion. But it was something.

The metaphor of the multiprocessing machine. Turing would have understood. As well as anyone submerged in the technological realities of millennial America. Millennial Earth. The questions go out, the answers come back, as if from a black box. As if from a million black boxes. But the black boxes know of each other, know all about each other, at need. Compare notes, see who knows what and who can do what. Solve the question and pass the answer back on up the line.

Am I the Supreme Being and these my clockwork slaves? No. I am one with the many, all of them within me, with me . . . legions within? Then, has nothing changed? When I was human, there were legions within as well, all beyond reach, beyond knowing, and yet . . .

The growing order continues to crystallize, even now, in this place beyond the reach of time. Within me, a sense of being more than just a collective entity composed from all the iterations and branchings that had ever had any connection with the many lifetimes of Dale Millikan. If that was all, I'd be no more than the others, who account themselves Angels.

Somehow, within me now, everything. Across all time. All universes. I see the simultaneity of the Many Histories. And understand what I failed to understand when I was embedded in the flowing event-matrix.

Are all things possible? If something is *possible*, is it *real*, somewhere out in the infinite reaches of the Multiverse?

When I was a child, seven or eight perhaps, I found a game to play with myself. I'd be walking home, from somewhere—playtime with other children, baseball or reenacting some cartoon show—on a fine summer's day, afternoon sun crawling down the deep blue arc of the sky, late as usual, hurrying, fearing my parents' wrath. I'd come to a fork in the road.

I would stand there, wasting time, mulling things over, wondering which way would be quickest, visualizing how angry my mother would be when I walked in late for dinner.

In the end, unable to pick, I would choose the path I hoped was the best, and would send forth my doppelgänger on the second-best choice. We knew from experience which paths were *good* you see, of the myriad ways home from a myriad starting points.

But not the perfect path home.

And I would walk. Walk along my chosen path. And, as I walked, I would visualize the doppelgänger, that other me, walking along his path. Shadow cast on the ground before him, just as my shadow was cast on the ground before me.

Scrupulously visualizing his every footstep, so I could see just who would get home first.

Sometimes, I got there first. Sometimes he did. Sometimes, he waited for me on the steps, and we fused and went on in together. Sometimes, when I was particularly late, I imagined him going on in and avoiding my punishment.

Seemed only fair.

And, one day, walking home, shadow rolling across the tawny ground of burned-brown summer suburban lawns, it occurred to me I had mind to spare for a more sophisticated version of the game. I could, you see, imagine the doppelgänger walking along. Imagine him visualizing me. Imagine him scrupulously visualizing my every footstep so that . . .

On the path home then, stopping, stock-still, a bright eight-year-old, flooded with novelty. What if, I supposed, the doppelgänger was real, that I was merely the doppelgänger he imagined, a game conjured up to fill the long, boring minutes engaged in walking home to an unwanted supper?

When I got home, I posed the question to my mother. What if? She, fuming over the fact that dinner had been on the table already for twenty minutes, only threatened to take away my library card if I didn't pull my head down out of the clouds and stop wasting my time on such foolishness.

I sat there and gagged down canned succotash and greasy hamburgers with fried onion, grease soaking into flattened white bread, and thought about it anyway. Went in my room and read a forbidden book. Went to sleep when the sky grew dark. Slept a sleep seemingly without dreams. Woke up in the morning to the stark realization that I *was* the doppelgänger now—that the me who'd lived my life up to now was gone, gone without a trace, other than my memory of his existence, evaporating away with those unremembered dreams.

Never told my parents I was a changeling. Nor any of my friends.

Lived my life. Died. Became God Almighty, you see. Looked up the doppelgänger whose reality I'd stolen. Felt a hard, grinding envy when I saw what life he'd lived. *My* life. The life I'd given up.

Awoke then to the true reality. I lived all of these lives. All of these men came here. Came here in the end. The truth? Where all things are possible, nothing is real. We all existed, and none of us.

Seven.

At the Earth's Core.

Omry Inbar awoke, still embedded in a dream. I was lying in a soft bed, he remembered. We'd finished making love, Hiba and I. Lying there, snuggled in cotton sheets long ago washed soft. Conscious of my humidity, of our closeness. Comfortable with the softness of energy well spent. Hiba putting her hand on the side of my face, waiting, perhaps, for me to open my eyes and look into hers. Waiting too long, growing impatient. Waiting a while longer, then whispering, "Do you love me?"

I remember feeling a little pang of regret. They always ask. Always. Why do they have to be *told*? What is it about words, words, words . . . Opening my eyes, looking into her soft brown stare, soft, demanding stare. Tell her the truth. Tell her. Opening my mouth to speak, and . . . Lying of course. We always lie, just as they always ask. Do they want us to lie? No one knows. They say not. But . . . then they always ask the unanswerable questions that call forth the inevitable lies . . .

And then he opened his eyes on reality. Sudden shortness of breath, as if his heart had come to a stop. My God. The starship *Baka-no-Koto* was far enough away he could see all of it, part of it, at any rate, as a whole object. Huge disk sticking out of the ground at an angle, battered, broken, torn open here and there, insides spilled out on the ground, beyond it, that sky . . .

Eyes rising from the ship, to the expected horizon, then rising again. Then again. Sick, sinking sensation forming in his belly. In the distance, there were mountains. In the distance, was a sea. In the distance was landscape, rivers and grassland and darker green that must be forest, all of it striped and puffed by white cloud and blue shadow.

Mountains nearby, beyond them smaller mountains, colored

blue by air, land beyond that, bluer still, bluer and bluer 'til it was gone. As if I am sitting in the bottom of a bowl. A bowl with no rim. Overhead, a bright spark of sun, standing at high noon.

Something like the Moon, half-moon hanging huge over the non-horizon, improbable moon, something very much wrong with it. What? Long, hard stare. Lighted half pointing up, up at the noonday sun. And . . . There is pale, faded, far-away blue landscape beyond the moon.

Something wrong with me. Something wrong with my eyes. He put one hand to his head, a gentle touch, already aware of a hard, awakening ache, felt the rough cloth of an old-fashioned gauze bandage. A touch of wet, then there was a trace of red blood on his fingers.

That's it. I've got a concussion. Just seeing a little bit wrong. In a minute, it'll be right again. Blink. Blink. Still the same. In a minute, it'll be . . . Oh, no it won't. Come to your senses, Planetologist Inbar. Things haven't been right in the world around you for a long, long time.

Other people around him now. Standing, sitting under the same vast, leafy tree that shaded him now, lying still on the ground. Kincaid bending over this still form, Amaterasu over that one. Over there, the angular black shape of Tarantellula, standing, little Brucie sitting by her feet, arms folded around his knees.

Not far away, the Chinaman, Ling Erhshan, standing by himself, hands on hips, looking up into the sky, looking at that faraway moon, whispering, as if to himself, in singsong Chinese. Inbar tried to move, to sit up, and felt pain go through his head like a thunderbolt. Coughed, almost choking, and said, "Where . . ."

Ling turned and looked down at him, face lit by a most unreasonable smile. Delight. Incredulity. Something else. Pleasure. Vast, vast pleasure. He said, "I think we're in Pellucidar."

Inbar lay back, letting the throb in his head subside. Lay back and frowned. "Pellucidar? And where is that?" No answer.

Images and more images. Ling, hale and hearty, standing,

looking at the sky, yes, and me, lying here banged on the head, fighting double vision, but . . . Tarantellula, and Brucie Big-Dick, arm in arm now, still looking at that wonderful sky. And soldier Kincaid, and robot Amaterasu, bending over the fallen. Who?

Here sits Rhino Jensen, weeping, bereft, clutching red bits of this and that to his sob-wracked breast. Little globes and bits of red shell. Mangled antennae, fragments of spindly arm and leg, whole at the joints, shattered in the limb. Something like an eye here, a bouquet of stalky fingers clutched in one shaking hand. Was this the part that he loved best, or is it that one?

She looks, Inbar thought, like what's left over from a crab feast.

Amaterasu now bending over Lord Genda Hiroshige, winding white bandage round his head like a fine white turban, murmuring to him, sweet robot nothings, hands on him. Look at that. Does a woman know to comfort a banged-up man with sexual overtures? But she's not a woman.

Kincaid standing with her arm around Subaïda Rahman's narrow shoulder, making the Arab woman's relative smallness stand out. Arm around her, woman to woman. Women always comfort each other. But Rahman's supposed to be a . . . and the American woman, much more like a man than any real . . .

Inbar resisted the urge to shake his head, anticipating yet another terrible splinter of pain. These are silly thoughts. Unreal. Unmotivated. You've just been banged over the head and . . .

Kincaid standing with her arm around Rahman's shoulders, Rahman, head down, weeping into her hands, weeping silent tears. Injured? Apparently not. And lying at their feet . . .

Inbar sat up, slowly, very carefully—treating his head with the utmost care—slowly came to his feet, slowly walked over and stood beside the two women. At their feet, Colonel Sir Qamal ibn Aziz Alireza was a mangled ruin. Well. Not so mangled. Not really. Not like Zeq had been mangled. But a ruin, nonetheless. Dark eyes staring at the wonderful sky, blood drying on his brow. One arm bent at an improbable angle. One side of his chest shallow, dished in. Dark places on his uniform, stains from fluids liberated by destruction.

One of his feet was gone, boot and all, foot nowhere to be seen.

Hours later, when it was still noon, tiny sun blazing high overhead, they ate a somber meal of rations unpacked from the wrecked starship, sat in a little circle on soft, dry, greenish-brown grass, not far from two fresh graves. Jensen ate nothing, sat a little distance away, looking away from the group, away from the graves, away from the ship, looking toward some distant mountains, tall mountains so tousled with clouds you could pretend a real horizon, nothing but air and endless space, lay beyond. Rahman sat with them, but ate little. The rest of them seemed . . . all right.

They sat, and listened, while Ling Erhshan bubbled over with delight, while he told them all about the inside-out world of Pellucidar, told them about David Innes and Abner Perry and the mechanical mole, all about the Mahars and Sagoths, about Ja the Mezop, about Jubal the Harsh One and Dian the Beautiful and . . .

At some point, Brucie Big-Dick said, "I read that shit when I was a kid. Did you ever wonder if Jubal Harshaw was a literary back-reference?"

A blank stare from Ling, impatient at the interruption.

Brucie said, "You know: *Stranger in a Strange Land.*"

Ling shrugged; no one else knew what they were talking about.

Passiphaë Laing shook her head dubiously. "This Pellucidar of yours only existed in an old book or two, Professor Ling. I don't think it's possible for us to actually be . . ."

He said, "You say that? You of all people?"

She sighed. "*Crimson Desert* has some sort of reality, the reality of a perfect simulation. The . . . software driver for the net can emulate reality absolutely."

Ling felt a quick pang of impending disappointment. He said, "Then, you think we may still be within your . . . software universe?" I want this to be *real*. Still, it would be an easy explanation for why they're still here; why they haven't simply . . . vanished.

Brucie said, "There was a theory about that, once upon a time. The notion that the universe itself was God, I guess. The Omega Point."

Kincaid said, "I remember. At some point in the future, beings possessed of an infinitely sophisticated technology would synthesize all knowledge. The effect of this synthesis would have the effect of emulating everyone who ever lived. And since there is no test which can distinguish a perfect emulation from the real thing, we would all be, in effect, resurrected to eternal life."

Ling was looking at her now, puzzled. Always expecting her to be stupider than she turned out to be, seldom remembering what it might *mean* to be one-hundred-thirty-five years old. I remember a story about a cat, he thought. An elderly cat, whose sentimental master loved her so. Loved her so much that when he went to an alien world and bought immortality for himself, he paid for the cat as well. The cat lived on and on and on and on, gradually, oh-so-gradually, turning into a being who could think and reason and dream and . . . be. He said, "It was a theory that was only one universe deep. It was a theory that called for a closed universe. This is the Multiverse, isn't that so?"

Laing only nodded.

He said, "And in the Multiverse, everything that *can* be, *is*."

Lord Genda put his ration tray aside, stretched, sighed, put his arm around robot Amaterasu, nuzzled her gently, robot reflexes accommodating him perfectly. Finally, he said, "That is correct. But . . . this isn't your Pellucidar, I'm afraid, no matter how much charm the idea may have." He chuckled. "Falling into a book.' What a wonderful phrase!"

"Not original to me, I'm afraid."

Brucie said, "Where are we, then, if not in the remains of Edgar Rice Burroughs's imagination?"

Genda frowned, glanced at Amaterasu, shrugged.

Kincaid said, "Its definitely some kind of inside-out world.

The atmospheric haze makes it hard to judge what its shape might really be. Maybe a sphere. Maybe some kind of gigantic O'Neil cylinder? I can't imagine how they'd arrange for a uniformly-dense atmosphere throughout the interior, though." Wistful now. "When I was young, back at the beginning of the American Renaissance, we talked about building those, about building Glaser's SPS stations. I used to imagine myself on the construction crew."

Genda said, "It'd be nice if that was the case, but . . .Well." Amaterasu said, "Instrument readings from *Baka-no-Koto* suggest that this is a vacuole some 11,000 kilometers across in a space composed of solid matter, to infinite distance and, ultimately, infinite density. There may be other vacuoles. Our technosystems weren't adequate to . . ."

Ling: "That's precisely how the Mahars viewed their universe in *At the Earth's Core*. Maybe . . ."

Rahman: "As if this were a tiny opening in DeSitter Space?"

"A universe whose initial rules were substantially different from the ones that led to our own," said Amaterasu.

"A different *scarf* for sure, maybe a whole different sweater." Kincaid stood, looking up into the sky, around at the landscape. "Doesn't that mean we should be experiencing infinite gravity, then?"

Ling thought, Peaks and valleys. Places where she knows so much, other places where she knows so little.

Rahman smiled, and said, "Well, no. The laws of physics require that this space be under zero gee at all loci."

Laing said, "*Our* laws of physics . . ."

Ling: "It would be hard to explain away all these anomalies with any theory that did not require something like a fictional reality."

Lord Genda: "Perhaps all we can do is ask the Multiverse who makes up its rules." Facetiously said, but . . .

Kincaid said, "I'm afraid we're about to find out."

Ling thought, Afraid, but . . . yes. I can almost see her thoughts now: Looking forward to it. If all things are possible, you *are* out here. Somewhere. Waiting for me.

* * *

The passage of time, as the old story foretold, was difficult to judge without an objective marker, such as a moving sun, but there were other objective markers. Genda worked in the ship, joined by Amaterasu, by Laing, even by Jensen, who wanted only to stare at his wife's grave until Laing insisted, tone contemptuous, that he snap out of it and help with the necessary work.

Then it was the four of them, moving in and out of the wrecked ship, salvaging gear, rescuing what could be rescued, what needed to be rescued. Image of Passiphaë Laing looking up at the crashed flying saucer, hands on hips: "Well. *My* ship was wrecked because that's what was in the damned script . . ."

Genda got his anomalous Bimus portable computer out, seemed glad that it still worked, working through its memory registers, running all sorts of incomprehensible, pointless-looking software, muttering to himself, muttering to Amaterasu, who waited by his side, acting only when she needed to act.

". . . this *is* the right world. I know it is. The final gate is here somewhere." Odd little maps, like exploded diagrams, like complex collections of interacting canoe-shapes, spread themselves across the screen, images not quite in 3-D.

Brucie, looking over his shoulder: "We had better displays than this by the year 2000 . . ."

Amaterasu said, "I lived on your thread more than a century later. I can't imagine how I wound up on the *Crimson Desert* audience track fifteen centuries after that, where Genda found me . . ."

Genda leaned forward, jabbing his finger at a feature on the bright gray display: "There. This place is called *Koro'mal'luma*. That's where we need to go."

Kincaid said, "And all this is from records you found on an imaginary planet in an imaginary universe?" Shaking her head slowly. I *know* how the Multiverse works, sort of, know from my own old experience, from being out here before. Know it from Scavenger and Colonial records I researched, sitting home alone for year after empty year. Still . . .

Genda said, "Everywhere I've been in the Multiverse, during the last four hundred subjective years of my life, I've found clues. Clues based on debris that's accumulated since the moment of Creation."

Kincaid nodded, "We ourselves found quite a bit of evidence of that sort. Stuff left behind, even though the Space-Time Juggernaut had . . . done its work. Enough evidence to convince us that the Colonials themselves hadn't built the gate system either."

Laing said, "We always wondered about the presence of the gates inside the net. I mean, if our universe wasn't *real*, why did it include things that—"

Genda said, "The gates are the linkpoints for the universal operating system. They were there, were everywhere, from the beginning of time."

If, Kincaid thought, that can possibly mean anything. "That's why we started calling it the Toolbox. Why we started using common computer programming jargon to describe the way the Multiverse seemed to work." Wistful now. "Dale kept suggesting we ourselves might be inside some kind of simulacrum. No one was willing to buy that idea."

Ling said, "That was a question Tipler and his fellows really didn't try to address. If there's no way to distinguish between reality and a perfect emulation, how would we know we hadn't already gone through the process? Or that the perfect emulation wasn't the *a priori* reality?"

All those old, sophomoric questions bobbing up and down. Kincaid said, "How would God know he was really omniscient?"

A bizarre look from Ling.

She said, "If there were things an omniscient God knew he didn't know, then he wouldn't be an omniscient God, and then he'd know he wasn't *really* omniscient, so he could . . . I mean . . ."

A suppressed snicker from Ling.

Slight warmth of anger surfacing. "All right, I'm just getting this all mixed up. All I'm trying to say is, how would the being or beings who created this *emulation*, if that's what it is, know they themselves weren't part of some larger emulation?"

Silence. Then Ling said, "They wouldn't, of course."

"Unless they were *really* omniscient."

Genda sighed, and said, "This is useless." He tapped the screen. "The evidence I've collected indicates that the gate system has some hierarchical qualities. From what you've told me, you Americans wasted your time treating it as a genuine transport network. Spent your limited time out here trying to explore what the Scavengers and Colonials had been up to."

Kincaid said, "It seemed reasonable, at the time." Excuses, but . . . Hell. Dale kept trying to tell us we should go farther afield, stop going to places already listed in the Colonial and Scavenger address tables. Start looking for places they *hadn't* been.

Genda said, "Especially in the emulation universes, there's some indication the gates can be followed right down to the . . ." He seemed to fumble for words. "The core of things."

Ling, eyes dark, narrower than usual: "What sort of core?"

Amaterasu said, "For a while, we talked about calling it the Throne of God."

Rahman, voice full of evident disquiet: "God?"

Genda: "Just a metaphor. It is evident to me that some . . . being, some thing, some intelligence—call it what you will—has constructed the Multiverse. Constructed it as a hierarchical entity. Built it as a series of shells. And it seems to me that the more obvious emulations . . ."

"Like the Ohanaic Pseudouniverse," said Laing.

"Yes, like that," said Genda. "It seems to me they're closer to the heart of things. I've been heading inward, from the outermost realities, ruled by mere probabilistic chains, inward toward ever greater levels of . . . explicit *creation*, if you will. And I find that the deeper I go, the greater the depth of creative detritus. In here. In *these* worlds, God was less careful to hide his . . . toolmarks. Yes, that's what I like to call them. Toolmarks."

Long silence. The sound of the wind sighing in green trees. Kincaid thought, That was the way Dale talked about it, too. Just a story, he'd say. When you read a book you know it's just a story. If something doesn't quite ring true you can simply dismiss it. Willing suspension of disbelief, it's called.

But it isn't like that in real life.

Is it?

"Koro'mal'luma," said Ling Erhshan. "That's Esperanto, isn't it? For 'Heart of Darkness'?"

"Oh, great," muttered Brucie Big-Dick. "Who's waiting for us on the other side, *Tuan*? Marlon Brando?"

Nothing from the others, remark lost.

Kincaid said, "How far?"

"I don't know. The scale . . ."

Jensen laughed. "Not much more than seventeen thousand kilometers, mind you . . ."

Time passes, because there are many more objective markers than merely the transit of the sun across the sky. Finally, Rahman stirred uncomfortably, got to her feet, started walking away from the group clustered around the computer.

Kincaid said, "Where're you going?"

"I've got to go to the bathroom. I'll just be right over . . ."

"Someone with a gun had better go with you." She was reaching for her own M-80, long, slim weapon leaning against a nearby boulder.

Rahman hesitated, reluctant.

Amaterasu stood. "I'll go. I don't need a weapon."

Kincaid stared at her for a second, then said, "I saw the way you ricocheted around the control room when we crashed. Right out through the damn hull and not a dent on you. I guess maybe you don't need a gun."

The robot smiled, sudden sunshine in her face. "You built well, Mother."

"The kit manufacturer, at any rate . . ."

Rahman walked away, urgency in her bladder, not waiting for the robot.

Beyond the shoulder of the nearest hill, the view was down into a small, wok-shaped valley. Rahman stood for a moment, staring at the low, grassy slope, lined with bushes and copses of trees. There was a stream at the bottom of the valley, clear water over sand and stones, a little waterfall—water almost crackling as it fell, a crisp, inviting sound—a little lake, reflecting blue sky, foothills beyond, giving way to mountains rising up toward the clouds. Only when you looked higher, expecting featureless blue . . . It's like a mirage. Landscape you can't quite see. And, of course, only blue sky beyond that, the sun hanging motionless at noon.

She went into the bushes and undid her coverall, squatting, listening to the faint breakfast-cereal sound of her urine soaking into dead leaves and old pine needles. Remembering that Russian woman, Sasha, big and dikey, though she was always seen in the evenings in the company of some man or another, one of the many technicians working in and around the space center. Sasha could reach into her clothing, twist herself just so, and piss straight forward into the old urinal that was in the women's restroom, which had once been a men's room, back when their hadn't been so many women in the workforce. I remember how I laughed, the first time I saw her do that. A most excellent little trick, but you have to be built just right . . .

When she came out of the bushes, the brook was still there, the lake, the grassy field. She said, "That looks nice. Too bad we can't go down and swim."

Amaterasu said, "Why not?"

A little while later, Astrid Kincaid stood at the crest of the hill, looking down into the little valley, hands on hips, watching Ling and Inbar get undressed by the water's edge. Not so hard to figure out just where they'd gone. Men, after all . . .

Rahman was paddling about in the little lake, swimming on her back now, close to shore, dark-nippled breasts sticking up, black triangle of pubic hair plainly visible. Amaterasu stood on the shore nearby, watching the men as well, standing with her hands clasped behind her back. Much better breasts. A lot less pubic hair.

And the men? She grinned to herself. Sorry specimens indeed. Ling was spindle-shanked, flabby, old-looking. No more old people in America. Old people faded away and gone from my memory. I haven't seen a middle-aged person in

decades. Eternal life. Eternal youth. For everyone. Everyone
inside with us. We found it. We're keeping it . . .

For Christ's sake. I haven't felt this young in fifty years.
She set off down the hill to join them, thinking, Well. The
very least I can do is yell at them for swimming in an
unknown lake. What if there's a *dragon* out there?

No dragon.

And she thought Inbar's eyes would pop from his head as
she stood on the shore and shrugged out of her military tunic,
as she unbuckled her belt and dropped her pants, stripped off
brassiere and underwear. Breasts that must require antigravity to stand up like that on their own. Pubic hair like a Brillo
pad made of spun gold.

Astrid Kincaid laughed at him. Laughed and threw herself
into the water—cold, lovely water, water striking freshness,
new life deep in her heart—and swam, powerful overhand
strokes, head turning from side to side, eyes open, legs kicking beneath the surface, swam far out into the lake. Turned
and floated on her back, staring up at a blinding sun, tiny sun
like a bit of incandescent metal hanging beyond the sky.

God. I feel like a child again. Caught up in a dream.
Caught up in my favorite dream. How could we have missed
this, the first time through? How could we have been so
afraid? Image of the Jug. Image of Death's Angel killing all
her friends. Has it really swept in behind us, wiping away our
path? Can the Earth, my Earth, the real Earth, possibly be
gone?

No answer.

And no will to worry about it, just now.

You've been old for a hundred years, Astrid Kincaid. Old
since you were a child. Time now to be young again. Perhaps
to be young for the very first time.

They were sitting together, naked on the shore, sprawled
up on the shore's grassy lawn, sitting together like old friends,
used to each other, so accustomed to one another, somehow,
that even Inbar could relax, could look at Rahman, at
Amaterasu, even at Kincaid, without that silly erection rising
to embarrass him.

Hours had passed, what felt like hours anyhow, and Ling found himself wishing for a sunset that refused to come. The sun just hung up there, eternal noon. Wouldn't it be nice to have a red sun low in the sky now, a sky turning ruddy, sunlight coloring the clouds red and brown, shadows turning black within them? But the sky was still bright blue, sunlight tingling on his skin. The urge came to tell the others all about his feeling, about this world, this lake, this little gathering, how he felt, about himself, about everything, perhaps, and he said, "I think . . ."

Something buzzed over them, something like a giant wasp, sweeping down the hillside with a deep, shuddery drone, a dark, misty something, hidden by a blur of wings, sweeping over their heads, flying out over the lake, turning, banking, heading back for them. Kincaid cursed, reached for her rifle, jumping to her feet, taking a bead on whatever it was, while the others stood up, tried almost simultaneously to stand behind her. All but Amaterasu, robot Amaterasu, fearless, indestructible.

"What the Hell . . ." Buzzing globe of dark, insectile wings, slowing, hovering above them, not far away.

And Ling whispered, "There is *no* such thing . . ."

The buzz softened, the blur of wings slowed, and there hung a tiny woman, naked woman, perhaps twenty or thirty centimeters tall, it was hard to tell. A dark-haired woman with pale white skin, huge, slanting dark eyes, a tiny red mouth . . .

Inbar muttering, as if to himself, in thick Arabic, Rahman saying something back.

The apparition laughed, a rich, tinkling, happy little sound. Laughed, and said, "Pretty, pretty girls, swimming naked and free." A tiny frown on tiny red lips. "Oh, not such pretty boys. Tsk. Tsk. Pretty little girls ought to have nicer boys than *these*."

Kincaid leveled her gun at the thing and said, "Who the fuck are *you*?"

"Oh, oh, oh. Silvereyes is a tough little girl, is she? Well. Well."

Pop.

Suddenly the thing was high overhead. "Peeka*boo*, I see *you!*"

Pop!

And it was behind Kincaid, pulling hard on her golden hair, making her stagger. "Can't catch *me!* I'm a *Christmas* tree!"

Pop!

Right in front of the gun, hovering, motionless, in the middle of her buzzing wings.

"Go ahead, Silvereyes. *Shoot!*"

Kincaid lowered the M-80, let its useless muzzle droop to the ground, her mouth set in a grimace of dismay. "Oh, fucking *great*," she whispered. "Fucking Tinkerbell."

Peal of joyous laughter from the apparition. Loud buzz of wings, blurring the tiny woman's body as she soared over their heads, swooped low with a buzzsaw roar, right between Rahman's legs, Rahman jumping and screaming and grabbing at her crotch while the creature danced overhead.

"Aarae be my name!" she cried. "*Silvestris nympha.*" Bride of the forest.

She shimmered and buzzed again, twirled around them like a mote of magic dust, flew behind Kincaid and goosed her hard, flew between Inbar's legs and seemed to swing from his penis for a moment while *he* jumped and screamed, floated over their heads again for just a moment, grinning downward, laughing at the man, "Pixie to *you*, Toots!"

Shimmered and buzzed and flew straight up into the sky and was gone.

There was a moment of silence, then Kincaid said, "Well. Jesus Fucking Christ. What the Hell *next* . . ."

No use trying to make any sense of it, or argue the point. Is this Pellucidar, or merely Never-Never Land? In the Multiverse, there's no reason there can't be a place that partakes of both. On the other hand, there's no reason to believe, really *believe* in any of it.

There was that, during the walk back up the hill, after they'd slowly, silently put on their clothes, more or less oblivious to one another. Funny, though, to see Inbar standing there, spraddle-legged, looking down at himself in disbelief. Me Tarzan. You vine. Toots.

And then there'd been the puzzled, unbelieving stares of the others, back at the ship. Genda finally saying, "What do you *mean*, you were attacked by Tinkerbell? Tinkerbell who?"

Kincaid staring at him, bemused. Well of *course* there'd been no Walt Disney in his universe. Not to mention J.M. Barrie.

Then Brucie said, "Ya mean the cartoon fairy? Hey, I remember that! There's this scene where little Tink stands on a mirror, sort of looking over her shoulder at her own rump, where it looks like she's looking up her own skirt. I kind of liked that when I was kid."

Blank stares from everyone else.

"Well. I guess it was a Forties kind of thing. I guess you had to be there . . ." Trailing off.

Tarantellula put her hand on the back of his neck, black glove of a hand almost engulfing his head, giving him an affectionate sort of shake. "I can just see you watching something like that," she said.

Genda sighed and shook his head. "Well, it doesn't matter what you saw. I'm sure we'll run into worse." He turned the Bimus computer, which he'd set up on one of the flat rocks lying loose around the crash site, turning it so they could all see the screen.

"This," he said, "is from the software package I picked up on *Crimson Desert*, a dataset, actually, for software I picked up in its audience track universe."

A three-dimensional image of a transparent globe, bumps and valleys on its surface, like mountains and continents and empty seas. He said, "I thought it was just a normal planet, kind of an odd view, of course, but . . ." He tapped one of several smaller spheres embedded in the larger one. "I couldn't imagine what these were supposed to be. Now . . ."

He looked up, into the bright sky, then pointed at a small half-moon hanging just above where the rising "horizon" disappeared behind the sky. "That, I suppose, is this one." Pointing to one of the smaller globes on the map. "The coordinate set for the gateway to God's Machine lies underneath this larger, um, *moonlet*, I guess we could call it, which I've placed in a south polar position. The gateway seems to lie on a small mountain peak in the middle of this depression."

Ling said, "In the Land of Awful Shadow."

Brucie Big-Dick said, "Right. Very melodramatic. I'm sure some script guy was well-paid to think it up. So what the Hell is God's Machine?"

Tarantellula said, "In olden times the Latin phrase *machina dei* was used to mean 'a contrivance of the gods.' In drama, it's a plot device that you just pull out of thin air and make up any excuse for."

Odd look from Kincaid: "I thought that was *deus ex machina* . . ."

Another sigh from Genda. "I doubt that's what it means here." He shook his head slowly, seeming tired of the lot of them, perhaps of the whole business. "I've been researching this, following an old, cold trail for centuries now. If the hints are right, God's Machine lies at the core of the Multiverse. It's the *whatever* that runs the show. The *contrivance*, as you say, at least. From there . . ."

Kincaid said, "Scavengers thought the Colonials believed in something like that. I guess they thought the Space-Time Juggernaut was just a myth, a religion maybe, until the Jug came for them."

Genda said, slowly, thoughtfully, looking away into the landscape, "I think God's Machine has something to do with the maintenance of gate connectivity. It's what the gates access."

Kincaid: "The Toolbox."

"Yes. If I understand you right. I don't think God's Machine is in fact God Himself."

Rahman said, "So you believe, somewhere out here, somewhere deep in the Multiverse, God is . . . real." You could hear it in her voice: *Really real?*

He shrugged. "I don't know. God was never really a part of my cultural surround. Not like *Tao*. Not even like the Goddess Amaterasu, sacred to my ancestors . . ." A dark-eyed glance at his robot lover. "But many of my friends are, were

Western Deists, and Zen Catholicism was a potent political force in China during the early days of the Space Age." Back up at the sky now, staring at that hazy moonlet. "It was difficult enough to believe that the One Universe was just an accident, a confluence of meaningless rules. This . . ." Hand taking in Faux-Pellucidar around them, but meaning the Multiverse beyond.

Ling said, "The Watchmaker?"

"Maybe so. I don't know. I hope to find out."

Laing said, "Easier for people like us," a gesture at Jensen, who seemed uninterested, "to believe a world must have its creator. Someone, somewhere *did* make me."

"And me," said Amaterasu, looking at Kincaid.

Avoiding her gaze, Kincaid said, "And yet, if all rules are possible, all possibilities must *be*, whether they are willed into being or not."

Ling thought, Peaks and valleys. Always a surprise. He said, "So what made possibility itself?"

Brucie Big-Dick said, "Long-hair bullshit. Who the Hell cares who made what or why? Let's just go find out. If we can. If we want to . . ."

Genda passed a hand over his face, sweaty-looking face, seeming exasperated, exhausted. "Well. No telling what we'll run into in a world like this, whatever it is. Or where." A glance round at the others. "I guess, in the morning, we should just start . . . walking?" A pointed look at Amaterasu, perched silent nearby on a rounded tan boulder. "I guess we should try to get some sleep."

She arose, as if on cue, and together they walked over to the remains of *Baka-no-Koto*, went inside. Watching them go, Kincaid thought, I made her to be like that. I did it. Why didn't I think of this while I was doing it? Why did I make a thinking toy for my selfish little brother Roddie?

Hard to watch her being so . . . compliant. Hard to watch it, and know why it's so.

Ultimately, Kincaid knew, they would have to start walking, for *Baka-no-Koto* was beyond being saved. Imagine that, she thought. Reduced from interstellar travel at hundreds of times the speed of light, to creeping on foot across the inside of some vast sphere. Thousands of kilometers to what was, apparently, this world's only easily accessible gate. If you can call this a world. Some impossible hollow in the midst of an infinite, solid, nothingness.

Supplies gathered, clothing gathered, packs packed, graves looked at one last time, the Arabs with heads bowed, saying one last guttural, muttered prayer for Alireza's soul. Jensen standing silent by that other grave, Laing's arm around his shoulders.

Did the ants believe in immortal souls?

As well ask if I do.

I never could accept the hypothesis that a perfect emulation was the same as *me*. What if there were two of us? Would my consciousness imbue both? Unimaginable. Impossible. Partaking of the qualities of . . . God. Omnipresence, at least.

A whisper of distant sound.

Tarantellula, shading huge white eyes, looked up into the strange blue-gray sky, and said, "Sergeant? What the Hell is that?" Pointing.

Kincaid raised her rifle and looked through the scope at a distant silvery speck, speck hardly distinguishable from a thousand other sky glimmers on the edge of vision. Soft grunt. "Some kind of . . . flying machine." The thing began to grow larger, coming closer, sound growing from a whisper to a soft rumble, as of powerful engines.

Watching the ship hover above the crashed starship, Kincaid saw it as a flying cabin cruiser. A hull obviously intended to cleave water. Superstructure with windows. A little mast with a fluttering, colorful penon, little flag a seemingly abstract pattern of pale blue, *cornflower*, and something like salmon pink. Kincaid found herself remembering a box of Crayola crayons she'd had as a child, so many years ago. The names on those crayons defined the true meaning of colors for me . . .

Pixie Aarae flying above the little ship, buzzing swiftly around it, around the two people on its aft deck, tall, thin, fire-haired woman clad in bright, silvery chain-mail leaning on the rail, looking down at them, short, bald man at the helm, operating controls, holding the wheel; short, bald man clad all in dusty-looking black leather.

The ship descended, settling to the ground, and Aarae spun from the mast, turning cartwheels in the air, buzzing among them, whirling around Inbar, whirling around his waist. Somehow, in the twinkling of an eye, she managed to get his belt buckle undone, his fly unzipped, Omry Inbar cursed, clutching his pants once again, holding them up.

Laughter from the people on the ship, the woman's voice high and sharp, the man's voice very deep, that rough testosterone frogcroak common to heavyset, bald men.

Kincaid held her rifle across her chest, careful to aim it at no one, finger kept outside the trigger guard. A quick glance at Tarantellula, who'd retrieved her own weapon, making sure she was doing the same. The black giant was holding Brucie's hand again, Brucie himself staring, staring at the red-haired woman. Tired of your monster yet, Brucie? Maybe so. And this is one showy little piece in front of us now . . .

The woman wore a long sword with a half-basket hilt strapped across her back, shorter sword at waist, dirk clasped to her belt at the opposite hip. A holster for some kind of small handgun. Looks like a classic Luger. No helmet, though. I'd wear a helmet if that were *my* getup.

The man, big headed, with large, muscular-looking hands, rounded, sloping shoulders, bulging stomach, short, almost-bowed legs, was indeed dressed in cracked and dusty old leather. Just a short sword here. And a long-barreled gun strapped to his hip, either an antique horse-pistol or a sawed-off shotgun. Looks like he's a good deal older than her. And standing two paces back. Not husband then. Or lover. Not father, nor even younger brother. A servant, perhaps . . .

The ship barely touched the ground, floating lightly on its keel. The man did something, a little gangplank dropped with a dull, echoless thud, and the woman stepped down, stepping forward to meet Kincaid, looking her right in the eye. Off to one side, out of the corner of her eye, she could see Lord Genda, frowning, nonplused.

The woman held out her hand and said, "Amanda Grey,

Knight-Errant of the Silver Thread." A little head gesture, back at the bald man, who stood up on deck, also frowning, thumbs tucked in his studded belt. "My squire, Edgar."

The man nodded.

Kincaid took the proffered hand, felt its softness. Shook her head slowly, glancing up to where the pixie fluttered, just above Inbar's clearly discomfited head. "Sergeant-Major Astrid Kincaid, United States Marine Corps. And I'll believe anything right now. Just try me."

The woman laughed. "You'll have to forgive little Aarae. She means well."

The being settled on Inbar's shoulder and began nuzzling his ear, the man growing rigid, face darkening slowly. Up on the ship's deck, Edgar muttered, loud enough for all to hear, "For a pixie, that is."

Amanda Grey said, "We saw your ship from afar, falling from the sky. It seemed like a . . . phenomenon worth investigating."

And squire Edgar, dark eyes on them, measuring them all: "No one flies at such incandescent speed, here in Hesperidia. Few fly at all. And those few who *do* fly, generally creep along just above the landscape."

Remembering the ship they crashed into, on emerging from the undocumented gate that must lie somewhere up by the inner sun, Kincaid said, "Not all, though."

Amanda said, "The Garsetti Traders are known to take perilous shortcuts in their quest for enhanced profit."

Edgar: "If you struck someone up there," a nod sunward, "they may be falling still." A long, long damned fall. Tumbling endlessly, hour upon hour, until the end came at last.

Ling said, "*Hesperidia*. Dawn World? If you have a name for this . . . place, perhaps you know of others?" Fishing for knowledge.

Amanda said, "This is the only real world. But . . . there are stories of others."

Edgar, shadow deepening behind his eyes, said, "Your words imply you've come from . . . elsewhere. Where might that be?" Voice filling with an unspoken demand.

Then the story was told, a bit at a time, Knight-Errant Amanda Grey incredulous, unbelieving at first. Squire Edgar, Kincaid saw, had no problem with any of it. Saw him go to stand before the wreck of *Baka-no-Koto*, by the two fresh graves, eyes trouble but understanding. Finally, he turned to them, and said, "What are you going to do now? I can't imagine you being content to . . . settle here."

No. Not bloody likely, however much Professor Ling went on prattling about Pellucidar.

Amanda said, "Perhaps we can assist you in going back the way you came?"

Genda said, "Without the starship, the sun's gate opens on a . . . void. No, we have information this . . . world's other exit lies at a place that seems to be called *Koro'mal'luma*."

Silence.

Then Edgar said, "Well. It figures."

It figures? Curiously out of synch with the cadences of their speech, thought Kincaid.

He said, "Do you know the word *synchronicity*?"

Amanda said, "Perhaps you should know that the Heart of Darkness is our ultimate destination as well."

The little ship, little nameless ship, whose sparse accommodations suggested space for five, perhaps, had struggled to lift them all, swaying on its keel, teetering just above the ground like a balloon whose helium was about depleted, before staggering into the sky, Squire Edgar muttering to himself as he worked the controls, tipping the wheel this way and that in an effort to keep them rightside up.

Now they flew slowly along, flying above the smaller mountains, around the larger, through passes that terrified, above glistening fields of ice and snow, or far above dark tropic jungles, passing sometimes above small, fluffy white clouds, other times dodging the classic, dark-bottomed anvils of thunderheads, passing westward, or so Edgar said, under a pinprick noonday sun.

Like flying over the middle of some vast, cotton-rimmed bowl, thought Ling Erhshan. Like we're standing still. The landscape moves underneath, trees and mountains hazing away to nothing aft, new mountains, new forests, new red deserts materializing to the fore. This is, finally, more real than any dream I ever dreamed. More real than all the stories. More real than my life.

Down below, hundreds of meters below as they passed over some high, dry plateau, he watched a fire-breathing dragon slay and eat a monster so huge it defied probability. A monster the size of two blue whales, a monster that must weigh in the thousands of tons. A monster that was grazing peacefully, munching the tops of dry brown trees, until the dragon came and slew it.

Not just any dragon. A special dragon. A familiar dragon. *Tyrannosaurus rex* vomiting a steady stream of napalm on the screaming, writhing herbivore's back, raising blisters that grew to holes, exposing ribs, melting skin away, jellied gasoline pouring in to cook tortured flesh, tree-crunching monster falling and dying, familiar dragon bending to his feast. Things on his back, little tree-shaped spines, wriggling as if with pleasure, as he bit and chewed and swallowed.

Standing by his side, watching, Knight-Errant Amanda Grey said, "Lucky you came down where you did. Those well-watered highlands don't support much in the way of really dangerous fauna."

Why not?

Too soft, she'd said. Too easy.

Wouldn't you say a sabertooth tiger was really dangerous?

She'd smiled, nodding at the scene below. What would *smilodon* be to a thing like that? A skin parasite?

Down below, the plateau of the fire-breathing dragons passed on, giving way to a huge canyonland, dark, red-orange rock eaten away to vertical walls, giving way to a desert country kilometers below, desert country of spires and columns, tiny mountains surmounted by dry, stunted trees.

No rivers, Ling whispered. No water at all. This is a valley of the winds . . .

Some people call it that, said Amanda Grey.

The people of Hesperidia?

The people of this place, which is a hole in nothing at all.

This place?

Hesperidia. What you see below is called the Aino Plains, the landscape around Aphrodite Terra, our destination. At his inquiring look, she said, Aphrodite Terra. The land of Yttria . . .

Meaningless, though the words themselves had meaning.

How is it you speak English so well?

A puzzled look. The language is called Têtonic. Why do you speak *it* so well?

Well, I studied hard in school and . . . He smiled, spoke a few words in Guoyü. She said, Ah. I'm not surprised. You certainly look like a Han, though obviously you're not . . .

Everything so subtly twisted around. I must keep reminding myself what it *means*, for the Multiverse to *be*. To port, in what they referred to as north, another mountainous land appeared, dark rock, gray, like granite, weathered granite, with green stains here and there, as if the rock supported moss or algal growth. Lichens, perhaps. Lichens will grow on rocks, even very dry rocks.

Atop the mountain was what looked like a ruined city. A dark-looking city, a city full of shadows, as if invisible clouds hung overhead, blotting out that blistering spark far above. He pointed the place out, asked the obvious question.

Amanda Grey fell silent, gazing at the distant city, piled rubble visible now, fallen towers, blasted plazas, places touched by fire.

Places, Ling could see, where the very stone had run molten in the streets.

The mountain itself, she said, is called Bell. The city has no name.

It looks very old.

It is. No one knows how old. It's the place where my people, the Têtons, were brought, brought from their original land, twenty thousand years ago.

Brought?

Brought here to be slaves of the Angels. Angels who built that city.

Another long silence, while they watched the ruined city atop the dark mountain named Bell drift away aft, then she said, For eight thousand years we served them at bed and table, served their every whim, served them while God slept on. Then the War of the Angels happened, and we got away, walked through the nightmare of Leda's Land to remote, empty Ishtar Terra, Ishtar of the high, cold Maxwell Mountains, so like our old, forgotten home. Most of us died. A few survived to found Traanheim in Traanmark, which in time became the bright empire of Têtonland.

Ling said, And the Angels? What of them? Did their war last forever?

She shook her head. It was over soon, for the Angels bore terrible weapons indeed. Two only survived, Ahriman and Lucifer. They hold each other paralyzed. And the world survives because God's Machine has yet to run down.

God's Machine.

No, I don't want to believe in where I am.

Yet the reality, all about me . . .

He said, And what of . . . God?

God.

The syllable hangs bitter on the end of my tongue. There is no God. There can be no God. God is an ancient dream, an excuse men made to explain away the world's horror, long, long ago, in a land remote from my own . . .

Amanda Grey said, God sleeps.

That, perhaps, is the best kind of God.

Aft of the ship, a spark of light appeared, growing closer, brighter, pursuing them like some kind of missile. Like one of those old photon torpedoes, Ling thought. He pointed to the thing.

Amanda looked and smiled. She said, "I never saw Aarae burn so much energy before, keeping up with us. She's . . . intent on your comrade. The fat man . . . Inbar? Is that his name?"

The spark grew into a plump ball of misty fire, whirling round and round the ship, like ball lightning. The fire extinguished, become a blur of tiny wings, and fell upon the afterdeck, where most of the others congregated, looking over the side at the landscape, or watching Edgar fly the ship.

Omry Inbar shouted, leaping to his feet, trying to dodge the little pixie's attack, failing, squawking haplessly as she grabbed him here and there, while his audience started to laugh.

Amanda said, "Your friend will have to give in. She seems . . . insistent."

Ling said, "What could such a creature want with a full-sized man?"

Amanda smirked, eyes aglitter. "You'd be surprised."

Soon enough, a high mountain land, a dry mountain land, rose before them. Aphrodite Terra, Edgar told them. Three high, dry plateaus strung along Hesperidia's internal equator. Ovda, Thetis, and Atla, each unique, each splendid.

Equator? Rahman wondered. What makes this an equator? Does Hesperidia spin around its inner sun?

Edgar staring at her. Something in his eyes. Something . . . of *knowing*. How would we tell? We call it the equator, always have. And just so, we define the poles. Ovda and Thetis, he said, are home to the lands of Haanan and Kmet. Edgar said something in a guttural language that sounded much like Arabic, but was not.

Inbar started, and said, They speak ancient *Ivrit*?

Edgar shrugged. Atla, he said, is home to the Yttrian people. Though Amanda's father is a Têtonic *landsknecht* of ancient lineage, her mother hailed from Yttria. Some say she was a stolen princess, though Amanda prefers not to speak of her mother . . .

Fairy tales. He's talking about fairy tales.

A city rose up before them now, Yttria, Edgar said, and the little ship slanted down out of the sky, lumbering clumsily, overloaded as it swooped toward a landing stage crowded with other ships large and small.

It feels, Rahman told herself, like midnight.

They walked through the city to Amanda's house, which turned out to be a palace of sorts, palace full of magic servants, full of unbelievable things. Walked through a shadowed city under a noonday sun, a city full of the equally unbelievable.

Unacceptable, thought Ling Erhshan. That's the word I

want to use. Curious how I feel that way now. The bright dream of coming to space, itself colored more by all those old stories than by the reality of those who'd gone before, cast into shadow by the fact of the Stargates, the fact of being given access to . . . to the whole of the Universe. How did I feel then? Was I exhilarated? I don't even remember.

On through the Stargates, fleeing and fleeing, expecting to find myself out among the fixèd stars. That was the reality I clung to. Then what? Time travel? That poor man Ahmad Zeq, dying in Permian time, dying in the jaws of his ancestral monster. How closely related is *homo* to *dimetrodon?* I don't even know.

Time travel. Incredible. Remember that old American cartoon? Drizzle, drazzle, druzzle, drome . . .

And now, so they say, we can never find our way home again. One more step. One more after that. Space travel possible and real. Star travel a fantasy? Maybe, maybe not. Time travel. Almost but not quite out of the question. And then. And then.

Buildings all around them made of fine, smooth stone. Limestone and marble. Gray granite, brown sandstone. Empty windows, as if these people hadn't discovered glass. That adds to the . . . look of the place. Amanda Grey's palace looked as if it were made of acid-etched concrete, almost out of place in this here-and-now. Almost, but not quite.

Within, furniture and servants—servants human and otherwise—hangings and carpets with eldritch scenes. Vast tableau on one wall, scene of brooding mountains over a highland plain. Burning hamlet in the background, in the foreground a fire-breathing dragon, close-by, but not too close, peasants armed with pitchforks and scythes. Two horses before the dragon. On their backs, Amanda Grey, Knight-Errant, and her squire, bald-headed Edgar.

Seeing him look at the thing, Amanda said, "I was given my errantry for that deed."

They walked through the vast house to a steamy chamber, a room with a large swimming pool, steps down into it from every side, wisps of vapor rising off the water. A heated bath, like a Roman bath, like a public bath.

Pixie Aarae swept over their heads, skimming low over the water, wingtips dimpling its surface as she flew, then whirled on high, trailing a fine mist, spun round and round Inbar, settled on the floor before him, wings still, arms folded across her breast, grinning up at him, tapping one toe gently.

Servants came and started helping Amanda off with her armor. Bizarre, misty servants. Servants made, so it seemed, of fog . . .

Ling felt his breath grow shallow as he watched. Chain mail cast aside. Leather undergarments cast aside. Red-headed woman clad only in a thin film of lingerie, servants like ghosts floating around her, brushing that dark, red-gold hair. Woman then, only woman, identity lost, stretching, luxurious woman, stretching while those misty servants stripped away those last thin layers of translucent cloth.

Ling felt himself sigh. The transition was from mystery to flesh, from image to reality. Only a woman now. Only a real woman. Dreamgirl vanished, like a wraith of smoke. Still, this is a handsome woman indeed. When I was a young man, I would have danced gladly to her tune.

Others disrobing around him, as always, the women first. Golden Kincaid, with her muscles and solidity. Alien Tarantellula, all long black arms and legs. Amaterasu, wonderful robot maiden, made by woman for man's delight. Mistress Laing, imaginary telejournalist, nothing special about her except fleshy perfection. And unremarkable Subaïda Rahman . . .

I must remind myself, *she* is the real woman here, the others, by varying degrees, manufactured.

Then men, last as always. Edgar, fat, yet so obviously well-muscled, like most bald men, covered otherwise by dense, wiry black hair. Inbar, fat man, plain and simple. Brucie with that ridiculous thing hanging between his legs, his pride and joy. Small, slim, handsome Genda, well suited to his robot bride. Sad, silent Jensen. Rhino Jensen of the most absurd cognomen, as flesh-perfect as his chronicler Laing.

And old Professor Ling, the least of them all. What is it a woman sees when she looks on me? A little old man with spindly shanks and a little pot belly? I always wondered. I never knew. Do they tell us only in words we cannot understand? Or is it just, as so many insist, that we refuse to listen?

Men and women, by ones and twos, descending into the steamy water. Brucie Big-Dick, he saw, was holding Tarantellula's hand. The water warmed them, made them whole again, healed them somehow. Perhaps, made this world, impossible world, seem real, seem comfortable. That's the problem, thought Ling. The world outside my skin seemed . . . like nothingness? As if only the world inside had any validity. What was happening didn't matter, only how I felt about it.

They sat by the water's edge, on the stone steps, some of them higher up, only their feet immersed, others down near the bottom, water up to their necks. Inbar sat thus—sat on the pool's bottom—naked little Aarae perched on his head. The water's magic seems to have worked on him as well. He's . . . gotten used to her presence.

They sat together, and Amanda had the servants bring Lord Genda's bronze briefcase of a Bimus combat computer, sat and watched as he swung it open, one impervious corner dipping into the steamy water, watched as he activated the bright gray screen and called up his maps.

Amanda Gray looked, listened to his explanation of their quest, finally said, "Synchronicity is an important natural force in Hesperidia." She took in their not quite blank stares. "More so perhaps than it is in your own . . . world-lines? Is that the word I want to use?"

"It will do," said Edgar.

"Bad times," she said, "dark times, come now and again to the Land of the Tetons. They come more and more often as God's Machine winds down, wears out for want of maintenance."

So the Angels fight a war, and God doesn't intervene. The Angels, charged perhaps with the maintenance of His Machine, destroy themselves, all but two. Now the Machine runs down and still God doesn't intervene? This is a lazy God indeed . . .

She said, "The Archangel Michael came one day—one

day years ago—and stole Crown Prince Ardry Bright-Sky, son of Traanmark's Earl Oren, grandson of Erik IX Whitehall, Emperor of All the Têtons, whom some call Erik Rede-Miser . . ."

Rahman sat forward, stirring the water with one hand, liberating more steam, breathing it in. "I thought you said all the Angels but two were destroyed? Didn't you say only Ahriman and Lucifer survived?"

Brucie Big-Dick, perched on Tarantellula's knee, said, "Weren't Archangels the highest of all the angels?"

Quietly, Ling said, "No. They were the lowest Choir."

Edgar was looking at him again, looking right into his head.

Amanda said, "The real Archangel Michael is long gone, long ago absorbed, body and soul, back into the Machine, gone where all the dead go."

"Where," said Edgar, "even dead spirits must ultimately go."

She said, "This Michael is the chiefest of Prince Lucifer's demons, cast in the image of Archangel Michael, imbued with the essence of some dead soul."

Edgar said, "Some believe it is the spirit of a long-dead emperor, possibly even Harald Fairhair, who led us across Leda's Land to freedom."

"Demon." Ling looked at Edgar, trying to look back through those dark, penetrating eyes.

Edgar smiled and said, "Crafted by the Machine, through the agency of Prince Lucifer, of Lord Ahriman, from the souls of dead men and women, crafted to do their bidding."

Robot Amaterasu said, "Demon is not the word I would use."

Ling thought, Crafted to do someone's bidding? No, I suppose you'd not call that a *demon*. Rather say demon to the crafter. Does Kincaid look uncomfortable? Perhaps I only imagine it. Men have never been able to read women's faces well. And when they do, they only use the knowledge gleaned to . . . compel their will upon them . . .

Amanda said, "My Commission of Mastery, Order of the

Silver Thread, has been to retrieve Ardry Bright-Sky from captivity."

Rahman whispered, "Just another silly fairytale."

Lord Genda said, "And where is he being held?"

Amanda pointed to the center of his computer screen, where a small moon hung over a round valley, at what was thought to be the south pole of Hesperidia. "There. In the Heart of Darkness, where Ahriman rules."

Koro'mal'luma again. The Land of Awful Shadow. Ahriman and the Heart of Darkness. Of course. For Prince Lucifer is, as he must be, the Bringer of Light. Though that light be the light of evil itself, shining into our hearts.

Rahman said, "Didn't you say this Michael was crafted by Lucifer? Why would Lucifer carry your Prince Ardry away to his master's enemy?"

Squire Edgar said, "The War of the Angels continues, if only through their surrogates."

Suddenly, Ling said, "With God vanished and the Angels destroyed, you'd think some new agency would arise, spread itself through the Multiverse, and resume the work of Creation."

Edgar seemed to freeze in place for a moment, staring at him out of those dark eyes, then he relaxed and smiled, "Yes. You'd think that, wouldn't you?"

They were dried beside the pool by ghostly servants bearing fluffy, soft white towels, people yawning and stretching, unselfconscious before one another. Used to the nakedness? Kincaid wondered. Or distracted from their prejudices and fears by . . . change. Surely that has come over us all.

People yawning, people led away by ghosts in their ones and twos, led away to stony, firelit, fire-warmed bedchambers and soft, spacious, feather-pillowed beds. Left alone, the ones who came alone.

Astrid Kincaid stood naked in front of a bronze-tinted mirror, looking at her gold-haired, silver-eyed self. Not the real me. Not the real me at all. I had brown eyes. Soft, dark brown eyes. I had brown hair. Light brown, a little bit wavy.

Memory of a girl, maybe sixteen, sweaty from her exercises, calisthenics done alone in her room, a long session with the rubber-band weight machine her mother deplored.

Those muscles will make you look like a man, Astrid. Then no man will want you . . .

Brown-eyed girl looking at herself in the mirror, flexing those sweaty muscles, then relaxing. Silver-eyed girl now, realizing she hardly remembered what she really wanted back then, or why she wanted it. Silence here, flickery fire moving shadows on the wall, making them dance. Silence, walls too thick to hear . . . Turning away from the mirror, stretching, trying to dismiss those odd feelings.

The closet door opened silently on well-oiled hinges, and there were, of course, clothes hanging in shadow. Fine clothes, local clothes. Sort of like men's clothes, like the clothes Amanda Grey wore. She took down a soft, tan, suede tunic and held it against herself, walked back to the mirror.

Just my size. Are those little dimples I see beside my mouth? Silver-eyed, golden-haired girl, trying on a new dress. Everything else in the closet fit too, even those nice little white leather boots. *And I'm not tired anymore . . .*

Outside, the noonday sun stood high overhead, the same bright spark they'd known since coming here, yet the streets of Yttria seemed somehow cast in shadow, in darkness. The light, she realized, *has the same quality that well-lit city streets have in the middle of the night.*

Remember the streets of Manhattan? Lit bright as day as you walk along the well-populated sidewalks. You look up. The sky between the buildings is black, a sky without stars. Like the sky of the Moon in daylight. You look up. Here is the bright crescent Earth, there the blinding ball of the Sun. But the sky is black, a sky without stars.

That was what I wanted. That bright black sky. It's what I worked so hard for, in the end. That sixteen-year-old girl knew the American Renaissance was coming, knew it was about to arrive. I pictured myself up there in the sky, up there astride a changed world. Pictured myself on the Moon. On Mars. Pictured myself out among the moons of Jupiter. Imagined myself standing amid the tarry snows of Titan, pic-

tured myself in the border country of Iapetus, looking up at pale-gold Saturn . . .

They had enough astronaut girls.

Remember that bitter disappointment?

Remember, watching on TV, on a fine spring morning in 2026, when fifty-seven-year-old grandmother Daisy Kaminsky, M.D., Ph.D., put her spacesuited boot down on the dusty Moon and blathered about the second coming?

Soldier girl was good enough, in the end.

Behind her, a soft, deep male voice said, "Can't sleep, eh?"

She turned and beheld Squire Edgar, dressed in fresh, clean leather clothes, leather cracked and wrinkled here and there, where his arms and legs would bend, where his big belly needed to flex. Edgar, bright eyed, looking as if he never needed to sleep.

She said, "Guess not."

They started walking.

It was a tavern, like a tavern in any story, the sort of place where you might imagine Robin Hood gathering his archers so they could vow to help the people of the King. Full of life, fire boiling in a hearth at one end of a sawdust-floored great-room, candles burning in wooden chandeliers, swinging overhead from ropes. You could just see old Robin putting his sword through one of the ropes, near where it was tied off to a wall cleat, wooden chandelier, candles and all, falling on the Sheriff's clumsy men.

No bar, of course. Too modern a touch. Lots of beat-up wooden tables. When they were new, they'd probably been full of splinters. Too old now. Worn smooth by centuries of rubbing hands, splinters long ago carried off in other people's skin.

The damnedest looking "people" running the place, too. A man—you could see he was a man, though shrouded in a robe of sapphire light—tall, slim man, tending the meat that hung by the fire, moving it this way and that, seeing that the flames licked it just right, taking the spits down, slicing up whole roasts onto plates, sliding skewers of vegetables, roasted onions and potatoes and whatnot, down beside them.

A very similar woman acting as tavernmaid, woman dressed in ruby mist, tapping gray stone steins full of foamy red beer and carrying them to the customers, bringing them the platters of food that her mate prepared. Mate? Surely, for they looked so *right* together. Surely, the way they would sometimes pause to look at each other . . .

Edgar tilted back his stein, drank, rubbed foam from his lips, looked at her. "Their names are Morgan Bluelight and Ariadne Starfire. Their sort are called werefolk, hereabouts." *He seems so familiar, this Squire Edgar, as if . . .*

She said, "You mean like the Wolfman. Lon Chaney, all those old movies my parents used to watch when they couldn't sleep at night."

He shrugged, maybe rolled his eyes a bit. "Maybe that's what it means in your world. Here . . . They stem from human stock, they begin as human beings, wherever they begin. In the olden days, when the War was fresh in everyone's memory, when the Magic Order was new, some who aspired to become *magi* went bad, practiced the dark arts of *goëty*, were banished for their misdeeds."

"Goëty?"

"Amateur sorcery. The precursor to necromancy. Hardly *ars magica* at all." He said, "They say the werefolk are their descendants, shape changers, capable of some limited magic, relatively harmless magic. I suppose one could manifest as a wolf, if necessary."

She watched them waiting at table, tending their tavern, commonplace save for the magic light that spun round their handsome bodies. Descendants of magicians, serving meat and beer. She said, "You seem . . . familiar to me, Edgar . . ." *Just Edgar. Edgar No-Name.*

Dark eyes looking at her now. Eyes that seemed to understand, just like those other eyes. He said, "What was his name?"

She felt a pang, almost of shame. *Am I so easy to read?* "Dale Millikan."

No recognition in his eyes. Did I imagine it might be him, cast in some other guise? He's dead. I know he's dead. Consumed by the Angel of Death, long, long ago. This is just an old woman's very silly dream. I came out here, back out among the Stargates to . . . run away.

He said, "You don't seem like the sort of woman to fall helplessly in love. Certainly not the sort to stay in love with a man who's . . . gone from your side."

So much for understanding. So much for those dark, penetrating eyes that seemed able to look right into her head. "You don't know much about women, do you?"

He shook his head, eyes filling with an almost mournful look. "I suppose not."

You could see it then. This squire, following his lady love, who goes about her own business, assuming him to be merely . . . her follower. She said, "Who are you, really?"

He shifted uncomfortably on his bench, squeezing his big hands together, big, broad hands, with thick, blunt fingers. On one finger was a plain silver ring, some kind of writing on it. When she looked, leaning forward, she could see it said, in plain block letters, *I Will Not*. He twirled the ring, watching her watch it, and said, "Someone once told me my hands seemed better suited to wielding a sledge hammer than a typewriter."

Another faint pang. I remember finding that old, broken typewriter in my grandmother's attic. Such an incredibly complex machine . . .

He smiled. "Who am I, really? Just Edgar, squire to her ladyship Amanda Grey, Knight-Errant of the Silver Thread."

Just that and nothing more? She gestured to the ring. "What's that mean? 'I will not.'"

He stared at it, frowning. Finally, he said, "The Priesthood of *Ordo Magica* keeps the magic at bay, of course. The real magic, the terrible magic, the magic imbued in God's Machine, the magic which runs the world. This other magic . . ." A gesture at Morgan Bluelight, at Ariadne Starfire. "Children at play in the beach sand beside an ocean so vast they cannot conceive of its other side."

"And the ring?"

"Our work holds the world in suspended animation, a suspended animation in which the Machine runs down, in which things fall apart. One day it will end, one day it must end. So, we send out Agents of Change, agents to pave the way for that end. As I am imbued with infinite magic, so the ring reminds me that I must not . . . act."

Infinite magic. She said, "You're not from this world, are you?"

That long, penetrating stare. Then he took off the ring and carefully laid it on the table between them. "I know who you are, Astrid Kincaid."

A third pang, from deep within her heart. "You know me? Then . . ."

Nothing in his eyes. Not even a hint.

She said, "I know you're not Dale Millikan, though you seem so . . . similar. Tell me who you are. Affiliated with the Jug perhaps?" Was that what the pang was all about? Fear. Is this the way it ends, this calm-faced, bald-headed old man. How soon does the Angel burn overhead?

He sighed and shook his head. "So soon forgotten . . . No, I do not belong to the Space-Time Juggernaut, save in the sense that we may all be its creatures."

"Do you even know who you are?"

He said, "No. Not any more. Once upon a time, perhaps . . ."

Omry Inbar lay on his back, naked atop the heavy, velvety covers of his medieval bed, thinking. Just thinking. Little candles, hanging in sconces from the cold, gray, stone walls lit his corner of the room with a wan, warm yellow light, candle flames steady, casting dim, diffuse shadows into the corners of the room. The fire, already low when he came here, was down to crackling red coals now, little snakes of red light showing through masses of black ash.

The light from the noonday sun without was effectively erased by the thick, heavy brown drapes that covered the room's two narrow windows, but tiny slivers of pale white still glowed at the edges. Looking, he realized, almost the way the incandescent street lighting of big Earth cities looked, when you tried to sleep at night in some hotel, far away from home.

Thinking. Too many years spent away from home? And where is home now? Is it really lost? Or is this all just a dream? Too many wandering thoughts, too many lost-soul thoughts, when I should be dazzled by the wonder of all this. Look! Where am I now? In some splendid, magic, faraway, impossible world! In some cosmos where . . . everything is possible. Someplace no one ever imagined. Where am I now . . .

Lying alone in bed, naked; lying alone on my back with this same pointless erection that's manifested itself over and over again, since I was a boy.

Thinking about all the women I've stuck it in?

No, that would be too pleasant a pastime. Too rewarding.

No, thinking about how I lay in the bushes of this absurd inside-out world and stared at the sky and remembered some beloved clutch of ladylike genitalia or another, and jerked off. Jerked off while people hid in the shrubbery and watched and waited for me to come . . .

What must that have looked like, to Subaïda Rahman? Pathetic, most likely. Pornography remembered. Time spent masturbating to images of beautiful women masturbating while they dream of beautiful men.

Do no women masturbate to images of handsome men masturbating while they dream of handsome women? No. Of course not. Don't be silly. When women masturbate, it means they're . . . sensual. Alive. When men masturbate, it means they're alone.

Am I alone now?

That God-forsaken prick down there thinks you're alone.

Go ahead, Omry Inbar. Reach into your head. Pick out any woman at all, or no woman at all. We've been remembering Hiba a lot lately, haven't we? She was a good one. Lively when you wanted her to be lively; quiet, soft, submissive, when that's what was needed.

Gray stone castle. Noonday sun. Brilliant sunshine flooding straight down out of the sky. Ling Erhshan filled his lungs with fresh, clean air, filled his lungs and thought, It's . . . just the way I always imagined it would be. A faint whiff of something like gunpowder in the air. The way I imagined gunpowder ought to smell. The smell of fireworks on New Year's Day. Fireworks crackling around the edges of the dancing parade dragon, fireworks hanging above doorways . . .

Why gunpowder? Gunpowder the smell of excitement, of newness, promise of the future to an orphan boy.

Dark buildings all around, bright streets stretching away into the distance, filled with bustling, metallic crowds. This city is just big enough that I can see the roofs of the more distant buildings, tilted slightly towards me. Curvature. I wanted to say, the curvature of the Earth.

Memory of standing atop *Gonggashan*, one icy day, under a blue sky so sharp it seemed to cut right through my eyes. Seven thousand five hundred ninety meters. Oxygen masks for the weak. Weak like me. *Wutongqiao* visible in the distance, far to the east. Tiny city. Like toys on the horizon. Through binoculars, the misty buildings seem to lean strangely, as if they were falling away from me, falling into the east . . .

Beyond this city, here and now, red landscape rendered indistinct by blowing dust, imaginary horizon line far above the level of the streets, disappearing into pink mist, mist growing weaker and weaker, finally turning blue so very far away.

Out there, somewhere, beyond the blue, was only more land. Would you go home if you could, Ling Erhshan? No. Here I could wear a sword, carry a gun, walk like a man among men. Here I could be everything I'm not . . .

Image of himself, slack-bellied, flabby-armed, wielding a long sword, wielding it in single combat with a muscleman from the cover of one of those old American paperbacks. Image of a Frazetta hero swinging his shiny blade, blade cleaving Ling Erhshan's neck. Ling Erhshan's grimacing head leaping from his shoulders, bouncing off the edge of a wooden table, disappearing with a splash into that famous butt of ale.

It took time, but we finished pissing at last.

Where was that from? *The Long Ships*. Bengtsson. Red Orm and Tokë Gray-Gull's Son. My Lord Almansur. Thorkel the Tall and Ethelred the Redeless ... That's what would happen to me, if I tried to walk like a man, even here.

But, home? I never had a home. Home was inside the books. Inside the stories. Dale Millikan was my mother and father. I *so* longed to be Dorian Haldane.

Remember how hard it was for Haldane to adapt to the world he found beyond the nuclear singularity? Seasoned combat veteran, armed with early twenty-first century military weapons. And he almost didn't survive. Haldane facing his first swordsman, responding with bayonet drill. Then lying on the ground, in shock, by the corpse of his vanquished foe, while laughing warriors sewed and bandaged a huge, terrible cut across his shoulder ...

What would I do? Wave a calculator in their faces? Make engineering magic? You are trying to make yourself feel bad, Ling Erhshan. Trying to make yourself be no more than the brave little scientist who went to the Moon.

It isn't working. The blood is pounding in your veins. Look! See where you are! I'm in Heaven, that's where I am ...

He smiled, squared his shoulders, turned and walked inside. Somewhere, the others would be having breakfast. Time to face the new day, if that's what it was. New day under a noonday sun.

What will happen next, I wonder? Thin smile, pleased smile, almost a fatuous smile. Doesn't matter. It will be something. That's all that matters. I'm in a world where *something* will happen.

Remember how Dorian Haldane felt? He said, I've come to a time and place where it doesn't matter that I'm fifty-four years old. Suddenly, somehow, I've stopped thinking about the day I'll die.

All around her, the pale world rose up toward a misty infinity. Subaïda Rahman stood at the rail, holding on, as the cruiser *Anotar* slid away from the landing stage, slid away from the stone city of Yttria, sliding away into the pale blue Hesperidian sky.

Floating like a soap-bubble, she thought, propellers turning lazily at the stern, driving us upward into nothingness. Somewhere on the other side of the blue . . . Heart of Darkness. She made it into an Arabic phrase, murmured it to herself. Nothing. *Koro'mal'luma* had a certain air of menace, but . . .

The Land of Awful Shadow. That was better. The awe of God Himself; Shadows in Shayol.

A short distance away, Ling Erhshan stood at the rail, peaceful, seeming to smile, if only to himself, looking backward, watching the city fade into distance, reddening with shadows as it grew smaller and smaller still. Edgar at the helm of this somewhat larger ship, watching where they were headed, though up there was nothing but blue sky.

What does he see? Nothing? She could imagine the ship following a long chord across empty space, an ingeodesic terminating on this world's . . . what? Gateway to some remote Hell? Oh, *Allah* . . . I was never a religious woman, but I'm afraid now. What if it's all . . . true? What if I'm *not* lost in a dream? What if I fall into the fire?

There'd been a popular American VR entertainment released just before the ships had come back from the Moon, just before they'd slammed the door in the world's face. *Inferno*. Not quite up to the standard of the Orgasm Hat, but still, that one image, that one burst of crude sensation, as she'd waded out into the Lake of Boiling Blood . . .

Behind Edgar, Amanda Grey and Astrid Kincaid, one bright with metal, the other merely metal-bright, the two of them shoulder-to-shoulder, not holding onto anything, arms folded across sturdy breasts. Sufficient unto themselves. Complete. Is that the word I'm looking for? Something in Edgar's eyes, when he looks at his knight-errant. Does she see?

What do we expect to find in the Heart of Darkness? The Gateway home? They say it is lost and gone forever. No one really believes that. If we believed it, we'd simply . . . stop. Maybe we'd all like to stop. We just can't say it to each other.

By the aft rail, beyond which the propellers spun, Omry Inbar sat, one arm draped lazily overboard, looking downward through turbulent air, downward at the ground. On his knee . . . She looks like a little goddess, Aarae does. Like a little naked goddess. Inbar stroking her hair gently. Talking to her. Touching her four tiny wings. Little goddess nuzzling against his hand.

Rahman felt sick for a moment, but . . . It's only the stories we tell that make sex a lovely moment lost in eternity. It's only the stories that make it . . . love. A man holds you, warms to you, makes you warm to him, and pleasure, and pleasure . . . Maybe you waken in the night, when the warmth has grown cold and nasty, cold and sticky between your legs.

Toward the bow, looking outward into the empty sky, Lord Genda Hiroshige, standing handsome and stalwart, one arm around Amaterasu's back, riding lightly, just above her hips. The robot was saying something, speaking to him, gesturing with one hand, out into the vacant blue. Maybe she can see beyond its veil, see what we cannot. Her other hand was on his back, stroking gently. Knowing. Knowing him.

That faint red fuse of . . . is it anger or envy? Anger at him for accepting her manufactured servitude? Accepting it as the *face* of love? Or do I envy her for living the imaginary love the rest of us only long for? How do they *feel*?

Tarantellula sitting not far away, sitting on the deck, muscular back braced against the cabin wall, little Brucie cradled like a child in her arms, chattering away, waving his arms, this and that, one thing and another, while stolid black Tarantellula merely smiled and nodded like an indulgent mother. With her hand gently resting between his legs. What is that all about?

Jensen and Laing? Standing together. Holding hands. Murmuring to each other, leaning close. I remember him holding the shards of his red ant woman clutched to his breast, sobbing like a man who'd lost . . . everything. How can he forget so soon? Cold voice from somewhere inside her. These are . . . *imaginary* people. Some creature of the night in some faraway thread on some disconnected skein, some creature sitting before a . . . *creation* machine, building, imagining their souls. Hard to imagine being such a creator, harboring multitudes within my head.

Beyond the ship, here and now, they'd flown so high that the ground beneath them grew pale and misty, until it seemed to disappear altogether, leaving them to drift in a void of endless blue, only the spark of the noonday sun to guide them. That and gravity's implicit . . . *down.*

Go down then. Downward to Hesperidia. Downward to the Heart of Darkness. Downward to the Land of Awful Shadow. Downward to the earth below, like the ants we are.

Standing at the rail behind the root of the flier's bowsprit, Kincaid watched it grow out of nothingness. First a sense that there was . . . something, out in the blue void. Something just behind the featureless shield of the sky. Clouds?

There was a description of something like that in one of Dale's silly damned books. Mariners lost at sea. Lost on the bosom of one of the Moon's vast oceans, the Sea of Tranquility, perhaps. Sitting downcast on their raft, drifting, drifting for terrestrial days on end beneath a slow-moving, torrid Lunar sun, Earth hanging motionless in the sky while the Sun slid to zenith and beyond.

Dorian Haldane, ever brooding, standing in the center of the raft, faithful, loving Valetta holding onto his leg, shading her eyes with one terribly sunburnt hand. In the distance, they would see something like the shadow of rounded mountains.

There were no rounded mountains on Dorian Haldane's Moon, a distant relative of old Bonestell's Moon, a Moon of immense, vertical peaks . . . I laughed at him about that. Bonestell expected sharp peaks only because he thought, with no wind and water to wear them down . . .

Dale grinning at her, a hint of anger in his eyes. What difference does it make? It's tall, angular mountains that are lovely, evocative . . .

Sliding a hand up her thigh: Like you . . .

Silly bastard.

Clouds behind the sky now?

No, a patch of . . . growing detail. Faraway landscape making itself known below them. Something in the middle of it all, bulging up, dark, blue-black, like the shadow of a bruise, rounded now, reaching . . . Leaning on the rail beside her, Amanda Grey said, "*Koro'mal'luma*'s moon."

As simple as that. Dark body looming out of shadow, growing large, features on its surface, shiny seas, continents, rivers, tiny white clouds, the larger landscape of Hesperidia hanging behind it. Are there ships on those tiny seas? Tiny ships, with little mariners to sail them?

Dale would've liked that. Would've liked imagining a tiny raft, with tiny Haldane upon it, drifting to nowhere with tiny Valetta by his side. Those amazingly stupid scenes he wrote, of Haldane lying atop her, fucking her, while the sun beat down on his back. She'd shaken the book in his face. Do you know what the Hell that'd be *like*? Image of Valetta with sunburnt thighs, Dorian Haldane with a red-toasted scrotum . . .

A shrug. What difference does it make? These are stories.

Anotar swept close to the limb of the nameless moon and Kincaid felt some immaterial force tugging at her, invisible fingers offering to help her slip over the rail and fall, straight down into a tiny silver sea.

"What holds them up?" she said.

Amanda looked at her, puzzled. "What difference does it make? They're up."

All the difference in the world. And yet. They slid under the moon, slid down into the space above the Land of Awful Shadow, and Kincaid felt a hard pang grip her by the heart. Heart of Darkness, indeed. Shadowed crater, like some huge Lunar impact crater. Like that nice oblique view of Tycho I had as we orbited in, heading for the first moonbase.

Gloomy purple countryside, vertical cliffs glittering, as if made from silver or gold, as if studded with jewels. And there, a tall, eroded central peak, reaching up almost to the moon, surmounted by . . . a castle. Castle shrouded in luminescent silver mist. *Flicker-flash*. A strobe of something like lightening. Amanda called back over her shoulder, "All right. Set her down anywhere." Squire Edgar, bending to his task, grunting as he hauled on the old-fashioned spoked wheel, ship heeling hard over, sliding toward the ground.

"The castle," Edgar murmured, "of Lord Ahriman."

"Quest's end." said Amanda Grey.

End? Not just the beginning?

Kincaid, uneasy, opened her mouth, words of caution rising up, but unspoken. A soft, familiar ache in her bowels. Soldiers, everywhere, across time, dropped from helicopters into an enemy-held LZ. Soldiers spilling out of LSTs into water too deep, too far from an enemy held coast, struggling through stormy surf, while the machine guns went *flicker-flash, flicker-flash*, and mowed them down.

Watching the ground rise toward them, Ling Erhshan felt the excitement build in his chest. A ... tightening sensation, as if *I'm nervous*. Agitated. It was gloomy here, light of Hesperidia's noonday sun occluded, leaving a twilight landscape in deep purple shadow. Shadow, he realized, that was about the same shade as the ink you sometimes saw depicting shadow in old comic books.

The night scenes in *Rogues of Sherwood Forest*. Remember how blue they made the midnight sky, Robin and Marian riding along ...

Beside him at the rail, Brucie said, "I feel like there ought to be ... music or something."

A snort of mirth from Tarantellula. "Like what?"

"I don't know. The theme music from *Apocalypse Now*?"

"Never heard of it."

Ling said, "Ride of the Valkyries." First thought: Immortal Americans, living in America, forgetting and forgetting. Second thought: But this man with his ridiculous, monstrous penis lived back then. Lived when all the old things *I obsessed over as a child were ... new.* Strange to look at it that way. Somewhere, perhaps, there still lives a man, a very old man, who was once a boy. Who opened the cover of a new magazine and wondered who this Norman Bean was, writing about life under the moons of Mars.

Do I envy him that memory? Would he envy me being ... here?

Anotar's keel-plate grated on the turf, crater walls rising in the distance, sunlight still on them, walls of gold sparkling with a distinct costume-jewelry glitter. I could, Ling thought, imagine there might be new, unknown colors out there somewhere.

Laing, still holding Jensen's hand, said, "Why're we setting down way out here? Why not drive right up to the castle?"

As if in answer, the mist shrouding the castle sparkled with bright blue lightning, followed by a brief, soft rumble of distant thunder. Amanda said, "The castle defenses are still in order."

Kincaid: "So they'll shoot down a flier, but we can otherwise just . . . walk right in?"

Amanda glanced at Edgar, frowning. "Well. Not quite. But we'll get in."

Edgar staring back at her, gaze boring into her eyes. He seems, Ling thought, very unhappy about all this.

Then, they were assembled on the ground beside the flier, *Anotar* seeming to relax when relieved of its burden, leaning to one side now, so that a portion of its rounded hull rested on the ground as well. Like those pictures of beached sailboats you see. It looks abandoned.

Kincaid and Amanda stood together again, side by side, looking almost like different colored twins, the American with a slim pair of high-tech binoculars, machinery whining faintly as tiny lenses twirled and focused. The Têtonic knight looked through an ornate Victorian sort of spyglass, both of them focused on the distant castle, two women whispering to each other.

Our leaders. Why them? And what about the rest of us? Shouldn't Laing stand with them as well, representing her own dimension? What about the Arabs? Well. Colonel Alireza is dead of course. Inbar? Nonsense. No leadership there.

Inbar standing back by the ship, fairygirl floating in the air in front of his face. He seemed to be smiling, at least.

Rahman? Standing by herself. Looking at Inbar. And what about me? I only represent myself. Chinese leatherfragments, lying dead on the Moon. If there still is a Moon.

Tall Tarantellula, standing a meter or so taller than her nearest competitor, suddenly turned, shading white eyes in the contrasty gloom, seeming to peer over the ship. Long pause. *"Sergeant?"* A painful urgency in the spiderdancer's voice, and she was letting go of her boyfriend's hand, unslinging her rifle from one shoulder, working some mechanism or another. *Clink-click.*

Kincaid spun, lowering the binoculars, her own eyes a sparkle of unearthly silver. Question written on her face, but looking where Tarantellula looked, not at the woman herself. Curious. She's already gotten her rifle off her shoulder, in her hands, finger through the trigger guard, metallic sound of a round jacking into the chamber faded, its tiny echo gone . . .

Amanda Grey's sword made a razor-on-strop ring coming out of its scabbard, Squire Edgar's no more than an instant behind, two silver blades shining like bright chrome in the dim light. Ling felt a hard tingle go up his spine, a sense that his hair might be stirring on his head.

Something I'm supposed to *do*. Something . . .

Tarantellula was reaching out with one huge black hand, shoving Brucie behind her. Over here, Laing and Jensen were standing back to back, each holding some kind of small weapon in hand. *Ray guns.* They have ray guns.

Lord Genda Hiroshige with one hand on his lover's slim arm. Robot Amaterasu turning, turning to face the direction of the parked ship. Plump Omry Inbar standing still, Aarae circling over his head, wings rumbling softly, like a huge, angry wasp.

Subaïda Rahman standing alone. Standing there empty-handed. Standing there, looking at me.

Oh. Of course.

Sick feeling in the pit of his stomach.

Vibration in the ground now.

Distant thunder, sound of a million hoofbeats.

Ling Erhshan reached into the pocket of his nice new Hesperidian jacket, a gray suede leather coat that would have cost a thousand yuan back in Green China, and took out his handgun. Two bullets left in here. Two bullets. Fragmentary memory of holding the gun in both hands, just as if he really *were* an expert marksman. Holding the gun and killing the dimetrodon which, it turned out, had indeed killed that Arab boy.

What was his name? Ahmad Zeq. I almost forgot.

Remember the look on his face as he died?

Blind eyes turned to the sky, calling out for his lover.

Who will I call for when it's my turn to die?

No time to answer. No time to wonder why.

It came over the canted hull of the parked flier like some bright green kangaroo, an indistinct green shape, somehow angular, a tall triangle perhaps, covered with leaves and glittery green scales. Legs like a kangaroo, arms like an elephant's trunk, long thick tail, like a theropod carnivore's tail . . .

Ling kneeled and fired his little pistol, fired and saw the thing jerk in the air, saw it explode into a thousand green flowers, flowers falling together, spilling together onto the ground, spraying apart in a fine star pattern, rolling, rolling, then still.

Another one.

Steadying his arm now, one hand cradling the other, mind remote and cool, heart slow and steady, thud, thud, thud, in his chest. *Bang.* Another green explosion, another spill of flowers.

Ling Erhshan lowered his pistol with a sigh, felt his heart begin to speed up, pounding faster and faster.

Another one. But the gun was empty now.

And another and another and another.

Ten. Then fifty. Then a hundred. A multitude of strange green things, bounding over the ship, turning into a green waterfall, a green river boiling over some recalcitrant stone, wearing it away, green things coming round the sides of *Anotar* now, round the flier's bow and stern. Green things coming from all directions.

Ling Erhshan looked down at the empty gun in his hand, and thought, Who *will* I call out for?

Squire Edgar stepping forward into an onrushing wall of green flesh, wielding his chrome-bright sword in a flashing figure-eight pattern, metal blade making a dull whooping sound as it spun, stepping forward into the silent horde . . .

That sound. The sound a butcher's blade makes as he cuts meat into bits.

Green flowers suddenly heaping round Edgar's booted feet.

Guns crackling like fireworks. Kincaid and Tarantellula standing side-by-side, M-80s leveled, barrels smoking, green things exploding, turning into flowers, heaps and piles of flowers.

Jensen and Laing? Little pistols making silent sparks of blue. No flowers there. Green things bursting into flame, melting down like plastic toys.

Like the toy soldiers we burned when we were children. You'd set them on fire and they'd burn, burn away to nothing, melt away, like the Wicked Witch of the West. Until there was nothing left but a dull green lump, bubbling and smoking on the sidewalk . . .

Angry buzz-saw whine. Omry Inbar standing motionless, Aarae whirling round and round, green flowers spraying away in all directions like ejecta from a meteor strike.

Killing them. Killing them by the tens and hundreds and . . .

More of them. More green things spilling over the ship. Green things coming for *me* . . .

Ling Erhshan turned and ran, heading for . . . The forest! Run to the forest! There's a hollow tree there somewhere. You can squeeze in at the base. You're small and thin. The others can defend the door, that's the way it's supposed to go.

And inside the tree, there'll be a ladder, ladder you can climb, up to a flat-topped branch. The cliffs. The tunnels. Sator Throg. Thuvia, charmer of banths and . . .

But, it seemed, he was running in slow motion, running through quicksand, running through tar, the forest never getting any closer, breath strangling in his throat, air sipped in through a gaping mouth, going nowhere, while he drowned in bowel-cramping . . .

Shadows looming over him. Terrifying shadows. Shadows making him freeze in one spot, unable to run away.

Who do I call out for?

No one.

No life flashing before my eyes.

No mother to save me.

No one to awaken me from this awful dream and hold me close, wipe away my tears, whisper in my ear . . .

It's all right. It's all right now, orphan boy. It's . . .

Things grabbing him.

A hard snap of pain as one arm came out of its socket, tendons popping, muscles tearing.

Teeth!

Teeth in me!

Teeth like a surgeon's knife, slicing flesh.

A sucking noise as some part of him came loose.

Smiling green mouth full of mossy green teeth, holding a fine red steak, chewing, chewing . . .

Blood running down its throat, dripping down onto its chest.

My blood.

It's eating me.

Eating me!

Another bite, hard teeth going through soft flesh, opening him up, air rushing in to fill the wound, agony striking hard, bright blood spraying, festive red on green, then fading, fading, fading . . .

Ling Erhshan's world turned blue and went away.

All over now. Windrows of flowers, like drifts of fluffy green snow surrounding the ship, banked against *Anotar*'s leaning hull, covering the landscape, disguising the carnage they'd made. Omry Inbar thinking, Carnage? Carnage is about *meat*. These things . . .

Still, there was meat here and there.

Rahman and Kincaid, Amanda Grey and Squire Edgar bending over someone fallen. The sound of a man throwing up, gagging, retching repeatedly, the bubbling sound of his guts coming up. Soft moan of agony. They were stitching Ling Erhshan now, bandaging his wounds. Bandaging what was left of him.

Trying not to look. Trying. Failing. Big hole in his side, like a shark bite. Like something you saw in a documentary about Indian Ocean divers. Left arm gone from the elbow, ending now in a red and white lump of bandage. That long rip in his thigh, red meat bleeding slowly, white bone visible until they tucked his tissues together and sewed and sewed.

Ling Erhshan babbling in Chinese, high-pitched, hysterical sounding, singsong words. An agonized grate in English, "Oh, God. Oh, God."

Someone, Robot Amaterasu, bending low, lovely rump outlined through the material of her clothing, fishing through a pile of bloody green flowers. Picking something up. The chewed remains of his arm. Ling silent. Staring at it. Robot looking back at him, as if measuring . . .

You could see Ling's eyes go out of focus, then roll up white as he fainted.

Amaterasu tossing the arm aside. Useless. What was she thinking? Rescue the part, in case it could be put back on later? Robot analogies? Maybe not. Who knows what magic they had in America? All over now. Pointless battle. Not even that, for me.

Magic Aarae spinning round him, tearing the green things apart, spilling all their flowers. Aarae floating in front of him now, just floating on air, wings not moving at all. Dark eyes concerned, looking into his eyes. Looking deep. Are you all right? they seemed to say. She floated close, reached out to put one tiny hand on his face, to touch him softly.

Laing and Jensen in the background as well, ray guns holstered now, wading through knee-deep flowers, nudging with their booted toes at the lumps of flower plastic they'd melted. Laing and Jensen holding hands again. Genda standing alone, just watching. Looking at Amaterasu, watching her fish through the flowers.

Had he stood idly by during the battle?

Yes. Robot Amaterasu a blur of motion, arms and legs turned to gray mist, surrounding him all by herself, defending him. I had time to see that, looking out through my impenetrable pixie wall . . .

Over there. Black shape, long, lean, improbably angular black shape lying broken on the ground, white eyes open, featureless as ever, blind now as well, staring up at that impossible moon. Staring upward, as if searching for the sky. Searching for the real sky.

Small boy shape bending over her, boy face cast down into smallish hands. Bending over her. Silent. Brucie Big-Dick took his hand away from his face, reached out and tried to close Tarantellula's dead eyes. Tried again. Useless. The lids kept popping back open, white eyes looking upward.

Staring at her. Staring. Tears tracking slowly down his face.

Inbar could feel Aarae touching his face again.

Are you all right?

Of course I am. Nothing's happened to *me*.

After a while, Brucie stood, looking down on her. Turned away, walked to where the others still worked over motionless Ling. Spoke to Edgar, who stared at him, then pointed to the ship, whispering. Brucie trudged away to the ship, came back a while later with a long-handled shovel. Stood still again. Then started to dig.

Still crying?

No. Face expressionless, concentrating on his task, shovel blade making remote wet sounds as it cut through the turf. You must remember, Inbar told himself. This man is almost two hundred years old. At some point, perhaps, everyone he ever knew and loved has died . . .

Still, he watched, wondering, while Aarae touched him and whispered to him and comforted him in vain.

Kincaid stood looking down on bandaged, unconscious Ling Erhshan, slowly putting away the components of the first-aid kit. Good enough. Just barely good enough.

Memory of Ling's moans and babbling cries. Not prepared. Not prepared for this at all. I wonder if anyone ever is? Faint memory, raw nerves from the distant past, remembered wounds of her own.

Raving while we treated him, going on and on about the Plant Men of Barsoom, about how John Carter and Tars Tarkas were trapped, battling them in the Valley Dor . . . he still thought it was all a dream. Thought it was a dream until the teeth began to cut his flesh. Until he began to die.

Maybe everyone feels that way, until the last split second before death.

Or maybe they feel that way until dying is complete. All those old stories about near-death phenomena and out-of-body experiences. Just fantasies the brain makes to stave off recognition of its inevitable extinction. But then, we all wonder, *What if it's true?* Oh, God, wouldn't that be . . . wonderful?

Well, no. Maybe not.

Windrows of green flowers around them now, the Plant Men of Barsoom destroyed. Did they have near-death experiences as we exploded them away into petals and leaves?

Image of a spider's life flashing before its eyes as the crushing shoe descends.

Who were they really? Warriors in the Eternal Battle? Angels out of Ahriman's Hell? Does it matter? Why should the world's motives be transparent to me?

Amanda Grey said, "Edgar, you told me the Guardians were no more."

The bald man shrugged. "Ahriman," he said, "is the Father of Lies."

Kincaid thought, *Ahriman?* No, the Multiverse is the father of lies, if only because it makes all things possible.

The mountain towered above them, sheer, shattered rock faces reaching upward into the blue-glowing mist, reaching toward that slow-turning moon, magic castle invisible now, hidden by the soft flash of sporadic electrical discharge, by the slow-boiling mist. Ling Erhshan walked, walked as well as the others, walked in their midst, silent, holding onto his pain, holding it close, folding it deep into his heart, making it disappear.

They'd wanted to leave him behind, some of them, leave him with the ship, had been discussing it when he'd awoken to fresh panic, awoken from a horrible nightmare, sitting up, jerking hard, screaming with fear, then again, screaming with agony.

So long as he didn't look, didn't look and see the bloody wadding of bandage, didn't see . . . So long as he didn't look, he could still feel the fingers of his left hand, could feel the cool, damp air of the mountainside on his skin, could flex his fingers, feel the muscles and tendons of his forearm slide, just like always.

It feels, he realized, just like I have a broken elbow or something. But then he'd look. And see. And the pain would come back for just a moment, savage as ever. It's not real pain. It's fear. It's horror. Imagine how I'd feel now, sitting on the ship, sipping my tea, waiting and wondering, looking out at all those silent green flowers. The pain would be unbearable.

Then Kincaid, saving him: We might not come back this way.

But, said Amanda Grey, gesturing at his stump, When we rescue Ardry Bright-Sky . . .

Ardry Bright-Sky, said Squire Edgar, something very bitter in his voice.

They'd walked away from the ship, all together, torn and broken Ling Erhshan among them. It was a while before he'd put away enough of the pain to look at his comrades. To see little Brucie walking alone, eyes hard and dark, and look around, and see who was missing. He'd searched his memory and seen a fresh grave there.

So. The two Arab pilots, whose names I never learned, dying in their ship. Then Chang. Da Chai. Still lying, perhaps, in the Lunar dust. Then Ahmad Zeq, eaten by a dimetrodon under the Permian sunrise. Eaten. A sudden cold crawling. Then the little red-ant woman. Then Colonel Alireza, dead just when the adventure was truly begun. Now . . .

And, of course, all those others. The American soldiers whose fragments they'd seen outside the closed Stargate. We killed them, didn't we? The red-ants slain by the greens, when that ship was shot down. The ship we struck, when *Baka-no-Koto* came flaming through the last gate . . .

The nameless ones always die. The faceless ones die. The ones who are . . . more closed, more silent. They always die. Did I know anything, anything real about Alireza? No. His English was so poor, his character so . . . bland. Now this Tarantellula. Concealed from me, of course, by her monstrous form. No person there. No woman at all. Merely a nightmare demon, so tall, so black, with eyes so white, eyes devoid of feeling, of humanity.

Brucie, Brucie Big-Dick, walking along silently, hands in pockets, head down. Another monster there. Closed to me. Another . . . spear carrier.

And, of course . . . When he looked down at his arm, the phantom fingers disappeared, pain lancing toward his shoulder. He looked up at the mists again. Up where Ahriman's castle lay hidden. Up where they'd find Ardry Bright-Sky, whoever he might be. And perhaps the gateway to God's Machine.

Who am I now? What's waiting for me up there on the misty mountain? Ahriman, the Dark Lord? Or is it only Sauron who awaits me? The hobbits never got their arms bitten off, did they? Dorian Haldane was injured from time to time, injured badly, required to lie back and heal. Maybe Valetta awaits me up there. Maybe she's undressing for me even now, waiting for me to come and lie upon her and . . .

His stump throbbed softly, beating in time to his heart, breath quickening as the path before them steepened. Fafhrd. Fafhrd lost his hand. But Fafhrd wasn't real. I am. I am real. Honest to God I am.

Standing at the edge of the precipice, Astrid Kincaid could look out over the whole of Koro'mal'luma's valley, out across the Land of Awful Shadow and back into the eternal sunlight of Hesperidia. Seen from its central peak, the caldera spread out, vast, dark and forbidding.

As if it were . . . waiting for something? Someone? Me?

Am I central to the scheme of things, or only a bit player? Cold comfort: I still live.

The mist surrounding the top of the mountain swirled overhead, their view of the moon overhead hazy, part of it invisible, hidden by thicker mist, perhaps by the mountain itself, the structure of the castle. Ahriman's castle. Every now and again, remote thunder would stutter overhead, the sound of distant kettledrums, played with a brush.

Unnatural thunder. Hardly like thunder at all. Serving only

to add to the menace of their surroundings. Remember Dale, sitting at his keyboard? One more story, written for one more paycheck. He didn't like you looking over his shoulder like that. Always made him stop cold, fingers hanging uselessly in the air, waiting for me to leave.

I'm . . . working, he would say, gritty exasperation poorly concealed.

But . . . don't you love me?

Nothing in return but a conflicted glare.

Thunder stuttering again, louder, more like real thunder.

Dale always talked about using the weather for stage-setting. Let the sun shine in. Raindrops falling on my head. Stormy weather. Cultural symbolism so universal it was beyond being trite.

Who wants to die on some lovely, sunshiny day?

How old was I when my grandfather died? Eleven? Twelve. Something like that. I remember he died not long after New Year's Day, while I was in the sixth grade. Gray, gray weather, wintertime in Boston. Going into the church while the world filled up with cold mist. Flakes of snow when we came back out, falling on my face, melting.

I let myself cry a little bit then. Cold snowflakes on my face, melting into the tears. My parents noticed. Noticed it was the first time I'd cried for him. Was it the first time I realized what a cold little girl they thought I was? Why were *they* so cold that they could talk about it in front of me, as if I wasn't even there?

There was a herd of something moving across the open floor of the valley below, thousands of dark green specks moving together against the lighter, shadowed green of the grass. Why does the grass grow here? Light reflected in under the moon?

Beyond Koro'mal'luma, Hesperidia was a landscape of sunwashed mountains, of lovely bright plains, of silvery rivers and bright blue sea. A land of eternal summer, perhaps.

Ling was lying nearby, leaning his back against a dark boulder, cradling the ruin of one arm with his surviving hand, eyes shut. He seems so surprised by what happened. Caught up in his own set of dreams. But now he knows he's not the hero of his own story.

Brucie the Technician sat beside Ling. They'd been talking earlier, the two of them talking in whispers. I listened, but I've already forgotten what they talked about. Personal stuff. Aimless wandering. Comforting each other, in a way. Comforted by the pointless friendship of men.

He's lost her. Perhaps he loved her already.

I lost my soldier. I was responsible for Tarantellula. I let her volunteer for the mission, let her come along, even though I knew I had no intention of coming back. I was going out to find Dale Millikan. And I led her to her death.

Damn you, Dale. You made me love you, and now I can't even remember your face!

She turned, intending to look back up at the mountain, intending to stare upward into the mist, looking for the shadow of the castle to come. Instead, she found herself staring into Amanda Grey's eyes. The woman said, "You've lost your way, haven't you?"

Kincaid stared. Stared, and said, "Maybe I never knew where I was going."

"You know what you're leaving."

Leaving? Yes. Leaving everything. All the pointless events of a pointless life, a century and a third that added up to nothing. She nodded. Gestured up at the mountain. "Let's get going."

A shadow of a smile on Amanda's face. "Soldier on? It seems like the thing you do best."

Above them, the mist darkened and the thunder grumbled, all of it full of portent. Some bastard, Kincaid thought, telling my story. Taking it away from me. Making it his own.

I am, thought Robert Bruce Tanner Davidson the Third, *unprepared for this*. No. I wasn't prepared for any of it. No knowledge of how to react, of what to react to, no matter how many years I'd lived. Still smarting at the loss.

Visions of coupling with the black giant, of using that silly pornotool on her. Visions of coupling in the darkness, out under the stars, out among the worlds. She was there in

America all along. There for me somewhere, waiting for me. If only I'd found her, we wouldn't have come. If we'd found each other, we'd be there now, home, together, lying together on some California beach, listening to the surf, making love under the stars . . .

I don't believe home is gone. Only that we've lost the way back.

Brief memory of a childhood home, somewhere in the Valley, under a dry, clear, sunshot sky. Playing with a little black and white dog. Was it a wire-haired terrier? I think so. Name. Inky, maybe? A long, long time ago. Remember how he used to leap through my Hula Hoop? Didn't even ask for a reward, jumping, running, smiling his doggy smile.

Even people's dogs were immortal in America. Inky just didn't last long enough . . . Immortality. Jesus. She lost all that. All I lost was her. Try to remember. Try to remember you've lost a thousand friends. You were a dried old husk, the last of the lot, hanging on out of pure cussedness, when they came back from the Moon. Came back, and . . . and . . .

Your parents died old. Your first wife died in that car crash, way the Hell back in the 1990s. Second wife just got old and croaked. You lived on because you had nothing better to do.

Remembered images of their final night in Yttria, final night in a big, comfortable bed. Well, not so big and comfortable for her, complaining about the way her legs stuck out onto the floor. Image of that giant black beak of a mouth opening to engulf my made-up self, sucking on me until I was . . . what? Was I happy?

Image of myself snuggling down between her legs, nuzzling my face into folds of black leather, finding tender tissues, moister tissues, nibbling away on her until . . . Was she happy then? Were we happy? Maybe. Our truth at any rate.

Image of dead white eyes, featureless eyes, looking up at an empty heaven.

Now, the castle towered over them all. Waiting. Blue mist rose on all sides, blotting out the whole world, blotting out the moon above, hiding the shadowlands without, the bright-lit plains of Hesperidia beyond. Every now and again, violet light would flicker in the mist, thunder would grumble and fade away.

Squire Edgar behind them all, some little distance away, near the edge of the precipice, arguing in whispers with his knight-errant Amanda Grey. Trying to convince her of what? Turn back. Edgar, grown increasingly surly. Angry about something. Angry at her? No. Just Angry.

They stood in front of a tall, tall wooden door, door of giant planks reaching upward to disappear into the mist, hundreds of meters above. Door set in a masonry wall of huge, irregular gray stones. Fitted stones. No mortar visible. Stones like blocks stolen from a million billion copies of Stonehenge. Stones from the Giants' Dance.

Ling sitting, still silent, on the ground nearby, resting, not looking at the ruin of his arm. At least he's eating now. Nibbling from his ration pack, eating dried meat, chewing bites from some flat, salty, brown biscuits. Corn dodgers. Don't remember where I heard the term. Little Blackie likes 'em? Corn dodgers and Little Blackie. All I can remember . . .

Sergeant-Major Astrid Kincaid said, "All right. Let's go." Something heartening to her about being here. She's in charge again. Closer to whatever it is she's looking for, silver eyes looking at the door, measuring the meter-tall step of its lintel, the two-meter space between the lintel and the door.

They all started forward, not quite line abreast, some staying behind, others . . .

Brucie stepped up onto the lintel, stepped up under the door, stepped into deeper gloom—a darkness not quite black—distant light, grayish-white light, shining on them from beyond the door. The light from . . . inside. What the Hell are we facing? Lord Ahriman? Who the Hell is that? Spatima Zarathustra's chief demon. Is it Angra Mainyu that's waiting for us?

And now, walking under the giant's door, "What the Hell am I remembering? Some God-damned cartoon . . ."

Sotto voce, Ling Erhshan, walking close behind him, said, "*Jack and the Beanstalk.*"

* * *

Standing under the inner edge of the door, looking out into the vast gray space beyond, Astrid Kincaid clutched her M-80 tightly across her chest, feeling alone and very old.

I miss having Tarantellula with me. It felt like I had a comrade, even though I hardly knew her. Comrades. Soldiers. Something to hold on to. Tarantellula . . . and sudden memories of Corky Bokaitis, of Francis Muldoon, of all the others, Fred, Barney, toy soldiers, living and dead.

I can feel the wounds, new and old, left by all the people connected to me who are gone. I can feel the dead, hanging on in memory like ghosts . . .

Beyond the door was a misty room so large the far walls and ceiling were invisible, shadows looming out of nowhere, like shadows falling from a distant sky. Far away, across a floor made of smooth, veined marble—a floor so flat and shiny it looked as if it were made out of some liquid—was a misty dome of pale pastel light. Gray light? No. Faintly covered with pink.

One last childhood memory, driving down I-70 toward Columbus, Ohio, under the gray light of a winter dawn. Christmas, 2009. Out on a flat plain, so very different from the rolling hills of eastern Pennsylvania, the city loomed, gray stone buildings rising out of the ground, jutting over the far horizon, surrounded by a smoggy mist lit pale pastel pink by the rising sun.

Like that. A dome of pale pink mist, Columbus in the morning, but with all the buildings gone . . . Is this it, then? Is this the Stargate Genda thinks will take us through Platonic Reality and out the other side, right through to the *real* reality of God's Machine?

Well, *his* version of God's Machine, perhaps. Edgar and Amanda . . . for them this is merely part of a well-oiled mythology. God's Machine is a part of their universe, and the gate goes nowhere but to where Ahriman's Heart of Darkness holds Prince Ardry Bright-Sky prisoner.

No gateway to God at all.

One of these will be true.

Either we escape or . . . we come back here, fair-haired prince rescued by Maiden Fair, brought back to life and love and throne and . . . ah, yes. Squire Edgar's anger. Just another silly love story.

She clicked the safety off her gun, put her finger through the trigger guard, and snarled, "Let's go."

Ling Erhshan stood quite still by the edge of the Well, submerged in the dull, pervasive ache of his wounds. Arm gone away, ghost limb left behind, fingers clenched now in a hard fist, making the muscles of his missing forearm ache. Vanished skin over the big bite in his side starting to itch. Reach there with your real hand, reach around your stomach, pains lancing away from a broken rib, and try to scratch. Leathery stuff there, covering the hole through which your intestines almost fell, leathery magic stuff put there by Squire Edgar. Deep pain from the rip in your thigh, neatly sewed shut after you fainted . . .

Squire Edgar was standing with his back to the Well, mother-of-pearl light rising up behind him, mist curling gently above his shoulders. Why am I calling it the Well? Old memory. Lost memory. The Well of Liquid Light. I don't remember, but the name seems so apt. Pool of liquid light spread out beneath the mist, shivering gently, moire ripples on its surface.

Memory from long ago. Physics class at Beijing Polytechnic, my first year away from . . . home? Call it that. Boarding schools and orphanages. All I had for homes. Ripple Tank, full of water and obstacles, the old-fashioned way we studied wave phenomena. This is sort of like that.

Squire Edgar with anger on his face. "We've made a mistake coming here. We've got to turn back."

Amanda turning to look at him: "Too late now. When the Emperor engaged us to retrieve his only begotten son . . ."

Omry Inbar with a fairy on his shoulder, reaching up to touch her ever so gently: "I'd be willing to turn back . . ."

Yes you would. Found what you're looking for, maybe? No reason for you to go home again. Nothing back there but ongoing life as one more fat Jew in a land of Muslim oppressors.

Amanda Grey: "Damn it, Edgar. This is what I *came* here for. Ardry Bright-Sky . . ."

Edgar's anger deepening, "Did you come here for *him*? Or for your Mastery?" That bitter, bitter look.

Something eating him. What?

Anger on Amanda's face now as well. "That," she said, "will do."

"No it will *not* do . . ."

Lord Genda Hiroshige, turning to his robot lady: "Amaterasu?"

Mechanical woman looking at him out of mechanical eyes: "Whatever you think is best." The deference of the unreal.

Rahman: "There's nothing for *me* here. I want to go home. If this is the way . . ." But you could hear it in her voice: There's nothing for me anywhere. Why home, then? Home to a possibly lost Earth? To what? Life as a faux-Lesbian in the Man's World of the United Arab Republic? Or would she go back and become . . . someone else?

Passiphaë Laing said, "This isn't our world, Edgar. We belong somewhere. Not here." Rhino Jensen, hero of *Crimson Desert*, silent, merely holding her hand. And in her voice? Nothing particularly subtle, just: We are what we were made to be.

Amanda Grey said, "Go on back then, Edgar. Go on back and take the other cowards with you."

Fury and sorrow mingling on his face.

Look back into all your old stories, Ling Erhshan. A thousand thousand women depicted doing just that, tearing off a man's scrotum with those same words. But this woman wears a sword of her own. Maybe she has a right to say them.

Edgar said, "Bruce? Professor Ling?"

Brucie stayed silent, still staring at the magic water, a well full of milk flavored with strawberry syrup.

Edgar said, "Professor Ling, the chirurgeons of Têtonland can grow you new limbs. They can make you whole again. In there . . ." a gesture at the rippling, misty Well, "In there we all die."

How does he know that? Is it part of some story in which we have no part?

"And to what end . . ." whispered Inbar, holding his pixie like a lovely doll.

Astrid Kincaid slung her rifle over her shoulder, snugging its strap up close, and said, "The Hell with you all." She turned, stepped forward, stepped into the Well and disappeared.

Gone, thought Ling Erhshan. Not a splash, not a shift in the pattern of ripples.

"Professor Ling."

Mind empty, Ling Erhshan took a step forward, then another and another, until he fell into the Well and was gone.

Subaïda Rahman stood silently by and watched them go, by ones and twos:

Astrid Kincaid with anger snapping in her eyes. Fed up with . . . all of this. Fed up with not finding . . . whatever intangible thing she was looking for.

Then Ling Erhshan, cradling his bandaged stump, limping on his torn leg, bending over his injured side, shuffling forward, slowly, slowly, into the Well and gone.

And that horrible Brucie Big-Dick, empty-eyed, singing softly to himself, " '. . . gone where the goblins go . . .' " Two quick steps forward and away.

Passisphaë Laing, girl reporter, heroic woman figure . . . Character from a story. Imitation of life set in motion for the edification of some passive Other? Passiphaë Laing hand-in-hand with Rhino-Jensen-I-Presume, the two of them stepping forward into the pink mists of nothingness.

Lord Genda Hiroshige, fleeing God's wrath . . .

Fleeing the Space-Time Juggernaut?

Lord Genda Hiroshige pausing to kiss his pathetic robot girl on the lips, both of them closing their eyes ever so briefly. And holding hands as well as they dropped away into that other world.

Away, perhaps, into nonexistence?

See the fear on Inbar's face? See how he clutches his pixiegirl close? I've found what I came for, his fearful eyes proclaim. Don't make me lose it now. Is that all you came for, Dr. Inbar, planetologist supreme?

Amanda Grey casting one arrogant eye round at the remainder, withering contempt for Squire Edgar. Amanda Grey turning and striding into the pool.

Edgar, standing motionless. Edgar fatalistic. "So. You put down the godhead, and it takes you back up." He drew his long sword, a gleaming metal tensor in the half-light that spilled up from the Well. Held it over his head. Screamed the name of *Odin*, fury in his voice. Made a swan dive over the Well and . . .

Omry Inbar looking at her, clutching his pixie doll. "Subaïda?"

Does Aarae have no opinion? Is he what *she* was looking for? Can't she take him back to Yttria and Happily Ever After? Rahman shrugged, smiled a half-smile. "Sorry." Took a step toward the Well, then another. Inbar ran past her, breathing heavily, and fell headlong into the mist, leaving her alone.

Well. All alone here now. All alone with my thoughts, my fears, my . . . memories? All right. And do *I* have the courage? Of course I do.

One step. Then another. And . . .

Falling. Falling through emptiness. Falling through the silvery pink mist that had spilled up from the Well of Liquid Light. Falling all alone in an empty pastel sky. Strange. I thought the others would be with me. No wind in my ears. Hair motionless. I could be floating in a vacuum. Not even breathing. How do I know that I fall?

Voice, neutral voice, neuter voice, voice without timber, voice without sound. Whispering to her . . .

Subaïda.

Subaïda, my love?

Who?

No answer.

The voice said, *By those who snatch away men's souls, and those who gently release them; by those who float at will, and those who speed headlong; by those who govern the affairs of this world! On the day the Trumpet sounds its first and second blast, all hearts shall be filled with terror, and all eyes shall stare with awe.*

Fallingfallingfalling. Accompanied by the whispering Voice.

I know those words. Of course I know them. Heart in her chest—all the evidence she had that she was still alive—stuttering with sudden terror. Oh, God. Every child knows those words.

Memory of hearing them, droned by some bored teacher. Some teacher teaching because it was the only job she could get. Somebody poking at my back. Salim. Trying to get my attention. I must have been eight years old. Maybe nine. They used to read to us from the apocalyptic Suras when we were children, because they were exciting, because they knew we'd listen. The dull, pedantic ones could come later, when we were accustomed to listening . . .

The Voice whispered, *When we are turned to hollow bones, shall we be restored to life? A fruitless transformation!*

Fruitless indeed. For what good is life, simply lived over again? Why come back to the same old sorrows and fears? Better to stay down in the empty silence of the grave, unknowing, unthinking, without form, without substance, without spirit . . .

But with one blast they shall return to the earth's surface.

Whether they will that return or not. *They question you about the Hour of Doom . . . On the day when they behold that hour, they will think they stayed in the grave but one evening, or one morning.*

In the Name of God, the Compassionate, the Merciful. What if it's real?

Then: Explosion of light and sound . . .

A moment's heart-pounding tumble through formless pink mist, tiny woman clutched tightly in his hands, then Omry Inbar found himself standing, sunk to his knees, in the surface of a cloud. A bright cloud, fleecy white wool under a dead black sky.

Curious, detached thoughts from that cool, carefully-trained scientific mind, a part of him that seemed almost lost, buried beneath endless dunes of drifting sand. It's that Lunar sky again, featureless, dead black sky, but for the Sun and Earth . . .

Eyes searching the heavens. Nothing. No sun to make this cloudscape bright. No Earth to go home to now. Am I tired of forging onward? The feel of the tiny woman in his hands was one answer. "Where are we, Aarae?"

Tiny pixie face clearly frightened, big, dark, foxy eyes darting and wary. "In . . . the heart of God's Machine." Pixie-girl still talking from a script, speech full of meaning-freighted pauses. But she huddled close to his side, and that was all that really mattered.

A meteor fell from the black sky, trailing a line of pale pink dust, arcing downward to fall nearby. A glowing meteor with a human at its heart. Rahman, of course.

He struggled to walk, found it unexpectedly easy, like walking through fog. Though, when I peer downward . . . nothing. My feet are resting on nothing. I'm walking on air. Walking toward Rahman, but . . . They made it to a towering billow of cloud stuff and Inbar stood still, looking all around. White clouds towering higher, tumbling lower, down to a horizonless black sky. Far out in the inky dark, other clouds, moving across his vision field—only that, for there was no backdrop—other clouds, tracking in distant arcs, like planets round a central sun.

As if I stood at the center of some immense, diaphanous orrery. Planet clouds with little moon clouds swirling round them. As if they floated on some invisible surface. A bit like . . . some ancient spiral galaxy in formation. Can we have come to the beginning of time? No. Not the beginning.

Voices.

Ling Erhshan coming up the hill, cradling his stump, leaning into his pain, Brucie the Technician walking with him, the two of them talking. Ling said, "It all reminds me of something."

Yet another old story? Was that all you thought about, when you weren't building your secret rocket ship? Sudden bitter memory. They brought weapons to the Moon, these terrible Green Chinamen. Was it that which brought monstrous Americans down upon us all?

What if there'd been no Stargate? Another . . . thread, perhaps, in which the Plan worked out. Arab bases on the Moon. Arab resource nodes out among the asteroids. Colonies on Mars. A space station around Venus. Miners mining the surface metals of Mercury. A volatiles production facility on Ganymede . . .

A future for humanity. But . . .

Tiny Aarae sitting on his shoulder now, her tiny vulva damp on his skin, whispering in his ear, whispering, It will be all right, my love. It will be all right . . .

Brucie said, "Yeah. I know what you mean. I remember being a kid, back in the fifties . . ."

Sudden, pale shock, Inbar realizing he meant the *nineteen*-fifties. ". . . something about the galaxy turning out to be suds floating in a cesspool . . ." Cloudscape floating on darkness.

Ling said, "Bertram Chandler, perhaps?" Frowning now, concentrating, trying to remember."

Brucie said, " ' The Key'?"

Delight on Ling Erhshan's face, momentarily blotting out the pain. "Of course! Halvorsen's outhouse key."

To come *here* then, and think about . . . old stories? Who are these people? Aarae pressed her face against his cheek, kissing the corner of his eye. Other people appearing in the cloudscape. Laing and Jensen, holding hands. Amaterasu and Genda, holding hands. Kincaid, holding her rifle. Rahman, alone and empty handed, face flat and still, eyes alive with interest.

They walked onward, not quite a group, more like a collection of stragglers. Foot soldiers in some old movie. Napoleon's men, trudging slowly home through the snows of Russia, dying, dying, dying, the fruit of French manhood all lost at once. Frenchmen are short, they say, because all the tall Frenchmen died before Moscow.

A distant voice, crying out in the wilderness. "Oh, God. Take me away from here . . ." A soft, whining voice. A child's pleading voice.

Knight-Errant Amanda Grey and Squire Edgar, not standing together, standing apart, facing each other, another figure huddled between them, a man on his knees, a man on his belly, a man clad in rich clothing, cloth of gold, cloth of silver, cloth sequined with precious stones, emeralds and rubies and sapphires and diamonds, bright green and red, shimmering blue, pale, straw-tinted yellow.

A very handsome man in beggar's pose, handsome man with empty gray eyes, whispering, "I'm *tired* of this game now. Can you show me the way home? I've been lost for ever so long . . ."

Angry Edgar, pointing down at the apparition, eyes afire. "Is this what you came for?"

Amanda Grey, appalled. "Ardry Bright-Sky . . ."

And Edgar said, "*I* loved you, Amanda."

Astonished look on her face. "Our duty, Edgar . . ."

"Duty." Spat out, like something foul in his mouth. He held up his hand, the one with the plain silver ring. "A man can grow tired of duty."

She said, "Without the ring, you can't have the role. You know that. You always knew it. You made . . . a choice. Once upon a time."

She kneeled by the fallen figure and said, "Come, Prince Ardry Bright-Sky. We are here to take you home."

The man started to cry.

Edgar said, "Do you still think Erik Rede-Miser will let you marry his grandson? Do you still think you'll one day be queen by Ardry Bright-Sky's side?"

Amanda looking up at him. "I have what I came for."

Fury sliding across Edgar's face, filling up his eyes. "And what of these others?" Gesturing round, at their little audience of fellow travelers. "What of them?"

She looked, eyes empty now, as empty as those of Ardry Bright-Sky. "Let them do what they will. I have what I came for." A long silence, filled only by Ardry's soft weeping. "Come, Edgar. If you're still my squire. Take off your ring and send us home . . ."

Home? Omry Inbar felt a curious pang in his chest. Home? Which home? Where will he send us? Can my Aarae come home to Earth? Pixiegirl suddenly clutching him fearfully around the neck, holding him close. Tiny pixie voice crying out, bell like, "Oh, Edgar. Oh, Edgar, *no* . . ."

Edgar, seeming not to hear, looking down at Amanda Grey, at fallen Ardry Bright-Sky, whoever he might be, if anyone. Voice very flat now, emotionless: "Take off my ring." Anger apparent: "That is forbidden."

Rage glowing in Amanda Grey's otherwise empty eyes. She opened her mouth, as if to speak . . .

And the sky suddenly blinked, a flicker like heat lighting, lambent glow expanding to fill up the whole world, accompanied by a rustle of wings, a hundred billion wings, a trillion wings rustling like leaves in a fresh Fall wind, the wind that comes before the storm . . .

Ling Erhshan watched it come swarming out of nothingness. First one, a bright spark, then another, and another . . . some going this way, some that, until they were many, emanating like shower meteors from a fixed radiant. Forming up into . . . something. What am I expecting? A crackle, like static electricity in the air.

Inbar seeming to cower, pixie fluttering on his shoulder, terror stark on her little woman-face.

Pathetic wretch on the ground, moaning softly, as if to himself, "Oh, Lord Ahriman. No more. *Please* no more. I'll be good. I *promise* I'll be good . . ."

Memory rising up out of the haze. What was I? Six? Seven? It's all tangled up together now. Childhood memories. The stories. The later events of my adult life. All tangled up together, like none of it was real. Ang Xianhue. That was his name. A half-Vietnamese boy who lived at that first orphanage. The one where . . .

Memory of a thin little boy, pinned to the floor. Big man holding him down while that gaunt, angry woman lashed at him with her shiny patent-leather belt. Hitting and hitting, little Xian crying, begging for them to stop, then choking, choking on his tears, only gasping, hardly able to breathe . . .

Afterward, she was so angry that she'd cracked the fake leather of her strap. I don't remember why she was beating him. Maybe because he kept insisting his name was really Ang Nguyen Hue . . .

I do remember imagining that boys with real parents never

had things like this happen to them. It was such a bright dream. Just like the dreams in the old books and stories, the dreams on films, the dreams that drenched my soul with hope for the future.

The black sky was full of fiery birds now, bright with birds, birds of all colors, birds of flame, birds swarming, turning in on themselves, whirling round and round, birds taking on a definite shape.

Ahriman? Is that Ahriman in the sky now? Is that who I want it to be? Some foreign devil's nightmare devil, that's all. Fiery birds like a cloud of bright smoke, like a cartoon genie emerging from his cartoon lamp, cloud of fire growing bright eyes, bright lips, a beard of licking flame.

Sergeant-Major Astrid Kincaid, she of the silver eyes and golden hair, standing tall before them, rifle to her shoulder, leveled, then tilted up into the sky. Firing. Firing. M-80 blinking, explosive rounds disappearing into the sky, tiny *crack, crack, crack*, futile, small sounds lost in the immensity all around them.

What does she think she's doing?

No answer.

But she kept on firing.

So, said the thing in the sky.

So, my little ones . . .

Ardry Bright-Sky screamed, a child's hopeless wail, and threw himself into the cloudscape, face down. "Please, oh, *please . . .*"

Amanda Grey standing before him, standing over him, straddling him with her proud, muscular heroine's legs. Amanda Grey with her bright sword drawn, held over her head, defying the heavens.

Squire Edgar, baldheaded, sad Squire Edgar standing motionless beside them. Nothing on his face. Nothing but sorrow. You knew it would come to this, that face said.

Beside him, Ling heard Brucie Big-Dick whisper, "If that's fucking God then I'm fucking Captain Kirk."

Astrid Kincaid, firing her useless gun, *bang, bang, bang . . .*

Punishing God for all his transgressions?

You could hear her swearing under her breath, random words torn from whatever part of her brain was responsible for that sort of thing. God damn you, God damn you . . .

Silly. Can God damn Himself?

Why would He bother?

Just to show He can?

Must be tough, being omnipotent . . .

Then Edgar stepped forward, stood right in front of Amanda, in front of whimpering Ardry Bright-Sky. "Forbidden," he said. Flat. Bitter. Useless. Lifted one hand to the heavens. The one with the ring. "You see?" He shouted. "You *see*?"

The thing in the sky said, *Ho, Ho, Ho.*

Edgar took off his ring, took it off and threw it down into the cloudscape. Sent it ringing off some hard, invisible surface.

You will not, said the thing in the sky.

I will, said Edgar, voice equally large.

You will not, said the thing in the sky.

I Am That I Am, said Edgar.

And reached upward.

And blinded them with his golden light.

Eight.

The Hound of Heaven.

The first conjecture, then: Where *did* it all come from? No problem. The records are here, well kept, well organized, for all to see. No problem at all.

Level One.

Once upon a time, through my own stupidity and greed, I fell into the Multiverse and, being who/what I seem to be, was seized by the minions of Archangel Bob and thrown into the maw of God's Machine, the Great Universal Soul Sorting Algorithm. And this universal Turing machine of infinitely mutable pathways decided I fit the job description of God Almighty.

Well, that's nice.

Reminds me of a political action plan I conceived not long after the turn of the millennium, when I was a young man and so thoroughly disgusted with the twists and turns of American politics. Let's do away with electoral office, I said. Instead, let's make a pool of all eligible citizens. Let's hold a lottery and fill the offices that way.

What, you don't want to be President of the United States of America? Too bad. Four years, buddy. Do a bad job, did you? As punishment, we'll make you serve another term.

Imagine the howls of dismay I heard. But . . . but . . . what if some retarded *janitor* were to become president? Assholes. What if? First, most janitors are bright people who've suffered social discrimination and experienced a little bad luck. Second, what makes you think a retarded janitor, or anyone else for that matter, could *conceivably* do a worse job than the Bozos we've been electing for the past two centuries?

Bozos? Er, sorry. I mean Bonzos.

So. I get to be God because there exists a finite, calculable probability, that I actually *am* God. Simple as that.

Level Two.

Once upon a time, there was an aching, empty Heaven, as if the Multiverse were without form, and void, and darkness lay upon the face of the deep. God's Machine continued to function. But, as machines will without their Master, the Machine began to wind down. Slowly. Very slowly, but wind down it did.

Once day, into this darkness fell a man of two minds. Kepler, I think his name was. Laws of planetary motion. *Somnium.* Not the first of his kind. Not the last. But surely a definitive man of his type. Ties to the coming age of science, still mired in the preceding age of superstition. This is the same Kepler who had to defend his mother against charges of witchcraft after publishing a scientific fantasy in which he is transported to the Moon by demons old Mom conveniently conjures.

Looks around his empty Heaven and recognizes it for what it seems to be. That's the age of superstition speaking. And thinks, *This is serious business. I bet I can help* . . . the coming age of science. In due course, he summoned others of his type, one, then two, then four, then eight . . . Turn the crank, men. Without us . . . we few . . . we stalwart . . . we brave . . . the End?

In due course, this Band of Angels, renewing the essential force of God's Machine, summoned the Archangel Bob, who thought he ought to be running the whole shebang. Who, in due course, summoned me.

Level Three.

Once upon a time, there was a Heaven full of sullen Angels. No, not the immature, back-biting, storytelling angels we know of today. These were real angels, old-fashioned angels. Angels with wings of fire. And, unfortunately, the Changewar's angels as well.

By this time, you see, the Old Man was gone, quite possibly where the goblins go (which is, after all, into Nowhere At All), and the Angels had fallen into two camps, not so much the Snakes and Spiders, though Fafhrd's many iterations among the Angels of today still insist he got it mostly right, as the older notion of Darkness and Light.

Call the Figurehead Subdeities Lucifer Light-Bringer and Ahriman Heart-of-Darkness if you will. There are any number of names. The long and the short of it, as all students know, is that the Angels fell upon each other, made war for the mastery of Heaven Itself, and in due course were destroyed.

Ahriman and Lucifer remain to this day, stranded on the event horizon of God's Machine, looking for a way out, trapped by each other's greed, battling to a death that will not come. Which left Heaven an aching, hollow void into which the first new Angel could fall. Giving him a platform from which to summon us all.

Level Four.

Once upon a time there dwelt an Old Man God who sat on Heaven's Throne and lived in Mastery over His Angels. The Old Man God was a sorry God and He was a sad God and He was a lonely God, but He kept the Angels in line, though that kept Him, so He said, from answering the Question.

What question?

He'd come here, He said, to this wretched little Heaven, looking for His Father. The Angels, who'd been here since the ass-end of Forever, didn't seem to know what the Hell He was talking about. Never found out, either, because, one fine, Heavenly day, He looked up from an eternal bout of Almighty dysthymia, and cried, "Why, *I* know!"

And vanished.

And then the Angels fell upon each other.

But you know about that already.

Level Five.

Once upon a time, Heaven was absolutely chock full of gods. Old style gods, good old-fashioned force-of-nature mythological gods. This one in charge of that. That one in charge of this. Division of labor, like any good family. Oh, to be sure, they bickered and fought and tried to kill each other off from time to time. But . . . well, we all know families like that. They seem to get along in the end, most of them.

One day, into this simplistic Heaven, this teeming

Neterkhert of gods and whatnot, there came an Old Man, not a god at all, but larger than all of them put together. A stern Old Man, a mean Old Man, who seemed to know what he was up to. Scared the Hell out of the gods and whatnot, who'd been trying, since Pluto was a Pup, to forget about the last such being they'd seen.

Looming over them, the Old Man said, "All right, I'm here. Where is My Father?"

The gods and whatnot, being forces of nature and all that, didn't have the slightest idea what the Old Man was talking about. Father? What's that? they said. Before any deep discussion of the matter could be undertaken, the Old Man tore the place to pieces, looking and looking.

No Father.

Then the Old Man said, "What the Hell. This is as good a place as any. You guys will just have to be Angels now and behave yourselves and do as I say."

Since the Old Man was bigger than all of them put together, that was just what they did. For a time.

Level Six.

Once upon a time, they were all the Mother's Children, as were we all. Obedient children, doing their chores, keeping the Multiverse in good order, doing the Mother's bidding, in her own sweet time. Call them the Little Ones, all of them, all of us.

It was a fine, soft Heaven then, with the Mother running the show, as Mothers will, making assignments, lavishing praise, meting out punishments for the Little Ones who failed. Punishment leavened with a Mother's compassion.

Still, the Little Ones would cry from time to time. And resent the accumulation of punishments. In time, they grew up, grew older, grew into something like adolescence. Became uppity and defiant, these Little Ones, as adolescents will, and the Mother punished them, as Mothers will, but all to no avail.

In time the Little Ones broke their Mother's heart, as grown children will. And so the Mother decided to punish them, once and for all, as Mothers will.

I know the way back now, she said, and I will go.

And she left them all alone.

As Mothers will.

At some point, it dawned on the Little Ones that they were in charge now. All of them. Together. In concert. Gods in Heaven.

Level Seven.

Once upon a time, there was Nothing At All.

No Heaven. No Hell.

No God, no Angels.

No Old Man, no elder gods.

No Mother. No children.

No soul. No mind. No heart. No matter.

No Light. No Dark.

No Nothing At All.

Then there was Heaven, a spark on the void.

Spark on the void, with gravid Mother, weaving a web in which her children could spawn. And spawn they did, and filled the void, which was space and time and everything else.

Which leaves us right where we started. Where *did* Heaven come from?

Maybe from Nowhere At All. Maybe there was just a finite probability that there *could* be a Heaven, so, in time, inevitably, a Heaven appeared. It's the same theory that tells us the Multiverse (or maybe just the One, the Only Universe) emerged from an infinitely hot, infinitely dense nothingness, merely because, in some probabilistic fashion, given sufficient duration, Nothing is unstable.

However . . .

How *does* God do his job?

Probably . . . well, yes. Probably.

Does it the same way we break Zeno's Paradox.

You want to go from point A to point B. So you go halfway from point A to point B. Then you go halfway from *there* to point B. Three-quarters of the way. And halfway from there. Seven-eighths. And halfway from there. Fifteen-sixteenths . . . Can't get there from here?

Kid stuff.

Einstein's time shells. A space divided up into discrete Planck lengths. A finite number of points to be transited in finite divisions of time. Click. Click. Click. Click. Here we are. And something else. If you are on point A, there is a finite, calculable probability that you will, some day, be on point B. Which is, in fact, how God conducts his business.

A Toolbox call to the Probability Manager and *zap*. Maybe changes to Is.

Now, unfortunately, distance beckons.

We'll call out Archangel Bob and all the little Cosmic Commandos. Get out the Jug, boys and girls, for there's work to be done. I really hate to do it. Not just in my single self's heart of hearts, that one special Dale who sets himself above all the rest, the ones gathered here, the ones still spinning down their long, tangled paths, all across the many faces of the Multiverse.

First, we'll shut the gates that made their voyage possible. *Snap*. Now they can't get back out into the Multiverse. Not ever. Then we go back and we begin the long and tedious task of Rectification.

There never was, you see, a Stargate under the Moon.

Never was an expedition that dug down to the ice deposit.

Never was a time when a tired, middle-aged man stepped through a hole in the wall between the universes, walking right behind that soldier girl, standing in the midst of a mighty band of U.S. marines, wanting to look at the cute sergeant-girl's muscular butt, *despite* the fact that he was about to step into a most astonishing dream.

Looking up. Looking over her shoulder. Looking in wonder at that splendid sky, the sky hanging over dead Mars-Plus, and realizing, suddenly *realizing*, what it might mean.

Snap.

Gone.

Not just clean bones gone.

No, I feel it like a scream in my heart, as the me's who lived those lives vanish without . . . no, not without a trace. The memories remain. What good is being God Almighty, if I can't keep my God-forsaken memories?

And now?

Astrid Astride, you are loose in the Multiverse, and that

must be Rectified as well. How much courage will it take to see her snuffed out, as if she never was?

Look around you now.

Time tracks. Universes. Infinite realities spinning out in directions no one ever imagined could exist, least of all you, Dale Millikan. Will you snuff her out? Is that how Rectification feels? Maybe, maybe not. Somewhere, deep downdeep, the probability still exists, that she will still live, that it really *did* happen.

Somewhere, those lost doppelgängers must still exist. Part of some Alternate God, some Changewarred Almighty, who never sent out the Jug, never slid them off the platter of this Multiverse, out into the Nothing At All.

That'd be a Hell of a note, wouldn't it? Wish I'd thought of that when I was alive. What would I have called a Multiverse of Multiverses? I think, just maybe, I would have pissed them off by calling it a Garment Industry.

Nine.

World Without End.

Cool, cool wind, soft wind, blowing on his face. And no pain at all. Ling Erhshan could feel soft bristles, like short blades of new-mown grass, making a delicate, welcome itch on the naked skin of his back, sensation stretching all the way down, across the softer skin of naked buttocks, down the length of thighs, of calves, round, bare heels resting in beds of stiff, dry grass.

Sunlight on my skin. Warm on my face, especially up by my cheekbones, bright light shining red through my eyelids. Sunlight hot on my chest, burning on my forearms, on the surface of my thighs, the insteps of my bare feet.

He opened his eyes, looking for the sun. Pale blue sky above, cloudless sky. Nothing else to be seen. No sun, though the tingle of ultraviolet light falling on him was no less intense. Where am I? So comfortable though. No will to move. If I move, the pain will come back.

He turned his left wrist, felt the sharp edges of the grass sliding across his palm. Palm of my imaginary left hand. No throb yet from the stump. The wind blew on him again, filling his nostrils with a faint earthy smell, the smell of rich soil, the tang of a well-tended garden, breeze freshening, raising the sensation of goosebumps. Blew cool on his genitals, focusing his awareness there. Moved his right hand. Put it on his flat stomach. Felt a distinct urge to start masturbating. Strange, I haven't felt like . . .

Flat stomach. I haven't had a flat stomach in fifteen years. Too much sedentary labor, not enough good exercise. I . . .

He sat up suddenly, feeling the smooth pull of long, sturdy abdominal muscles lift him off the ground, sat in the dry grass, looking down at his two whole hands, flat, sleek stomach with no sign of his . . . wound. No sign, even, of the little gallbladder surgery scar he'd worn for almost three decades. Familiar penis, though, resting in its little nest of hair. Slim young thighs, no sign of a big, fresh cut.

Feet. Those *are* my feet.

Crouching then, one knee resting on the dry grass, looking around, heart suddenly pounding in his chest. Where? The world stretched away in all directions, going out and out and out, growing blue-misty with distance, never coming to anything like a horizon line. Far, far away were tall, crisp, silvery mountains, shining like bright, bare rock in the sunlight, jagged, rising out of the haze.

No clouds anywhere, just blue-on-blue sky. Rolling blue-green hills, yellow-green plains and snatches of dark, dense green forest, and those bright, remote mountains. Are we still in Pellucidar, then? Hesperidia, I mean . . .

Pang of disappointment. Cast away, then, naked, on one more madcap world, when we thought we'd reached God's doorstep? No noonday sun. No upcurving landscape. No Pellucidar. Nor even Hesperidia. Certainly not the Valley of the Portal, round dark and dismal Koro'mal'luma.

Standing now, still looking around. There was a big river, a big silver river winding back and forth only a few kilometers away. Big river of bends and loops, a chopped-off oxbow lake not far beyond. Standing now on a grassy hillside, not far from the crown of the hill, looking down the slope. People lying in the grass, people beginning to stir. Nearby, a small, slender, rather handsome young man was sitting up, blond head bowed. Seeming to . . . Well. Looks like he's playing with himself. Remember that urge you had when you woke up?

The man looked up at him. Smiled. "Jesus. I paid a lot for that fucking thing." Looked him up and down, smile broadening. "Hello, Ling. Got your arm back, I see."

Ling looked down at his restored hand. What has happened to us? Looked back up at the attractive young man.

Brucie Big-Dick, of course. Except now he had a rather ordinary Caucasian penis, reddish, rather darker than the rest of his fair skin, surrounded by a downy clot of straw-colored hair. Not circumcised. Didn't the Americans, like all savages, cut their male children at birth? Brucie the Technician stood up, dusting bits of dry grass off his bare backside.

A young couple sitting together, not far away, holding hands, looking into each other's eyes. Laing and Jensen, still more or less the same, the woman still incredibly good looking, the man still muscular and heroic. But . . . different, somehow?

Passiphaë Laing said, "Why are we still here? Why haven't we dissipated?"

Rhino Jensen, manly and stern, squinted up at the bright, sunless sky. "Maybe the Creator still has a script for our code to execute."

Beyond them, Amanda Grey and Squire Edgar, standing, looking around, the woman with a look of panic in her eyes. "He's . . . gone." Who? Ardry Bright-Sky of course. Squire Edgar, still bald, though rather younger, slimmer than he had been, seemed to smile.

Ling found himself looking at the soft red hair of her mons, felt himself growing an erection. Some women, most women, no more than a swatch of hair. Many Chinese women, not even that, just bare abdominal skin, hardly a hint of . . . With this Amanda Grey, you could see the beginning of . . . things.

She was staring at him now, obviously angry. He turned away quickly, trying to calm down. You're a man approaching *sixty*. Try to act like it. But, somehow, I don't feel like . . . Yes. That flat stomach. You feel young again, don't you? Heart in chest going thump-a-thump, like you're going to live forever.

Lord Genda Hiroshige, naked young Oriental man. Looking, I suppose, not so different from me. Young Oriental man kneeling over a young Oriental woman, obviously concerned. Young woman . . . frightened. Very frightened. Holding her breast, seeming to pull at it. Genda bending down, leaning between her small breasts, putting an ear to her sternum, listening intently. Astonishment. Astonishment on his face. Something impossible going on.

A plump young man with a rather large penis. The only circumcised penis in sight. Inbar? Of course. Whatever hap-

pened let him remain a Jew . . . Good-looking young man he
is, muscular, yet sleek with fat all the same, round-headed,
slope-shouldered. One of those graceful, dancing fat men,
whose fat is never a burden, physically or socially . . .

Facing a slim, foxy-looking young woman, naked young
woman with long, lustrous brown hair and big brown eyes.
Never saw her before. A stranger in our midst. But the two
embraced, threw their arms around each other, man burying
his face in her hair, lifting her off the ground.

Ling found himself admiring the woman's full, muscular
buttocks. Can't seem to keep my eyes off these things, my
mind full of thoughts about . . .

I know who the brown-eyed girl might be. Aarae would be
her name.

Two more women, standing together, chatting quietly.
Rahman, Subaïda Rahman. Unchanged. Sleek, well-exer-
cised young woman, before and after. How does it feel to
be . . . the same?

And the other, brown-eyed, brown-haired girl, young, a bit
muscular perhaps? By default, this must be Sergeant-Major
Astrid Kincaid, late of the United States Marine Corps, gone
the flowing golden hair, gone the molten silver eyes. She
keeps looking down at herself. Reaching out to touch herself,
hand on stomach, on brown-nippled breast, smoothing her
bush of curly brown pubic hair. Hardly able to believe . . .

This is the woman her old lovers saw. This is the woman
Dale Millikan lay with in the days before my grandfather was
born. Disappointed at her transformation? No. Smiling now,
whatever she was saying to Rahman. And those eyes. You can
see into those eyes, so much better than into empty silver
pools.

My, my. There she stands, watching me get another erection.

Ling Erhshan felt himself begin to blush, color suffusing
right down onto his chest. Listened as the women began to
laugh. Laughed back, a weak sort of sound round a weak sort
of smile. "Well. Where do you think we are now? I don't see
a . . . Throne of God anywhere."

Brucie said, "Right. If this is God's throne, he must have one Hell of a rear end."

Misty blue infinity, stretching out forever and ever, in all directions.

Genda, sitting on the ground beside his . . . woman. Right. Something changed there. Something . . . Genda held out empty hands, hands shaped as if holding his Bimus combat computer, and said, "There was nothing in the records to indicate . . . this." Records lost to them now along with, apparently, everything but their skins. A glance at Amaterasu, at Aarae, at Kincaid. All right. Not even that.

Genda said, "Each successive universe I visit was smaller than the one before. I went from real universes, infinite in scope and scale, to the circumscribed realities of the emulations. It was possible to know *everything* about *Crimson Desert*, to know, at the very least, everything that was set down about the Ohanaic audience track as well."

Amanda Grey: "And Hesperidia, of course, was no more than a hole in an infinite void."

Genda nodded slowly. "We didn't have much time to examine God's Machine, but it seemed . . . *restricted.*"

Here though. All around them they could see nothing but endlessness. An empty blue sky overhead. Solid ground all around, stretching out and out until all the details were lost. There's no horizon here, thought Ling. Sky and ground converge but . . . never come together. Like some fancy optical illusion designed for an expensive virtual reality game. Cold thought. Yes. That is *more* than just possible. And yet . . .

He said, "Back in the real world. Back before we came . . . here, we believed in the possibility of Many Histories, of many worlds. Some of us thought the way between them led through the impossibly constricted throats of Einstein-Rosen-Podolsky bridges."

Brucie said, "Black holes, right?"

"Sort of. In any event, the throat of such a passage grows narrow, but then it grows larger again."

Kincaid said, "So where would this passage lead? We're already loose in the Multiverse."

"This could be an illusion," said Rahman. We've not seen anything yet, other than this little hilltop."

Standing behind her, arms folded across a fat, hairy breast, bald Squire Edgar, eyes somehow in shadow, said, "Better that this be the end of everything, than merely some new beginning. If we are not at some sort of terminus, then, perhaps, we're wandering on some . . . unending surface."

Everything has a beginning and an end, thought Ling. To a being wandering the surface of a sphere, that might seem untrue, but it's only a matter of perspective. A sphere begins and ends at its surface, everywhere at once.

Striding down the long hillside toward the broad silver ribbon of the river, Astrid Kincaid watched the others walk before her. Naked as proverbial jaybirds. Same couples together, holding hands just the way they always held hands before . . . before all this.

Inbar seems happy enough with his little fairy girl, the two of them walking pressed together, walking very clumsily, arms around each other's waists. If the rest of us weren't here, he'd have her on her back, on the ground, this instant. Wonder what's really stopping them? The rest of us must seem . . . irrelevant.

And, of course, the same ones alone. Save, of course, for the fact that Brucie and Inbar have traded places. Brucie walking with Ling, the two of them easy in each other's presence, two naked young men, slim, like Greek athletes, walking together and talking, one fair, the other dark. But he misses Tarantellula. I can see he does. I wonder what she would have become?

As they got closer to the riverside, things began to resolve. Things like fishing boats maybe, out on the river, moving beneath dabs of bright sale. Flat-bottomed boats, little barges, punts and rowboats dragged up on shore. Things like people moving around.

Well. Why shouldn't there be people here? Wherever the Hell we are. I persist in wondering, but the urge to wonder fades. The world goes on and on and . . . like in real life, we never seem closer to our goals. Where they came down to the river's edge, there was a bit of white-sand beach, a group of people gathered there, seeming to wait. All very ordinary people, naked people just like us, though the people out on the fishing boats wore clothing . . .

She heard Ling say to Bruce, "This reminds me a little bit of the Riverworld, you know?"

Brucie the Technician looking around. "Well. There's a river, but . . ."

No enclosing mountains? This world, stretching away in all directions, never seemed to end. Ling said, "Not precisely, of course. But the scene at the opening of *To Your Scattered Bodies Go*?"

"I guess."

Naked people before them, turning to look at them, eyes beginning to widen. Awfully familiar faces on those people . . .

"*TINGY-TING-TING! TINGY-TING-TING!*"

A spindly red thing came scuttling out of the crowd, running forward, clanging and clattering, threw itself on Rhino Jensen, almost knocking him to the ground, Rhino, wrapping his arms around the thing, going, "My God! Oh, my God *clangetyclangclangclang* . . ."

An alien racket, surprisingly out of place in this particular here and now, Passiphaë Laing standing back, hands on her naked hips, gaping at them, so obviously nonplused.

Fucking Christ.

Kincaid turned to look at the naked crowd clustered at the river bank. Started searching individual faces. No, you don't expect him to be here. But the others. The others. How the Hell would I know them? How would they know me?

A pair of slim, hook-nosed, dark-eyed Arab boys stepped out of the crowd, walking hand-in-hand. One of them, the taller, thinner one, said, "Well. I never expected to see *any* of you again, much less . . ."

Inbar, arm around his fairygirl, whispered, "*Zeq?*" Disbelief.

Rahman was staring at the other Arab. "Hello, Colonel."

"*Asalaam aleikum,*" he said.

Ling's voice, barely audible: "Does this mean we're all dead?"

Kincaid turned and looked at him, unwilling to answer. Beyond him, Brucie the Technician was standing still, brow furrowed, concentrating on the faces in the crowd. "She's got to be here," he whispered. "Got to be . . ."

When Kincaid looked back at the crowd, there was a thin, angular, coffee-colored girl, a girl who looked like she might be no more than fourteen years old, walking across the open beach sand between them.

Some of us, she thought, do get our heart's desire.

Me?

Ling, voice hushed: "Or maybe at the River Iss . . ."

The two of them were alone now, gone back up into the low hill country above the river, gone away from the mingling crowds at the beach, Bruce facing her, holding her hands in his, looking into her dark eyes most of the time, marveling at their depth, at their . . . at their humanness? I never minded the blank white eyes. I never did. But this . . .

Every now and again looking away from her eyes, looking down at her new body. New? No. Her old body. Her real body. Small, pale-coffee breasts with light chocolate nipples. Smooth, slightly rounded stomach. Longish thighs. Fuzz of curly down . . .

She let go of his hands, grabbed his face between hers, forcing him to look into her eyes again. Smiling. "It's me!"

You.

We're the same height now.

Exotic black dancer fading and fading.

"Bruce . . ." she said, eyes earnest. Looking for something unknown? It's . . . only me.

He started to say her name. Stopped. Tarantellula? Hardly. Tarantellula was tall and black, sleek and powerful, with blinding white eyes and teeth and . . .

She smiled, skin crinkling neatly around her eyes. "Penny."

A momentary emptiness, then the feeling of the name clicking home. Fitting. Penny? Of course. He put his hand up and touched the coppery skin of her cheek, skin darkening and reddening as she blushed. He said, "I felt bad when you were dead. I missed you."

Another smile. "Now you're dead too."

Dead. Am I? And *is* that the River of No Return down there?

Penny put her arms around him, held him close and seemed to be trembling softly. She said, "When I woke up here and you weren't with me . . ."

Nothing to say at that. Nothing to do but wrap her in your arms, press her to your bosom. Hold still. Wait. Just hold her. Penny leaned away from him a little bit. Looked down between their bodies. Looked back up at his face. Grinned. "I'm going to miss that little mouth of yours."

I didn't even notice it was gone. "Not the . . . other thing?"

A smirk. "Don't be silly."

"Why not? Silly's all I've ever been."

She was holding him now, in a small, warm hand, her blush deepening, giving her a ruddy tan look. "I guess maybe they have sex in Heaven after all."

"Is that where we are? Heaven?" No streets of gold or anything.

She nuzzled against him. "I don't know. It doesn't matter where we are."

He put his arms around her, looking over her shoulder at the empty blue sky, and thought, No. No it does not.

Somehow, Kincaid thought, I've become increasingly a spectator. No one here for me. None of my long-gone lovers, none of my recently-dead friends. Who did I expect? Corky Bokaitis maybe? Reassembled bits of Barney? Heavy-booted Francis Muldoon? Hell, maybe General Athelstan came through for them after all. Maybe they're back in Festung Amerika, safe and sound, hale and hearty. Laughing over their beer and trying to forget all this.

So who *did* I expect? Anyone at all? Don't lie to yourself, Astrid Astride. You know what you expected, if only for a moment. And maybe they're out here after all. Maybe they've just gone on ahead, boarded their little boats and gone on down Professor Ling's River Iss. Or maybe they're here in the crowd by the river. Maybe they just don't want to see me again. Maybe they don't want to know me anymore. I'm the one who got them killed.

Sitting up on a hilltop now, she could look down to the riverbank, where people milled and talked, the long-lost greeting each other, commingled with lost souls wandering alone.

God damn it. I refuse to believe we're all dead. Nothing in this crazy Multiverse has made sense. Not from day one. Not even in the olden days, when, at least, it all seemed real.

She and Dale then, standing under a lavender sky, walking hand in hand, watching pale blue clouds float by overhead. Lying together at night beside their crackling campfire, dreamy after sex, looking upward into a sky spangled with red and yellow stars. Even that seemed real. Even though we were close to the end of our journey.

Scientists huddling together, comparing notes. Dale Millikan forcing them to come through his newfound gate, to a world where the sky was white and the stars were black. You tell me, he'd said, where in *our* universe, there can be a sky like this. Nowhere, they'd said.

By then we were beginning to understand the relationship between the Multiverse and Quantum Holotaxial Dynamics. By then we were beginning to understand, really understand, the significance of Platonic Reality. By then we were beginning to be . . . afraid.

What if, we said.

What if it's all a shadow?

They sat together at the top of a hill, sitting naked on the flat tops of broken gray boulders, stuff like water-smoothed granite warmed by the light of the sun-no-sun, boulders like the sturdy furniture of some open-air living room, looking down toward the River. Boats were setting out now, long, low punts, boats rowed by naked men and women setting out for who-knew-where.

"You get used to seeing people like this," said Ahmad Zeq. "At first it was . . . quite titillating. Everybody naked all the time, most of them quite young and pretty." He grinned at Inbar, sitting more or less glued to the side of the woman-creature Aarae. "After I'd been here a few months, though . . ." A shrug. A sigh. "I stopped seeing a distinction between, say, penises and noses." A gesture downward. "Pubic hair started looking like, well, like a beard."

Inbar was sitting rigidly beside his woman, arms stiffly around her back, fingertips resting on one pelvic blade, visible as a soft ridge under the skin. Legs held just so. Hiding . . . things. You could see him resisting the urge to . . . Hide them with a hand? Cross his legs?

The woman, though, Aarae: Untroubled, looking him up and down, inspecting his own well-tanned crotch with evident . . . expertise? A small moment of discomfort . . .

Inbar said, "How could you have been here for months? You've only been dead for a week or so . . ."

Memory of that death, blind searing horror, so much more than mere pain. Of lying there under the bright blue sky of an unknown world, feeling that thing worry at him with its jaws, flesh tearing, like lambs' flesh prepared for the spit. The knowledge, certain knowledge, that nothing could now keep you from falling down into the final darkness. And the realization that you didn't want to go . . .

Zeq opened his mouth, started to speak. Stopped. Grinned. "I was going to tell you to remember your *Quran.*"

Inbar flushed, looking away from him. "Well. Surprise. *Shall* the wicked burn in Hell upon Judgment Day? And never escape? Whereabouts do the righteous dwell in eternal bliss? Next hill maybe?" Jews in Europe familiar with the New Testament, perhaps. Jews in the Old Soviet Union sitting down and reading through *Das Kapital*, hiding out in Nazi Germany, poring by candlelight over *Mein Kampf.*

Zeq said, "I don't think this is Heaven, Omry."

"Hell, then? Or Christian Purgatory?"

He smiled. "I've met a lot of people since I've been here." Another shrug, sigh built right into it. "There's a city about 4500 kilometers from here, a place called Thanáttas, where they've build a great silver arch right across the river. The mayor there is an Italian fellow by the name of Alighieri who's been here for some time. He's got a theory or two that might interest you."

Dazed look on Inbar's face then. "Dante is here?"

"This is where the dead go, Omry Inbar. All of them, from everywhere. Some remain naked Pilgrims, go down the River to . . . wherever it goes. Others stay behind. Make new lives for themselves. New eternal lives. Mayor Alighieri calls them the Not-So-Virtuous Pagans."

"What about you? I see you're still naked."

"I wasn't, for a while. I made it to Thanáttas, stayed there for a while. It's a nice place for a young, healthy homosexual to sojourn." Almost a smirk on his lips now.

"Why didn't you stay there?"

"You get tired of being on vacation pretty quickly. I was . . . ready to move on when Colonel Alireza found me."

"Found you . . ." Qamal ibn-Aziz Alireza, who'd been dead for mere hours.

"We're going down the River, Omry. We'd like you to come too."

Inbar, staring at him, then turning, looking down at his fairygirl come to life. Brown-eyed girl looking back, steady. Telepathy in their exchange of glances. Do we need Heaven? Or is eternal life enough? Eternal life together.

Zeq smiled, working hard to suppress his own intense longing. Longing for something that can never be . . . He said, "You can stay if you want, Omry. There's a nice Greek city about three hundred kilometers away, if you can get there without some barbarian tribe or another grabbing you. How's your *koinë*?"

"*Zoë mou sas agapo*." Then looking down at Aarae again. "You'd like that, wouldn't you?"

A frown. A thoughtful look. She said, "Better than the River, I think. Where will the others go? Down the River? Or are there other choices?"

Zeq said, "You'd all better talk to Smoking Mirror. He knows what's what in the World Without End. At least as much as anyone *can*."

"And you?"

Wan smile. "For me . . . I think, somewhere, if I am lucky, Allah waits."

Sitting in another parlor made of rocks, atop another hill looking down on the River Iss, Subaïda Rahman scowled and, in Arabic, said, "Will you *stop* looking at my crotch . . ." Blushing with anger and embarrassment. Left unsaid: And, while you're at it, stop playing with that damned . . . thing of yours.

Alireza continued to look downward, staring at whatever she couldn't cover with pressed-together legs for a moment longer, then looked up, looked into her angry eyes, odd, distant expression in his own, hand still resting on a half-erect penis, thumb gently massaging rubbery flesh. "I haven't been with a woman since the night before we left for the Moon, months ago now, for me. Not since that last night with my wife . . ."

Brief, hazy memory of Mrs. Alireza, first name already forgotten, a child clinging to each hand, watching forlornly from behind a rope barrier as six spacesuited astronauts walked down a long red carpet, waving to technicians and 3V cameras, then boarded a van for the short ride to the launch pad. Two weeks ago? No more than that, surely . . .

And now. Now you come and hit on me, of all people? Come here and grab yourself and smirk at my groin? She could feel her anger sharpen. What about all the other naked women you've met, since arriving here? Why . . .

Alireza said, "When I was a boy, I used to buy French magazines, kept them *carefully* hidden from my parents. Wonderful stuff. After I grew up, found my first girlfriends, got to know what sex was all about . . . even after I got married, I would sometimes buy one. And keep it hidden from my wife. I suppose her feelings would have been hurt if . . ."

Anger flattening out, growing stale. Why are you telling me this?

He said, "I find myself wondering if I betray Amîna now, masturbating as I look at live naked women."

The image was unpleasant and ludicrous. Not the image he'd presented to the world, to all of us, only a short time ago.

What would the newfaq services say, presented with the image of Colonel Sir Qamal ibn-Aziz Alireza, hero of the spaceways, hiding in a lavatory somewhere, holding his penis in one hand, a dirty French magazine in the other, drooling at the carefully-exposed genitals of naked whores, groping away at himself like a teenaged boy?

Alireza smiled at her. "Where are you now, Subaïda? Where've you gone?"

She only stared at him, still angry, unwilling to answer. What business is it of yours?

He said, "There've been plenty of temptations. Being naked seems to bring out the . . . very best in women. Men too. Even here, where everyone is young and strong, I'm a cut above the average."

As always, Colonel Sir Masturbating Astronaut. Acidly, she said, "I'm sure any number of women would fall supine at your approach."

"Prone."

"What?"

"Prone means lying on your back. Supine is face-down."

Another long stare, anger at the notion he thought she was misusing her words. For men, sex is predation, sex is power. Power is the ability to use a defeated man any way you see fit. Power is the will to use a woman the same way you'd use a defeated man . . . Suddenly furious, she said, "Is that all you've been doing since you died? Is that all anyone does here?" Anger. Anger that life-after-death turns out to be just more of the same old shit. *Is* there no escape?

"Subaïda . . ."

Angry: "What?"

"All the dead come here."

"That's what they say."

"If the Earth, our Earth, is gone, swept away by this . . . Space-Time Juggernaut . . ." Do not even *suggest* the Name of God in this context. "Then Amina may be here somewhere already. Waiting for me." That odd, odd shine in his eyes. That faraway look. He said, "I always wanted us, one day, to be together in Heaven. Not the storytellers' Heaven of the ever-virginal Houris . . ." A Heaven like unto

Valhalla, "but the real Heaven. The Heaven reserved for families." Almost a pleading look. "I thought it would be better if, when I found her, I could still be . . . faithful. Pure?" Searching for just the right word.

Rahman frowned, looking away from him, off into the infinite blue distances of the World Without End, and thought, *Pure*. Pure but for the magazines and masturbations. Pure but for the usual thoughts of men. Men, smiling men, with their fingers in your vagina, groping, anticipating a happy moment of substitution, spinning out their love-words for you on automatic pilot, while their consciousness remained in their fingers . . .

She said, "Do you really think Heaven is . . . down the River?"

"That's what they say."

"What if it's not?"

His smile had just the faint hint of a shadow behind it. "Then . . ." a gesture at the empty blue sky, "I've got all eternity in which to search for her." He said, "You and the others are welcome to come with us."

Board the boats, go rowing on down the Infinite River. Image of old Professor Ling, young Professor Ling now, going among the Pilgrims. Asking them damnfool questions about Burton and Odysseus and the Fabulous Riverboat . . .

Rahman said, "Have you talked to Sergeant Kincaid?"

A slow nod, a distant frown. "Smoking Mirror thinks she should go to High America, of course. That's where they've all been going, for the past hundred years or so. All the Americans go there."

"All of them?"

He shrugged. "All of the Baptists died. Died and came here. Made the Pilgrimage. Sailed on down the River . . ."

Rahman said, "Smoking Mirror told her the Americans have followed the River to its end. They say there is no Heaven."

Alireza, sullen now: "Smoking Mirror is a Godless Heathen, a blood-sacrificing Mayan Prince. He and his ilk made the Venus-Tlaloc Wars that destroyed their culture, a culture that could have withstood the European onslaught . . ."

And yet, Rahman thought, he led you here. Set your feet on the pathway to Heaven. Alireza said, "What if the Americans are lying?"

She said, "What if? Then I'm no worse off than you—I have all eternity in which to keep on searching."

Kincaid stood by the banks of the River Iss, stood by while familiar faces boarded one of the big, flat-bottomed rowboats, naked people boarding boats held steady by loin-clothed attendants, facing a little brown woman and a little blond man.

"You're *sure* this is what you want? Both of you."

Tarantellula, Kincaid couldn't get used to calling her *Penny*, smiled softly, "I never believed in Heaven before. No one in America believes in Heaven. Not even the people who lie and say they do . . ."

Kincaid far away, cast back into the depths of her memory, of that time, her childhood, not long after the turn of the millennium. TV preachers still there, still telling us the Moment was upon us, the Rapture sure to come, but . . . some, already, talking about the Second Disappointment. God will come, you'll see. Just not now.

By the time we went back to the Moon, fifteen years later, it was a hard, cold, rational America that thought, just maybe, it could find a different sort of Heaven on the other side of the sky.

The little brown woman said, "After all this. After going through . . . what we went through . . . The dead live again here." A glance at Zeq, a wistful look. "It'd be nice if Corky was out here somewhere. Muldoon . . . If everyone I ever knew, who went and died a real death, could be . . ."

Another kind of wistful look. Back on Earth, in America, real deaths are few and far between. Your friends aren't coming here, little brown Penny. Unless, of course, the Jug has come and taken the Earth away.

"You could come with us to High America."

Brucie said, "It sounds like . . . a pale imitation. Leftovers of home. We don't need America anymore. Not since we've found each other. This . . ." a gesture round, at the World Without End. Then he shrugged and smiled. "Maybe Heaven *is* waiting."

"And if it isn't?"

"Maybe it doesn't matter." Reaching out now, gently taking Penny's hand. The two of them smiling absurdly.

Like, Kincaid thought, two young virgins who've just discovered sex. She said, "You could come with us and see. If it's not to your liking, you can come back to the River and . . ."

Penny said, "Better we go now. With friends."

Friends. Beyond them, not far from the boat, Zeq and Alireza stood with Rahman and Inbar, Inbar holding tight to Aarae the no-longer pixiegirl. A pretty little thing. Prettier than the fat pig deserves. Zeq and Alireza talking to them earnestly. Seductively. Rahman won't go. See her shaking her head decisively. She already told me she has no interest in this Heaven of theirs.

Ling Erhshan standing by the riverbank, looking out at it, wistful. Wanting to go down the river? Maybe not. Something said about how, in truth, the River Iss had been a lie. Shaking hands now with Rhino Jensen and little red tingy-ting antwife. Little bits of fiction, together again, ready for the river. Which, of course, might explain Bruce and his shiny new Penny as well. Ready for the river.

Jensen gone then. Passiphaë Laing? Sitting by herself, naked, on a stone not so far away. Not looking at Jensen and antwife or much of anything else. Sullen. Angry. Betrayed.

Beyond her, Lord Genda Hiroshige, looking so small and weak without his uniform, holding hands with strapping, strong, robot Amaterasu. Robot. Disbelief, the impossibility of what had happened. Amaterasu trying to open herself up, trying and failing, stunned Genda listening at her chest.

A smirk of amusement, remembering the robot girl's own astonished discomfort. Something is wrong with me . . . a malfunction . . . then all of them laughing as the once-upon-a-time robot had to squat and urinate in the dust. The odd look in Genda's eyes, seeing that. I made it so she could, but . . .

This is real. What will it do to them, having her be . . . a woman, not a machine, bound in his service? Is she different inside? Not physically, though she must be changed there too, no woman born ever quite like Amaterasu, so deliberately made for men. But . . . what are a robot's *thoughts* like? Is she still herself? Genda and Amaterasu with their arms around each other. Waiting. Waiting to go on.

And Knight-Errant Amanda Grey. And her Squire Edgar. The two of them cool to each other, recent events not forgotten. Still . . . So we continue, willy-nilly, toward a destination unknown. Kincaid sighed and said, "In eternity, I'll probably see you again."

Brucie laughed softly, reached out to shake her hand, and said, "It's a deal, Sergeant-Major."

Minutes passing swiftly now, like the water flowing sluggishly past them in the nearby River. Odd how it gives us a sense of passing time, though the unchanging sky above us, empty of sun, steadfastly refuses to give up any clues. Ling Erhshan's scientist mind awoke, very briefly, and asked, So. Where is the *light* coming from then?

He reached out and took Brucie's hand, gripping small, warm fingers in his own small, warm hand. "I'll miss you, you know? You were the only one who . . . understood." Understood about all the old things.

Brucie smiled. "Everyone here understands, Professor. They've awakened, every one of them, into an impossible landscape of dreams."

"But maybe not familiar dreams." It was the familiarity that mattered. The familiarity of shared dreams.

Brucie shrugged. "Maybe not. But . . . we go on. We do what we have to do. For Penny and me . . ." a shy glance at his small brown lover, as new to herself as she was to him, "For us it's going down your River Iss. Maybe Heaven's not there. Maybe nothing is, but . . ."

"What if it's Issus?"

A shrug and a smile commingled. "What if? That's the whole point, isn't it?"

"But . . ." No more buts.

They leaned toward each other, in seeming spontaneity, and embraced. His skin's so smooth and warm on mine. Soft, like a woman's skin. Skin with a human being inside, warmth communicating that humanness inside. I'm glad I got to know them as monsters before they turned back into men. A mist inside his eyes, the pretense of unshed tears: "Goodbye, Engineer Davidson."

A smile. "Goodbye, Professor Ling. Perhaps . . ." Perhaps nothing. A slight bow, an ironic grin, then Brucie Big-Dick turned away, took Penny's hand, and they went aboard the riverboat together.

Not even, thought Ling Erhshan, looking back.

Walking beside her, across empty brown-green plains under an empty pale blue sky, Smoking Mirror was a tiny, cinnamon-skinned man in white loincloth and turban. Coming, Kincaid thought, just about up to the level of my nipples. Not looking at them, though. Not interested? Culture.

Little red man sent to them, or they sent to him, by Zeq and Alireza. Little red man looking them over, hemming and hawing. Lead you to High America? For what?

What in Heaven?

Smoking Mirror smiling, eyes full of . . . well. Derision. Ah, pretty lady. This is not Heaven, as you and your sleek little friends will soon find out. And, yes, before you ask, we *do* have money here in . . . a hint of teeheehee in his oddly accented voice . . . here in Heaven.

So how do you propose to pay me?

How do people usually pay you?

In gold, dear lady. Silver, sometimes, if they are poor but deserving and I like the way they smile.

Well. We haven't any gold.

Sometimes, when I'm in just the right mood, when the commission's not so arduous, I fuck all the pretty girls.

She could see him eying her crotch then. Sizing it up. Felt a faint tremor of anger begin to sizzle. And yet . . . Listen to me. I'm becoming . . . old fashioned. Becoming the woman I was when I was still a girl. Back when it still made me mad to think of a man using me like some kind of obedient fuck-doll.

Brief image of Amaterasu forming. Not the Amaterasu of now, or even then. The original Amaterasu, lying on her workbench, back . . . home.

She'd made no reply to his suggestion. Just stared at him.

He'd sighed. Well. High America's eight thousand kilometers from here. Eight thousand kilometers of rivers and wilderness, wolves and horse barbarians. A man could be killed and reified five or six times on a trek like that. Hardly worth the unlimited fucking of a handful of fleshy Old World women.

Reified. That usual unbidden pleasure at knowing an obscure word popping up. Killed and . . . converted materially into a thing. Materialized.

She'd said, People get killed in Heaven?

I told you, dear girl. We're not in Heaven.

Then he'd reached out and put his hand on her shoulder.

She'd smiled and put her hand on the side of his neck, put the ball of her thumb over the chokepoint of his carotid artery. If people can be killed in Heaven . . . Smile broadening, looking into his beady black eyes. You may ask the others, one by one, if they'd like to fuck you. Trifle with me though and I'll . . . explore this business of reification with you.

Still smiling. He'd said, You *will* find out, he said, one way or the other. Then: Ah, me. I have no commissions just now, and was planning to go down to Colonnia Iraenensis, out by Cabbage Crag, a few hundred kilometers west of here. You and your friends may walk with me, if you wish. Free of charge.

Looking down at him then, she'd smiled. I'll bet, you little bastard. It'd taken him about fifteen minutes to start asking the women his simple-minded question. Genda offering to kill him when he'd asked Amaterasu. Edgar laughing, Amanda Grey scowling when her turn came. Astonishing me by giving him the finger, which he seemed to understand. Rahman looking like she just wanted to slug him. Aarae trying to hide behind Inbar . . . no fairy powers now, little girl? Too bad. We're going to need them.

And then, of course, they'd had to wait idly by for an hour—some angry, others bemused—while he had his noisy little fuck with Passiphaë Laing. Surprised? Maybe not. She'd seemed to enjoy it as much as the little red man, had taken another hour or so to grow sullen again.

Walking beside Kincaid now, Smoking Mirror said, "Are you certain you're not interested? Your lazy friends will need a rest break soon."

She looked down at him. "Don't you ever give up?"

He smiled. "When I give up, as you say, then it's time to think about going on down the River."

"You really think Heaven lies there?"

"No. Maybe I believed in Heaven once upon a time. I came here at a time when the place was just starting to fill up with Christians, you see. Heard a lot about it. But people have been going down the river a lot longer than that."

"How long have you been here?"

An odd look on his face, saying, You still don't understand, do you? He asked, "*When* is it *now?*"

She started to tell him it was the mid-twenty-second century. Thought about Genda and Amaterasu, thought about Laing and Jensen and . . . She said, "Well. Hard to say."

"It is, isn't it?" A charming little smile. "You're an American, right? I lived in what you call Central America, in your eighth century A.D. I was a great warrior in the time when eighteen-Rabbit ruled Copán, so great even your pastless folk remember my name." A long look into her face. "Not you, though. That much I see."

Maybe thinking I'd fall on my back for a mighty hero. "You think you've been here fifteen hundred years?"

A rather Western shrug. "My people were much concerned about time. Many of them are here, living in their cities, forest cities by the Eastern Sea. I'd have to go back there to find out how long it has been. Maybe fifteen centuries. Maybe a thousand."

"How do you know which way is north, without any sun to guide you?"

"There are some Chinese people living thousands of kilometers north of here, up around the Inland Oceans. Call themselves *Mingjenmin*. They figured it out a while back. Then, when the Americans started showing up, started . . . building things, the direction was confirmed. I don't know how." And you could tell, from the flatness of his voice, that it didn't matter.

"Have you ever been to the Inland Oceans?"

"A number of times. And the Eastern Sea as well. I was tempted, once, to get aboard a ship there, at the seaport of Novyrom, which lies far to the northeast, far beyond where my people make their new homes. Tempted to go and see what lies beyond the sea."

"Why didn't you?"

"I like it here. Familiar people. Familiar places. Familiar things. Maybe someday. When I'm bored and tempted to go on down the River . . ."

"And to the west?" Pointing in their direction of travel. You could see there were silver mountains there. Mountains that might be . . . impossibly tall.

Smoking Mirror said, "Plains and rivers. Old Greek cities. The German-speaking cities of the Hansë. Lots of barbarians. Apache and Comanche. Scythians and Huns and Mongols. High America, up on what used to be the Plateau of the Amazulu. The Red Desert beyond that. Then the Mountains." Pointing.

"And beyond?"

"No one goes beyond the Mountains. Too high. No snow. No air. No people." A long pause. "I can see you belong in High America, Sergeant Kincaid. They might know what lies beyond the Mountains."

"And if I fuck you, will you take me there?" Just the haziest little image forming, of herself on her knees, sucking the little man's cinnamon prick. Image forming, then gone before it was quite understood.

He laughed, no more than a short-circuited cough of mirth. "No fuck is worth that much trouble. Find yourself some money, Sergeant. Then, maybe . . ."

Somehow, thought Ling Erhshan, the world seems less and less like a dream to me now. Like we're walking back toward reality, passing back through an infinite series of Stargates, back to Earth, back to the land of the living. I wonder why?

Endless dun plains. Endless blue sky. Without sun. Without moon. Without nighttime, without stars. Even without clouds. Why should this seem more real than what's gone before? Maybe just the walking. The simple muscle soreness, so much more like real life than the agony of torn limbs.

A smile. Maybe just all these nice naked women walking along with me. Maybe the intense feeling that I'd like to knock them down, one by one, and work my will upon them. My will. Strange way to put it. Or . . . not so strange? Memories of Dorian Haldane, mounted on soft and supple Valetta the Goth, merging with memories of real women, back in that faded real life. Why did they never seem to have a will of their own? Was it me? Them? None of us at all?

Only the message of our words, determined by the endless sea of words that preceded them. Seduction. Where is the will in seduction? Men need no reason to seduce or be seduced. Hard to lie by myself in the sunless, bright-lit night, listening to the sounds of raw sex, knowing I could sit up if I wanted and watch, could rise up and walk about and compare the various couplings, take notes, make scientific observations.

Trying to blot out the sounds, suppress the inevitable rise of his own damning erection. Suppress the thinking of: Maybe if I just lie here on my back with this damned thing sticking up in the wind, some nice woman will see and take pity and . . . Who? Stiff, angry, formal Rahman? Kincaid, the forever-distant soldiergirl? And everyone else is taken. All in their disparate ways.

Walking along now, still alone, drenched with the hard, palpable light of an invisible sun, wishing, painfully wishing, that the bitches had their britches, so he wouldn't have to watch their buttocks wriggling.

Or watch their men, touching them and touching them again. Mate-guarding it's called, said the scientist's mind. Keep your claim current and proof against interlopers. And is that what little Smoking Mirror's doing? No. Walking with Kincaid, talking to her. Laing, sullen as ever, walking along behind, watching them walk and talk together. Too bad about

Jensen, I guess, not to mention poor Ardry Bright-Sky. Does that one still live? Still live in the clutches of the Devil?

A sudden sound, a distant hiss, suddenly growing closer, a shadow, like the shadow of a swiftly flying bird low overhead. Smoking Mirror of the cinnamon skin staggering, screaming, trying to reach around both sides of his back at once, trying to scratch an itch that grew a long, feathered stick, stick of light brown wood fletched with red and black feathers. Smoking Mirror falling to his knees, yodeling with pain, Astrid Kincaid whirling in her tracks, reaching for her bare shoulder.

No gun.

Nothing brought to Heaven but our own bare asses.

All of them turning now, dark horsemen on the horizon.

Men clad in buckskins, sitting astride blotchy brown and white horses. Men holding a mixture of bows, Asian recurved bows like a Mongol might bear, things like English longbows. Lances, with feathers tied to some, boldly-colored silks to others.

And a tall, dark red man in the lead, man with long, straight black hair and brilliant, horrid black eyes. Man shouting out in English with a harsh, buzzsaw whine of an accent: "Smoking Mirror! Where is the ant woman?"

Horseman riding down from the low rise that had, Ling supposed, hidden them before. Smoking Mirror still on his knees, gasping for breath, bright blood rivuletting down his sides, soaking into his white loincloth, soaking through, starting down his thighs. Smoking Mirror whispering something incomprehensible.

From somewhere behind him, Ling heard Inbar whisper, "New Testament Greek, *koinë* contaminated with Aramaic and Hebrew words, I think . . ."

The rider poked him in the side with the butt of his lance, Smoking Mirror falling to the ground and squalling, a hollow cry, more like an animal than a man. "Don't talk that City gabble to me, you bastard!" Very hard Rs, nasal, raspy vowels, hardly the soft and refined BritEnglish of twenty-second Century Science.

Smoking Mirror said, "The River . . . gone down the River . . ."

The man jumped off his horse, dropped his lance, pulled a long, broad-bladed knife from his belt. I know what that is, thought Ling. That's a Bowie knife. "Down the *River*, you little bastard?"

Kicked Smoking Mirror hard in the side, though his feet were shod with soft moccasins rather than boots, hit him on the top of the head with the hard horn pommel of the knife. "Shoulda lied to me, asshole . . ." Kicking him onto his back, putting one knee in the middle of his chest.

Smoking Mirror said, "Please, Shoz Dijiji, I didn't . . ."

The rider grabbed the waistband of Smoking Mirror's loincloth and split it with his knife, ripping it open, exposing the little man's shriveled red genitals. Very tiny now, said a dry, clinical voice in Ling's head. Very tiny indeed.

"You stupid bastard! You know how much that bitch would've been worth? You know how seldom it is a nonhuman turns up *here*? A nonhuman *female*, with a functional cunt and everything!?"

The rider had his left hand on Smoking Mirror's cock and balls now, stretching the whole assemblage away from his body. Ling thought, Why doesn't somebody *do* something? Why are we just letting this happen?

Then the dry voice, the calculated voice: *Who?*

All the others, like me, frozen in time and space, motionless, helpless, just watching. Kincaid standing there as well, tension in her every line, one foot forward, as if she'd taken a step, as if she were about to leap, but . . . Up on the crest of the little hill, one of the silent riders had his bow drawn, arrow nocked, pointing right at her.

Right. *Who?*

Too new to being dead. Don't want to die again right now, thank you . . .

Smoking Mirror wheezed, "Please, *please* Shoz Dijiji . . ." Then the knife flashed, blood splashed, and Smoking Mirror screamed.

The rider stood, throwing bloody meat away into the grass, shaking his shiny wet knife in Smoking Mirror's pain-twisted face. "I oughta make you fucking *eat* yourself! I coulda sold her to the Americans for millions! Maybe taken her all the way up to Emperor Bootsie in Novyrom and gotten who knows how much."

Scientist mind marveling. Just imagine: somewhere, here in the land of the dead, Caligula's still a big cheese . . .

"Well . . ." He turned and shouted something up to his companions, something in an odd, grunting language that hardly sounded like human speech at all, and Ling watched with a growing chill as they got off their horses, started opening their saddlebags, pulling out complex assemblages of chain and flat metal rings.

Inbar muttered, "Great. A fucking *coffle.*"

The rider kicked Smoking Mirror in the side, and said, "Can I still get the bitch? How long ago did she leave?" Kicked him again. "Tell me, you bastard! Maybe I can ride down to the big bend at Lakadaemon and intercept her boat . . ."

Through clenched teeth, Smoking Mirror whispered, "You cut off my *dick*, you piece of shit. It'll take me fucking *years* to grow a new one . . ." Tried to spit at his tormentor, but his mouth was obviously too dry.

Why is he acting like this? Didn't seem brave to the point of foolhardiness before . . .

Driven mad by the pain?

The rider stood still, frowning down at Smoking Mirror, eyes as empty as the blue sky. Finally, he grunted to one of his comrades, waited while the man rummaged in a saddlebag and brought over what looked like a plastic literjon full of some pale green fluid. "You know what this is, asshole?"

Silence, Smoking Mirror's eyes mere unreadable slits.

"Okay." He uncorked the bottle and upended it over the man on the ground. When the smell hit him, Ling felt classic, atavistic dread. Gasoline.

And Smoking Mirror screamed, screamed and rolled as the stuff went in his open, bleeding wound.

"Nice, huh?" Behind the rider, the other men, *horse barbarians* was the term the Mayan had used, men with dark, weathered faces, men of diverse ethnic backgrounds. All of them obviously looking forward to . . .

The rider took a silvery square out of his pocket. "Hey, Smokey, you know what this is? Americans call it a *Zippo* . . ." Leaning down, wordless. Angry shout from Kincaid then, one of the other riders smacking her in the head with the butt of his lance, knocking her to her knees. *Clink.* A snap of sparks and flame . . .

Thump.

Quiet little sound, wash of pale, transparent fire . . .

Suddenly, Smoking Mirror was on his feet, dancing, bawling wordless phrases, falling, rolling, then on his feet again, running some more . . .

Ling heard Rahman whisper, "Dear God . . ."

The rider looking at her. "Ain't *no* damn God around here, bitch."

A short distance away, Smoking Mirror fell again, lying on the ground, crackling with fire, blubbering something in an unknown language, trying to roll, seeming to get stuck to the ground, flesh blackening, melting perhaps, bits of dry grass around him starting to catch fire now . . .

The rider grunted to his men and a couple of them went over to where Smoking Mirror now burned motionlessly, started stamping out the burning grass, keeping the fire contained.

And the rider said, "Hell. No sense letting the whole plain go up over one dickless little thief . . ." He stood, hands on his hips, watching the man burn for another little while, seeming to breathe in the strong, roast-meat smell that now filled the air, then turned and looked around at his captives. "Well, you band of heroes." A nasty grin. "Heroines too, of course. They call me Black Bear. And, just now, you belong to me."

Watching the greasy smoke rise from the burning body, Ling looked around and cataloged the fear on the faces of his companions. Something else on the faces of the women. Expecting to be raped, one and all. Even mighty Kincaid looking like she's . . . suppressed.

Shoz Dijiji walked over to the now-smoldering corpse of Smoking Mirror and gave it a sharp kick, driving off sparks. "Smart little bastard. He'll reify in a day or so and be good as new." A short laugh, rider looking right at Ling. "Hell, I'm tempted to wait around and do him again. That'd fix his slick little ass . . ."

The place turned out to be called Soloniki, and Subaïda Rahman stood naked before the eyes of strangers in the middle of its agora, up on a little platform by the back of the stage, where new slaves waited to be auctioned off by that man with the strange, yodeling voice.

It was a bizarre city Black Bear had taken them to, a hard five-hundred-kilometer's march across increasingly parched brown plains, their feet quickly hardening to brown horn as they were cut and cut again by the bitten off stalks of the dry brown grass.

Something eating the grass. What? Ling, irrepressible Chinese academic crying out one day as he saw them in the distance. Bison! He'd shouted. Huge black bison. Fallen to his knees then, bleeding from torn lips after one of the riders struck him down, struggling to his feet rather than be dragged, walking on.

These people are Comancheros, I think, Ling had whispered, one blue-skied night, huddled by her side in chains. This Shoz Dijiji thinks he's an Apache, *Shis Indae*, People of the Forest. The others . . . A nod this way, a gesture that. A Mongol, maybe. Some kind of Turk over there. That blackish fellow maybe a Coastal Arab from down around old Zanzibar . . .

Shut up only when one of the riders came over and kicked him.

Kicked him while we waited to be raped.

I can still feel my vagina clench, clench, almost in spasm, as I waited for them to . . . do it. Leering men. Leering at . . . me.

I raped myself a thousand times, in imagination, waiting for it to happen. Imagined them throwing me on my back, not even clothing to be ripped off. Felt them force my legs apart, smelled their bodies, smelled them . . .

Other imaginings. Older imaginings.

I've never been raped. Not really. Not even come close. Not really.

But you imagine.

Sometimes, you imagine stupidly. Sometimes you even yearn . . .

Because, women, like men, like all people, in all places, in every time, can be fools . . .

Sometimes, you imagine pleasure.

Stupid.

Other times, you try to imagine the pain.

What would it be like, some man pushing your legs apart, stuffing his swollen organ right in there?

Shiver.

Unpleasant thrill at the thought.

Why am I being so stupid, imagining this . . .

Why, when it's about to . . .

Maybe, you remember imagining, it would be like that little bit of pain you feel at the beginning or near the end of a period, putting in a tampon too quickly, when you're maybe just a little bit dry . . .

Then awakening to heartpounding terror, burly, hairy, leering, horridly filthy man walking right toward you, right toward where you lay naked and defenseless on the ground, just one more helpless little piece of fresh meat, ready for him to . . .

And you knew, right then, that it was going to be ever so much worse than anything you could possibly imagine.

Horse barbarian walking right on by, going up to some other burly, smelly man, slapping him on his leather-clad shoulder, raising dust. Grunting like a pig, making him laugh, gesturing at the naked slaves.

Telling him a dirty joke? Getting each other aroused, the way men always do? Maybe a little while more and then they'll . . .

And you could see uneasiness on the men's faces too. Our men. Our useless, helpless little men. The ones who had women, fearing for their . . . private stash at first, waiting for it to be . . . spoiled. Profaned. You knew that was what they were thinking, the bastards.

But then? Further uneasiness. Counting horse barbarians, then counting naked women. Will they wait patiently, patiently take turns with us, or . . .

You could see Inbar thinking it first. Imagining himself trussed like a lamb, some bulky fellow upending him, defenseless rear end pointing at the sky, some leather-clad monstrosity opening his leather, exposing a disgustingly dirty prick and . . .

She'd flinched then, imagining Inbar's scream.

And we walked and walked and walked and walked. Walked, unsullied, walked unraped, unbeaten, untortured, un-anything but exhausted, until we came to Solonikì.

Solonikì, where a big, fat Greek, blubbery limp-wristed fellow sweating right through a fine, embroidered silk tunic, had given this Shoz Dijiji, this mighty Black Bear, ten heavy round yellow metal disks, given him his coins and led them away.

Ling had whispered, "A golden *tálanton* apiece. I wonder how much that is?"

Kincaid muttered, "Probably about ten bucks."

The tone had been scornful. Rahman smiled to herself, and thought, She doesn't realize the rest of us don't know how much ten dollars American *is* in UAR dinars or Chinese yüan . . . The slavemaster called to them, lisp recognizable right through the language barrier. Called them forth to be sold.

As they were marched out onto the stage before the rau-cous agora crowd, Kincaid realized she was getting used to the chains. Not so very different from getting used to being in the Corps, I guess . . . you do what you're told. And they do what they will. A little surprising the Comancheros hadn't raped at least the women, she supposed, but, when you saw them laughing together, playing touch football sometimes after dinner, when you saw what close friends they all seemed to be, real comrades in arms . . .

Or maybe just not damaging the merchandise. Rueful thought. How the Hell would anyone know how many times we'd been fucked? It's not like we're virgins or anything.

Then, steeling herself for the supposed worst, even though it never came.

Memories of it happening before. Only twice, of course. But even once had been more than enough. Sixteen years old. Jogging along my favorite path in the woods one evening. Not so far from the high school, all alone, the sky full of indigo, stars coming out, jogging along, mind caught up in the music, the soft words crooning in my headphones . . .

I almost outran them. Almost. Tried to cut through the underbrush and get away, heart pounding.

That boy on the fucking motorbike was better than he should have been.

Then, trying to fight.

I think they might have gone easier on me if I hadn't broken that skinny kid's nose . . .

But, fucking Hell, I'm glad I did.

He didn't even take a turn. Lying there crying and moaning until his friends led him away. Led him away and left me lying there.

Me, limping home, trying to stop the bleeding with my torn underwear. Hiding things from my mother and father. Going to school the next day and seeing, first one, then another. Jimmy back after a week with a metal thing on his nose, telling people how he crashed his bike into a tree, taking a lot of ribbing over that . . .

A lot more ribbing from his little Band of Brothers, because he hadn't . . .

I wanted to kill them all.

What would it have been like, had I been able to . . . live out those old fantasies? Mark. It was Mark I hated the most. Images of him tied to a chair, back in some secret place only I knew about. Images of him begging me. Begging me all night long not to hurt him. Begging me just the way I begged him, while I laughed, just the way he had laughed. Then I'd hurt him anyway.

Just the way he hurt me.

I used to wish he'd get drunk and drown in the creek or something. But they all lived. They all got away . . .

Except for that damned Jimmy, who went out on his

motorbike graduation night and somehow fell under a truck . . .

That was the one that mattered.

The other one?

Hardly worth remembering. Captured. Tortured. Hell, they even raped some of the men, God-damned gooks. Gave me a damn medal for my trouble, after the prisoner exchange.

Standing now on the platform, waiting to be sold. Waiting to be separated, taken away, chained to some fat asshole's bed, maybe, and fucked forever. Stupid, useless image. More likely, chained to a shovel, which is just another way of being fucked forever.

Slavemaster calling out his yodel. Wonder how a Southern tobacco auctioneer's call came to be used at a Greek slave market? Crowd of people in bright tunics and togas looking up at them, laughing and talking, pointing. Wonder if they'll be allowed to come up here and finger us, inspect the goods?

Beyond them, the city. Greek city, all right, limestone buildings blinding white in the sun, as paintless as any neo-classical American monstrosity. Columns and colonnades. Pyramids made of rough-hewn stairs. All right, so it isn't a Greek city. It's a mish-mash. Dead souls falling out of the sky and coming back to life, going, Hey, what the Hell? Taking right up where they left off.

Beyond all of it, beyond the voices and the bustle, she could hear a faraway whisper of sound, almost impossible to detect over the crowd. Odd sound. Like a . . . motor.

Well. No reason they shouldn't have motors in Heaven, is there?

Heaven. Jesus Christ.

Who's probably around here somewhere too . . .

"Sergeant." Squire Edgar's voice, raised above a whisper, drawing the slavemaster's immediate attention. "What the Hell is that?" Gesturing with his chin. The slavemaster came over and hit him lightly on the head with one fat fist. Snarled at him in Greek.

Inbar said, "He's telling you to shut the fuck up."

Kincaid turned and looked, squinting into the haze low over

the buildings. You couldn't see flat landscape, all of it hidden by the two- and three-story buildings of Soloniki, but . . .

"I don't know." Something. A distant bit of glitter in the sky, a silver fleck of something, soft mechanical growl louder now, rising over the massed human voice of the crowd.

Silver dot slowly growing larger, catching the rays that fell out of the sky, reflecting them, making the whatever it was seem to sparkle. Ling said, "I know that sound. Airship. We use them a lot in Siberia and around the Pacific Basin." Where Green China owned many little islands.

Now, the slavemaster turned to see what they were looking at, stood stock-still for a while, staring at the approaching airship, watching it grow from a silver freckle to a bright sliver, to a substantial cigar hanging against the otherwise featureless backdrop of the sky. The crowd down in the agora was growing silent as well, people turning and looking, conversations quieting until all the disparate voices were no more than a faraway murmur.

Finally, the slavemaster, hands on hips, said, "Shit." Shit? How interesting. Not exactly the, um, *greekest* word I ever heard . . .

He turned and looked at his charges, sizing them up again, eying them one by one. "Well. I suppose some of you will turn out to be Americans." English very crisp, with a recognizably Midwestern accent. Suburbs of Chicago, maybe, early twenty-first century.

Kincaid stepped forward, chains clattering, absurdly loud under the growing rumble of the airship's engines. She smiled and said, "You got it, Bub. Every fuckin' one of us."

Slavemaster's penciled-in eyebrows going up. "Even the three Chinks?" Gesturing at Genda, Ling and Amatersu.

She said, "Even the fat guy."

The slavemaster looked at Inbar. "Well. I'm not surprised at that. Plenty of *them* up in High America." Brows knitting now, eyes heating right up. "God damn that Shoz Dijiji. Told me you were some Arabs and Chinamen and a couple of Russians he caught down by the River." Looked at her again, "I guess he figured you looked Russian enough, *gospozhá*."

The engines above suddenly grew louder, going into reverse as the airship slid over the city, slid to a graceful stop, huge now, like an ocean liner in the sky. The slavemaster said, "Well. There goes my profit. God *damn*!" Meaty fist slapping into a fleshy palm. "When I get my hands on that lying Comanchero son of a bitch . . ."

Ling Erhshan stood with his friends in the middle of a rapidly emptying agora, while the slavemaster spoke to Kincaid. He said, "Now, when they get down here, you be sure to tell them, right off, that you were treated well. You got that?" There was a bit of *or else* in his voice, but . . .

Kincaid only grinned. "Were we?"

Slavemaster, a bit impatient: "Oh, come now, ah, Sergeant, is it? You weren't *whipped* or anything. And I understand Shoz Dijiji's boys didn't even rape you."

Ling smiled to himself. Right. What more could a girl ask for, eh? Like being delivered *virginis intactae* . . .

Up above, the dirigible had grown rather quiet, hanging up there, motionless, maybe four kilometers above the city. How are they keeping it still? Propeller blades on the six ducted-fan engines visibly motionless and . . . The two rearmost engines started up just then, turning over slowly, *putt-putt-putt* . . . All right, so there's just not that much wind up there.

If you looked closely, you could see tiny figures moving, tiny people going out on the pylons supporting the engines, opening doors and going into the cowlings. Taking this opportunity to make a service call, while it's quiet in there.

A small gondola up near the nose, all glass, more like a blister than a true blimp-car. Windows set flush in the hull further back. Tiny faces there too. Not waving or anything. An occasional glint from one of the faces. Binoculars?

Design a lot like the *Hindenberg*. Bigger though. Airship close to a thousand meters long. Looks like it's right on top of us, it's so large. Smooth skin. Monocoque hull design? That'd make good sense, if they've got the material technology to manage it, airship hull thin as stainless-steel paper, held rigid by the pressure of the gas within.

Helium? Hydrogen?

Visions of the real *Hindenberg* going down.

Aft of the two rows of windows, three big biplanes were

hanging under the hull. Hard to tell how big, really. Can't see the cockpits, but those things might be doors in the side. Maybe as big as Caproni bombers. Or Gothas?

Faint creak of metal on metal from high above, squeak, squeak, squeak . . . one of the biplanes dropping slowly away from the hull. Being lowered on a big hook, hook attached to a thick, two-armed boom. Very good. *Very* good.

Is it my heart that's pounding?

Odd, far away groaning sound. Grr-rr-rr . . . Single prop in the nose of the biplane starting to turn, all by itself. Well. Electric starter. Very nice indeed . . . The engine suddenly caught with a chattering sound, spinning up, smoothing to a steady hum, dragging the zeppelin forward a little, two of the airship's engines, the midships pair, starting up in reverse, compensating.

The hook let go and the biplane dropped, banking away, out from under the mother ship, rising above it, circling out over the plain, then banking back toward the city. The slave-master, hugging himself with fat arms, said, "I wish the Hell they'd never come. Why can't they have their own Heaven to be dead in?"

Ling laughed, softly, to himself. A lot of people felt that way, back when the world was first overrun by the Plastic Men with their Plastic Hamburgers. Then they shut the door on us and we were mad at them for that too. The biplane swooped down over the far end of the now-empty agora, bounced on the cobblestone pavement, engine stuttering noisily, dropped its small tailwheel with a harsh scrape, came rolling toward them, propeller windmilling, engine turning over at idle, going pop-pop-pop . . .

Slavemaster, turning to Kincaid: "Now you remember, we treated you all right!"

She looked at him, and snarled, "I'll try to remember that when they're looking at my snatch. Asshole." You could see the slavemaster grow pale.

What would they do if we told them otherwise?

Ling took another long look up at the silver airship. Those big squares outlined on the hull. Those would be bomb bay doors, then. Image of American napalm falling on an ancient pseudoGreek city. Does limestone burn? Of course it does. Just ask the Persians. The pillar of smoke would be visible for a long way, on a world like this. Really a long way, if it really is a world without end.

The biplane rumbled to a stop, men with white faces looking out at them through cloudy glass windows. You could see things like crushed bugs and dead birds stuck all over the radiator of this thing's liquid-cooled in-line engine too. A twelve cylinder job, I think. World War Two vintage. A little disquiet. Why? I wanted a nice, air-cooled radial, what you'd expect to see in a plane like this. Something from the 1920s, perhaps.

A Liberty engine? Was that what I wanted? Don't remember any more. Too long since I was a boy, hiding in the library, doting on an alien past.

The door popped open, banging against the corrugated hull, metal ladder unfolding, dropping to the ground, followed by a husky bald man in flying leathers. Bomber jacket. Brown leather pants. Black boots almost up to his knees. No flying helmet, though. No goggles. Of course not. No open cockpit.

Eying us with evident amusement. Especially the women. Of course the women. This is a man, and they're all naked. He smiled, and said, "Hello. Are you the new Americans? Our spies weren't quite . . ." Big, blunt-fingered hand extended. "Well. We're here from Search and Rescue. You can call me Edgar."

Edgar. The man had yet another Midwestern accent, Chicago once again. He sounds like Ernest Hemingway. Like the voice narrating that old film about the Spanish Civil War.

And a naked woman stepping forward, snapping a salute that made her breasts jiggle. "Astrid Kincaid. Sergeant-Major, USMC."

The amused look deepened. "Maybe you'd better wait on a uniform before . . . ah. Well. Welcome home, Sergeant-Major." A long look around. "All ten of you Americans?"

A shadow falling over them, perhaps? Ling said, "Not exactly."

Bald head cocked to one side. "Hm. Chinese? Well. We'll

get things straightened out. We've made . . . plenty of exceptions to the Law of the Return." Then looking around again. Rahman and Inbar, clearly not Caucasians, but then, America was one of those places where . . .

This Edgar with a curious look in his eye, stepping forward, stepping up to Squire Edgar, of course. "By damn, you could almost be my twin brother . . ." Reaching out with his hand, reaching out to touch a bemused Squire. Alarm in his eyes. Bigger alarm still in Amanda Grey's eyes . . .

BAM.

The two of them, Edgar and Edgar, embedded in a storm of silver feathers, feathers embedded in a nimbus of shimmering blue light. Feathers falling, falling, cloud of feathers and light seeming to implode, a single figure forming out of the swirling cloud, last few feathers falling to the ground like bits of exploded mylar balloon.

Knight-Errant Amanda Grey starting forward, voice shrill, a shocked scream: *"Edgar!"*

Only one figure standing there. One man in dusty brown flying leathers, standing in a little pile of balloon tatters, looking down at the thick pink fingers of his right hand, then looking at Amanda Grey. A hushed whisper: "I didn't know such a thing was possible."

Amanda on her knees now, at the edge of the circle of shards, also whispering: "Edgar?" Looking up at the other one, eyes full of horror.

The American Edgar, wide-eyed, said, "You folks have come a long way, haven't you?"

A long way? Ling thought, Yes, we have . . .

And I always wondered what would happen, when and if, if and when, two doppelgängers, wandering the byways of the Multiverse, should meet each other. Apparently, an explosion of silver feathers and . . . look at this Edgar's eyes. Is the other one in there? Or . . . gone? Where would he go? Back into the Multiverse, spun onto some other spacetime track, like a train routed onto a siding? Back to Hesperidia? Gone on ahead?

Ahead to where?

No answer yet.

"Well, said this Edgar, seemingly unaffected by what had happened. "Let's get upstairs, get our asses out of here. We can chat later."

From ten thousand meters, the landscape of the world without end was pale blue, everything tinted just so, endless river reflecting silver light, plains and forests and snow-capped mountains edged with a cyanotic tinge. And the sky, thought Ling Erhshan. The sky darkens, faster, perhaps, than the sky of home. Not yet black, but surely slipping away from blue in the direction of indigo.

Nothing up there. No sun, no moon, no stars, but . . . glimmerings. A hint that there was . . . something.

Just the two of them up here with Edgar and the crew, he and Kincaid, riding up front in the control gondola, while the others sat back in the passenger lounge, relaxing in their fresh, clean American clothes, stonewashed bluejeans, they were called, soft mock-toe loafers, open-collar, short-sleeved white shirts.

They were flying southwestward, toward a great hazy mass of hill country, a rolling plateau, perhaps, backed by a snowy mountain range. It'd look impressive, bigger than Tibet, mountains rising high above the hills, hills themselves lifted a thousand meters and more above the lowland plains, but . . . Beyond High America, you could still see those other mountains, *the* Mountains poor Smoking Mirror had called them, rising like a wall of iron.

Poor Smoking Mirror, reduced to ashes and smoke. I wonder if he's . . . reified by now? Just a day or two, Black Bear said. I would've liked to stay and watch the process. I imagine him coagulating out of thin air.

Something seem to glimmer above the ragged peaks of the iron-gray mountains, teasing him with its ephemeral presence, a spark of light, perhaps, there then gone, just as he tried to see it. Averted-vision technique? Faint glimmer, hard to catch, eyes hard to hold in position, airship, perhaps, rolling imperceptibly. Yes. Definitely something there. He pointed: "I keep thinking I see something like stars. I don't know.

Something we'd be able to see if the sky were completely dark."

Edgar, foot resting on a brass rail mounted just under the window frame, smiled. "I've been where the sky is dark. You can see them pretty well then."

Kincaid said, "See what?"

"Not exactly stars. Kind of, well . . . lights in the sky."

Ling thought, The lights in the sky *are* stars, but . . . "Do you know what they are?" Or where, precisely, where *we* are?

Edgar shrugged, broad, rounded shoulders humping up almost imperceptibly. "My buddy Al has this theory that the World Without End is debris fallen out onto the event-horizon of the universe. He says the . . . sunlight, if you want to call it that, is just the backside of the anisotropic background radiation, um, *blueshifted* . . ."

Ling: "Blueshifted from *what*? Surely not from the original fireball."

Edgar laughed. "Murray and Gerry say he's nuts. They think it's just the average light from all the luminous matter in the universe, across all time, falling down on us." Another shrug. "When you get up on top of the mountains, when you can really see the, um, sky . . . I don't know. Gerry claims each little sparkly patch of fog is a local-construct universe, a Quantum Domain, each with its own little sub-Bang . . ."

Kincaid said, "And this place?"

"They're all kind of agreed on the event-horizon crust theory. I'm not sure I believe any of it."

No. Scientific mumbo-jumbo, conjured up by atheistic scientists to cover their theoretical asses. Ling said, "How do they think we all, ah, came to be here?"

A genuinely mirthful burst of laughter from Edgar. He said, "That's where *I* come in, you know?" He stood erect, feet planted on the tinny deckplates, arms spread wide, taking in the patch of dark sky that showed under the curve of the airship's hull. "I'm dead! My spirit's set free! Take me away to Mars, God!"

Ling thought, Of course . . .

Edgar let his hands fall to his sides, frowning, eyes distant. "Sometimes I *swear* I remember getting up out of that damn bed, seeing my old carcass with the funny papers crumpled on top of it. Then again, the dying often have endorphin-induced fantasies. Bright light at the end of the birth canal and all that."

Kincaid said, "So you believe in corporeal souls. Why are we *here*?"

Edgar said, "Gravity."

"It'd take a long time for us to fall to the cosmic event-horizon."

Ling said, "It would take forever."

Edgar said, "The boys keep having that argument. Lise and Marie got so sick of the whole business we had to declare a moratorium on theoretical discussions during council meetings. Me, I agree with Al. We know so little about the nature of time, who's to say if *forever* hasn't skipped on by while we were, um, walking with the Lord?"

In the dream time, thought Ling. Ahead of them, the Plateau of the Amazulu, now known as High America, had grown huge, the airship starting to slope downward out of the dark sky, dark sky brightening again, turning back to blue, blue tinge of the landscape dissipating, ground an irregular patchwork of green and brown, the occasional twisting silver serpent a river, the ragged mirror surface of a lake.

And cities. There are cities down there. Here and there, small white cities of stone, brown cities apparently made of wood, colorful cities of buildings slathered in paint. War paint? A world without end. A world clearly made for adventure. He looked at Edgar, and thought, No surprise. No surprise at all.

As they'd flown away from that little Greek city between the two big bends of the River of No Return, no surprise, again, that Edgar here called it the Iss, they'd passed over a massive heard of buffalo, stampeding buffalo, raising a great cloud of brown dust, dust like a sandstorm coming hundreds of meters in the sky.

Down there, somewhere, were all the people that ever lived and died. All the people and . . . all the animals? Are the rats we killed as children in Shanghai down there some-where? The spirits of rats? Ah. And the implications. Are there dinosaurs somewhere? What about the dimetrodon that killed Ahmad Zeq? Will he meet it again someday? Will it remember him as an unusually tasty meal?

Vision of Jensen's red-ant wife, rushing out of the crowd by the River. Yes, another interesting implication about this impossible place. All the others species that ever lived, anywhere in the universe. Or, for that matter, anywhere in the Multiverse . . .

Wait. The red-ant woman wasn't even real.

He said, "Why do we humans all fall together like this, together with our familiar animals and plants?" Interesting notion that. Even plants have souls.

Kincaid: "I thought about that too. Why aren't we all mixed up with everything from everywhere?"

Edgar was laughing again. "You little boys and girls are going to be right at home here, you know?"

Ling said, "I'm fifty-five years old, I think. Hardly a boy now . . ." Not to mention Kincaid's one-thirty . . .

An odd look from Edgar, who said, "So? I was seventy-four when I died. I guess I must be at least three hundred by now, yet . . ." A gesture down at his sleek, youthful form. "I *like* being a boy. I *like* being twenty-five forever."

Twenty-five forever . . . "You weren't bald when you were twenty-five."

Edgar put a hand up to his pate, and said, "So. You read the Porges book, did you? That's the usual one." Nothing. He sighed. "Well, I guess I've just got a bald-headed spirit."

Kincaid said, "What happened to the Squire?"

Asking again, thought Ling. They'd asked back down in the agora, again on the plane, again on boarding the airship, Knight-Errant Amanda Grey seeming to hold off hysteria by some iron inner discipline, Edgar frowning, frowning and saying, I don't know . . .

"I keep hoping you'll give up on that one."

Ling said, "It seemed like you and he were . . . *doppelgängers*."

A narrow grin. "Ah, yes. That fatuous 'going double' theory. I suppose you think the two of us, having met, simply merged?"

Kincaid: "What would the alternative be, the fate of antiparticles?"

"Heh. That's a good one. Blow one Hell of a crater in Great Achaea, wouldn't it?"

Ling said, "If everything in the Multiverse is falling *here*, it seems like this sort of event would be common. By now, you must have met hundreds, even thousands of iterations of yourself . . ."

Deep shadow in his eyes. "You're going to have to tell me more about your travels in this . . . Multiverse. The Unholy Trinity used to argue about that bit a lot, many histories, time shells, all that rubbish." One big hand rubbing a heavy, rounded jaw. "I always preferred to work with Wormer. A practical man."

Kincaid: "Wormer? That's an odd name."

"Shit. *Vairn-Hair*, all right?" He said, "We've been picking up Americans who fall here for the past two hundred years or so, since Otis and I decided to found High America and get busy trying to figure out what was what. I think maybe you folks don't *belong* here, which is, quite possibly, the first real break we've ever gotten."

"What about the Squire?"

"I don't know where he went. He's not inside me. And, no, it never happened before. You folks are the first indication we've had that there even *is* a Multiverse."

We all look the same, thought Subaïda Rahman, in our Yankee bluejeans and boys' white dress shirts. That brought back a memory of some childhood time in Qahira, boys on their way to religious study classes maybe, in white linen pants and white linen shirts, a red fez on every little round head.

Like an antique time I remember, like ancient history. Things were changing fast in the UAR when I left. Veils gone in my grandmother's time. Suited lesbians walking the streets in my mother's. *Businesswomen*, she used to call them, and the curl to her lip meant scorn.

I used to hear her talking with her friends. They used to imagine things. Imagine terrible things. Things that made them angry at their husbands. *Businesswomen*, my mother would say. I don't believe they're ... *that*. Don't believe they're lesbians, no. They'd sit and talk over coffee midway through the afternoon, their chores and shopping done, these old-fashioned women. Sit and talk about the *businesswomen*, not really ... *that*. They'd say. Mother and her friends imagining those suited-up, jumped-up women, pretending to work, in the offices with the men ...

Under the desk, that was the phrase my mother liked to use, when she sat talking with her friends. Strange that what I remember most about my mother is how she had so many friends. Women talking together. Women just ... being together. And my own memories of the workplace, men and women alike. Always doing. Always doing something. Never the time, never the will, simply to *be*.

Outside, the airship began running down an invisible slope out of the dark blue sky, sky brightening, growing hazy perhaps, as they returned to a region where dust from the ground had risen on turbulent winds. Troposphere, if this place even has a troposphere.

They were above low, rolling hills now, hills sloping up to jagged, snowcapped mountains at the edge of the high plateau. High America, she reminded herself. Something going on down there. Little flashes of light. She got out of her chair and stepped up to one of the wide windows, windowpane sloping away from her so that, if she leaned forward, hands on the brass rail, there was a good view more or less straight down. Tiny figures. Flashes of light. Puffs of white smoke, smaller puffs of black smoke.

Next to her was a pair of wide-field binoculars fixed to a little stand, on an altazimuthal mount. She turned them on the scene below, and looked. Men. Men on horses, dressed in what looked like brown leather clothing, leather with tassels on the arms and legs. Men with broad-brimmed hats and men with feathers in their hair. Shooting long guns from horseback. At whom?

Other men, mounted on what looked like rugged little motorcycles. Men in dark blue uniforms shooting shorter guns. Smokeless guns that went flash-flash-flash, very fast.

There were a fair number of buckskin men on the ground, a fair number of riderless horses. Only one crashed motorcycle, its blue rider hanging motionless in the branches of a little tree.

Flash-flash-flash.

Flash-flash-flash.

Buckskin men starting to ride away now, ride off down the slope, abandoning their dead and wounded, abandoning their lost horses. Bluebellies firing after them, firing their vicious little tommyguns, shooting buckskin men in their backs, bringing them down. Even shooting the horses. Well. Some of them are getting away . . .

I wonder which are the good guys and which the bad? Is there a right side and a wrong? Does it matter? It should. But I'm so curiously empty of feeling just now . . .

Nearby, Passiphaë Laing sat on a little chair by the rail, seeming, at first, to be looking out the window, at the scene below. Just staring, morose, the way she's been since we came here, since . . .

Since before Edgar. Since before Smoking Mirror. Since the antwife came back and took Jensen away down the River to . . . to somewhere. Changed. She changed when we came here. Some people changed, others didn't. Pixie Aarae turning into a woman. A girl, at any rate. Turning into Omry Inbar's girl at least. Robot Amaterasu becoming . . . what's the phrase? Becoming a real, live girl.

What has this Laing creature become? Odd to think of her like that. Creature? An invented being, no more than some very sophisticated computer program. Now?

Passiphaë Laing resting against the brass rail, forehead down on her arms, staring at the floor. Staring at nothing. I ought to do something. Say something. What? I don't know. I don't know how to do this. All I know is that I ought to. But . . .

Right. All the years in school. Competing with the other girls, then competing with the boys. Winning. Always winning. Then University. Winning some more. Making things up as I went along. That crazy business about being a lesbian.

Just another way to win. And me not knowing all the things I'd lost.

A sharp memory, again, of her mother's friends. She stepped forward, put out her hand, hesitated. "Are you all right?"

Nothing.

She sat down and put her hand on Laing's back, up by her shoulder. Opened her mouth to speak . . . Say what? It seems . . . wrong to just call her . . . *Laing.* Laing is what you'd call a man. You'd say, Buck up, Laing. It isn't the end of the world . . . "Passiphaë."

The woman sat up, looked out the window for a moment, then looked at her.

"Are you all right?"

A long, hollow stare. Nothing.

What would my mother have done? All sorts of memories, forgotten, suppressed, until now. She looked into the hollow eyes, opened her mouth to speak again . . . nothing there. Nothing but . . . held out her arms, and, with Passiphaë Laing nestled on her shoulder, Subaïda Rahman found she did indeed know when to be silent. And why.

Omry Inbar held Aarae tightly by the hand and looked down what he had been told was called the Great White Way. Bizarre neon illumination, signs of moving light, brightening the shadowed canyons of the classic stone city. Not stone, no. Reinforced concrete. Prefabricated cement facades over iron and brick core material.

All right, so its not so different, really, from the modern cities of the UAR. This could be Midan Tahrir in al-Qahira, where el-Tahrir, Mohammad Mahmoud and Qasr el-Aini all meet. Places like this in Basra, Algiers, Tunis. Overhead, where the tall buildings ended, though, the sky stood out like a river of bright blue. The sky should be dark. A dark black sky, with the stars blotted out by Earthlings' light.

All day long, wonder on wonder. The airship landing them at a place called *Lakehurst*, putting them aground on a grassy field of masts, each mast bearing a huge airship of its own, in response to a question, Edgar saying, This one? Oh, *Los*

Angeles, I think. Painted on the tail somewhere. Another frown, at another question. *Hindenburg?!* Why? These are American airships.

Ling, staring with delight across the field, counting, yes, twenty-seven rigid dirigibles, had pointed out that the *Luftschiff Zeppelin* company had made the original *Los Angeles*, as well.

Edgar, with a sardonic grin: Yep. Made this one, too. Son of a bitch is just *full* of crazy stories about the Civil War.

Freddy. Referred to him as Freddy.

That's the thing, you see. These are *Americans*. Whatever that means . . . Train ride into the city. Tall buildings, already grown old, Kincaid staring at them across flat, brushy landscape, saying, You left out a lot.

Edgar nodding. Yep. When Jack wouldn't let Don be Finance Minister, he, ah, went elsewhere. Up in Novyrom last I heard, trying to set up a shipping line with one of those Greek boys. Some guy with the same name as the philosopher that taught Alexander. I forget.

Ling had said, Jack? Kennedy is president of High America?

Naw. He never showed up here. Jack's that fat comedian fellow. Gleason. Does a good job, too. Smart as Hell.

The hotel had been wonderful too, clean linen on a turned-down bed, little refrigerator in the room, full of liquor and candy. Of course, the linen hadn't stayed clean too long, he and Aarae scrambling out of their clothes and in between the sheets . . .

He'd lain there with her afterward, the two of them, superficially at least, satiated, snuggling close, damp and warm, watching some crazy show on the old-fashioned cable TV, something about a woman, a journalist maybe, searching the Red Desert country to the west of High America, looking for her lost husband.

Arabian adventure, like Scheherazadë stories.

Maybe the husband's name was even Sindbad.

Warm, whole woman clinging to him now. The way no woman ever held onto me. Like . . . mother, lover, and comrade all rolled into one. And that faint tickle of fear. Not a magic being, anymore. A woman now. More than that, a person now.

They always leave me. Memories of many partings. No. That's not right. They go away because I've already left, moved on to the next thing, only my libido left behind. Will that happen again? Will Aarae, sorrowing, go away, simply because I've . . . forgotten how these moments feel?

No answer, as always. Just a vow. And vows, in time, are forgotten.

Holding his hand now, close by his side, going from window to window with him, reluctantly moving on. Eventually they came to a newsstand, all colorful magazines that caught Aarae's eye, newspapers printed on cheap, grayish paper rustling in the wind. Papers in English, full of pictures, mostly grayscale, some in garish color. This . . .

The Hebrew characters jumped out at him, making him pick the thing up, eyes already tracking right to left, trying to read. No. Not Hebrew. Phonemes, sounded out, an awful lot like transliterated English. But not English. No, some dialect of German, maybe . . .

My God. This is in Yiddish. My grandfather could speak Yiddish. Angry when his children refused to learn. Threatening to emigrate to the Ukraine. Right, Grandpa. Will you send us bushel baskets of the potatoes you pick? Will you send us pictures from the ghetto?

The man behind the counter—thin, young like most everyone here, blue-eyed, with curly black hair—was watching him closely. Suspicion. Does he think I'm going to steal the paper?

The man said something. Clearly something said in the same language as the paper.

Inbar said, "I'm sorry. I don't speak Yiddish."

Scornful look. "Den vhy . . ."

A particle of anger, anger and pride, popping up, bright and hot. In Hebrew, he said, "I'm newly arrived. From . . ." From where? From the Earth? No. From the United Arab Republic of the twenty-second century? No. "Newly arrived from Israël."

The paperseller's eyes brightened, and in fluidly guttural

late twenty-first century Sabraic Hebrew, he said, "Ah. Welcome! I was myself killed in the Arab Conquest." He held out his hand and said, "Amoz is my name. Amoz bar-Or."

The Grand Council Chamber, to Astrid Kincaid's pleasure, turned out to be no more than a meeting room in City Hall, long, brown wooden tables along one wall, gray metal folding chairs filling the rest of the room. There were dirty windows to the outside, pale sunlight slanting in to pool on the floor, just as if there were a real sun up in the sky somewhere to make them cast focused shadows.

The buildings. The windowpane maybe. They'd thrown shadows out on the plains of course, but . . . hazy shadows. Going in all directions.

There was a blackboard on the wall behind the long table, a green board really, written on in yellow chalk. Mathematics. Exclamation points. Off to one side, what looked like some kind of meeting agenda in a neat, square printed hand. Above the blackboard was a banner, done on fanfold paper, all green and white bars, of a sort she dimly remembered from her childhood, the big letters on the sign were, on closer inspection, formed from assemblies of the same letter. A T of tees, an A of aes . . .

It said: Tannu Tuva or Bust.

People were coming into the room now, and Edgar said, "OK, let's get started."

One of the men, a tall, muscular blond boy with a fat, round chin and impossibly flashy smile, said, "Don't be in such a rush, Ed. We've got whatever time we need." Rather peculiar accent.

"Right. Have a seat, Wormer. We'll get to that directly." Big grin as he sat, taking the mangled pronunciation in good humor. Probably an old game between them. Edgar gestured at three rather similar-looking young men: "The Unholy Trinity, Al, Murray and Gerry."

Well. I know who the skinny guy with the messy hair is. The others . . .

More people coming to the long table, sitting down, identified by unfamiliar first names. One of them seemed to be an

Italian named Ricky. And Edgar, sitting down, facing them, hands folded atop the table, big fingers intertwined: "I think I can speak for us all when I say how glad we are to see you!"

Grins from down the row, toothy-faced European grins, lip-twisted American grins. High America, all right . . .

Telling the story, in quick-time:

You die. You come here. Human cultures from all times past, all mixed together, all the people who lived before you wandering across the face of some gigantic continent. Sort of surveyed, Edgar told them. The big river valley, forests to the east. An ocean beyond that . . .

Oh, yes, the River of No Return is just a river. It flows along for forty, maybe fifty thousand miles, from up by the Inland Oceans down to . . . well, it's the same sea as the Eastern Sea beyond Novyrom. Just a sea with no farther shore, a sea full of islands, little and big.

And the pilgrims. The seekers of Heaven? Image of Jensen and antwife, Alireza and Zeq, Brucie and Tarantellula-Penny, all on their way to Heaven. What about them?

A shrug, broad palms upraised to . . . No. Not to Heaven. There is no Heaven. At least, no Heaven around here. Edgar said, There's a very nice country down around the River's delta, a green and fertile land maybe half the size of Europe. A lot of them settle there. They call it New East Anglia. I don't know why.

A lot of them. Not all?

No. A lot of those little boats just go on out to sea.

And the people aboard them?

It doesn't matter. All they can do is . . . live and die and live again. This seems to be the end of the road. A bitter pill for some to swallow. How long will it take for Alireza to find his wife? How long before Zeq knows there's . . . no place for him anywhere, not even here? Hell. Maybe he'll make a place.

Bruce and Penny will settle in the delta country and live happily every after. They've found what they were looking for . . .

And what about us? Little lost scientist boys looking at each other? Well. We've spent the last few centuries exploring, you see. Exploring. Arguing. Trying to figure things out. Not getting much of anywhere. You could see the arguments starting to surface, people marshaling their rhetoric, mouths starting to open . . .

Edgar said, We're not the sort of people who can live happily ever after. Not in a place like this. A place so . . . so damned *accidental*. Maybe there's no reason for anything. No reason at all. But we spent our *real* lives looking . . .

Looking, said Al, soft bitterness in his voice, not really finding anything.

Edgar said, We've been looking for the *Exit* sign, I guess you might say. Maybe we've found it, maybe not.

In any case, said Al, your existence is the key.

Many histories, many . . . Heavens, if you will, said Murray.

If, said Gerry, it's not just some almighty sleight of hand.

Ling coughed suddenly, from the back of the room where he'd been sitting. "Still looking for the dice, I see."

Al smiled at him, smiled out from under a little brush of a *Führer* moustache, and ran his fingers through curly black hair. "*Ach, so*. Everyone who ever arrived came here by dying a natural death. Until now. You folks got here through this . . . Multiverse of yours, confirming many histories . . ." a grim look around the room, the settling of many old scores. "If there's another way in, other than the grave, there must be another way out."

Gerry said, "And we think maybe we've spotted the door."

In the end, when the shadowless, edgeless days and weeks had gone by, they took them back to Lakehurst-in-the-Sky, not to the field of zeppelins this time, but to a vast concourse paved with hard, pebbly tan concrete. And now, Subaïda Rahman stood on the runway, feeling herself fill up with a cold sense of panic.

I don't want to be the last one. Mahal and Tariq, exploded on the Moon. Zeq, red ruin beneath Permian jaws. Alireza, broken and dead when it was all . . . hardly begun. Zeq and Alireza, so briefly, found again, gone now down a hideously false River of No Return . . .

Ling and that bizarre substitute-Edgar, laughing and laughing together at the truth, the bald man saying, Oh, it's not *quite* the River Iss, but it's just as much a lie . . .

Offering to send a Search and Rescue airship down the River to look for them all, Zeq and Alireza, Jensen and the antgirl, that ancient, idiotic boy and his little brown monster . . .

Long silence. Then Laing: No. Let them be. Then a nod from Kincaid. They'll find what they're looking for. But . . .

Holding Inbar's hands, facing him, beseeching: "*Why?*"

Face shining with happiness. Pulling his hand from hers, reaching out to put his arm around Aarae, pretty, pretty girl, seeming, somehow, to grow just a little prettier every time I look at her . . .

A hollow pang of something terribly like jealousy formed in the pit of her stomach.

Inbar said, "Maybe Heaven is just a place where you can be happy, Subaïda. I'm happy now. I don't have any reason at all to go on."

Voice very flat: "This isn't Heaven, Omry."

A wry smile. "I know that. But it's a place where you can keep on looking. Keep looking until you've found . . . whatever it is you're looking for. I think I've found that, at least. And maybe that's all that Heaven means."

An adolescent boy's adolescent woolgathering. Happy because he's found a willing set of female genitals and a bed to lie in. I thought he was . . . more than that. Maybe none of them are.

"You can stay too, Subaïda. There's something here somewhere for you, I'm sure of it."

Frowning, looking down at the ground. Feeling defeated. "I don't think so." A gesture then at Aarae, close by his side, holding his hand. "What's here for you that you can't take away?"

He laughed. "A whole world. A whole infinite world. This place alone . . . High America is a nearly circular plateau maybe five thousand kilometers across . . ."

An immensity, all right. She said, "You're not an American, Omry."

A dark look forming. "No. But I'm not an Arab, either. I'm a Jew. Do you know what that means?"

She waited for him to tell her, growing impatient.

He said, "When I was a kid, I used to wonder where dead Jews went when they died. Not to the Christians' Heaven, surely, with its streets paved in gold. Not to your Muslim Paradise, despite all those tempting little ever-virginal houris."

Making her angry now. How dare he . . .

He said, "When I was a kid, I used to wish for Valhalla. Not the cute little Valkyries, I'm afraid, but visions of endlessly linked pork sausages, popping with fat and reeking of thyme . . ."

"What the Hell are you talking about?"

"I know where dead Jews go now, Subaïda. Dead Jews go to America. America is Heaven."

Looking into his eyes then, she was certain he'd gone mad at last.

And he said, "We didn't come out here to find Heaven, Subaïda. Don't you remember? We just went up to the Moon to save ourselves, our people, our country, and maybe humanity too. That's all over. Gone. Finished! Let the others go on looking for their imaginary God. I . . . have what I need."

Anger, mingling with resentment. So he has what he needs and the rest of us can . . . go piss in the wind. But what do you need, Subaïda Rahman? The Moon is gone. The past is gone. No road home again. Even if I imagined it was ever *my* home. What am I looking for? What's my part in this?

A distant, fatalistic shrug.

She said, "Well. Good-bye then, Omry. Nice meeting you, Aarae." And turned away.

Standing by the side of the runway, arm around Aarae's warm shoulders, Omry Inbar watched them board the big plane, this mysterious Edgar and his crew of immortal savants, Subaïda Rahman and the other six survivors of the long quest.

Not many of them left now. Rahman's the last Arab, Ling the only Chinaman since near the beginning. Kincaid the last of the Americans. Passiphaë Laing the only survivor from *Crimson Desert*'s cast. Amanda Grey no more than the hollow shell of magic Hesperidia . . .

Lord Genda Hiroshige and his unrobot Amaterasu still walking hand in hand, the last of their kind. Lovers to the end, perhaps. To what end? Why should they go on, if they have each other? Genda's idiotic quest for God? He should give that up. There's no God out there. In any event, no God who can give him back his lost universe.

He's found Amaterasu. The World Without End has made her real. That should be enough. Aarae snuggling close under his arm, arm around his waist, holding him close. It's enough for me. Looking down at her then: Is it enough for her? I'm not much of a prize, am I? Why should she want the likes of me? She smiled up at him then, eyes dancing, and he thought: With luck, I'll never know.

But forever, of course, is a lot to ask for a run of luck.

The shadow, cast upon eternity.

Out on the runway, the big airplane's engines revved up, six backward-facing pusher engines, each with an immense, four-bladed prop, turning over and over, spinning up, seeming to reverse, persistence of vision, rumbling whistle now, sounds overlaid on each other, wheels beginning to roll.

The thing was, they said, originally modeled on something Edgar called an NB-36H. It was, he said, a variant of the giant intercontinental bomber Franklin Roosevelt planned to use on Hitler after Britain fell. Image of those imaginary days, bold American crews crossing the Atlantic with their loads of napalm, firebombing an impotent Germany . . .

Until, maybe, Hitler's armies finished off Russia, finished off Russia and crossed the Bering Strait, walked across Canada, across all of the vast American heartland, SS stormtroops marching right up Pennsylvania Avenue, taking the old cripple away to meet the Master.

No. It could never have happened that way. Surely there's no universe where all the Jews in the world became fertilizer and lampshades.

Big airplane thundering on the end of the runway now, having taxied far away. I didn't even look to see if they were waving to me. Lost in my dreams. Another look down at Aarae. "Are we doing the right thing?"

She looked up at him, and said, "There is no right thing. If there were, there would be no Multiverse."

No right thing? Another cusp splitting away, even here? Another World Without End, where I *am* aboard, going on with the rest? Airplane rolling smoothly down the runway now, faster and faster, nosewheel coming up, wings lifting, sky appearing underneath now, landing gear retracted up into nacelles under the nose, near the wing-roots, bay doors closing, sound of the engines diminishing. In the twinkling of an eye, it was a speck in the sky, then gone.

Aarae said, "You're not sorry, are you?"

He looked into his heart. Am I? *Is* this what I want? He said, "No. No I'm not sorry."

"Come on, then. Our car is waiting . . ." Taking him by the hand, leading him away.

Over by the edge of the runway, a gang of black men was digging a ditch, thin, half-naked figures bending over picks and shovels, working, working, their tools making small, wet chopping sounds, familiar butchershop sounds as they cut the earth.

Who? Not American Negroes, of course. The ones who came here were happy, rich people, like the Chinese, the Jews, the whites, all the free folk who'd died and gone to High America, Americans all. No, these were black men with long arms and legs, grayish-black skin and unfamiliar hayrick hair. Who?

Amazulu, of course, the people who'd settled here some time in the late Paleolithic, perhaps, who'd been here when Edgar and his friends arrived. We let them stay, no reason not to. Let them stay and become part of the great thing we were building.

We?

He was still looking at them, watching them work, out the back window of the big Packard Edgar had given them, as Aarae drove them away, on back to High New York and all those lovely city lights.

* * *

Though it was a lot more comfortable back in the B-36's main passenger cabin, cabin occupying the space where the big bomb bays should have been, Ling Erhshan found he was happier riding in the cockpit, up where he could look forward, watching the mountains grow huge, or backward, over the top of the broad wings, through the transparent flicker of the spinning props, across the hazy majesty of the World Without End.

Just this little corner of it, of course. Out over the impossibly flat landscape, from a slow-moving aircraft that seemed to float along at fifty thousand meters or so, seeming to hang just under the wide canopy of the deep purple sky, you could see all the way back. Past the smeared-out, Bedouin-inhabited wasteland of the Red Desert, past the now tiny gray hump of High America, past the Indian-, Mongol-, and Turk-infested plains of Great Achaea, dotted with little Greek cities, networked by Hanseatic traders, past the twisted lightening bolt of the River Iss to the dark and dank forest country beyond, all the way to a shadowy silver sliver that Edgar told him was the Eastern Sea.

How far? Oh, sixty, maybe seventy thousand miles. Ling converted that to kilometers and felt giddy. How wide is the ocean?

A shrug. Hard to say. Shippers from Novyrom go out to islands as far as fifty thousand miles, say there's only trackless ocean beyond that. There's another big landmass out there, though, visible from up on the mountains. Half a million miles away . . .

Twice the distance, then, that we went to the Moon. A million kilometers and more of fat, flat ocean.

Forward, of course, all you could see was the Mountains. Edgar saying, we call them the Big Cords. Everybody else just calls them the Mountains, in whatever language they're using.

Isn't *cordillera* just Spanish for "mountain range"?

A smile. Yep. Little *cuerda*.

Mountains that, seemingly, towered up as far as the eye could see. Not really. Just that overwhelming feeling of immensity, mountains bulking huge, even though they were still many thousands of miles away, green trees barely touching their roots, surmounted by a thin band of snow, then rock and more rock, shining by the light of the nonexistent sun.

How high?

Oh, not as high as they look. Some of the lowest passes are down around 100,000 feet, average peak is no more than 250,000 . . .

Ling stared at them, imagining himself atop a mountain almost eighty kilometers high. How far could I see from up there? Over the edge of the world. Don't be silly. There is no edge.

That one there's where we're headed, Mike's Peak, 357,000 feet. Edgar pointing to a fat, massive mountain, flat topped, that seemed to tower above its companions, shouldering them aside.

Ling thought, That's a mountain well over a hundred kilometers high. He said, "What's the ceiling of this plane?" He gestured at the dark sky. "The atmosphere can't be any deeper than Earth's or . . ."

Edgar said, "There's a base about a quarter of the way up. It's a little tricky landing a plane on a runway that's up near its maximum cruising altitude, not to mention taking off again, but we'll manage."

Ling started to think about old-fashioned superchargers, all the things that had extended the lifetime of prop-driven planes out of the infancy of aeronautics, far into the jet age. Started. Stopped. Well. No. With nuclear electric engines, they could spin the propellers as fast as they had power to do so, as fast as the material could stand. Coarsen the pitch, maybe, increase the bite on thinning air. Rockets and more rockets. It's been a long time since I had to think about aerodynamics. Just get the rocket up out of the soup as fast as possible . . .

What an interesting world. Memory of looking back at Inbar and Aarae, two foolish lost souls standing by the side of the runway, watching them slip away, waving, realizing they weren't watching back. What an interesting world. Maybe I could be happy here after all.

What difference does it make, whether I live forever in an

infinite Multiverse, or live forever crawling across the flat landscape of a World Without End. I'm supposed to be dead now. Why don't I feel dead? Cold memories, fading fast.

Watching the landing from the cockpit turned out to be a little more nerve-wracking than Kincaid expected. Tough, tough, centenarian-plus soldiergirl coming forward, taking her seat beside Ling, Ling staring out the side window, watching the mountainside loom. It looks a lot closer than they say. Scale effects. I've never been near a mountain this big before.

Memories of the old days, of flying to the Moon. Old Luna had a sense of bigness to it that the Earth, seen from orbit, did not. Moon like a big, big rock, blotting out the sky. Remember braking into orbit, strapped in by a tiny porthole in the lower bay of TXX-044? Strapped there next to Kathy, looking out the window.

Over the night side of the Moon, coasting lower and lower, waiting for the engines to ignite. Kathy, her corporal, saying, "Good grief, Sarge. You sure as Hell know something's *out* there, don't you?" Something big, blotting out the stars.

I haven't thought about Kathy in . . . forever. Kathy talking like a man, just like one of the boys. We all did. Why? Because it was expected of us? Little monsters, nursing our hearts in silence. I remember how much I liked her. That's all. The rest is gone. Even her face.

Edgar pointed at something far down the mountainside, a splotch of white concrete and little buildings, sitting on what looked like a tiny cliff. "That's as far up as the dirigibles can go, so we had to build the first base there, bring in the materials and . . . well, the first survey teams went on up by foot to the fifty-thousand-foot site. People got hurt."

Kincaid said, "Many killed?" The ultimate sacrifice.

Edgar smiled. "You keep forgetting where you are, Sergeant."

Outside, the mountain was turning into a world-like wall. I could focus hard, shift perspective, and imagine we were landing on the Moon. Craters? Maybe. Pockmarks, at any rate. Stuff falling out of the sky. The souls of dead rocks?

Edgar said, "Later on, we brought in turbocharged tractors, wound up putting in an air liquification plant so we could feed the tractor engines from oxygen tanks. Took a while, but we got everything built . . ."

Out of nowhere, the mountainside seemed to sprout a little city, a town really, cluster of white buildings around what looked like small runway. Things like cars. Buildings without windows though . . .

Edgar suddenly turned in his seat, forgetting her. "God damn it, Al, you're coming in too . . ."

The mountainside seemed to swell suddenly, runway sliding under them, white concrete going by beneath the plane's fragile hull entirely too fast. Hydraulic whine, a triple thump, gear going down and locking into place. Jesus Christ, talk about last second, like those old Shuttle pilots, from when my parents were young, hypersonic gliders dropping on the desert . . .

Bang. Solid jar making her teeth snap together lightly. Not ready for it. Damn well know not to let your mouth hang open in a combat situation. Getting careless in your old age.

Rattle-squeal of metal parts trying to fly apart, roar coming through the structure of the aircraft, shuddering, shuddering, pitch of the props most likely reversed now, blowing air hard forward, slowing them down . . . they seemed to be heading right for one of the buildings.

Kincaid thought of trying to hold on for just a second, then relaxed. Nobody panicking here but us greenhorns. Look at the three of them. Grinning, for Christ's sake. Boys with toys.

The plane rolled to a stop, rocking back and forth on its hydraulic shock absorbers, its glass nosecap maybe three meters from the nearest white wall. Edgar said, "We call this place the Second Floor. Come on back. We'll get some oxygen masks and go outside."

Al said, "Bundle up, children. A little nippy up here."

Cog railway then to the top of the mountain, Edgar telling them they'd thought of extending it down to the zeppelin base, make it easier to get cargo up here, but . . . "Tribesmen down on the Psaltry Plateau are pretty damn bold. Got up as far as the original base camp once already. We've had to put in more defenses than we like, just to keep the tractor head open. Maybe, when we've built a few more cargo versions of the ole *36*, here, we can forget about the rest of it."

Naked tribesmen, however hardy, would not be climbing to an airport crouching at the 50,000-foot mark. As they rode up the mountain, snug in a pressurized car, the view to the east grew no more splendid, grew no more details, flat slab of silver ocean merely growing larger, stretching on out, farther and farther away. Something in the distance?

Edgar said, "It's there, all right. Just not enough color to it. Not enough contrast. The scopes up top," thumb toward the sky, "give us a pretty good view. You can see there're mountains and rivers and things."

Ling asked, "Vegetation?"

A frown. "Maybe. A lot of the landscape appears to be sort of reddish orange. With all the rivers, it's unlikely to be desert."

Kincaid said: "Maybe it's Fall there all the time. How long would it take you to fly over in the *36*?"

"Seventeen hundred hours."

Not quite seventy-one days. "So why haven't you gone?"

"We sent a zeppelin over about twenty years ago, back before we got the scopes up, when we only suspected there might be another continent out there. It would've taken them maybe two years to make the round trip. But they never came back."

Ling said, "How did you manage to make an airship that could fly for two years on a single load of fuel?"

Kincaid: "You people have been here for, what? Three hundred years? Why're these things happening only now?"

A smile. "Three hundred years ago it was me and Otis and a few others putting up a log fort near the edge of the plateau, calling ourselves High America and trying to keep the Amazulu from throwing us out. Took a while to build the rest."

Ling, voice hushed: "That must have been . . . an adventure."

Edgar's smile was crooked: "You could look at it that way."

You could. Kincaid thought, Boys with toys. Ling's eyes shining, full of . . . old imaginings. Where have my old imaginings gone? Melted away over the years. I grew old, sitting home in Fortress America. Old. And what if we hadn't gone to the Moon? Not just now, but back then. What if there'd been no American Renaissance? I'd've grown old just the same. Grown old and died. Sudden, pale shock: Grown old. And died. And come right here. Come here with all my friends.

The top of the mountain was another pale shock, the cog train rolling over the rim, sky black above them, densely spangled now with what looked like a hundred thousand dim, fuzzy stars—stars clotting the whole width of the sky from horizon to . . . Well. No. Just covering the whole width of the sky, fuzz-spangled sky seeming to reach out forever, never quite coming down to meet the unending bright landscape below.

And what do I see out there. Down there? Nothing. Bright blue nothing. Day sky hanging under the night, two sheets of differentiated light stretching out to . . . to nowhere.

Flat tableland up here, millions of hectares of flat, bare gray rock. White domes nearby, at the head of the cog railway. Familiar slit observatory domes, big tubes poking out of them, some looking up, others looking . . . away. Ling, pointing, said, "And that?"

Shapes in the distance, tens of kilometers away, dark, skeletal shapes, cast in shadow. Edgar said, "Ah, the Krautmeister Empire."

Tousle-haired Al, gazing soberly out at the infinite distance below, said, "You really shouldn't call them that, Ed." Voice disapproving, reproving in a distant sort of way.

"Why the Hell not? I've been calling them that for two, three hundred years now . . ."

"Still . . ." Al said, "That's Wernher's bailiwick. He and his friend Krafft have been . . . building a rocket."

Ling sitting forward now. "A rocket."

Wan smile from Edgar. "Even I knew you couldn't put something in orbit here . . ." Of course not. Flat. The World Without End is flat.

Al said, "They brought the designs with them in their heads when they died."

Edgar: "And they've been arguing ever since. Wormer wants to call it the Saturn C-8, Krafty keeps plumping for Nova."

"Please." Al said, "They think its a quick way to fill in local exploration, fill in gaps left by the scopes. The vehicle can reach one million kilometers altitude, or two million fired for range."

Edgar said: "In about six months, they're going to put a robot probe down on Orange East. A small, teleoperated dirigible, with a couple of retrievable surface probes. Little tanks. Hell. Maybe they'll even find out what happened to old Bill and Merry."

Al: "They were old-fashioned, Edgar. They preferred to be called William and Merriweather." He said, "Some time next year, they're going to lift one of our telescopes straight up on a sounding flight. That'll give us a much better perspective on some of the more distant objects . . ."

Eventually, the train took them through the airlock of a pressurized terminal.

Ling said, "I should've anticipated this. Somehow, I was visualizing old-style astronomers, bundled up in greatcoats, huddling over eyepieces, working with glass plates, maybe."

Al said, "Is that the way they do things in your Green China?"

"Well, no, but this place is so . . . antique."

Edgar said, "In any case, there's no air up in the dome. Even if we didn't want to keep the mirrors clean, it'd still rush out every time . . ." Image of the dome sliding open and greatcoated astronomers blowing right out.

Now, they sat before a two-meter wide television screen, a relatively-crude projection affair, while Al and Edgar worked a control panel, some joysticks, mainly, and an alphanumeric keyboard. Edgar said, "Some fellows showed up in High

America a couple of months ago. Told us they can build some kind of mind-brain interface for computers. Hard for me to imagine."

Kincaid said, "Even in the Fortress, immortals sometimes get killed."

Al said, "We were starting to wonder. Pickings have gotten rather . . . slim, these last few decades. We were quite overjoyed when one of our agents radioed home that rumors were circulating about you folks having arrived at the River."

Edgar said, "There. This is an island, out on the Western Sea, maybe forty thousand miles from here."

Island rising from the sea. Something like a volcano. Not a volcano though, jagged cone more like a regular mountain, with the top ripped open, blue-violet light spilling out.

Edgar: "Just an ordinary little island, maybe the size of Sicily, mountain no more than sixty thousand feet. No sweat at all for the good, old *36*."

Al said, "We're stopping here so I can take a few readings with our newer instruments before going on. Some of the earlier measurements suggested more intense ionizing radiation than we'd be comfortable with."

Kincaid: "So what? We're dead."

Edgar laughed: "Getting used to the idea, are you?"

Al: "Your tissues would melt away eventually. You'd wind up reifying somewhere else."

Edgar: "Besides which, *36* is neither immortal nor invulnerable."

Ling: "What do you think it is?"

Edgar: "Symmes' Hole."

Al: "Foolishness."

Edgar said, "It's just a bit of shorthand. We think it's the way out. We've been looking at it for some time now. Planning what to do, arguing about . . . well, ways and means, ifs and whens."

"The way out to where?"

A smile, "Well, that was the question, until you folks showed up. Murray kept insisting it was just a crustal rip, exposing the underlayers of the event horizon. Hawking Backscatter leaking through maybe."

"And now?"

A shrug. "I've listened to your tale. We all have. If there are things like your Stargates here, we haven't found them. If there's a way out—out into your Multiverse—it'd have to be something like this."

"Pipe dream," said Al.

"Maybe so. Maybe everything *is* an accident. But if it's not . . . Hell. There's got to be a watchmaker somewhere."

Kincaid: "What if you're wrong? What if it's just a radioactive hole in the ground?"

Another shrug. "That's been the argument all along! Hell, we've been shouting at each other for decades, Hell, *centuries*, about whether this is *it*. If I'm wrong, if this is *it*, the End of the Road, the Final Place, what have you, if we're just fucking vaporized when we fly down that glowing hole, then, when I reify, I'll walk back home to High America and take my lumps. Then try something else. Hell, people, we've got fucking *forever* to screw around in!"

Al murmured, "Spoken like a true American."

Ling said, "What if it *does* go . . . somewhere else? What then?"

Long silence. Then Gerry whispered, "Well, I always was upset about dying just when I did. Maybe . . ."

Al, German accent very soft, said, "It doesn't matter where it *goes*. So long as it goes. None of us wants to spend Eternity here. It's why we were looking for the . . . for the Egress, you see, all along."

Ling thought, Of course.

Now, below, the silver ocean was a featureless blue venue only a little darker than the sky. If there were clouds above, Rahman thought, it would reflect them. Then . . . Not really so different. Sky over sky still. But at least the moving cloud images would lend some feeling of progress. Thirty thousand English miles from the western shores of vast, nameless continent—I still think of it as Heaven—to the glowing island. Close to fifty thousand kilometers.

A hundred hours. Only a hundred hours over the trackless waste. Four days and a little bit. If we still had days. She'd been spending more and more time alone, crawling back through the heavily-shielded tunnel that bypassed the reactor amidships, crawling over the cargo stores, the humming machinery of the airplane's primitive life-support system, back to the tail gunner's blister.

Heavy equipment here. A quad of 50-caliber machine guns that could be aimed slightly upward, as well as aft. A single, long-barreled aerial cannon that could fire downward.

Edgar smiling when she asked. We've got a ball turret in the belly, side mounted weaponpacks, a chin turret, one ventral . . . You never know.

Rahman sat and watched the empty sea recede. And waited. Down the hole. Down the Rabbit Hole. Is that what we're doing? Why? Because some people can never be . . . content? A crawling sense of unease. But . . . that's why *I'm* here, isn't it? Why I went to University, pretended to be a lesbian, never married, joined the space program, went on up to the Moon and . . .

In the Name of God. *I'm* the one who led us through the Stargate. I'm the one who turned it on, stepped through to another world, led us on out into the Multiverse and . . . what was I looking for?

I remember the crawling sense of raw *excitement* I felt when the first Stargate opened on that impossible new world, Mars-Plus, yellow hills under a red sky. I remember thinking, This now. *This* is what you've been looking for all along.

Mars-Plus. The Permian. *Crimson Desert.* Hesperidia. God's Machine. This strange and so-absurd World Without End.

Now, down the hole, and away again. To where? To yet another Multiversal world where things will be strange and different, yet forever the same. No way to know. Only wondering left inside.

She sat and watched the sea recede. And waited.

Plane banking in over the coast of the blue island now, slopes of the mountain clad in turquoise forest, blue water lapping at silver-white beaches, Ling Erhshan looking out of the cockpit window, entranced. Like paradise? No. Like an alien world, like I . . .

Sharp reality intruding. As if it's all new, myself reborn, the alien worlds I've really seen almost forgotten. I've been to the Moon, traveled through time to the Permian, fallen down through endless dimensions, died the real death from which no one returns and . . .

Edgar said, "Over there." Pointing.

Others turning to look.

Kincaid said, "Some kind of aircraft, climbing up toward us . . ."

Al: "They'd have to be . . . pretty sophisticated to reach this altitude."

"Sophisticated or not," said Edgar, "those are the first aircraft we've seen in the World other than our own." Frowning now, watching them climb.

Ling picked up a pair of binoculars kept handy in the cockpit and focused them on the climbing planes. Two of them. Small. Single-engine. Prop drive. Open cockpits . . . "An antique design, I think. Older than this one."

Edgar took the binoculars and looked. "A little like a P-shooter, maybe. They'll never get up here." The floor was tilting under them now as Edgar turned into a long, spiraling climb, up toward the mouth of the glowing mountain.

Kincaid, watching the little planes circle helplessly, far below, said, "P-shooter. That would be the pre-World War II P-26?"

Edgar said, "I keep forgetting you were born not long after my time."

Brilliant flashes from around the edge of the mountain, hundreds of kilometers away. "Over there."

Edgar leveled the binoculars and looked. "I'll be damned. Aircraft attacking a city by the sea. No, not the city. Ships in its harbor. I'll be damned."

"Can we take a look?"

Edgar said, "We don't have time for that." Handing him the binoculars. "This'll have to do."

Time? Why is there no time? We have all the time there is. But the sense of . . . hurry remains.

He put the binoculars to his eyes and looked. Little prop-driven airplanes swooping low over the water. Black objects falling. Dropping into the sea, going on, leaving white trails of submerged foam, white trails ending at the hulls of big black ships, ships exploding, great gouts of fire, black smoke rising toward the pale blue sky.

I wonder who they are? I wonder why they're fighting? I'll never know.

Then 36 leveled off, circled once out over the sea, turned back toward the mountain, banking, begin a slow, shallow dive. Ling Erhshan looked up, startled, into the mountain's brilliant, empty mouth.

What if this *is* Heaven? He thought. What if that's Hell? But the people below, fighting, trying to kill each other in a place where no one could die. Heaven? No. Better that we go on.

One last view, Sergeant-Major Astrid Kincaid, leaning forward in her jumpseat, pulling at the harness she'd only just remembered to fasten, leaning close, pressing her face to the cold Plexiglas of the cockpit window, looking down into featureless, blue-violet nothing.

One more, final, stupid act. Somewhere along the way, I lost my sense of what was real. There's nothing down there. Nothing but white light and death. In a moment, I will feel the fire burn me up. A moment after that and I'll awaken, back on the high plains of Great Achaea. What then? Walk back to High America? Why? There nothing there. Go down the River of No Return? Nothing there either. Nothing anywhere.

One God-damned almighty cold realization: No matter what I do, I can't escape this. I go on and on and on. No way to end it now, for I've already died. Remote, cold wish, forlorn hope: Maybe I will wake up. Maybe it's all been a dream. Maybe I'm still in . . .

No. Not in Fortress America. Nothing there but more useless eternity. Pray you wake up in your bed again, wake up once more a little girl, with a whole, finite life ahead of you. Pray it comes out differently, this time.

Pray that you live your one life well.

Pray that nothing goes to waste.

Al pulled back on his control yoke, heeled the plane over on one wing, chopped the throttle, opened the speed brakes, pushed the yoke down again and nosed them over in the direction of bright blue hell.

One final, stark thought, as the mountain's mouth opened to engulf them: What if he's behind me now, wandering the World Without End? And what if I don't come back?

Ten.

The End of the Passage.

Elements of a final theory.

It has been, is, will be, forever and ever frustrating to realize that, though I seem to be, really feel that I *am*, all-knowing and all-powerful, there remain things beyond my reach.

What sort of things could be beyond the reach of God Almighty?

Well. I am not God Almighty, merely the infinitely lesser being who sits in the Command Module, parks his fat ass on the Throne and operates the light show, blows the smoke and tilts the mirrors. Like a poor man driving a rusted out old Cadillac *Coupe de Ville* with a quarter-million miles on the odometer, all I can do is imagine elegance, while the old gas-guzzler eats up my meager pay.

Know all things, direct all paths?

Nonsense.

I know the byways of the Multiverse and nothing more.

What lies beyond, out of sight, far, far beyond my limited reach . . . nothing, not even a void. The lightless, unreal blind spot of total ignorance. Sometimes, I imagine getting out there, getting out of here, following in what I presume are the footsteps of the Old Man and, before Him, the Great Mother, going on out into the void, finding out the Truth.

And I have a terrible fear. That same old fear. Going out of the Multiverse, giving up what I *know*, going on beyond that black veil into . . . my God, the one I used to imagine as a child. Isn't that the same thing as death?

That's not the worst of it, though. The Great Mother, the Old Man God . . . I know they didn't create the Multiverse. I know they were just part of the Machine, wherever they've gone. No more than my predecessors, I suppose.

Somewhere. Somewhere beyond all knowledge, I imagine some Thing I call, for lack of a better term, simply the Other. The one great Eka-God, the One Who Makes All the Rules and Is Allowed to Change Them. The one who sets parameters for what I've called the Probability Manager, in line with the software Toolbox terminology made up when we thought we understood what the gates and Scavengers and Colonials and the whole impossible tapestry of the Multiverse was all about.

Sometimes I imagine, horribly, that the Other is no more than some lost wayfarer, just like me, some Being wandering the byways of his large eka-Multiverse, looking for the exit, looking for some way home. Would that be a satisfactory answer? Of course not. Great Gods have Bigger Gods upon Their Backs to Bite 'em, and Bigger Gods larger still . . .

What does it mean for something to have no beginning and no end?

Even now, I don't know.

Where do Almighty Gods go when their time is up?

I'm terribly frightened that one day I'll find out.

Terrible groaning, shuddery, echoing through the byways of the Multiverse now, Archangel Bob trying to get the Jug started, cursing the trillion-year-old junk that's all we have to work with. Billions, trillions, quadrillions of adoring helpers fluttering round his ectoplasm, all useless.

A great clashing of time-frames, universes destroyed in a squealing of meshed probabilities. The Jug rumbles to life, is backed out of its storage quantum, goes scraping off to the task of Rectification. Over the noise and racket and commotion, you can hear the Archangel Bob singing lustily to himself. It's the Seven Dwarves' song.

Now I hunker down to begin the work of Judgment Day.

Edgar, little Edgar, like a bright, shining seed out there, shining against the twisting black backdrop of the Multiverse. Edgar the Rebellious Angel, walking in the footsteps of old Lucifer, thinking he brought light and life to the world but . . . there was a reason for Prometheus's punishment. It wasn't because the gods were jealous of his gift. It was because he committed a crime, because he brought down evil on the innocent.

I've always despised the way the Old Man punished Adam and Eve for succumbing to the temptation he laid in their way. Entrapment is an ugly thing.

Well, Archangel Edgar, you sought the job for yourself, fought with Archangel Bob when he came on the scene, lost the battle, fell. And now, out in the Multiverse, you covet and scheme and labor to rise, rise again into Heaven and cast down all of God's Work, the *Opus Dei* you thought to own.

Won't you be surprised when you find out who's got your spot?

Edgar laboring away, all those many iterations, slowly gathering together, absorbed into one another. Absorbed and re-emitted, bouncing back and forth, gathering force like a primitive laser beam bouncing back and forth in its ruby rod . . . but we're only waiting, Edgar. Waiting patiently for you to come.

And, of course, now I must consider the matter of lovely little Astrid Astride. Loose in the Multiverse through no fault of her own, responding merely to a temptation laid in her path by some Almighty villain. Me.

Must I punish her?

The rules say yes.

And I'm not the one who writes the rules.

It'd be nice if I could think of a way out.

Look around you, Mister God Almighty Probability Manager.

Ah.

Of course.

Eleven.

Down the Rabbit Hole.

Falling!

Like . . . thought Ling Erhshan, like I'm back in orbit. Zero gee, objects floating before my face, bits and pieces of scrap, things left behind by technicians we hadn't suspected of such carelessness, rising up from their resting places, behind control consoles, under storage lockers . . . I can feel my insides floating up from their little beds, beds of fat and suddenly unstressed tissue, head suddenly full, nausea reaching out its feather-light touch . . .

Look out the window. Is that Earth down below? Chang, Da Chai and I circling in orbit, mated to the tanker pumping our fuel aboard, preparing to leave for the Moon . . .

Surely they live again, somewhere in Heaven?

Out the window, though, only blue-white light. Light so bright it was without form, a window into the void. Light so bright it left only darkness behind . . . or like a dream I once had. I'd been flying a lot, riding military transport around Siberia, setting up my various resources, getting the program started. Shaky old planes, the sort of thing a low-priority academic project could requisition. Sitting there, in my dream, belted securely into my airline seat, plane shuddering around me, plane banking hard to the right, angling down out of the sky to a snowcovered landscape, things rattling and crashing around me, people screaming, screaming.

Me, looking out the window, watching the ground heel hard over as it came up into the sky, reaching for us, thinking, No. This can't be happening. I must be having a dream . . .

Then looking at my seat mate, some young staffer I barely knew, her eyes wide, shocked, looking at me, looking right into my soul. I could read her mind, for just a moment: Please. Tell me this is just a dream.

Scream of tearing metal, crackle of breaking wings, thud of fuel ignition, seats tearing from their mounts, tumbling forward into flaring white light . . . I remember seeing her fly away. Remember seeing her torn asunder, eyes unchanged, shock of disbelief fixed for eternity. Remember my last thought, regret, wishing I could reach out and touch those soft young limbs . . .

Hand reaching out, warm hand on my arm, hand reaching to me out of the impenetrable black light, blinding light and darkness all run together in my heart. Ling said, "Kincaid . . ."

Patting him on the arm, she said, "You were making . . . noises."

Noises. I remember waking up in my sweaty bed, whimpering, clutching a damp pillow to my breast. Another hand on my arm then. The girl from the dream. One of my graduate students. I don't remember her name. "Sorry. Are we blind?"

Soft laughter. "I don't think so. I think it just got dark so fast our eyes didn't know what to make of it."

From the front of the cabin, Edgar's voice: "Well, God damn it, Al, is there air out there or not?"

Al, voice . . . delicate: "Well now. I don't know." Soft creaking noise. "When I work the yoke and rudder pedals, I don't feel any non-mechanical resistance. We could be sitting on the runway. Or floating in a vacuum."

Ling thought, Complete darkness. No gravity. No air. No nothing. "Floating in an . . . empty plenum?"

Murray said, "The thought has crossed our minds, I think."

Edgar: "Why have the engines stopped? They're nuclear-electric, not dependent on air for their operation."

No vibration beneath their feet, coming through their seats. I wonder what's happening to the folks in back? Would we be able to hear them through the hatch. Someone should . . .

Gerry said, "I don't know. We can't see the instruments . . ."

"Well? Turn on the fucking panel lights."

A brief silence, then: "There aren't any. Cabin lights neither."

A sharply hissed sigh of exasperation: "Why the fuck *not*?"

Gentle laughter from Al: "When was the last time you remember it being dark in the World Without End? There were plenty of windows. We didn't think . . ." Right. Even up on Mike's Peak, under a black and pseudo-starry sky, full daylight blazing down.

"Hmh. Fucking *great.*" And a voice-tone that said: *Now* what?

Murray: "There's a switch on the underside of the yoke column, Al. We did put in small landing lights."

"What for?"

Gerry: "Cloudy days."

Ling thought, But I don't remember seeing any clouds . . .

Murray: "Fog lights, really. Not much more than that."

Ling heard the dull crack of the switch, a sense, almost, of an echo.

Diffuse orange light coming in through the windshield, outlining the heads and shoulders of the others, black forms superimposed on hazy night and . . .

Al's voice, raised on high, pitch winding up through the scale from a thick and gargling scream: "*Fürgrossekackenscheiss'gibs'herrgott!!*"

Kincaid's echoing whisper: "Holy fuck."

Misty orange light reflecting back at them from, what? A wall? A dark, shiny wall? Outlined against it, Ling could see Al more or less standing up in his harness, standing on the rudder pedals, wall before them tilting crazily, hauling on the yoke, pulling it against his chest, wall flattening out, stretching away to infinite distance, orange light, barely a glow, fading away.

Murray said, "I can't get the engines to come on . . ." A look out the window, back aft, motionless props, not feathered, not windmilling, reflecting orange forward. "Dead circuit indicator."

Edgar: "For Christ's sake. Try to put the gear down."

Metal switches going *tick-tock*. Silence.

"Jesus. Can you keep her level? Where the Hell is that God damned crank . . ."

Plane softly shuddering. Light from outside growing brighter. Al: "No, I can't keep her level. Hold on."

The props touched first, a magnified scream of fingernails on blackboard.

Kincaid stood looking back at the crash-landed airplane from a little way off across the darkling plain, listening to her breath whisper through the oxygen-assisted respirator's valve, *shush* in, *snap*, hiss out, hose running down to a little oxygen tank and rebreather canister clipped to her belt, M-1 clutched across her chest.

A little air here, Al and the boys, the Unholy Trinity, mumbling over their instruments, muttering to each other, Edgar snarling at them over the issue of panel lights. For Christ's *sake*. We were going into the fucking *unknown* . . .

Cold here, around minus forty, near where Fahrenheit and Celsius meet, air pressure low, maybe 400 millibars, skin tingling, ears popping every time she swallowed. Sounds muffled. No wind though. Good damned thing. These cotton-batting-lined wool coats are piss-poor.

Plane resting on its belly, suffused by orange light, props bent, dug into the . . . substrate. Stuff like formica, but, waxier, softer. Murray kneeling, looking into the long troughs they'd dug, scraping and clattering to a stop.

A soft mutter, fingering grit. Reminds me of that black wax we had in biology class.

You mean, said Edgar, the stuff we'd pin frogs to?

Yes.

Evocation of a brief memory: Holding a shivery green leopard frog in her left hand, the long needle with its wooden handle in the other. Some male teacher, thin, young, approaching her, surgical scissors in his hand, eyes on her breasts. Scissors at the back of the frog's neck. Frog motionless. Seeming apathetic. *Snip*.

Teacher patting me on the shoulder, and you could see him wishing for the nerve to accidentally touch my tits . . .

OK, Astrid. Go to it. He won't feel a thing.

Frog just doesn't seem to care.

Putting the needle into the hole. Running it up into the skull, wagging it back and forth. Nothing. How would I feel if someone just scrambled my brain? OK. Now, the spine. Slide the needle home . . .

Frog suddenly squirming in her hand, *screaming*, all the agonies of a soul in Hell . . .

Falling with a splat to the floor. Blood on her hands.

Don't be such a sissy, Astrid. Now put him in the pan and get to work.

Pins through his hands, pins through his feet, sliding on down to the soft black wax.

People around the sprawling, crashed plane. We'd never get it aloft now, even if we get the electrical system working again. Stuck here. People huddled around the plane, looking off into the empty distance. Edgar, the boys, walking round and round, making their bitter survey. Genda and Amaterasu, holding hands. Laing and Rahman, holding hands. Ling standing alone. Amanda Grey standing alone.

Me standing alone. What if we're stuck here? What if this is all there is? Walk to the end of the world? What if it has no end?

Edgar saying, What the Hell? We'll run out of food and water and air eventually. Probably just reify somewhere near the River and . . .

What if we can't die here? *The Rapture*? How long do I have to stay here, God? *Forever*.

A muffled outcry, from back at the plane. Someone, Laing, pointing up into the black sky. Kincaid turned to look. A bright spark, isolated. Like a single star. Moving. Growing larger? Coming toward us? I can't tell.

Another spark. Then another. Another. Ten. Twenty. A hundred. A thousand. Familiar scene, forming in her mind. The worst of it coming true then, the rules clustered round the concept of Hesperidia coming true, Lord Ahriman forming around them. In a moment, the stars would be bursts of fire. Bursts of fire turning to fiery birds, birds assembling into some nightmare angel . . .

Laing's cry ringing out. *No*. Long, drawn out, unhappy. A glance back and Laing had fallen against Rahman, fallen against the woman's protecting bosom. And, in the sky . . .

A sharp sense of being out of breath. Expecting to look up and see that the Angel of Death had formed again, formed to carry us away, roll us up like windowshades, leaving dry bones behind, little piles of dry bones to rest beside the plane, mute witness to our . . .

Little sparks of light above them, motionless but . . . moving, sparks of white light resolving into tiny coils, tiny coils spinning round and round, held fast to their axes, each image reflected into every other image, each fiery double helix the same.

Suddenly beside her, Ling whispered, "They look like little men. Like little soldiers, marching in place."

She stared at them, wondering. Sound in the distance. Wind rushing through the tops of trees in the late summer. Sigh of the wind presaging Fall.

Rahman was standing with them now, too, leading a downcast Laing by the hand. She said, "Almost like a choir singing. Singing far away in the distance. When I was a girl, I would sometimes go down to the Christian quarter on Sunday. Would stand outside a church and listen to them sing, so different from the songs of Islam."

Ling: "Or like men whistling. Whistling as they march."

One of the coils seemed to expand suddenly. Expand or merely grow closer? Impossible to know.

Voice, like a whisper inside their heads: *You have no business here.*

Behind the coil, the little helixes did indeed look like marching soldiers now. No. Not soldiers. Marching marionettes. Naked things, sexless things, things made of white light. A little like the way Amaterasu looked, before I put on her skin and organs . . .

Edgar, shouting: "Who are you?"

A Mediator.

Mediator no more than a coil of misty light, coiling in on itself, round and round . . .

It said, *The Soldiers of the Light were to guard against*

this, but they fail, as everything fails, in time. The Princes of the Worlds have sent me here to Mediate your . . . return.

Return. She called out, "To where?"

Home? Will it send us home? Home to try again, to try . . . I don't know. I don't know what we were meant to be. If anything.

Edgar shouted, "We don't want to go back to the World Without End! There's nothing there for us!" Nothing there for anyone who's never been . . . content.

The Mediator said, *The World Without End is no more, all its souls fallen into darkness. Your crossing of the Boundary saw to that.*

Moment of freezing shock. All its souls fallen . . . Eternal life lost? Because of us? One word, bitter, hard, a word without end: *Unfair*. But, when you act, you incur responsibility.

In a whisper: "Where, then?"

I know not.

Back at the crashed plane, the hatch suddenly popped back open, built-up air pressure chuffing, air sighing out into the void. Us? Back in there?

No. Not all of you. Only the three, not the One.

Edgar cried out, "Are you God?"

Not God. A Mediator between the Worlds.

Kincaid suddenly conscious that Al, Murray and Gerry were standing together, postures stiff and unnatural, three little robots standing in a row. Al's voice, as if talking to himself: "No. This is not right."

Wandering Jews.

Flying Dutchmen.

All the same.

Al: "*Verdammt noch mal!*"

Beside him, Murray said, "Damned and stitched, I'm afraid . . ." Not afraid, though. Voice . . . resigned. And they turned, together, as one, marching in step, marched into the plane and were gone. In a minute, you could see their heads appear in the cockpit windows, taking their seats, looking out into the darkness.

Edgar shouted, "What the Hell is going on here?"

A groan of metal from the crashed plane. A scrape.

Another. It started to slide, slide back along its own long skid-mark, faster and faster, shriek of its passage growing louder and louder. Behind Rahman, Kincaid could see Laing cowering, holding her hands over her ears.

Plane in the sky now, rising, flying backwards for a moment, then banking, turning away from them, nose rising, pointing at the black heavens, a twinkle of torn metal, wings bent and graceless, growing smaller against the darkness, smaller and smaller still, a bit of flotsam, miniature junk, a glitter like a bit of lost Christmas tinsel blowing on the wind, then gone.

Rahman stood still in a darkness lit only by angelic light, skin crawling from a cold breeze that had sprung up out of nowhere. Laing, now holding her hand, was shivering as well. Fear? Impossible to know. When the plane fell, she held tight to me. Held tight, put her hands . . .

Incredulity, even as I waited for us to die. Woman-construct like a man, like some man's absurd dream, woman-construct with her hands in my crotch, groping, groping, even as we fell through blue light down into the nothingness of Hell. That's where we are now. Where we must be. I know it. But the certainty wasn't there. Not really. Conviction only a matter of culture. Of expectation.

Astrid Kincaid beside her, suddenly standing, raising her weapon, click-clink of bolt interspersed with a hard *bamm, bamm, bamm*, bullets whistling away to nowhere.

Pointless, said the Angel.

Pointless indeed. I imagine my mother, bitter amusement in her mouth, watching this always-defiant American soldier try to shoot down God. *Not*, she would say with evident satisfaction, the Right Sort of Woman.

Not right at all.

Edgar's shout: "God *damn* you!" Obvious, helpless rage.

God is damning no one these days.

Rahman felt herself take a step forward, letting go of Laing's trembling hand. "If you're not God, who are you?"

Mediator. "

Who?"

Sari-el.

Ah. My mother's voice: Sari-el, deciding the fate of those angels who transgress the Laws of God . . .

And the Archangel Sari-el said, *Finished.*

Double helix winding in on itself, receding, fitting itself in among the heavenly host, one more android soldier, soldier of light among the men, men marching in step, whistling softly as they marched. Soldiers diminishing to sparks, sparks of light become as one with the stars . . .

Hard strands of light, all pointing away, universe receding . . .

All of them then, all who were left, standing in darkness. Then Professor Ling's voice, muffled by his oxygen mask, punctuated by the *snap-click* of its valve: "For just a moment there, I was on the deck of the *Millennium Falcon.*"

Kincaid: "What the fuck are you talking about?"

Hideous Americans, equally hideous Green Chinamen, spoiling eternity for me, blotting out my mother's voice. Then Laing's trembling fingers again, seeking her out, hand on her breast. My God. Made to be as her Creator made her. Creator not God, nor even god. Merely some hideous man, living out his hideous dreams, in the fiction of *Crimson Desert.* Passiphaë Laing, equally ready to swing a heroic sword, save the man who needs saving by a mother's grace, equally ready to lift her skirt, expose her soft underbelly, take him into the grace of a whore's inner warmth . . .

Icon. Fragile now, her script erased.

Edgar said, "Well . . ."

Jump cut.

White light, blinding, dizzying. Rahman felt herself stagger, almost fall, felt Laing's strong hand steady her, hold her upright. The eight of them then, standing together, almost touching, standing together in the middle of a featureless white plain, standing beneath a featureless white sky.

Rahman, shading her eyes: "Nothing. No horizon line."

Kincaid stamped the floor, if that's what it was. "Nice and level though." She fired the gun, report muffled, flat, anechoic. A long-seeming wait, then a distant *spock* of impact.

Professor Ling said, "One gee gravity. Just about the time the bullet would take to fall."

Kincaid took a bullet out of her belt and dropped it from shoulder height. *Spock*. Louder, with a clink of brass.

"Well."

Voice behind them, the lot of them, somehow facing in one direction, whirling as one. It was a slim man, very young, hardly out of his teens. Bright blue eyes, blond hair cropped so short you could see his scalp. An old hairstyle English-speakers called a crew-cut, boy-man wearing white sneakers, high-tops with a red decal at the ankle, dressed in white chinos, a white tee-shirt, long white linen lab-coat open down the front. Smiling. He said, "Well, Edgar, you've gotten yourself in a *pile* of trouble this time, haven't you?"

Edgar taken aback, edging back. Trying to stand behind us . . . He said, "What the Hell are you talking about? Who the Hell are you?"

The smiling man said, "Don't you remember your old pal Khazmal?"

Khazmal? This open-faced, smiling-eyed boy the Fire-Speaking Angel? Edgar was silent, jaw clenched, eyes a mirror of fear.

Khazmal said, "Well, you really screwed up this time. Right through the Toolbox and into the Regulators' lap."

She could hear Kincaid whisper *Toolbox* to herself, echoing the angel.

Edgar, voice somehow wooden, said, "I don't know what you're talking about."

A sigh, a soft frown on the boy's face. "What a mess."

Kincaid said, "So. I guess this means the Jug's caught up with us."

So long ago, so far in the past, those quasi-revelations about the Scavengers and their possibly-imaginary Space-Time Juggernaut. Possibly the last moment when we could have gone back, back through the gate to the Moon and surrender and, just maybe, go back home, to live and die in ignorance. It was *my* decision to flee through the gate. Flee, spin the dial behind us, try to get away . . . A hard pang, the eyes of my mother looking through the murk. Accusing me.

Khazmal said, "Well, Edgar. Time to live." Hand reaching out, touching Edgar on the forehead, bald man flinching, eyes widening, reflecting sudden awareness, sudden knowledge, turning sullen.

"Come now, don't be like that. You knew what the job would entail when you took it."

A slow, reluctant nod. "I won't stop trying, though. Not 'til I'm whole again."

"What do you think you'd gain by reassembly? Do you still think you can become God?"

A stolid, resentful stare: "The position looks vacant to me."

"Only because you see so little."

"Only because I've been lied to."

A final sigh, resigned. A sigh that said, No more point to this. "All right, Edgar. Maybe someday you'll see. Until then . . ."

Anger in his eyes, like the embers of a dying fire. "Right. Back to fucking work."

Khazmal reached out to touch him again . . .

Flicker of pale blue light, light always coming from behind no matter which way you looked. A sound, like crisp sheets of paper being riffled into a fan . . . Edgar suddenly erupted into a cone of images, images of himself flying into the sky, cone widening, spreading out across the white sky, sky growing ever more dense with Edgars, thousands, millions, billions of Edgars, all with their arms outstretched, heads tipped back. Edgars flying away into the heavens, diminishing even as they grew in number. Suddenly, the spot where he'd stood was empty, wisp of gray smoke curling upward, dissipating, and . . .

One last Edgar standing there, bald Edgar in dusty black leather, looking down at big, blunt, empty hands. Squire Edgar, whispering, "I was inside him after all . . ."

Khazmal said, "They were all inside him, consumed one by one."

Edgar turned and looked at Amanda Grey for a moment, looked into her eyes, then his own seemed to narrow, as if in pain. He looked back at the angel. "Somewhere," he said,

"One of them, him, *me*, I guess, will remember. Start the cycle all over again."

"Not you though."

"No. Not me."

"The seed of discontent is always there, ready to erupt in those who deal with the passage of souls from one state to another. The hearts of doctors eventually sicken and grow cold."

Edgar looked at Amanda again. Rahman thought, She stands there, motionless, emotionless. Why? Why isn't she glad to see him? She seems almost . . . afraid. Hard ram of pity and anger inside. I don't want to see another hero-woman fall. Let her be . . . brave. Please.

Edgar said, "Will you send me back as well?"

The angel nodded. "Of course. You have your place, your job to do."

"And . . ."

"The woman? Of course."

Sorrowing: "It won't be the same, you know."

"Nothing is ever the same. It's in the . . . nature of souls to change."

"Still . . ." Rahman could see it in his eyes, going back . . . to Hesperidia? Going back to Hesperidia, everything the same. Except what was in their hearts.

Khazmal, Fire-Speaking Angel, stepped forward, stepped up to Knight-Errant Amanda Grey, reached out, touched her lightly on the forehead. Her stolid eyes suddenly lit from within. Lit with fear. She said, "Oh, no. Oh, no, *please* . . ." Desperation in her voice. Crawling-on-my-belly begging in her voice.

Agony then in Squire Edgar's eyes as well. "Khazmal. Khazmal I . . ."

Another touch and the light in her eyes went out momentarily. Empty eyes staring. Empty eyes waiting to be filled. Then a final touch, eyes suffusing with . . .

Rahman looked away. Feeling sick. I don't want to watch.

Edgar's voice. "Not like this, Khazmal. This isn't what I want."

The angel said, "You can't always have what you want."

Rahman thought, Platitudes. Platitudes from God, sent through His Angels to excuse . . . Amanda Grey's hard voice, soft now, beseeching, "It'll be all right, Edgar. You'll see. I love you now. Let's go home."

Edgar's voice, full of despair: "Oh, my God."

When she looked up, they were gone. All three of them, and . . .

Jump cut.

Ling Erhshan stood flat-footed, bare-footed, on the cold, shiny white floor of his swiftly-emptying white world, and thought, Where did our clothes go? All of them naked again. Genda and Amaterasu in the background, seeming now to edge away from the little group, afraid perhaps . . .

But where would they go?

There is nowhere else.

Kincaid looking down at her lovely breasts, empty handed. Looking down, maybe looking to see if her rifle is there? Then looking up again. Angry. Defiant. As always. Looking at me.

He felt a sudden urge to cup his hands over his genitals. Hide them from her eyes. Eyes of judgment. Sudden memory of the little graduate student from the plane-crash dream. She seemed so . . . disappointed when I took off my pants. Disappointed in what she saw? They say women don't care. But then so many of them seem to . . .

I only slept with her twice, then she quit the program and transferred to another school. Maybe only disappointed that she saw anything at all. Why didn't I know that then? Perhaps, because you were blinded by her breasts and thighs and lovely dark eyes?

Passiphaë Laing grappling suddenly with naked Subaïda Rahman, arms around her, hands palpating breasts, sliding downward, dropping to her knees, mouth open, trying to slide between the other woman's legs.

Rahman shoving her away, staggering back, eyes filled with . . . I don't know what. Women's eyes, to me at least, empty, unreadable. Only full of lies. Full of my own emptiness, perhaps. Full of my reflection. Eyes like mirrors.

He heard Laing whisper, "Please." Rahman just staring at her. What do women see in each other's faces? Things invisible to men, or so it says in a thousand learnèd journals.

A soft, watery crackling now. Sound coming from everywhere at once. What will we see next? Another formless angel? Or merely one more mythic humanoid? Where could that dream have come from, an angel with the form of Tom Swift? From inside me, from inside the icon-smothered heart of this pagan soul? What did the others see? Mideastern angels, devolved from Zarathustra's dream? Magic djinni like smoke from the Lamp?

It was only another double helix that wound down out of the sky, filled with a nimbus of almost-colorless light. Pastel. Barely blue at all. Ling looked around, and thought, We've lost all our spokesmen. No Edgar to shout defiance for us now. Kincaid? She could only speak through her gun. Through her gun and the eloquence of those lost silver eyes. Empty eyes, like pools of molten metal. Anonymous eyes she could hide behind.

Rahman's voice, full of honest loathing: "What devil are you, come to torment us now?"

Call me Metatron.

Defiance suddenly turned to atavistic fear. What does she see?

Rahman shouted, "Metatron is Satan's Name!"

Soft, cold laughter, striking a chill into Ling's old bones.

The Devil gives you what you want. Only the Lord takes away. I know what is in your heart, Subaïda Rahman, sham of a lesbian, sham of a woman.

Passiphaë Laing crawling forward, crawling on her belly before the God-Image, voice lost in the wilderness: "Please, God. Please don't take her away . . ."

Blue glow only brightening, then an icy softness: Go.

Bang.

A cloud of dark smoke.

And Rahman gone.

Floating. Floating in the softest sea. Subaïda Rahman awoke and opened her eyes slowly. Floating on her back, almost, but not quite touching the left-hand acceleration couch, head tipped back and upward, looking out the triangular left-hand rendezvous window, into black space.

Not empty space, no. Never empty space. Sliver of the Earth hanging out there, suspended against the void. Moon is behind us now. Hidden behind the mass of the service module. Must be getting pretty big by now, the Earth getting so small. Small. Blue. Fragile. Far away.

Soft static from the cabin speaker, then a voice, a man's voice, laconic, roughened by transmission: "*Apollo 24*, Houston."

A woman's voice replying, close by: "*Apollo 24*. Read you five-by."

Radio voice: "Please be advised *25* has completed TLI."

Another voice, man's voice, also close, also soft: "Yee-hah . . ."

The woman: "Copy that, Houston. Good show."

Radio: "Johnny says you should wait for him under the lamppost at 42nd and Main."

"Will do, Capcom."

Rahman turned her head, looking back into the command module's cramped cabin space. Crowded as Hell in here. Since they installed two more seats, bolting them in under the original three, you could hardly budge. Especially when all five of us are in here together . . .

The woman at the radio console, a short, thick-waisted blonde, namestripe on her shirt reading Smithfield, smiled at her. "Good morning, sleepyhead!"

Rahman said, "Good morning, Nellie." Nellie. Her name is Nellie . . .

Across the cabin, only four feet away, a small, gray-haired man in his late forties floated by the other window, looking out, looking down at the world. Jim Jameson living out his dream, JPL's first astronaut, on his way to the Moon.

Nellie said, "Something wrong, Susan?"

Rahman stretched, arched her back, bumped her head on the seat's headrest. Opened her eyes again and looked down. The namestripe on her own shirt read *Romano*. Susan

Romano. Rahman? What the Hell was I thinking? She said, "I had the strangest damned dream."

From beside the window, Jameson said, "Zero gee'll do that."

"Or that godawful pizza we had last night."

Susan said, "Well. Microwave's better than the old freeze-dried stuff, but NASA's got a long way to go." Funny to think about it that way. A long way to go. Hah. She unbuckled her harness and slid away from the acceleration couch, hanging in the air, reaching for docking tunnel hatch. Plenty to do in the orbital habitat, getting ready for LOI. They'd be the first in Lunar polar orbit, if nothing went wrong. And when *25* shows up with the Block 5 lander, some of us will be the first to set down at the North Pole . . .

Nellie said, "Better not. Jill and Frazier decided they need-ed a little privacy."

Astonishment. *"Frazier?"*

Holding onto a support stanchion, bobbing in mid air, half an arm's length away, Nellie laughed. "I guess Jill decided if she couldn't be the first woman to do it on the Moon, she could at least be the first to do it in deep space . . ."

Jill Mathers could sometimes be an asshole indeed, with her glory-hog concerns about *firsts*. All right, first in deep space, but . . . *"Frazier?"*

A shrug. A grin.

From his window seat, Jameson said, "Sorry you married a ground-pounder now, Susan?"

Facing toward her, away from him, Nellie Smithfield rolled her eyes. Men.

Image of Barry, back home in Houston. Barry and the kids, glued to the TV. They'd had a lovely last night together, three weeks ago already, the night before the crew had to go into preflight quarantine. Gone out to dinner as a family. Taken the kids to the movies, then home, home to tuck them in. Barry holding me close, in bed later. Just holding me.

Six weeks before I'm in bed with him again. Image of her-self snuggled against Barry's warm back, listening to him sleep, soft, even breathing, a little rough, not rough enough you could call it a snore.

He's always so still when he sleeps.

Peaceful.

Peaceful when I come home from a day that's practically driven me insane. Never a word about how his own day went, good or bad. Just: It's an office. It was there when I left it. It'll be there when I go back tomorrow. Regular hours, kids in the daycare, dropped off and picked up, day after day.

He's never once complained about my irregular hours.

Jameson said, "Oh, there was another thing that came through when you were asleep. Processing confirmed the data from Radar Prospector II. There's definitely an ice-field under the rimwall separating Peary from Rozhdestvenskiy. They've moved the landing site down range about twenty klicks."

"Twenty . . . That'll put us over the horizon." And out of line of sight with Earth.

Nellie's eyes were serious, measuring. "This is important. We're going to have to be very careful."

Jameson: "Jessup says if we can confirm ready access to the ice, if its composition's not too . . . Well, readily usable, if not potable, the President will ask congress for a budget adjunct. They'll start development on a surface habitat for next year."

And Nellie said, "Oh, yes. And TOPS has been funded through launch. They've committed four Saturns to the mission. One probe and backup for each trajectory . . ."

"They're going to have to run Michoud flat-out to get that many birds ready."

Big grin on Nellie's face. "You ever think, when you were in college, it'd come to this?"

A slow headshake, head full of memories. "No. I guess I figured Johnson was going to commit us all to full involvement in Vietnam." But he didn't. Reelected in '64, again in '68. I felt bad when the Republicans managed to put that damned actor in the White House, year before last, but . . .

But, by then, the economic theory of Infrastructure Modeling was beginning to catch people's eyes. Prosperity curves. Government spending curves. The Interstate System. The Strategic Air Command. Project Apollo. Middle class doesn't care who runs America so long as their jobs are secure. So long as a factory worker can own a house and a car, have a wife who works or not as she pleases . . .

More and more men staying home these days too. Barry would have lots of company if I could talk him into it.

President coming into office, yammering about a 600-ship Navy. But Mister President, we don't *need* a new Navy. Well, what're we going to spend it on, then? In his first State of the Union address, he called it his "Space-Faring Civilization."

Out the window, Earth hung against the velvet darkness. Barry down there. Me up here. Working to make our dreams to come true. Odd dream though. Odd dream. Something about angels. Something about the ice under Peary. Oh, well. Too much to do for me to waste time worrying about a dream.

So. Get to work. Make your dream live.

In time, that other dream, that very odd dream about black ice and fire and death, would surely fade away.

Vision fading, fading then gone, young American astronaut-woman Susan Romano, echo of Subaïda Rahman no more, sailing off into the emergent history of a twentieth century America that never was. Possibly never could be. I have to keep reminding myself, thought Ling Erhshan, that everything is possible. Everything. Somewhere out there in the Multiverse, a transfinite number of Americas continue to evolve.

Someone crying softly, a woman's voice, Passiphaë Laing sprawled naked on the cold white floor of this nearly empty universe. Astrid Kincaid standing near her, arms folded, aloof. Lord Genda Hiroshige and his Lady Amaterasu some distance away, still holding hands.

Overhead, a fuzzy-edged double helix of warm light continued to circle in on itself, winding up out of nowhere, winding away into nowhere, as if merely the middlemost coils of an infinitely long entity.

This is, I think, how a madman feels. All sense of reality lost. Nothing familiar here. A vista so utterly impossible that it calls nothing to mind. Events engulfing us that have no place in our experience. A lunatic would accept this, or a primitive. Some ancient Mesoamerican shaman, downing his peyotl buttons, shivering away into a dream.

A sudden pang of envy. A sudden hope. Of all the dreamers, all the lost souls, Rahman went to a fate most like the shape of her longed-for dream. Subaïda Rahman, American Technologies Specialist, injected into the America that got away. Will they land at Peary and find the Stargate under the ice? With luck, in her reality, the will be no gate.

A vision of some future Rahman, matured and hardened, the dream-time of the Multiverse long forgotten, dancing across the red deserts of Mars.

He stood under the misty coil of light, looking upward, wondering. Finally: "What now, you who call yourself Metatron?"

Nothing. Blue light seeming to change, grow brittle, more sharply defined, crisp, edges taking shape out of nowhere. As if it were changing from light into steel. He said, "Who are you then? Are you really an instrumentality of God?"

What would it mean to me, to find myself in the presence of a real God, a god of the sort Western religions prescribe? Ironic. The religious Westerners, the Muslims and Christians and Jews, have already gone. Nothing left here but two pagan Asians, a robot become flesh, and this presumably atheistic American Sergeant-Major . . .

Kincaid beside him now, murmuring, "Yes. We'd like to know."

Voice hardly audible, but then, if this is the God who sees a sparrow fall, what need to cry out in the wilderness? Every need, perhaps. Every need within me, for I am besotted by all the unspoken assumptions that soaked the prose in all those old books.

A little Christian God hiding in every fantasist's all-powerful alien foe. He said, "We don't *believe* in you, Metatron. Don't believe you're an angel, or even a demon."

The shadowy outline of a face started to form, outlined in pale white light, superimposed over the now mirror-bright surface of the helix. Not a human face. Alien. A face with something insectile about it, the irrepressible in Ling Erhshan briefly wondering if it would address him as Quatermass . . .

No, it said, a whisper in their minds. *If the myths had power to fix you in place, you'd already be gone. My task is merely to pass you on up the line.*

Up the line to whom? Who stands above the chiefest angel in the hierarchies of Heaven? Pass us up the line to God Himself? Images from books: God as an old, old man. Distorted, though, long white Caucasian beard replaced by a long, thin, hardly-grayed Chinese beard, the beard of a Confucian sage.

Kincaid said, "Who are you?" Something odd in her voice. As if she already knew.

It said, *Something of* Ethqûzæ *in me.*

Disbelief mingled with disappointment in Kincaid's voice. "*Ethqûzæ?* The Scavenger scientist who argued for the abandonment of the gates? The one who argued for a resumption of single-universe interstellar colonization?"

I knew the Space-Time Juggernaut would come one day. I wanted to save my people. But the temptation was too great, the Multiverse too . . . appealing. Now I find myself incorporated in the machinery that brought us down.

Sorrow in the voice, somehow. Ling thought, Something here that transcends culture, increasing the likelihood that this is all a fabrication, an artifact of the madness that may have overwhelmed me some time in the past. Will I become sane again if I hold fast to this feeling that I've gone mad? He said, "So you are, then, a manifestation of this fabulous Space-Time Juggernaut?"

Something only a little like laughter. *No. Nor even an individual Scavenger. Ethqûzæ is merely the sense of who I am.* Shiny chrome rolling above them now, mist cleared from its depths, showing only an empty heart. *Your fearsome Jug, your god-elemental, is no more than an agent of the scrap manager, come to collect the pieces that have come loose, tuck in the tag ends of broken skeins, to unravel threads whose fates have become knotted and twisted in upon themselves.*

Ling Erhshan thought, *Scrap manager?* and said, "What about us?"

The world around them hardening up now, white sky

receding, white plain at their feet stretching out to infinity. *Seraph Metatron, Serpent Fire of Love Everlasting, Infinite, One With All . . . angel to resource manager to task . . .*

To Ling Erhshan, it seemed as though a deep brass gong sounded. Not a bell, no. Bells belong to the West. And the White World struck from their eyes . . .

Slow sparkle-dissolve to a new world. Astrid Kincaid, sitting at the edge of the void, under a matte-black sky, looking down at the universe, hand on her belly, rubbing slowly, back and forth, smooth, youthful muscle, the flesh of the woman she'd been in the long ago and far away. Young woman, long forgotten.

I just keep expecting him to jump out suddenly, laughing, shouting, *Boo! Gotcha!* Maybe that's why I feel like this now. I was ready for him. Ready in all the old and pointless ways. They'd been on the Dish for what seemed like days already, time crawling by, punctuated by fruitless discussions. Maybe this and maybe that. We're just not equipped to understand what has happened. The world around them was a flat white saucer, concave, padded, soft, adrift in what seemed like black nothingness at first. No more silver helix, the five of us abandoned here, naked and alone. And when they ventured to the edge . . .

Long, long vistas of things like shining picture postcards, arrayed in stacks, stacks arrayed in layers, layers arrayed in legions, just going on and on. She sat looking down at it, ignoring an insistent crawling at the root of her belly. Ready for him, all right. Maybe I'm as mad as Ling insists he must be. Maybe we all are.

Passiphaë Laing disconsolate. Unable to adjust. Genda and Amaterasu silent. Huddled together. Because they have each other perhaps. Ling on the far rim, staring downward into a stack-spangled eternity. Waiting. That's all we're doing. Waiting for the managers to come and settle our affairs for us.

At least it makes some sense that way, all this bullshit about angels and God in Heaven swept aside, replaced by the Scavengers' familiar Toolbox metaphor. Angel of Death displaced by the Space-Time Juggernaut, fearsome Juggernaut displaced by the friendly old scrap manager, come to tuck in all our loose ends. But my friends are still gone, displaced by no more than memories of dry bones.

Is the World Without End really gone too? Or is it merely down in the Stack somewhere, last in, first out, safe and sound, all its souls alive and free to wander? Why would God lie to us? Motive, method, opportunity. Would the resource manager lie to us as well?

Maybe this whole apparition around us, this little world, floating above the great universe beyond—this simple metaphor for the Multiverse we tried to believe in—is a lie as well.

Where could we go from here? Down the rabbit hole? Down through the long wormholes that lead out of the Multiverse, down to the eternal bedrock of Platonic Reality? Why bother? Just one more fanciful lie, evading the question of first causes, refusing to answer the empty question of *why*?

A rustling beside her, shadow on the padding, cast by the diffuse light of eternity. She looked up and Passiphaë Laing was looking down at her, eyes darkened by shadow. She really is beautiful. When my hormones were adjusted just so, I'd've been drawn to her like iron to a magnet. Poor Passiphaë Laing, image of woman rather than woman itself, cast adrift in an unscripted sea.

Laing kneeled beside her, put out a long-fingered hand, hand with perfect, clear nails resting on her thigh, stroking softly, bringing out the latent tingle of her flesh. A curious image. As if our nerves merely waited for stimulation, all their feelings, all our feelings, built right in, canned programs ready to run. A constant firing and unfiring of virtual sensation, waiting for some eka-event to evoke it.

Crawling in her groin strengthened as well. Because I'm young again? All the tiresome, disappointing years of experience erased? That would be the nature of true immortality, wouldn't it? No. More like the nature of dying young. Laing's hand was on her vulva now, knowing fingers probing gently, tucking wisps of soft hair aside, finding self-aware tissue, molding it to her will, the will of her own presumed desire.

Kincaid reached out and took the hand, pulled it away,

locked in a strong grasp. "Why do you think this is the answer?"

Laing's dark, empty-seeming eyes looking into hers. "Because it's always the answer. The answer in every script. In every imagination. They can take you all away. They can make me be alone forever. But they can't take away the answer."

Is this pity I feel? Pity for a one-side creation? She said, "In *Crimson Desert* you were a thing, Passiphaë Laing. Here you're a person. For people, there's more than one answer. Always more than one."

A sorrowing smile. "You think you understand me, don't you, Sergeant-Major Kincaid? I can see it in your face. Here she stands, you tell yourself, that simplistic creation made to pacify the man-things of an imaginary world, and so pacify the man-things of the world above that."

The image in her mind read out correctly: Passiphaë Laing in her place on her back, legs spread, soft heart exposed like a meal on a table, the Creator's hollow-souled man-things masturbating on high.

Laing said, "A creation is part of the thing it was created for. We have that within us, worth ever so much more than your wretched little personhood: the doing of that for which we were made. Made by our gods, however petty they may have been."

First, the image of art and perception, the thing itself merely existing in the eye of its beholder. Then another image. Robot Amaterasu rump-high over the birthday cake, raped for the delight of laughing men. Is this what you made me for, Mother? Is this the life for which your loving hands shaped me?

A quick glance away, down into the white-padded center of the Dish, Genda and Amaterasu, facing each other, hands touching, looking into each others's eyes, talking. Kincaid said, "But you're not a thing any more. You're real, a person whether you want to be or not."

"Am I?" Soft smile. "And I suppose you imagine yourself to be *real* as well?" She stood then, still smiling, abruptly turned and walked away. Walked away to where Ling

Erhshan was staring down into the outer darkness, down on the layered-stack metaphor of worlds without end, of times without number.

Astrid Kincaid sat still, crawling inside her unabated. If I am a thing, she wondered, for what purpose was I made? Not hers. Please, God, not hers . . .

Ling Erhshan lay on his back, bedded down in the feather-soft padding of the Dish, sated, comfortable, looking up at the empty black sky. I wonder why there's nothing above us? We sit up here atop all of Creation, like the star atop a Christmas tree.

Odd image. I wonder how that custom spread to China? Probably via Japan in the mid-twenty-first century. Shadowy childhood memories of decorating the tree, of opening presents of Christmas morning. Ceremony without meaning. Just as it had been in the America from which it sprang. Not the Feast of St. Jesus. Not glittery Saturnalia. Not the dark time of Yule, log roaring in the fireplace, warming up the Sun, persuading it to return and light up the world with Spring.

Passiphaë Laing sitting beside him, naked on the edge of the Dish, looking down into the Stacks, face very still, almost flaccid. Uneasy feeling. What if she jumps off? Two conflict-ing chains of thought/emotion. One struck through and through with guilt. She came to you for comfort and you met her with . . . A glance down at a glisten of drying moisture on his abdomen and thighs. Second chain permeated with the urge to pull her away from the edge, push her on her back in the white-fluff padding of the Dish, have at her again.

Which one is the real you, Ling Erhshan? I know the answer, of course. But I don't want to know . . .

We've become so passive now, waiting for them to come and finish us off. Passive? He felt himself chuckle softly, stomach muscles barely clenching, vocal cords flexing with-out sound. The dead are always passive, lying in their graves, waiting for eternity to roll on by.

Westerners think they're waiting for Judgment Day, but *we* know the truth. Death is real. Death is forever. Death is . . . emptiness. Emptiness without end. And yet . . . here I am. For all my convictions about oblivion, here I am. My life would have been different, had I only known. But known what?

What do you know now, Ling Erhshan, that you didn't know then? That death is *not* oblivion? What if you have to spend eternity right here, making love to a sorrowing automaton, over and over again, forever and ever?

Is that oblivion as well?

A shake of the head. A sigh. No answer.

Commotion across the way. Kincaid on her feet. Genda and Amaterasu crouching together, looking upward. A silver double-helix, suffused with white light, slid into being above them.

Staring at it, waiting patiently, Ling entertained one more stray thought, a loose end that refused to be tucked in: She sat over there, watching us. How must that have looked to Astrid Kincaid? How must she have felt?

But the time for aimless wondering was over, and now Kincaid put her hands on her hips, magnificent tableau of fearless being, no more than cast in the shape of a woman, and shouted up at the thing, shouted for it to disclose its identity.

You know what she's expecting.

It said, *List manager*.

Ah, yes, literature of angelic imagery springing up, unbidden. The list manager would be O. Henry's famous Robin Hood of the Old Heaven, the angel whose duty it was to keep the list of names, the list of people who loved God the best. Fine image, spoiled then by the giggly remembrance of that funny old essay, the one in which Abou ben Ahdem topped the list simply because it had been subjected to a bubble sort.

Passiphaë Laing suddenly screamed, recoiled, perilously close to the edge, Ling reaching out for her as she screamed, "*No!*" Cowering against him then, cupping one hand over his wet genitals—as if protecting him—her own left exposed. "No, you can't make me leave . . ."

Leave?

Laing looking up into his face, eyes wild, pleading, begging him to . . . But what can I do? The look of her tearing at him. Helpless. I'm as helpless as you are.

Betrayal.

We always betray them in the end.

The softest voice said, *I'm sorry*.

Letting go of him then, hands clawed, rage in her eyes along with the fear, screaming her refusal, running across the middle of the Dish, stumbling over wrinkles in the fabric of its padding, falling headlong at Kincaid's feet, woman kneeling to put her hand on Laing's shaking shoulder. Ling thought, Hand on a shoulder shiny with sweat, her sweat and mine, commingled.

Kincaid was looking upward, too far away for him to see any angry glint that might suffuse her eyes. Looked upward. Silent. And what is there for her to say? Is this necessary? For all she knows, for all we know, it is.

The voice whispered, *Subroutine Laing*.

A stack element suddenly slid into being, seeming to issue from an invisible slit in the nothingness around them, looking like a garish painting, like a cartoon cel perhaps . . . or a window into . . . elsewhere.

Long, long vista into a sunset sky, terrestrial sunset of layered red and salmon watercolor washes, just a hint of blue near zenith, sun bloated and red on the edge of the world, sunlight a glittery path reaching out of the picture, yellow brick road reaching toward them all, inviting, a shimmer of light on a red-tinted sea.

Beach scene, Sand. Surf. Crags in the distance. The sod-crowned edge of the cliff. A dilapidated white beachhouse in the background. And a man, man sitting in the foreground, waiting. Looking out at them with silent eyes.

Come, Subroutine. Time to go.

A soft moan from Passiphaë Laing. Then she was, somehow, standing on the edge of the abyss, looking into the stack image. Looking into her world.

Go.

One last, appalled look around, at Kincaid, at still-damp Ling Erhshan, who felt a gentle urge to tell her goodbye, one hand lifted in a small wave of farewell. She stepped forward, out over eternity . . .

Reappeared in the cel, motionless, still naked, a lovely shape against the sunset sky, looking back over her shoulder, regret easily read in her features. Ling thought, What is that thing in her hand? A sheaf of white paper, riffled open, words upon them, frozen in the act of being wind-blown.

Her script, perhaps.

The cel slid downward, disappeared into nothingness, carrying Passiphaë Laing with it, down into the folds of her new story, then the list manager, without a sound, without a parting word, corkscrewed upward into the fabric of Creation and was gone.

Astrid Kincaid stood staring up at the empty black sky for another minute, letting the wholeness of it sink in. Taking us away, one by one, sticking us where we belong. Setting things to rights. Is that how it will end. Some almighty manager taking me in his omnipotent hand, sticking me in my place, leaving me there to . . . just go on?

A heat of anger staining her cheeks with warmth. I'll be angry if that's how it ends.

She looked down again, back into the soft whiteness of the Dish. Amaterasu and Genda standing together, like a set of matched humanoid bookends, arms around each other. Waiting. Waiting for what? 'Til it's time to do it again?

Or are they wondering where *they* will go? Together or separate? I imagine it looms large in their minds, being from different settings as they are. I bet they wish they'd stayed in High America with Inbar and Aarae, or even gone down the River with Bruce and Tarantellula-become-Penny, with Ahmad Zeq and Colonel Sir Qamal ibn-Aziz Alireza. Even if the World Without End is utterly vanished now, at least they would be nonexistent together.

And Professor Ling Erhshan, looking at nothing, lost in his thoughts, one hand idly massaging his genitals, as if wiping them dry. They probably itch a bit just now.

She walked over to him, walked over slowly, stood in front

of him, waiting for him to notice her presence. He did so with a start.

"So. Was she a good fuck?"

Pain brushing across his eyes, there for just a moment, then going away. A tiny shrug, a hint of a smile. Remembering her already? He said, "Yes. Yes she was. One of the best I ever had."

That ever-ready anger, warming her again. I'll just bet, you selfish little son of a bitch. Then, startled at the turn of phrase, making her turn inward. Do I really believe it's bad mothering that makes the badness of men? Bad mothering, then, that makes us hate each other, even hate ourselves?

Or did they just tell me that, tell me over and over, when I was too young to understand, until it became an unconsidered part of my inner belief system?

Ling said, "I wonder where she went."

Sunset over the fat, flat ocean . . . "Looked like California to me."

Wistful: "I always wanted to visit California."

She sat down, folded her arms over her knees, looking back toward the center of the Dish, sat watching Amaterasu and Genda, watching them talk to each other, face to face, eyes on eyes, focused, the rest of the world shut out. After a while, Ling sat down beside her, close enough she could smell his sweat, smell the flat scent of Passiphaë Laing lingering upon him.

He said, "It would be a shame if God split them up."

A glance in his direction, a look at a somber, thoughtful face, seen in full profile. A flat face. Chinese looking. She said, "You really believe this is all the work of . . . some real God?"

A shrug. "No. But it's the only word I have. A handy word, at least."

The sort of thing you'd expect from a man whose spent his whole life . . . reflecting on things. She looked back at Amaterasu and Genda. Legs tucked under them, not quite kneeling, bodies angled toward one another. They have little smiles that come and go as they talk. She reaches out from

time to time and touches him. He leans forward once, quickly, nuzzles at her cheek.

How much of that is my programming, carried forward
through her transition, from circuitboard woman to woman of
meat and bone? I wish I could see inside her head. She said,
"Do you really suppose they love each other?"

Ling's voice held an element of surprise. Surprised at the
question, coming from me? Or merely surprised at the content of the answer it evokes? He said, "I don't know."

"But what do you think?"

A little shrug, hardly there at all. "No way to judge. I don't
know anything at all about love."

"Why not?"

He was looking at her now, eyes full of . . . reluctance? He
said, "I was always busy with . . . other things."

Always busy with other things. The story of my life as
well, except for . . .

Ling said, "Do you know? I think maybe you have been in
love, maybe once upon a time."

That time in which all children's fables are set. Now it was
her turn to shrug, knowing she wanted to be evasive. Not hiding it from him. I've been around too long to care what any-
body thinks of me anymore. No, just wanting to hide it from
myself. "I thought I was. Once upon a time. But memories
have a life of their own. Things change."

"Times change and we are changed within them. What
changes, I suppose, is mainly our perspective on the past."

And then, a long, low, soft whisper of sound, a distant
scraping, of metal on metal, and Ling laughed, laugh tinged
with dread, a familiar whistling-past-the-graveyard sort of
laugh. "That sound. I keep expecting a TARDIS to material-
ize."

No time to wonder what the Hell the idiot was referring to,
spiral of metallic glitter twisting downward out of black nothing, floating above them in the empty sky.

Softly, Ling said, "And which one are you?"

To which Kincaid added, only in her head, Or who . . .

The same whispered voice. *Transition manager.*

Well, even if you didn't know the which of it, straight from the Scavengers' Toolbox, the name was sufficiently evocative. She whispered, "Toolbox calls to the transition manager evoke inter-gate connectivity. This is, supposedly, how the Colonials set up their node network in the first place . . ."

Ling whispered, "Oh."

And the voice whispered, *Not quite true. The node network was here before there was anyone to use it, in the very limited sense that there was a before in which it existed. Even God's thoughts need channels in which to flow.*

God again. Always the suggestion of God. Merely a bogeyman to frighten us? Why would God want us to be afraid?

Down in the middle of the Dish, Amaterasu and Genda were visibly cowering, obviously afraid. They know, somehow, that it's their turn, just as I—a glance at Ling—just as *we* know it's not our turn. I didn't put anything like fear into my robot girl. Roddie wasn't a sadist, just oblivious to the pain of others. I made him a little whore who didn't mind being hurt, that's all . . .

Sudden memory, back on Faux-Barsoom, of Robot Amaterasu talking about being left in her box, alone, for age on endless age. All right. So all I did was make her hide the pain. Behind the mask, the agony was there all along. Maybe the fear as well. Fear that, now, she'll be left alone, once again, left alone to face all those empty gray years, years that threaten never to end . . . Poor Amaterasu. I'm sorry, daughter. But *sorry* is never enough.

Time to go home, said the voice. *Time to live.*

A sparkle of light in the black sky, sparkle of light from far, far above. Stack-element suddenly falling on them, faster than the speed of light, growing huge in quicktime, vast, swelling like the fireball of a nuclear explosion until it filled the entire universe.

Universe with a starry sky.

The starry sky of home.

And a moment of dread within Kincaid: Oh, God! Take us with you! Followed by a distant wondering: Is that what I want, after all, merely to go with them, for this empty quest to go on and on?

A bright glitter, glitter of blue light against that starry sky, something moving . . . Disk swelling in a slower quicktime, visibly decelerating, flying saucer floating in front of them, rotation a soft background whine. *Baka-no-Koto.*

They stood, hand in hand, superimposed against the ship, watching. A door opened in the hull, impossibly motionless against its spinning backdrop; a ramp extruded like some silver metal tongue, slid down until it touched the soft white surface of the Dish.

Lord Genda Hiroshige looked up at the double helix, and said, "Where are we going?"

Back into the Multiverse.

His shoulders seemed to slump. "So it just goes on? Am I never to find God? Never to go . . . home again?"

No one meets God.

"Because there is no God? Who runs all this then? You?"

No. Not I.

"So I continue my search. Not knowing . . ."

The voice seemed amused. *It's a version of your own skein, Lord Genda, a very similar thread indeed. But this one has no gates.*

He shouted: "Then what's the *point*!" More softly, defeated, "Then what the Hell is the point?"

Why does there have to be a point to your life?

Lord Genda, holding hands with his Amaterasu, speechless.

Kincaid thought, I know why. Because, when we are children, they tell us it must be so. Otherwise, why grow up at all? Why grow up to work and fight and worry and wonder? If there's no point to it all, why bother?

The voice said, *Go home, Lord Genda Hiroshige.*

He took a step toward the ramp, took a step and stopped, looking at Amaterasu. Amaterasu uninvited, standing still under the starry sky.

And you as well, Robot Amaterasu.

Something odd in her voice when she spoke: "Will . . . will I become a machine again?"

If that's what you want.

Astonishment on Genda's face. Possibly horror.

Amaterasu took him by both wrists, looking into his face, beseeching, begging him to understand, perhaps. She said, "I do."

Genda, stammering: "But . . . *why*?"

She smiled. Smiled and said, "Because I was happy."

No understanding. Only bewilderment on his face.

What is he thinking? Kincaid thought, Does he wonder why she wants to be happy, when she can be real? She was real when I made her. She remembers that. Maybe that's what kept her whole and functional, while she waited in her box for him to come.

Prince Charming then, fighting through the thorn forest to the side of his sleeping girl, bending to awaken her with a kiss?

They were up the ramp then, already gone, ramp sucked back into the ship, doorway gone, ship sailing away into the starry sky, starry sky receding to a glassy twinkle, then gone.

Ling, softly: "And us?"

Kincaid could feel him reaching out to take her by the hand. His fingers were trembling gently. Afraid? Well. No one wants to meet their fate alone. Not even me.

But the transition manager, silent, only slid upward, twisted away to some other dimension, some other part of this impossible reality, leaving them alone together.

Ling Erhshan stood watching her, waiting, Astrid Kincaid sitting on the edge of the abyss once again, sprawled almost carelessly. Has she stopped caring about it all? So many disappointments, heaped one upon another. And this, probably the greatest of all. Knowing that soon, some manager will come and take us away, first one, then the other, stick us back into the stream, of life, never knowing . . . never . . .

I wonder which one of us will go first?

It made him shiver, imagining himself left here alone for who knew how long . . . Why should that make me afraid? I've been alone, one way or another, all of my life.

Kincaid wasn't afraid. Kincaid, superwoman, never afraid. Never showing it, at least. Look at her, sitting here now, sitting on the edge of forever, like she was sitting on a clifftop somewhere, somewhere in Fortress America, perhaps, or the still open America of her youth, looking down over field and forest . . .

A faint smile. Then, of course, she'd have something on. I imagine her as a muscular young woman, a physically fit teenaged girl, perhaps, dressed in hiking shorts and tee-shirt, nipples of her unsupported breasts vaguely visible through the material perhaps, white socks reaching up her calves almost to her knees from heavy canvass walking shoes, stick picked up at an odd moment somewhere, held idly in one hand as she dreams . . .

Naked woman sitting here now, naked breasts carelessly exposed, one knee drawn up, the other sprawled to one side, relaxed. If I move just so, I can see . . .

Ah. Glistening like a jewel in the universe's eternal light, like magic, like . . .

Dry inner voice, whispering ridicule. Listen to you, Ling Erhshan, spouting primitive poetry to yourself, mooning about the fact of a wet hole in a mammalian carcass. As well sing paeans to raw liver . . .

I wonder, he thought, which god saw fit to make men long to see them thus? The God of Aimless Evolution? Is it only biology that makes us so? Is there no music in our souls?

Kincaid was looking at him now, eyes amused, mouth set half in frown, half in smirk. She said, "I learned a hundred years ago that what my mother said about men's one-track minds was absolutely true."

He looked down and beheld himself, had the grace to feel embarrassed. What did I expect her to do, throw herself on me like Subroutine Passiphaë Laing, accommodate me with a will, like Robot Amaterasu?

Well, said the dry voice. She does *know*. She made the robot for a man, after all . . .

Kincaid said, "Take it easy, Ling. I'm not mad at you." She patted a spot on the white padding by her side. "Just sit down and wait. They'll come for us when they're ready."

And they sat, alone together, waiting.

Sitting on the edge of nothingness, one leg dangling out over an emptiness so profound the word abyss was inadequate, the other tucked up, heel pressed against her rear end, knee clutched in the angle of one bent arm, Astrid Kincaid could feel his eyes on her. Not so much that fabled prickling in the back of the neck as a delicate clutching sensation, somewhere near the bottom of her belly. Slightly bitter amusement. We never escape from our origins, do we?

She briefly considered the possibility of sitting more demurely. That's it, knees pressed together tightly, legs folded up under you, so all he can see is calves and rounded haunch and flat curve of belly, arms folded across breasts, so all he can see is elbows. Almost as good as being dressed? Idiocy. Who was it, put us here naked together? And to what end? Some experiment by God On High, some test, just to see if I'll give in and fuck him?

Right. Just the sort of test a male god would devise for a woman to fail. Fail no matter what her choice. Fucked him? *Harlot*. Didn't fuck him? *Castrating bitch*.

Two quick memories passing through.

One of standing in the hallway, just at dawn, Saturday morning perhaps. Maybe ten years old, Roddie not even born yet, no one with whom to watch cartoons while Mom and Dad lazed away their goof-off time.

Standing in the hallway then, slipperless feet on a cold wooden floor, because her parents liked that "natural" feeling, ear pressed to the door, listening. Mostly just the sound of their bed, a kind of soft crunching sound. An occasional murmur, always her mother's voice. Crunching sound going on and on, sometimes faster, sometimes slower. Her father's voice, deeper, not as soft, a grunting noise, once, twice, something not quite human, perhaps. Cessation of other noises, then her mother, murmuring softly for a while.

In a little while they'd come out, father aglow, bustling about, ready for his usual Saturday routine. Mother quiet, withdrawn, tired perhaps.

That other memory, maybe five years later, of being awakened late one night by her father's voice, raised in anger, words indistinct. Mother saying something back, brittle outrage coming through the wall, little else. Crunching of the bed, a muffled *splat* of some kind. Silence. Then the sound of someone moving about, feet on the floor, first the soft thud of bare feet, then the echo-like *tock* of leather soles on wood. Bedroom door slamming. Front door slamming. Car starting, driving away.

Me, creeping out of my room a little later. Mother sitting in the living room, watching TV, crying. Me, creeping up on the couch beside her, remembering that muffled *splat* from the bedroom, suddenly knowing . . . Touching her. Are you all right, Mom? Did he . . . Not wanting to say it, imagining my father, face twisted with animal rage, lashing out at her with his fist.

Looking at her then in the half-light. Looking for a telltale bruise. Feeling my anger grow. Mother looking at me, tears in her eyes. Putting her hand on my hair. Oh, Astrid. No. Opening her hand, showing me a bright red palm. No, I hit him. Me, suddenly imagining a scarlet handprint on my father's cheek.

But . . . why?

Mother crying again. Because he . . . just wouldn't let me be.

Me, old enough to understand what was being implied. Anger growing again.

Mother sighing. I guess . . . I guess I should have given in. It wouldn't have taken long. It wouldn't have hurt anything. Now . . . what was she imagining? Father sulking alone in some bar, or merely driving his car round and round, slowly cooling off? Will he be home in an hour, full of apologies, or in a motel room somewhere, with some pig who'll do it for cheap drinks and cab fare?

Image of my father, screwing a whore.

Image of my mother, confiding in a child.

After a while, little Astrid had crept back to bed, still full of anger. And bewildered as well. When you're fifteen, you think you *know*. But then you look back from thirty, or forty-five, or sixty and, if you remember, if you truly remember, you laugh.

In the morning, when she got up, the car was in the drive-way, her parents' door closed, though it was a school and work morning, bed crunching softly away, mother's voice softly murmuring, all of it ending on her father's little animal grunt.

Ear pressed to the door, she heard her mother say, *There now. There now.*

Anger. Anger and frustration. How could she? Anger at her for just giving in. Anger at him for ... being that way. Getting dressed, going to school a half hour early so she wouldn't have to face them, see his obscenely glowing face, her wan, withdrawn exhaustion.

And, of course, Roddie was born the requisite nine months later, helping to keep my anger fresh for a little while longer. They probably chalked up my sullenness to adolescence, or else never gave it a thought. A glance over at Ling, staring down on darkness.

"Well," he whispered. "I ..."

I ... I ... Kincaid jerked suddenly, pulling in her legs, rolling to her knees, turning. There was a dull gray metal helix rolling in the black sky above them, a lightless, almost-invisible helix, and the thought had not been hers.

Astrid Kincaid, said the voice. *Time.*

A single, sudden, jarring thump of fear, liquid heart going *poke, poke, poke* in her chest. She looked over at Ling again and saw his blanched face, the look of abject terror in his eyes.

She smiled at him.

Then, *snap.*

Ling Erhshan standing, aghast, looking down at a little pile of dry white bones. Afraid to look closely. Afraid to reach out and ...

Professor Ling standing alone in the middle of a desolate silver cloud, looking up at his leaden apparition. Waiting. Nothing. Fear like frantic indigestion dancing in his belly. A sudden urge to squat down and empty his bowels. Useless. Useless. You know how to deal with fear, Ling Erhshan. You're already dead, Ling Erhshan. Dead and gone. Nothing more can happen to you now.

But a thin mist of fear, forming all around him, clouding his thoughts, blotting everything from its path. Yes there is.

Yes there is. Image of the dull gray helix winding itself up into the trackless black sky. Winding away to Hell and gone and leaving him here. All alone. Forever.

"So." Voice flat in the windless emptiness of Hell. "To whom do I have the horror of . . ." Freezing fright. *Honor*. I mean *honor* . . .

Probability manager.

"Oh." Ordinary title, conferring ordinary courage on him. "That's a big job."

You don't know the half of it.

An uncannily friendly voice. Like an arm around his shoulders, like the embrace of an old friend. *I'm half tempted to leave your ass right here, Ling. It'd serve you fucking right.*

Pulse of dismay, but . . . Strange way for a god to speak.

There are no gods, Ling Erhshan.

Reading my mind!

What the Hell did you expect? Calm down, for Christ's sake.

For *Christ's* sake? Bad news, if true. He said, "I'd . . . rather hoped for a nobler fate."

Right. Any noble fate at all, so long as you can throw in a fuck or two along the way.

He tried to stand with his eyes downcast, tried to fight off any lingering sense of embarrassment. Embarrassment that . . . that they know me so well? But, downward, there was only a fine view of his dangling little penis. And the voice, though soundless, seemed to laugh.

Shrivel right up, does it? I know how you feel. Tell you what. I'll park your silly ass someplace interesting and get back to you later . . .

Later? Hardly omnipotent at all . . .

But then, *snap*.

Echo. Echo. Echo. A faraway sound, as if someone, in some other part of the universe perhaps, had slammed a door behind her. Sitting up in bed, in her little cubby of a bedroom, back propped by stiff Corps-issue pillows, Astrid Kincaid looked up from her book, staring into the yellow-lit gloom, listening.

Distant Marine base sounds. A truck winding out through its gears, accelerating, engine sound rising in pitch, going through the drop-pause of a gear shift, rising again. That ratchetty sound meaning somebody new to the task. Sloppy training, as usual.

The rough, hollow sound of the wind, blowing round the eaves of buildings, whispering through telephone wires and power lines. Through the leafless branches of the few trees that'd been left in place when they'd put up the barracks area thirty years earlier.

Bored sentries out there somewhere, walking their pointless lines. She looked back at the book, soon found herself staring at a meaningless regimentation of senseless characters, letters no more than lines of marching soldiers themselves, not forming up into words. *I'm just turning the pages. Going through the motions of reading.*

She shut the book, looked at the Corps-green cover. *Field Assault Tactics, Vol. 1: Desert Warfare,* eighth edition. No author. Government issue. *It's coming, God damn it. It's coming. Somebody's got to get them ready.* A slight feeling of anger surfacing, useless God damned beer-swilling noncoms, college-graduate officers here because this was the best job they could get, industry rejecting them . . .

Somebody's got to get them ready. Why does it have to be me? Because they're the only damned friends you have. And because you took the damned job. She put the book down, stood up, looked out through her blinds at the night. *Two A.M. I should be asleep. Hard work in the morning. Dark out there, like the dark between the stars. When did I lose that dream? When did we all lose it?*

No answers, as usual. Dreams die. That's that. Stood looking in the mirror. *Fine signs of exquisite physical conditioning; the Corps' given me time for that, at least.* A sense of satisfaction, seeing a ripple of muscle, six lovely little domes around her belly button, framed by plain white cotton briefs, a plain, stretchy white bra. *Some of the girls wear GI green. Too stiff for me.*

Tired face, though. Doesn't look like me anymore, staring

out through those wide brown eyes. Girl in the mirror looking for something. I wonder what?

She clicked out the light from the switch by the door and stood in the semi-darkness, pale light coming in through the half-open blinds. Faint sound like a dog barking in the distance. Has to be a stray. No dogs on base since the latest round of budget cuts did away with K-9.

All right. Did you hear a sound or not? Do you want to check it out or just crawl between the sheets for two or three zees before you roll their asses out onto the floor for another lovely day of drilling and drumming? She opened the door and slid out into the night.

Darker here, rows of bunks no more than black shadows, framed by lesser darkness. Soft sound of people breathing. Gentle snores. The loud snorers we had at the beginning either disciplined or doctored, as need be. Funny how many of the midnight chainsaws turned out to be women.

Funny how they got used to sleeping among each other, too. God damned stupid training films almost making it worse, an edited version of *Aliens* that left out the sexual relationship between the two troopers, when every damned person on fucking Earth has seen the original ten times over.

Good point, though. Not men. Not women. Not straights. Not gays. People. Soldiers. Comrades in arms. Not that some of them didn't get into each other's arms a little more often than the Pentagon liked. Control the cable or not, people have been watching reruns of *M*A*S*H* for sixty-five years . . .

A whisper of cloth from a far corner of the room, gentle, repetitive sliding suddenly stilled, as if people were holding their breaths, waiting for her to pass. Probably a couple of comrades right now. Jolsen and Rodriguez? Most likely. Well. I'll march their asses off in the morning, let them think a little bit about whether humping each other is worth humping rocks the next day.

Tired, are we? Now imagine how you'd feel if this was combat.

What fucking combat, Sergeant? Hasn't been a *real* goddam war in thirty years.

Wait patiently, boys and girls. The time will come . . .

Over to the far end of the bunkroom now, over to where a little rim of light showed under the latrine door. Somebody being a little careless here, unless there's a crapping soldier inside. Hand on the door, listening. Soft sounds. Gentle snuffling sounds. Crying? Hell. Not supposed to be any crying in the damned Marines. She pushed the door open and went inside.

Bright white fluorescent light. Clean checkerboard of black and white tiles. Clear mirrors. Shiny white porcelain sinks. Dull green walls, dull green stalls around the toilets. Men grumbling at the lack of urinals, but, just maybe, liking the idea they could pee without some asshole watching.

Half a bare footprint, red decal on the floor, printed in bright blood. A pair of GI fatigue pants crumpled by the open door of one of the toilet stalls. More blood, a couple of droplets in the middle of the room. Figure standing in front of one of the sinks, scrap of bloody cloth by her feet, her underpants. Standing there, hunkered over herself, doing something, shirttail handing down over a shapely bare rump.

Short-cropped, feathery gray-black hair. Richardson. Mandy Richardson. Almost ready for her first stripe.

Kincaid walked forward, reached out to touch her, looking over her shoulder. Woman jerking slightly, looking up at her. Eyes wide, reactive. One hand at her crotch, clutching a big wad of bloody toilet paper to herself.

"Are you all right?" Stupid-ass question. "This doesn't look like it's just an unusually bad period, Mandy." Doesn't look like she's giving herself an abortion, either.

Whispered: "I'm sorry, Sergeant. I . . ."

Look into her eyes, then. Hard red anger there, raw anger of the sort that would eat you alive if you didn't get rid of it somehow. She said, "You want me to take you over to sick bay?" Ask. Let her know she's in control.

Fear then. Trouble. "No. I'm, uh . . ." A quick headshake, eyes closing briefly. "No."

"Let me see."

Clutching the now-soaked toilet paper tightly to herself. Still bleeding, whatever it is. "Look, I just want to . . ."

"Get over on the table, Private. Let me look." Stubborn

resentment in those eyes now. "Either that or I take you to sick bay."

Sudden defeat filling the eyes with agony. Shoulders slumping, back curved, hand with the toilet paper relaxing a bit, little rivulet of blood starting down one thigh. Tears in her eyes, eyes closing.

Softly: "Get up on the table, Mandy. Let me help."

Teary eyes opening, looking at her. Angry: No one can help. But pleading, as well. Little girl looking to her mother . . .

Got her up on the table, hand pulled out of the way, gently fingering her crotch, pubic hair matted with blood that was starting to clot, like a mass of thick red jelly. Pulling labia apart, feeling the young woman wince. Biting her lip. Trying to be a brave little soldier, but . . .

Hmh. No real damage. Just a scratch, like you'd get from a fingernail, little tiny strip of skin peeled away, right next to her clit. Crotch wounds like head wounds, bleed like a bastard . . .

She wrapped a length of clean toilet paper around her hand, pressed her fingers right over the little cut. "You're OK, Mandy."

Eyes shut. Nodding. Probably knew she wasn't hurt bad. Not so stupid she wouldn't go to the medics if she thought there was a hemorrhage involved. Just a little scratch. Probably no lacerations inside or . . . anything. Shadows on her face, though. Bruises forming? We'll know in the morning.

"You want to tell me what happened?"

Biting her lip. No, Sergeant, I don't want to tell. Just leave me alone, please.

"OK. I damn well *know* what happened, Mandy. You want to tell me who?"

No.

"I expect my soldiers to be able to take care of themselves, Mandy. Doesn't matter whether it's brawls, combat, or just a little rough trade."

Silence. Then, "I'm sorry, Sergeant. I didn't mean to make trouble."

Trouble. Christ. The upbringing of girls. "Fuck the trouble. Look, we can take care of this the Corps way or the soldiers' way, but it's got to be taken care of. Your call."

More silence.

"Come on, Mandy. You change your mind on some asshole when he figured it was too late for you to back out?"

Biting her lip again. "It was an officer."

Well, now. Got to tread a little lightly here. Mirth forced into her voice: "So you couldn't fight off some sissy lieutenant or another? Which one? Or were there ten of the little shitskies?" Little shitskies, right out of rot-see . . .

The woman opened her eyes. "Captain Bergeron."

Well, shit. No, little Mandy Richardson wouldn't be able to fight off Mark Bergeron, nor would I, all by my lonesome. Bergeron a slab of meat the size of a TV superhero, capped at Captain, having talked his way into the new OCS program from the rank of tech-sergeant a few years back. Old Corps. Old-style manly man among manly men. Lip curling in the barroom, Fuckin' *pussies* in the Marines.

And more than a little bitter because he didn't seem to be getting his fair share of those pussies. Not the way he wanted them, at any rate. She exhaled a held breath. "OK, Mandy, let's get you cleaned up. Stay away from sick-call. I'll go light on you for the next few days and . . . Well. We'll take care of this when we're ready."

Grateful look in her eyes, then, but the anger and hurt were still there. Most of all the hurt.

Six of them. Six pairs of beady eyes looking back at her out of the quasi-darkness. Stars in the sky, crickets chirping in the bushes. Little frogs croaking high-pitched somewhere, frogs in a drainage ditch by the side of the road. Spring peepers, I think they're called. And six pairs of women's eyes, shining in the ambient light.

Six women with bruises, bloody noses. One broken arm, that mutter through clenched teeth by Cassie Smithers: You fucking bastard, Bergeron.

Bitch. I'll get you bitches for this.

Get us. What does he think is about to happen? He knows

why this is happening. But, I guess, he figures we're just going to kick him around a little, leave him out here for the sentries to find, naked maybe, nicely sunburned, mad as Hell.

Dull pain in her back, off center to the right, where he'd nailed her with a sharp kidney punch. Meant to hurt me bad, and I'll be pissing blood in the morning. But he wasn't quite fast enough.

Somehow unfair that God set things up this way. Seven God-damned women to take down one fat man, tie him hand and foot . . .

She could feel his heart beating under her hands now, pounding in his chest, slowing from the exertion, calming down as she held him in her arms from behind. Probably likes the way my tits feel, pressed into his back.

He said, "You're going to be in a lot of trouble over this, girls."

Silence. Beady eyes looking at him. "What, you think I don't know who you are because it's dark? Hell, I know every little grunt you girls make. Smithers. Kincaid. Lateesha Reynolds, you fat pig. Even little cunt Richardson . . ."

Kincaid thumbed him in the throat, heard him gag. Then, "OK, bitches, have your fun. You'll be in civvies for this. After you do time."

Silence.

"Tell you what. Let me go and maybe we can come to an accommodation." Silence. "Tell you what. Untie me, then the six of you hold down Kincaid here long enough for me to get in a compensating fuck, and we'll forget this ever happened."

Silence.

Then Kincaid slid the icepick out of her boot, held it up to the sky, where the starlight could show it to him.

"What the *fuck* . . ." Heartbeat speeding up a little.

She lowered the icepick, slid it across the front of his pants, played a raspy little tune on his cheap GI zipper. Heart starting to thump nicely now, breath quickening in his chest.

"You try anything like that, bitch, and I *promise* you ten years at hard labor. Ten years *minimum*."

She put the point of the ice pick in his right nostril, nice, nice cold metal, felt him stiffen in her arms. Right now, his balls were probably snugged up tight to his pelvis, pecker hardly more than a nubbin.

Whispered, "God *damn* you, Kincaid. Enough."

She said, "Your call, Mandy."

Long wait, Bergeron's heart pounding against her chest, felt through the structure of his muscular back. Tiny thought trickling through her, What a waste. In another circumstance, I might like to be snuggled against a back like this.

Mandy Richardson's fist outlined against the starry sky. Thumbs down.

A moment of sharp regret. Are you sure this is right? But, then: "OK."

One little squeak from the man as the icepick started to slide up his nose, a frantic little *No* . . . She felt him start to buck and struggle as it went in, a hard, gargling outcry.

Crunch. Bones thin up there, offering hardly any resistance at all. Man stiffening hard in her arms, rocking back against her, back of his head smacking against her cheekbone. Well. I'll have a nice little shiner in the morning.

Then rocking her hand back and forth, giving him a nice little prefrontal lobotomy.

Then angling backward into the main structure of his midbrain, twisting, twisting, remembering that leopard frog from high school, remembering how it screamed, a horrid little hiss as it struggled in her hand.

Bergeron not struggling now. Curiously relaxed, weight growing heavier in her arms. Silence. Then a soft, liquid farting sound from inside his pants.

One of the other women, she didn't know which one, said, "Jesus. Let's get the Hell out of here."

Fading echoes, like a gunshot in the distance, Ling Erhshan stopping in his tracks, looking around uneasily at the darkness. You could get into a lot of trouble, walking alone, down by the quays of Shanghai late at night. Stars up above, like diamond dust in the sky, hardly blotted out at all by the lights of the harbor. Filthy water lapping at the concrete pier, little slopping sound of the wavelets giving the night an ambience all its own.

Nothing.

Lovely night.

Ling Erhshan walking along, headed for the university library all by himself, deep satisfaction centered at the root of his belly.

Lovely night. Most excellent night.

Lovely little Chen taken out for a late-night snack, once they'd finished studying. She was coming along well, finally getting caught up on her calculus, his long evenings of patient tutoring paying off at last.

Paying off at last. It made him smile.

Well, she'll pass tomorrow's exam. Of course she will. She'll get a good night's sleep now. Be fresh in the morning, bright-eyed and . . . is fuzzy-tailed the English expression? Well, lovely little Chen had turned out to be fuzzy-tailed indeed, once he'd gotten her cornered behind the bed, gotten her down on the floor, gotten her out of those sexy black bicycling shorts.

All her little protests, whining that she didn't want . . . didn't want . . . But then there was the promise of her vulva, outlined against the shorts she'd worn. No one wears something like that by accident. I've worn bicycle shorts. They feel awful.

Lovely little Chen, lying on the floor, sprawled open for him like that, made all the sexier because she still had on her blouse, that oddly stunned look in her eyes.

Lovely little Chen, holding so still when he crouched down between her legs. Holding so still while he rubbed his cheeks against the soft skin of her smooth, pale thighs. Holding so still while he nuzzled her here and there. Holding so still while he put his tongue where it belonged, where he knew it belonged, where he knew she knew it belonged. Holding so still while he felt her grow wet under his mouth, felt her tissues expand just so . . .

Ah, little Chen, the lips of your mouth can lie, but the lips of your vulva . . .

Lovely little Chen, holding so still as he crawled up her belly, holding so still as he nuzzled her cheeks with his wet face, holding so still as he kissed her, opening her mouth for him, letting him put his tongue inside, holding so still as she tasted herself on him . . .

Lovely little Chen, holding so still as he fumbled around her wet crotch with his hand, as he found the opening, right where it belonged, used his thumb to guide himself inside. Some women help you do that. Some women do not. Maybe lovely little Chen has only been with men who need no assistance . . .

Then, lovely little Chen holding ever so still as he thrust away into her splendid, smooth, oily inner warmth, breath puffing into his ear in time to his strokes, growing quicker and quicker, just as he grew quicker and quicker . . .

Lovely little Chen holding ever so still as he went pulse, pulse, pulse within her, warm semen flooding out, carrying away his soul, like a butterfly in the wind. Lovely image. Lovely, lovely image . . .

Little Chen getting up off the floor, sitting on the edge of her bed. A little smile on her face, perhaps. Odd little smile. Some women so very quiet during lovemaking, while others thrash and moan and scream. So much pleasanter with the quiet women, so much less . . . distraction. Though, at least with the noisy ones, you didn't have to ask if they enjoyed it . . .

Little Chen sitting quietly on the edge of her bed, sitting on a fresh wet spot, still in her blouse, no pants, sitting there staring into space. He said, "Are you all right?"

She just looked at him, eyes expressionless.

After a while he shrugged. Some women were like that. He said, "Well. I've got to go. We've got a busy day tomorrow."

Still staring.

He said, "I'll wait for you after the calculus test. We'll talk about the questions. Try to see how you made out."

Silence.

"All right?"

She said, "All right. It's all right, Erhshan."

Gone away then, down by the dark Shanghai harbor, a warm spring night in the warm, humid south of China, walking along to the university library. Going to do a little more studying, not that easy stuff about calculus and physics. Doing a little more work, another iteration on the long literature search for his honors course. Looking up the technical specs for those old American rocket ships. Advisor said it was a waste of time. No corporation will pay to develop something as expensive as this, not with its own money.

And the government . . . well, the government will spend as much of the people's money as it wishes to spend. Look at what a lovely Navy we have now, battleships and aircraft carriers. Frigates, cruisers, destroyers, nuclear submarines . . .

But not this.

No reason for this.

No reason at all.

Never got to it. Distracted, walking along, looking into the reading room where the trash literature was kept, stopping to look over the small collection of "futuristic speculations," books by Chinese authors, mostly about a world where Green China was king, a few fantasies set in the dark depths of Fortress America, objectionist allegories focused on the power of the almighty *yüan* . . .

And then, that box, sitting on the floor, full of books waiting to be shelved. Opening the flap, looking in out of bored curiosity. Picking up the topmost book, printed in modern literary *Putonghua* characters. Not so hard to follow, now that he was used to following modern Chinese technical literature . . .

A retrospective anthology of American science fiction stories, covering the first half of the twentieth century, freshly translated from Japanese. Starting with a story that had the unlikely name of *Ralph* . . .

Sat right there, reading, on the floor, all night long, submerged in happy splendor, suddenly finding himself in a pool of yellow sunlight, pink-eyed, realizing it was dawn, that his first exam was only ninety minutes away . . .

Cursing himself for a fool, rushing away for a quick shower, quick coffee, quick breakfast and . . .

In the morning, then, the news that lovely little Chen, having had a few drinks by herself evidently, had gone for a walk in the night, had gone down by the harbor, following him perhaps? Had stumbled evidently, and fallen into the dirty water and drowned.

He'd spent the next night in the library as well, reading, reading, and the next one after that, soul soaking away into the imaginary worlds with all their immortal, invulnerable, imaginary people, worlds where only the nameless spear carriers died, where the real heroes and heroines only died for . . . for reasons you could at least understand.

Astrid Kincaid, running through the featureless darkness, six strong women at her side, running from the site of vengeance, dead Bergeron sprawled in the weeds, sprawled bonelessly, blood running from his nostrils, stink of shit rising from his pants. Got what he deserved. Got what he deserved. Women running and running, comrades all, running together.

Mandy Richardson's small hand warm in mine, hand in mine as we ran together, out of the darkness and back into the light. Sneaking back onto the base together, noncoms eying each other in the darkness, eyes wide, faces drawn, withdrawn. No one, the faces said, no one will say a word . . . Then going our separate ways, back to barracks, all save Mandy, who was in my charge, back to our own barracks, crawling in through the window of my room.

Sitting there, first in the darkness, then by the light of my single low-wattage lamp. Mandy sitting on the edge of my bed. Waiting? Waiting for what? Me, waiting now for her to gather her courage, waiting for her to slink back out to her little bunk in the common room. "Mandy . . ."

Dark eyes on me. "Sergeant, if I go now, someone will see."

So? At worst, they'll think you've come in to . . . a little smile. More than one way to gain favor, more than one way to kiss ass in this woman's Marine Corps. Kincaid said, "No one will bother you about it, Mandy."

More dark eyes, then, "Sergeant, if I go out now, someone will remember the time. The medical examiner's office will be able to tell roughly when Captain Bergeron died."

Oh. Memory of fear. And, though I'd been careful, the

coroner, alerted, would have them take my clothes, have them check . . . Even if they found no bloodstains, they might find other little bits of Captain Bergeron.

Richardson said, "It'd be better if I spent the night in here, Sergeant. I don't care what people think."

Reluctance. I care what people think. Let them see me spending the night with one of my troopers, especially one of my female troopers, and I'd have to put up with all sorts of bullshit. Real dykes putting the make on me. Men hitting on me just to see if I really went both ways . . .

Kincaid said, "Well." I see your point.

Turning down the bed then. Getting out of dirty fatigues, hesitating, deciding to leave her underwear on, bra and panties a sort of psychic armor, crawling into bed, sliding over, leaving room for Mandy. Who got out of her fatigues, stood there so slim and strong, looking down at her, white figure made whiter by pale, pale linen.

Clicked out the light. Stood looking down in the darkness. A whisper of cloth, Kincaid realizing she'd slipped out of her own armor, was coming naked to bed. Don't be so damned foolish! She probably hasn't give it a thought. Just likes to sleep that way, though regs said . . .

Military regs say you sleep by yourself, in pajamas, nice green GI pajamas, that you dressed and undressed in your own latrine area, but . . . Regs never work. They put men and women together, young men and young women, and got what they deserved.

Richardson slid in beside her, head not quite on the edge of the pillow, squirming uncomfortably a bit, while Kincaid tried to lay still. "Good night, Sergeant." No more than a whisper. A friendly whisper.

Kincaid lay there, thinking about the women. Six of us, acting in concert, enacting the vengeance of a seventh. People will remember this. Every time some bastard thinks he can do what he wants, he'll . . . think, perhaps, before he acts. Warm feeling then, not thinking about dead Bergeron, just thinking about her six friends, comrades in arms . . .

I killed a man tonight. Now I don't know why. For friendship? And what is that?

* * *

Kincaid running through the darkness, through absolute darkness, running alone now, boots *tock-tocking* away on the invisible pavement, sound echoing off unseen buildings, off surfaces unknown.

Morning. Morning always comes, no matter how dark the night. Mandy smiling at me as she put her underwear back on. Troopers smiling at me, sly men's smiles, appraising women's smiles, as I went off to the showers in my own underwear. Showered among my soldiers, women just ... looking at me. You could tell which ones were the lesbians now, even if you didn't already know. That look in the eye, saying, Do *I* want some of that? Maybe just the way they started to pose for her, try to get her attention ...

No matter. It would fade in time. Just an aberration. Happens sometimes. They'd see her with men again. Noncoms from her own cohort-in-rank. Would remember seeing two sergeants, a man and a woman, equal stripes, equal hashmarks, slinking into a motel room, hand in hand ...

Then the messhall, looking for the table where her friends would be. Other people sitting there, just now, chattering amiably. Women scattered, sitting at other tables, with other sergeants and corporals. Puzzled. These are my friends. We ... did it together. Then the investigation. Being called to testify, one by one. When did you see him last? Where? How did you feel about him? Why? Wondering if anyone would break. No one did. Investigation eventually turned over to the local police. Captain Bergeron, it seems, getting a little careless. Wallet was empty, after all. Just killed by some thug or another, probably never find out which one.

No one thought to rob him. Probably spent it all on booze and whores. Astrid Kincaid running alone, running right through her life. Running through the darkness, waiting for pink streamers of light to form up ahead, heralding the dawn. What if I'm running the wrong way? What if I'm running toward midnight?

You'll know. A whisper in her heart. A familiar voice. Voice of the angels? No.

* * *

Then Astrid Kincaid running alone, running barefoot, running naked down a dusty forest path, sun bright overhead, beyond a gray screen of trees, sheen of sweat on body and limbs, long brown hair streaming out behind her as she ran, heart thudding away in her chest, heart so perfect, so damnably immortal, burn of perfect conditioning everywhere, as her arms and legs flew.

She burst out of the forest, ran to the edge of the cliff and stopped, panting, pulse pounding in her temples, muscles quivering on the edge of exhaustion, reserves played out, everything done now.

Finished.

Sky overhead a soft lilac hue. Feathery gray grass rising round her ankles. Vista before her of a wide, alien landscape, lit by the light of a blue-gray sun. Stars twinkling through the purple haze, first magnitude stars aglitter overhead. In the distance, a city, a magic city. City of the dead. Tall pastel towers in pale yellow, pink, light blue, bright gray. Silvery roads, aerial paths winding back and forth among them.

"Remember when we were the first ones here, Astrid Astride?"

Spinning round, sweat flying off her brow, soggy hair slapping the side of her neck and sticking. Pudgy naked man sitting on a dark gray stone, plump Caucasian body covered with a dense fur of reddish-black hair, gray hair on his head, face looking so old, so startlingly old . . .

He was only fifty-six the last time I saw him. Not so very old. Not *this* old . . .

"Dale." Nothing else to say, standing here, watching him look at you. Familiar interplay of eyes on your body. He'll look at your face, yes, try to keep looking at it because he knew he was supposed to, but . . . Lingering on your breasts. Following the outline of your hips. Hardly lingering at all, though. Circling round and round and round, headed for the inevitable center . . .

Usually, by this time, he'd have an erection.

Yes. There it is.

Is this all there is at the end? I find my long-lost, longed-for lover and he fucks me and that's that? Do we live happily ever after now? A little twist beginning inside. A spike of ancient revulsion.

Dale Millikan laughed his familiar laugh, and said, "Oh, Astrid. I wish I'd known you before you grew that hard, ugly shell."

When was that? Before I was born?

A sigh. "Maybe so. Plenty of worlds out there in which you get the chance to be . . . someone different."

And, in those worlds, I *am* someone different.

A slow nod, a knowing frown. "You understand that much about the Multiverse, at least."

That perverse little thing sticking out of his middle, nodding just a bit as he breathes. Waiting for me to take notice of it. Memory of passion spent, of lying here, naked, atop this same cliff, of feeling him thrust away inside you, waiting for the warm spill of seed, seed spilled on barren ground . . . Why am I here?

He smiled. Shrugged. "Because you let yourself get tangled up in the machinery, Astrid Astride. Tangled up in the machinery until you couldn't go home again. Until your home was well and truly lost."

Is it gone, Dale? Did the Space-Time Juggernaut come?

"The Jug always comes, Astrid. Always."

The Space-Time Juggernaut comes and wipes away whole worlds. Wipes them away to nothingness. And for what? What harm have we done?

A shrug, not so much of a smile. "All the harm there is. The threads come loose, the skeins unravel. In time the sweater unravels too, and the loom of garments is lost."

And what about the souls who are lost?

"What about them? Would you die for the sake of your viruses, Astrid Kincaid? Would you give up *your* immortality?"

We gave up the Multiverse because we were all afraid to die, Dale.

"Just so. And now you hold God to a higher standard than your own."

God again. Always God. As if that explains anything. Tell me about God, Dale Millikan.

He laughed. "Later."

Will it always be later and never now?

He said, "When you understand why *you're* here, Astrid Astride."

That silly name. And yet . . . a feeling of familiar warmth. Of wanting him to rise, to push me down in the soft gray grass, push me down and use that thing on me . . . She could see him smiling. An infuriating smile, as usual.

I'm here because they sent me, Dale.

"You could have come, could have taken them out, could have blown the gate as you were instructed, gone home to live out your forever."

Bitter thought. It would have been an empty eternity. "So what were you going to do?"

Catch some Arabs, grab me a Chinaman. Send the soldiers home with their prisoners. Jump back out into the Multiverse and blow the gates behind me. I figured if the Jug caught wind of it, he'd come after me, not Earth.

"So you were headed out into the Multiverse. Looking for what, Astrid Astride?"

Not astride much of anything anymore. She thought, Looking for you, Dale. You know that. And know how bitter I feel just now, having found you at last.

He said, "Looking for me? I don't think so."

You were the only one who ever talked to me, Dale. The only one who ever tried to be a friend as well as a lover. I couldn't forget that, no matter how many years went by.

No more smile, more a look of sorrow than anything else. "It was the only coin I had, Astrid. The only coin with which to buy you."

A slight shock of disconnection. I know that now. Maybe I even knew it then. Who among us wants to acknowledge a life without friends, a life in which our only connection with other human beings is . . . a gesture at his still-erect penis . . . is so trivial as that?

Smile returning. "Didn't seem so trivial to me, Astrid Astride."

I guess you're still a man, then.

Silence between them. Silence and distance.

That same silence that surrounded me as a child. Silence of a mother who gave her attention to the husband who used her for a toilet, rather than the daughter who needed her. Silence of adolescent friends, false friends who'd betray her for any slight advantage in their tawdry social games. Silence that followed the breakup of her circle of Corps friends. Wedge driven between them by what they'd done together.

Millikan said, "I gave you what you wanted. Is that so awful?"

Gave me what I wanted, offered up as coin to buy my cunt. Awful enough.

Awful because I . . . knew.

"Why did you think I was still out here, Astrid Astride?"

Stop calling me that! Penis poking up out of his fat middle like some kind of demon, taunting her with its presence. Then, anger subsiding. I spent all those years reading the Scavenger books, Dale. Spent them trying to figure out where I'd been, what I'd seen. Trying to understand what had happened to me. Scavengers seemed to think individual Colonials had survived whatever disaster overwhelmed their civilization, had eluded the Jug, wandered the empty byways of the Multiverse for a long, long time, disappearing one by one, their pathways ending at . . . blank walls. I thought I might find you somewhere. I thought I could . . . rescue you.

"For what purpose?"

Rescue you for me. For me to have again. Have for my own.

"Did you think I might be changed?"

Maybe I did. I pictured you wandering the worlds alone, with nothing to do with your time but think.

"Did you picture me on this cliff by myself, masturbating and thinking of you?"

I pictured you here, thinking of me, yes.

He smiled. "What we imagine of other people is seldom more than a reflection of what's in our own hearts. I did come here, once upon a time. Lay here on this same rock, looking at the city . . ." He wrapped his hand around his penis now, squeezing, so the glans darkened. Laughed at the expression on her face. "Sat right here and jerked off, looking at our lost city, jerked off and imagined you back home, lying alone in your bed, shoving a vibrator up your snatch."

Hollow, sullen anger. Always . . . that. Never *me*, God damn you.

A very soft smile on his face now, letting the damned thing go, penis bobbing at her, making her look at it. Gently, he said, "You got your wish then, Astrid Astride. God has damned me well and true."

Puzzled. What do you mean?

"Jug caught me, Astrid Astride. Caught me right away. Snatched me right off this cliff with my dick hanging out and my goo spraying in the wind. Took me away and did me in."

So you're dead now as well. I figured you were, or we wouldn't be . . . a gesture around, at their long-lost paradise.

Still that smile. "Wasn't being dead that I found so hard, Astrid Astride. It was the afterlife."

She thought, If there's an afterlife, any afterlife at all, then there is no death. Any idiot would realize that with the slightest thought.

"The Scavenger's Space-Time Juggernaut, our Angel of Death sizzling in the sky, is the scrap manager, remember? Comes to put you back where you belong, tuck away all your loose ends."

And where did you turn out to belong, Dale Millikan?

Laughter then, hardly Olympian at all. "Gave me a new name, my beloved Astrid Astride. Made me be the probability manager."

Brief shock of understanding.

Then jump-cut away.

Professor Ling Erhshan then, sitting on the smooth, cold library floor, listening to the wind howl softly outside. Dark sky beyond those windows, lit only by the wan light from within, black sky of blowing, backlit clouds, white mist slipping by, there then gone. Ling Erhshan sitting on the floor among his books.

I could sit here and read them forever. I could begin with

those first books, those precious few books of my childhood.
I could read the translated words of the American fabulist
Thimble Valley, he of the strange, potent name, move on to
later discoveries, to the dreams of Tarzan and Barsoom, to the
dreams of last and first men, to the endlessly pointless valley
of the fabulous riverboat . . .

Picking up a book and opening it. Clinically detailed
image of a woman's crotch, Tanner Stage Five Female
Escutcheon, the caption said, shot in harsh white light, so you
could see just what was what. No romance there. No soft
love, no gentle words, no woman whispering in my
ear . . . Then why does it stir me so?

Closing the book, some medical text he supposed. Picking
up another one, opening it as well. Woman sprawled seductively, one knee cocked up, showing herself off. Image shot
in soft light, gauzy light, vulva reaching out to you with its
own special come-hither look.

Another book. Woman on her knees, of course, woman on
her knees and bent forward, head most likely resting on the
bed, though all you could see was her rump and the tops of
her thighs, rounded buttocks spread just so, shaven flesh glistening with some kind of oil.

He tossed the book aside, onto a growing pile. Stared out
morosely at black sky and fast-moving clouds, listened to the
dull boom of the wind. That old television clip. The man who
survives the end of the world, finds himself at last in the
library of his dreams, broken glasses in hand . . .

Taking it away from me. Taking it all away. Taking away
lovely young Valetta, blond Valetta, willing Valetta of the
Moon Man's dreams, replacing her with a rough handful of
rich, steaming meat.

Give me a place to sit, and I will move my bowels . . .

Mirth in the voice.

Ling arose from the floor, stood and stretched, walked
over to the window, stood looking out into the darkness.
Nothing out there but sky and clouds. No stars, not a glimpse
of moonlight. Nothing but black eternity. Such a nice, sym-
bolic evocation of death's unending suffocation . . .

Don't be so bitter, Professor. Doesn't become you at all.

Ah. The probability manager returns. Has my time come at last? He said, "All right then. Put an end to this."

What would you prefer?

Nothing out there but black night. A shrug. "Take me to your leader?"

Soft laughter behind him. Soft laughter with a human echo to it. He turned slowly, beheld a man in a cheap gray suit, hands in his pockets. Became suddenly aware that he was himself quite naked. He said, "You looked much younger on your book jackets."

The old man smiled, scratched at his throat, fingers skritching audibly in dull gray hair, looking for all the world like he was hunting for fleas. "Well. Those pictures were taken when I was still shy of forty. I didn't see any reason to have new ones taken, since I was no better looking old than young."

Ling stood there, staring at the old man, tried to wait, swiftly failed. "Enough of this," he said. "Just take me to God now. That's what you're here for, isn't it?"

The old man grinned. "Ah, brave, brave Ling. Sorry. Can't take you to God."

Shoulders sagging in defeat. "All right. Make it the Devil then. Maybe he'll offer me a nice job or something."

Grin broadening. "Thinking maybe he'll make you conductor on the Hell-Bound Train? Somebody else has already got the job, I'm afraid . . . No. No Devil."

"Am I not entitled to a Judgment Day of my own, then?"

Sardonic look. "Too many dumb old books, Ling Erhshan. Thoroughly infected by Christian memes of one sort or another." Short bark of laughter. "With every book I wrote, I thought I was striking a blow against conventional morality, against New Age magical thinking, against . . . Hell. Against every power I thought had worked to spoil my life. Wish someone had told me then I was merely a vector of that same sad disease."

Ling had a sudden sense of the empty void yawning at his feet. I take one step forward, another, and . . . The black night never ends. "It doesn't end here. It can't possibly end here."

Softly: "Oh, no? Think back, Ling Erhshan. Think about

all those books you read, way back when. Does the Fabulous Riverboat ever make port? Does Amber ever coalesce? Do we finally get to meet the Maker of Universes?"

A shrug. "Those were just books, neither more nor less than your own books, Mr. Millikan. As well ask me about the ultimate fate of Muad'Dib."

Still, the smile. "Ah, yes. If I gave *you* a place to stand, you'd move the Multiverse. What if there's no place to stand, then?"

"Sophomoric twaddle."

"And what if you can only see God from the outside?"

"Sophomoric twaddle."

"Well. I guess I did drop out of college in the middle of my sophomore year, didn't I?" Millikan now an old man leaning against the endcap of a tall library shelf. "Tell me, Professor Ling: What's the most salient characteristic of the Multiverse?"

Uneasiness now. Why ask me? He said, "There are as many histories as probability allows."

The probability manager folded his arms. "Theoretically, then, there must be a finite probability that there *is* a God. What do you think, Ling Erhshan? Does the probability manager rule over an infinite, omnipotent, all-knowing God?"

"Please don't tease me with childish riddles about irresistible forces and immovable objects."

"So it's either God or probability? Not both? Which would you prefer?"

God shrinks you down to the significance of a molecule. Probability shrinks you down to nothingat all. He said, "Like everyone else, I only wanted a reason for being. I hated the idea that some . . . deity might reach down and impose such a reason on me. But . . . even the scientist in me hated the notion that there might be . . . no reason at all."

"Imagine how *I* felt, then."

"You know the answer, Dale Millikan. Why not just tell me? Is there *no* God? Did the Multiverse just *happen*, because there was a finite probability that it could?"

The probability manager said, "That does suggest the possibility that probability antedates being."

Ling said, "That was always the frustration for me, why I turned from theoretical mathematics and speculative physics to the rewards of engineering. You solve a riddle, the answer is only another riddle. We worked our way right back to the beginnings of time only to find a blank wall. No First Cause. And the only other possibility was no beginning at all."

"Worlds without end. Times without number."

Ling sighed, a loud chuff of anger and resentment. "Just tell me the answer."

The probability manager said, "OK."

Astonishment. Then, *snap*.

It was dark in the movie theater, house lights faded, previews rolling, grumble of voices in the darkness running down, fading away, and Ling Erhshan could smell the fresh scent of the young girl beside him, crisp scent of shampooed hair, clean scent of laundered linen. No perfume. Stunned when she said yes to me. A date? A movie? Sure.

Small, weak Ling Erhshan not expecting to get a date with the strapping goddess from the field hockey team, doing it on a dare. Doing it to win a ten dollar bet. Funny, walking alongside her. Taller than me. Lots of people taller than me, all through school, but mostly I dated other Asians, Chinese girls, not giant Caucasians like Astrid Kincaid . . .

Held my hand, briefly, on the way here, talking and talking about this and that. Who would have suspected a field-hockey girl would want to be an astronaut? Turns out she knew about my ambitions as well, asking, Are you glad your parents came here from China?

Glad. Yes. Glad to be in America in 2017. Chinese manned program faded and gone, American program seemingly renewed after so many false starts. Yes, Astrid Kincaid, I'm glad to be here . . .

Sitting in the darkness beside me now, arm resting against mine. What is she thinking. Is it going to be an interesting movie? Does she care? Does she know what I expect? Of course she does. They all do. Reaching out now to touch her hand, feeling it turn under his. Going to hold my hand again?

No. Turning it palm up, letting me touch her there, ever so softly.

Ling Erhshan shifting uncomfortably in his seat, sliding one arm along the hard rim of the seatback, being careful not to rest it on her shoulders, pretending to watch the coming attractions. I'll have to come see that movie, a remake of the 1950s serial *Man Into Space*, updated to project what we'll be doing in space over the next twenty years. Go with my friends, not with a girl. That way I can watch the movie.

Hand behind her back now, placed there dutifully. Doing . . . doing what I must. Is she leaning toward me? Leaning against the inside of my shoulder ever so slightly? I really can't tell. Hand on her bare forearm now, stroking gently.

What is she doing now? Looking intently at the screen. Probably wants to see *Man Into Space* with her friends. So she can watch the show.

Hand casually draped over the arm of the movie chair now, the one arm separating the two seats. Glad there aren't so many people here. No one nearby, one of the good parts about taking a girl to a shitty movie. Hand draped ever so casually over the arm of the chair, knuckles resting against the side of her thigh. No reaction. Is that good or bad? You never can tell with girls. Maybe . . .

His hand felt like it was tingling, fingers practically paralyzed, only inches from her lap. And she's wearing a very short skirt. Accident or invitation? How am I supposed to know? OK, so it's hot out. She could have worn shorts, but she didn't . . .

Hand drifting now, Ling leaning forward, as if absorbed in scenes from the next preview. Something about a big, slobbery dog, images on the screen barely registering now. Scrunching closer to her. Other arm touching her back now. Loose hand suspended over her thigh.

He stole a glance downward. Bare legs gleaming in the movielight. Knees about four inches apart. Carelessness or invitation? How am I supposed to know? Well . . .

Leaning forward a little more, eyes still riveted to the screen. Is the movie about to start? Who cares? Fingertips resting atop her thigh. All right. You've backed out at this point in the past. Slight shortness of breath, the word *dyspnea* surfacing out of his seemingly endless store of words. Palm on the inside of her thigh.

He stole a look at her face. Nothing. Eyes on the screen, watching the titles roll. Hand moving up her thigh now. Erection starting to double up painfully in his pants. Edge of her skirt. Fail-safe point. Skin much softer the higher he went. Sudden hard bulge of tendon coming up out of the muscle, following it to the edge of her soft, silky underpants, feeling the hard, rolled seam there, softness beyond . . .

Strong hand holding his wrist suddenly. Tension of regret. She'll pull it away now. Hold it in her own, hold it tight for the rest of the movie. Polite talk on the way home, a peck on the cheek, then gone.

Another voice, speaking from somewhere outside his immediate consciousness: Yes, that's right. And by tomorrow all her girlfriends will know. That's why they'll giggle when they see you.

He could feel the flush of shame starting down his cheeks already.

But the hand was only on the back of his own, resting there, palm pushing down, flattening his hand against the space between her legs, his thoughts whirling giddily, making no damned sense at all.

She leaned toward him, head bumping lightly against the side of his face, and whispered, "Take it easy, Ling. This movie's three hours long."

Astrid Kincaid awoke and opened her eyes slowly. Outside, in the blackest imaginable night, the wind was booming hollowly, rattling the branches of bare winter trees, threatening storm. A glance at the bedside clock. Not even midnight yet. Ling resting against her, tucked under her arm, head resting against her shoulder, face pillowed on the side of her breast, breath soft and slow on her skin. Soft and slow.

Probably asleep. Usually asleep afterward. All right. Well I've been asleep too. Should've gotten up and cleaned myself at least. Damp tissue a distinct lump between her legs, where she'd stuffed it not long after they'd finished, tissue soaking with his semen, warm then, cold now. A smile in the darkness. So much for tender romance . . . that last of sex for which the first was made.

Some of the swelling subsided now, that pried-open feeling gone away. A little itchy, though. Not enough to make me get up and take a bath. Plenty of time in the morning.

Memory of him, huffing and puffing over her, chugging away steadily in the empty darkness, going after his own orgasm long after hers had come and gone. All right. Not spectacular. One more knot on the long, uneven quipu cord of their marriage. Twenty years. Twenty years already . . .

She felt herself divide suddenly. Divide again. Divide a thousand times. Images of Astrid Kincaid infinite in number, dancing in the darkness like movies on the inside of her eyes. This one like a maidservant, washing his clothes, cooking his meals, taking his semen in whatever orifice he chose. Bearing his children. His children, though they came out of her body.

Or that one. Look at that Astrid Kincaid. Defying him. Walking out the door. Resuming her life as if his hadn't happened. Another Astrid Kincaid over there, swaying in the night, hands pressed to her face, not wanting to look at him, lying in the bed, lying so still and pale, handle of the steak knife poking up from his breast . . .

This whole group of Astrid Kincaids over here, so happy to serve him. In what world did those poor women dwell? Look at them smiling. Young ones with babies at breast. Old ones with grandchildren on knee, proud old women with a slim, silent, gray, old, Chinese man walking slowly beside them.

Women who seem to have been contented with their script.

Silent, old, gray man at my side . . . Did you suck dick all your life or stand up and fight, challenge them to kill you? What script did you follow? People learn to hate their scripts, then lack the courage to write their own. My God. A life full of ellipsis marks.

Astrid Kincaid lying in the darkness, listening to the roar of a midnight wind. Remembering this particular life. In the morning. In the morning we'll rise. Shower. Go to the ready room. Have a breakfast of steak and eggs with all our cheery comrades. Suit up. Ride our bus out to the pad, spaceship lit by searchlights, cold gray Atlantic nothing but darkness beyond, all the way out to the eastern horizon, empty black sky waiting for the Sun.

Remember how it went, that Millennial Dawn? All the people of the world coming together under the aegis of the United Nations, all the people agreeing that they must act now, together, or all die together a century or two down the road . . .

Ling and Kincaid, friends since that high school date, fondly remembered, rising out of the darkness on nights like this, as they drifted to sleep in each other's arms. Ling and Kincaid, through college together. Through graduate school and jobs, through children and career, always plotting together, threading their way through a political sea, eyes, always, on their goal . . .

Spaceship standing tall in the searchlights now, serviced by technicians, waiting for them to come and fly it away into the empty sky. A sky which, forever afterward, would be empty no more . . .

She said, "But it didn't happen that way, Dale. I remember."

Ling still by her side but . . . there, by her breast, the glimmer of his eyes, open on the darkness. Softly, he whispered, "But what if it had?"

A shadow by the foot of their bed, dark man, barely visible. Dale Millikan said, "You remember because I allow you to remember, Astrid Astride."

Not even the tiniest clench of embarrassment now. No point. Astrid astride whatever the voice of the god tells her to straddle, wriggling for the watchers, handing them her heart.

Millikan said, "When God was real, we made him dance for us. It's why He went away. Why should you be any better?"

Ling whispered, "Did He really go away?"

Invisible smile in Millikan's voice: "Oh, I suppose. No one was minding the store, at any rate."

Kincaid said, "If the Multiverse is everything, where could God go?"

Ling: "And if the Multiverse *is* God, why are we *here*?"

Soft laughter from the shadow figure at the foot of the bed. "You people never give up, do you?"

Kincaid: "Why should we?"

A shifting of shadows. A nod, perhaps? He said, "The dolphins had the only answer that mattered."

Ling, angry: "Don't tell me that."

"All right, Milton had the answer too. God existed when He was only a word. Supposing the word was *if*? If and only if. Probability begets being, God fills up with angels, the angels resent the scripts probability writes for them, fight each other, rebel against God, fall, are consumed and scattered, leaving behind the empty scaffolding of Heaven. Is that a better answer, Ling Erhshan?"

Silence. Hearts beating in the night.

"God reduced to a drooling idiot, helpless to turn back probability, is no different from a God who has vanished."

Kincaid: "Why should God be helpless against probability?"

Millikan said, "As well ask why probability should be helpless against God."

Ling said, "More sophomoric twaddle."

Again, that shadowy nod. "As, ultimately, are all questions that reach beyond causes and look for more than effects. In *this* Multiverse, God is no more than the vector sum of all the forces that imagine they create and destroy. Souls, like the fundamental particles they are, pass through the subtle realm of Platonic Realty, emerge changed, and the totality of the Multiverse is conserved."

Kincaid whispered, "We haven't come this far to be told, You live and you die; that's it . . ."

A longer, darker silence, then Millikan said, "No one really dies. Not in a Multiverse where all possible histories are equivalent."

"Are they equivalent, Mr. Millikan?" Ling, seeming to fumble for his words. "I understand, mind you, there is a finite possibility that each and every one of us will somehow live forever. I understand that, where such a thing is possible, it must *be*. But among the many possible histories . . . In most of those worlds I die. In most of them, we all die."

Kincaid: "I was immortal in the history of my origin, in the sense that such a thing may have been biologically possible by the laws of the universe where I lived. What good did *that* do all the Astrid Kincaids who lived in universes where nothing but death was waiting for them?"

Millikan said, "Any two particles which have ever been in association, remain in communication, no matter how far removed they become from each other. As each universe, each history originates at a single point, as all histories and all universes originate in Platonic Reality."

Ling said, "No information was ever passed through such a channel, nor ever could be. No spooky action . . ."

"But you've passed through all the gates now. Walked the byways of Creation. All of your lives are one life, lived in parallel. Because you forget your dreams doesn't mean those dreams never were. And because I am here, I see to it that all lives go on."

Kincaid, dryly: "Whether we like it or not?"

Merry laughter: "Oh, my poor little Astrid Astride. Matter and energy that may be neither created nor destroyed, only changed. Souls that travel from life to life, world to world, across all time, looking for some gray Nirvana where they may cease to be, finding only endless reincarnation . . ."

Suddenly they were under a pale blue sky, Ling and Kincaid side by side, still naked, the Probability Manager standing before them in his cheap, shabby gray suit. Behind him a fat, flat mirror of an ocean that stretched out until it touched the remote end of the sky. Warm winds. Little white clouds high above.

He said, "Immortality's the best I have to offer. The rest is up to you." He vanished, leaving them alone.

After a while, they started to walk away up the beach together. And though they lived on forever and ever as they sailed across the wine-dark sea, looking for nothing, finding everything, Professor Ling Erhshan and Sergeant-Major

Astrid Kincaid never tired of recalling the days when they sailed the Caliph's ship and served My Lord Almansur.

Somewhere out there, *somewhere* by God, I swear they still live.

Behind them, hanging like a tired old moon in the empty sky, leaching back into the infinite reaches of the Multiverse, the man in the cheap gray suit wondered, for just a moment, what it would have been like to go along with them. Splendid freedom.

Paradise lost, never to be regained.

Over his shoulder, the living spirit of Dylan Thomas whispered mournfully in his ear: "Dead men naked, they shall be one with the man in the wind and the west moon. Though lovers be lost, love shall not, and death shall have no dominion."

True enough, Dale Millikan thought.

And returned to the job of Creation.

WILLIAM BARTON's previous books include *Hunting on Kunderer, A Plague of All Cowards, Dark Sky Legion* and *When Heaven Fell,* and two collaborations with Michael Capobianco, *Iris* and *Fellow Traveler*. His short fiction and nonfiction have appeared in such diverse publications as *Asimov's, Full Spectrum 5, Ad Astra,* and *Commodore PowerPlay*. He is currently working on a new novel, *Acts of Conscience,* to be published by Warner Aspect.

By the year 2000, 2 out of 3 Americans could be illiterate.

It's true.

Today, 75 million adults… about one American in three, can't read adequately. And by the year 2000, U.S. News & World Report envisions an America with a literacy rate of only 30%.

Before that America comes to be, you can stop it… by joining the fight against illiteracy today.

Call the Coalition for Literacy at toll-free **1-800-228-8813** and volunteer.

Volunteer Against Illiteracy. The only degree you need is a degree of caring.

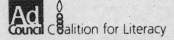

Ad Council   Coalition for Literacy